CHICAGO,

THE WINDIGO CITY

Praise for Mark Everett Stone

Chicago, The Windigo City

"I am looking forward to seeing where Mark Everett Stone will take these characters in future novels as the stories along with the characters have gone from strength to strength and I hope that this continues."
—Michelle Herbert, Fantasy Book Review, UK

"Mark Everett Stone has hit another home run …. The action is non-stop, and the magical/technical gadgets are incredibly imaginative. Fans of this series will not be disappointed. The BSI series remains one of my absolute favorites, and I'm looking forward to the next installment."
—M. E. Franco, author of the Dion Series

I Left My Haunt in San Francisco

"The third in a series, *I Left My Haunt in San Francisco* is lively and smart. It is packed with action and just enough goop and gore to please fans of the genre without turning away newcomers to this subset of modern fantasy demon-busting …. Stone's book moves fast and reads quickly. It is well-written and nicely paced, with a few short rest stops built in to allow the reader to catch his breath, all to better appreciate the at-times purple but always entertaining prose …. It is just great, grand fun."
—Mark McLaughlin, ForeWord Reviews

"Another high impact, fast moving story from Mark Everett Stone. I am really enjoying seeing his growth as a writer reflected in the strength of his characters and am looking forward to seeing what the future holds for Kal."
—Michelle Herbert, Fantasy Book Review

"Kal Hakala is at his finest, throwing out one liners and sarcasm like candy at the local town parade. There's even some nifty new gadgets that would make Q green with envy. Stone concocts his tale with a generous helping of spells and weaponry, a dash of some familiar faces, a smidgen of new folks on the team, and tops it off with plenty of awesome battles with the Things That Go Bump in the Night .... A dish best read in one sitting because you won't be able to put this one down."

—Shay Fabro, award-winning author of the *Portal of Destiny* series

"The third episode of the Files of the BSI series is told with Mark Stone's trademark tongue in cheek humor. It keeps you wanting more with each turn of the page, to not only uncover the mysteries of the story, but also to enjoy Kal's quick but cynical wit."

—CP Bialois, author of *Call of Poseidon*, The Sword and the Flame series, and *Skeleton Key*

The Judas Line

★ "This delightful Catholicism-infused quest fantasy stars a likable and original duo. Fr. Michael Engle, a pragmatic Catholic priest, and Jude, who has a considerably more uncertain relationship with God, are unlikely friends, but when a blood-covered Jude runs into Mike's church asking for help, Mike listens to him, believes him, and joins him on a quest to find the Holy Grail, which Jude hopes will help him destroy a legendary and dangerous family heirloom. Along the way they encounter Cain, the Norse gods (drinking and watching *Bridge over the River Kwai*), and a Valkyrie with the requisite 'chainmail-covered pillowy breasts.' When Mephistopheles shows up, Jude manages to label him an Arch-Fiend of Hell without irony and without irritating the reader. Stone's depiction of magic is realistic and intelligent and his treatment of Catholicism refreshingly informed and three-dimensional. Even the obligatory near-apocalyptic ending is coherent, surprising, and exciting."

—Publishers Weekly Starred Review

"This evil mystery is a heavenly read! *The Judas Line* creates a believable mystery which links the ancient past to the present. By building on the ancient story of the betrayal of Jesus Christ by Judas, Market Everett Stone crafts a dark versus light drama which will keep

readers hooked. I loved how Stone makes Jude an unwilling member of the darkest family threatening mankind. Simply brilliant!"
—Elizabeth Crowley, Fresh Fiction

"A fast-paced book which does not lack for history or adventure. The inclusion of death and destruction are a given and it is good that there is a lot of humour instilled throughout. I would say that if you're a fan of Jim Butcher's *Dresden Files*, you will enjoy Mark Everett Stone's work. Recommended."
—Michelle Herbert, Fantasy Book Review

"Evil does not die so easily. *The Judas Line* is a novel following Jude Oliver and the long family line that lies behind him, specializing in assassination, using the artifact known as the silver. Jude Oliver must find the origins and stories of his family to be able to end the Silver's legacy for good, with only a single Catholic priest by his side. Blending paranormal and biblical ideas, *The Judas Line* is a riveting thriller that should prove hard to put down."
—Midwest Book Review

"I have come to expect a lot from this remarkably talented writer, but Mark manages to please yet again by bringing new elements to his latest work. *The Judas Line* is, as anticipated, a lightning-paced thriller that is equal parts non-stop action and intelligent musing. This is, in fact, a surprisingly introspective book that delves into many interesting questions about the nature of good, evil, and faith. It's an enthralling read certain to delight and entertain, a well-crafted gem worthy of a place on any bookshelf."
—Michelle Izmaylov, author of *The Galacteran Legacy: Galaxy Watch*

"Mark Everett Stone takes the classic good versus evil plot line and puts his own unique spin on it. He effortlessly merges bible canon with the world and people he's created, adding off-the-wall humor to help break the tension. This book makes you laugh while making you think about the nature of evil and the power of faith."
—Jamie White, author of *The Life and Times of No One in Particular*

★★★★★ "A fast-paced read, with nail-biting moments and some humor thrown in. The characters were compelling, I often find myself picturing them in my head .... I can't recommend this book enough."
—Lisa McCourt Hollar, Jezri's Nightmares

"Once in a great while, a book comes along that challenges you to think outside the box. *The Judas Line* is one of those books. I was absolutely amazed at the way Mark Everett Stone has taken religious stories and beliefs and intertwined his own tale of power, evil, friendship, sacrifice and redemption. The action is nonstop and the characters will stay with you long after you finish the last page."
—M.E. Franco, author *Where Will You Run?*

"The pacing is flawless in every respect .... Never before have I found a work of fiction to be so captivating. It picks you up, sits you down, and it does not let you even think about getting back up. A word of warning: Hide your pocketbooks, because once you read this, you will spend your next paycheck on every Mark Everett Stone book available."
—Grace Knight, author of *Sun And Moon* (2013)

What Happens in Vegas, Dies in Vegas

★★★★★ "*Things To Do In Denver When Your Un-Dead* was one of the most refreshing and original books I have read in a long time and the sequel is just as exciting as the first. In fact it may just be better than the first .... Exceptionally well-written and entertaining."
—Jerzri's Nightmares

"Vegas is non-stop action that will leave you with whiplash.... Stone leaves you gasping for breath by the end and of course, enjoys taunting the reader with the prospect of a third book in the series, which I will be waiting anxiously to read."
—Shay Fabbro, award-winning author

★★★★★ "A cracking good yarn from first to final page, no question .... Mark has cemented himself solidly into the position

of Master in my self-created niche of Paranormal Suspense Thriller writing. His command of his art grows exponentially with each work of his that I read....Two very enthusiastic thumbs up for a job well and properly done."
—Jeffrey Hollar, The Latinum Vault

"Don't expect a minute of down-time, for Stone is a zero tolerance taskmaster who brings a complicated plotline and well fleshed-out characters to heel and makes it look easy. What you *can* expect is for Stone to surprise you repeatedly, satisfy you completely and leave you wanting more."
—AJ Aalto, author of *Touched*

Things to Do in Denver When You're Un-Dead

★ ★ ★ ★ ★ "If you crave a really enjoyable Paranormal Suspense Thriller to read, THIS is your book. It grabs you from the very first page and drags you along (snarling for you to keep up) and dumps you at the feet of one of THE most unexpected plot twists of an ending that I have ever read."
—Jeffrey Hollar, The Latinum Vault

"If you like quick wit, sadistic charm, and bad-ass gadgets, then you will enjoy the hell out of this book."
—Shay Fabbro, award-winning author

★ ★ ★ ★ ★ "An absolute pleasure to read. It is witty, funny, dramatic and a well thought out paranormal with very fine storytelling. I couldn't put it down!"
—Clarrissa Lee Moon, author of the series, *The Nightwolves* and *Celeste Nites*

"I have really enjoyed reading this book .... The story could just be one of guns, blood and guts and magic, but ... Mark Everett Stone has made these characters seem real."
—Michele Herbert, Fantasy Book Review

"This is not a story for the faint of heart or stomach, nor for those wanting a plot with any connection to reality. Personally, I'm really looking forward to the promised sequel."
—Gordon Long, TCM Reviews

"A fantastic read and very easy to follow. The way Mark combines magicians, zombies and super ghouls with a Bogart-style ultra sarcastic officer of the 'Bureau' makes you want to keep on reading. I highly recommend this for everyone—not just those into stories of the un-dead."
—G.R. Holton, author of *Soleri, Guardian's Alliance* and *Deep Screams*

"Five stars, two thumbs, fantastic! From the moment I began the first page to the final flip of the last, I was hooked .... The writing is sharp, fast and engaging."
—Patti Larsen, author of *Fresco, Wasteland, The Diamond City*, and *The Ghost Boy of MacKenzie House*

"The blending of dark twisted humor in this chilling tale is utterly perfect, written with a sure hand. Comedic timing is everything, and author Stone has perfected the classic one-liner.... Make no mistake folks, this isn't for the faint hearted ... the sarcasm is used as a brief respite in the fastest paced action horror that I have read in a very long time."
—Suzannah Burke, aka Stacey Danson, author of *Empty Chairs*

"In a first and quite brilliant novel, Stone proves himself equally adept at feverishly fast-paced action, edgy wit and banter, and the weaving of a richly satisfying and fresh world of mystery and intrigue. Write on, my friend."
—Michelle Izmaylov, author of *The Galacteran Legacy: Galaxy Watch*

CHICAGO,

THE WINDIGO CITY

From the Files of the BSI
Book Four

MARK EVERETT STONE

CAMEL
PRESS
Seattle, WA

Camel Press
PO Box 70515
Seattle, WA 98127

For more information go to: www.camelpress.com
www.markeverettstone.com

Cover design by Sabrina Sun

Chicago, The Windigo City
Copyright © 2014 by Mark Everett Stone

ISBN: 978-1-60381-929-9 (Trade Paper)
ISBN: 978-1-60381-930-5 (eBook)

Library of Congress Control Number: 2013950442

Printed in the United States of America

This one's for Mom….

ACKNOWLEDGMENTS

I WANT TO THANK ALL those who have been an inspiration to me and who have encouraged me while writing this series: The amazing AJ Aalto, M.E. Franco, Jeff and Lisa Hollar, John Booth, Cp Bialois, Jaime White and, of course, my best friend Dave Nihsen. Thanks man.

As for any geographical or structural anomalies between the really real Chicago and the one herein, it's all my fault.

Also by the Author

Things to Do in Denver When You're Un-Dead

What Happens in Vegas, Dies in Vegas

I Left My Haunt in San Francisco

The Judas Line

CONTENTS

CANTON

KAL

CHAPTER ONE

———•———

Why BB Wears Glasses

"**A**RE YOU READY?" JEANIE'S BREATH tickled my neck, sending shivers along the length of my body and raising goose bumps. I vowed that she could only do that on months with vowels in them.

I grinned and kissed her forehead. "Again? You are *insatiable*."

Two small but powerful fingers skittered across the scars littering my chest and pulled out a hair.

"Owie!"

"Don't be such a baby," she said, nipping at my shoulder with sharp and very white teeth. "You know what I meant. Are you ready to go back to work?"

"Guess so," I mumbled, feeling a yawning pit in my stomach as recent events played out in my mind.

A couple of months earlier, the deeply disturbed father of a serial rapist I'd shot ten years ago beat the everloving tar out of me, scattering my teeth like Chiclets. I was pretty sure I swallowed a few. He'd also taken a DeWalt variable speed power drill to my kneecaps and I had come a gnat's whisker from an up close and personal look at the afterlife. Since then I had been on forced leave, in spite of being fully healed and sporting a brand-new set of titanium/porcelain dental implants that added an extra hundred watts to my smile. No amount of arguing could convince my boss, BB, that I was fine and ready for work. I had to wait until I had his say-so.

"Two months," he had said, staring at me with his patented stern expression, eyes glittering like polished gray pebbles behind his wire rims. "Then you can come back. No more, no less and no arguments."

I'm pretty stubborn, but BB was in a class all by himself.

My girlfriend, a refugee from England circa 1943—a stunning chocolate brown vision who'd had the misfortune to fall for me during a unique time-traveling episode in my career—gave me a look of concern mixed with exasperation, but kept her mouth shut. Instead, she exited our bed and headed toward the shower, leaving me wondering what I'd said. The more primal parts of me appreciated the view. Figuring that contrition was the better part of valor, I followed Jeanie into the marble-tiled shower, needles of hot water scouring my pale, tender hide.

"What did I do this time?" I asked, staring at her back and her shapely … assets.

She didn't bother to turn around. "You almost didn't come back to me last time and you can't go back to work if you're not sure."

I was well aware of that. Of the other four team members I'd taken to San Francisco, only one returned, and while my best friend Canton Alsate suffered no injuries, I had been nearly pounded into guacamole. Three out of five dead, a near catastrophic result for the Bureau of Supernatural Investigation, especially since their numbers had been so devastated by a rogue Agent the previous year. Now the BSI had to make do with Green Peas—raw recruits who had to pass my personal brand of training—and former Agents—who also needed to pass training because they were out-of-shape and used to a life of luxury. It was a freaking miracle that no crises had developed during my eight-week absence.

"Understood," I said to the back of her neck, giving it a small kiss. "But I *did* come back."

Jeanie turned and encircled me with her powerful arms, hugging me tight and tilting her head back to stare into my baby blues with her huge brown eyes. "I need more than a mumbled aside to reassure me that you're going to be okay." Her thick English dialect lent her words a throaty sexiness that had me on the express train to Horny Town.

Using every ounce of willpower I could harness before my runaway endocrine system could hit full steam, I derailed my amorous train of thought and answered her with all due gravity. "It will be back to work training Green Peas, hon. I seriously doubt BB will send me on another mission for a while and everything's been quiet. In fact, we might not see another Supernatural outbreak for a while. No, I'm going to be stuck training Green Peas and former Agents and be bored outta my tree doing so."

She still looked unconvinced, running her hands over my thickly scarred torso—wide, melted-looking patches of skin that were mirrored front to back, a reminder of a run-in with a red-headed psychopath. "So if something comes up, do you promise to refuse the mission?"

I kissed her hard, reveling in a succulent lower lip sandwich. When we came up for air I said, "You know that's not an option. All I can do is ask to be recused from a mission, but it's the Director's call."

With a sigh, Jeanie laid her head on my chest, water spraying off her soft, black hair. Using a Spell she had developed—she is one of the BSI's most gifted Magicians—she grew her hair out seven inches in seven days, long luxurious locks that she magically straightened and coiffed. It never needed hair spray or restyling. If I weren't already rich, I'd be thinking of how much we could make curing male pattern baldness.

I luxuriated in the feel of her soft skin, firm breasts and the subtle hardness of her long muscles. She was perfect, the whole length of her, fitting with me … two puzzle pieces created just for each other.

We lay together for a long time, my pale, pale skin a stark contrast to her dark form, a yin to her yang. Total opposites, black and white, male and female, yet so much alike, both of us cogs in the wheel of the Bureau … lifers to the cause.

Said cause was to protect humanity against those Supernaturals who would commit harm and heartache. The Bureau had been created as a defense against the World Under, that other place where the Supernaturals exist. I reckoned it wasn't a very nice place because they keep trying to enter our world and the results were usually a loss of human life, perpetrated in various grotesque and inventive ways. Usually clean-up involves a supersized mop and bucket.

I had been a part of the Bureau for more than ten years, performing a job that should have killed me long ago. Not to appear immodest, but I was the best of the best when it came to fighting Supernaturals. In a job where the attrition rate was fifty percent or so, I was a living, breathing anomaly, a miracle of the modern age. It didn't hurt that I had my sister's soul stuck to mine like a spiritual symbiote, giving me superhuman strength and speed in the form of an incandescent, berserker rage that I could control. Although, thanks to an accumulation of cellular damage, I had to quit the rage business cold turkey, only calling upon her magic when absolutely necessary. Apparently her magic could only go so far to heal the stress the rage put on my flesh.

Jeanie and I stayed in the shower for almost an hour, making sure we were clean, scrubbing all the nooks and crannies that needed scrubbing and a few that didn't. One thing led to another and the shower stopped being about getting clean, becoming instead about intimacy and holding the world a bay for a little while longer, pretending we were the only two people in existence.

After toweling each other off (which also took much longer than necessary), we dressed in shorts, sneakers and t-shirts. It was Training Day and mama Hakala's little boy was going to run some Green Peas into the ground. Two months of vacation meant that I needed get some extra miles in as well and I knew that by the end of business I would be huffing and puffing like the Big Bad Wolf with a horrid case of asthma.

Before leaving, I put what looked to be a small, skin-colored, circular bandage behind my right ear. It was a bone-induction microphone that allowed me to receive messages from the boss. Another was applied to my throat, a subvocal mic that would allow me to communicate with those wearing receivers, if necessary.

Active only on the subvocal range—talking subvocally took time and patience to learn, but was vital when silence on an op could mean the difference between life and death—those mics kept the various Agents at Warehouse (BSI Headquarters) in contact at all times in case of emergency.

Such paranoia stemmed from a particularly nasty incident. A few months ago, a serial killer and former Agent, Margaret Whitcombe, murdered about half the Bureau's one hundred Agents. I had the pleasure of ending her crime spree with extreme prejudice, the cost being a certain amount of hurt she put on me, now evidenced in spiraling scars around my torso, shoulders, and upper arms. My body was a roadmap of pain and suffering that no amount of therapy or vodka could erase.

The second I put the circular receiver behind my ear, a low level *thrum* hit my brain and my heart plummeted. I activated my throat mic with a soft tap. *"Go for Kal."*

The voice of Andrea, BB's Receptionist, vibrated against my skull. "*Agent Hakala, please see the Director as soon as possible, please.*"

Jeanie saw the look on my face and hers fell five stories and landed with a *splat*. "It's BB," she said quietly.

"Yeah, the boss."

She flipped a hand toward the door of our apartment. "Go then, and tell him that if he's sending you on another mission, I want to talk to him."

Great. Just what I needed, my girlfriend chewing out the boss. Personally, if it came down to those two butting heads, my money was on Jeanie.

A peck on the cheek later and I shuffled out the door to see what was what.

Warehouse was exactly what the name implied ... a big damn warehouse custom designed to house, train, entertain, train, and retrain Agents when not out in the field. Each Agent had an apartment suited to their needs and plenty of food and recreation. We fought hard and we played hard. It was my job to see that the Agents lived through the fighting bits so they could commence playing.

Once out of the living area, or DORMS, I traveled down the ferociously long and drab hallway toward ADMIN, BB's stronghold, the office at the end of Warehouse, the pot of gold at the end of the rainbow. Along the way I was scanned both technologically and magically, my identity checked and re-checked. If I was not who I was supposed to be, if the scans came back UNKNOWN or SUPERNATURAL, then what was left of me would be swept into a dustbin, or frozen in Carbonite.

At the end of the hallway, I placed my hand on a small black panel next to the ADMIN door, a sophisticated DNA scanner and aura reader. Again, if I was not who I said I was … well, see above.

It's not paranoia if they're really out to get you.

Once through that door, I came face to face with the Receptionist Andrea. Note the capital R. Being a Receptionist means that you are the last line of defense between what dangers may arise and the people or place you are meant to safeguard. All Receptionists are fit, hard women with killer smiles, bad attitudes, and itchy trigger fingers … not to mention, they are much smarter than the average Agent. Not only did they serve as ferocious defenders, they performed psychological evaluations on all Agents to make sure we were relatively sane. Or at least crazy in a way the Bureau could use.

When I entered, Andrea had one hand below the level of her desk on the grip of a double-barreled shotgun loaded with silver deer slugs aimed at my most tender bits. She was wearing a purple blouse that matched the stones in the dangly earrings half-hidden by her shoulder-length blonde hair.

Wordlessly, I *slowly* placed my hands on the desk and let the silver Spell Shapes set deep in the wood confirm my identity one last time. Precious metals and gemstones serve as batteries in the magical world—the more pure, the more precious, the more magical energy they can absorb. There are enough diamonds residing in the vaults in Antwerp to absorb the kind of magical energy needed to wipe Helsinki off the face of the Earth.

When her computer emitted a soft chime, I breathed a sigh of relief. It only took one mistake to terminally end my career. Not that there have been *any* mistakes of such magnitude in the Bureau's history, but, as my dad was fond of saying, "There's always a first time."

"You're cleared, sir. The Director will see you now." Her voice slid in and out of my ears like silk, supercharging my testosterone, but having a girlfriend who can turn you into a tree frog puts a damper on casual flirtation.

I gave Andrea a carefully neutral smile and entered BB's office.

A long trip across soft burgundy cut pile carpeting later and I was seated in front of his large mahogany desk, possibly the most technologically advanced piece of equipment on the planet. Not that you could tell .... It looked exactly like an expensive desk, which was part of its innate coolness. I knew that that desk could inform BB of events a hemisphere away, order his morning latte, pay his bills, do his taxes, perform *10 petaflops*—a FLOP is a FLoating-point OPeration, or instruction per second; a petaflop is 10 to-the-*fifteenth* power of instructions per second, way cool—and tell him what I had for breakfast on March 10th of 1997. The only thing it couldn't do was go back in time and kill Hitler.

To me, it was all science fiction; my only education in computers was a course in COBOL in high school.

BB, aka Benjamin Bauer, looked at me over the top of his gold wire rims, studying me intently. Well into his forties, he still kept in tip-top shape instead of letting himself go to seed like most desk-jockeys were wont to do. What was left of his hair was slowly turning gray and the crow's feet decorating the corners of his eyes were a little deeper, more pronounced, but he still retained the same air of vitality and youth that had so impressed me when we first met. Back then he'd been my team leader and one serious bad-ass. Since then his bad-assness had multiplied by fifty.

"How do you feel, Kal?" he asked in a smooth tenor.

"Fine, boss," I answered calmly, waiting for him to spill what bad news was housed in his bald dome.

"Good." He leaned back and kept staring. It was unnerving as hell.

I waited for the proverbial shoe to drop, but it never did. Finally, I broke. "What's going on, boss?"

His smile was slight, almost nonexistent, but it was there if you looked hard enough. "I am evaluating you."

Great. "And how are you doing that?'

He shook his head. "I'll get to that in a moment. First I want to talk to you about something you might find rather interesting. You remember the little trick with the soul gem? The one you used to run away from the Bureau?"

How could I forget? Alex, the best and brightest Magician to come along in a generation, had crafted a Spell stone out of quartz and placed it inside a wristwatch. When I died, it housed my soul and cast a preservation Spell on my corpse so I didn't rot. Alex then healed my body and, using the quartz, placed my soul back in my body, resurrecting me. I don't recommend it as a party trick.

"Yeah, of course. I practically invented the damn thing."

BB sighed. "We've been employing the same methods for the past few months, but with no results. None."

My blood chilled and goose bumps pebbled my skin. "You've been trying to bring Agents back from the dead?"

"Yes. We even tried it with Agent Wilkes after his death in San Francisco. The preservation Spell went off without a hitch, but the Spell gem used to store his soul didn't work. He remained stone dead. Care to venture any ideas as to why?"

Wilkes. Former football rival turned colleague and friend. Former Army Ranger and a damn fine Agent in his own right, he was killed in that op turned nasty in San Francisco. I still missed the big lug and his infectious smile.

Why did resurrection work for me and not for the Bureau? I gave that a good hard think for a moment, the answer eluding me .... I could feel it slipping and sliding around in my mind, but the more I considered it, the more it became like nailing Jell-O to the wall. Finally, just as I was about to throw in the towel, it hit me.

"My sister." So obvious, no wonder I had so much difficulty figuring it out.

My sister Leena was the reason I joined the Bureau ten years after her murder at the hands (or tentacles) of the Finnish quasi-deity Iku-

Turso. Unbeknownst to me, she was a budding Magician who hadn't quite popped her magical cherry yet, but on her death, in a fit of pain, terror and rage, her spirit had latched onto mine, slumbering until it could come to my aid.

Not too long ago I finally had my revenge: I stuffed the bastard back into the World Under, where other, much stronger, beings had been lying in wait for centuries. Maybe he owed them money or something, but I didn't care .... He was gone and I finally achieved a small measure of peace.

Speaking of peace, let's not forget my girlfriend, Jeanie Morrow, one of the reasons I was still relatively sane. Less than a year ago I was a freewheeling bachelor, using women for sex, absolutely convinced that relationships kill Agents. Only when meeting the Colonel Tolkien and his wife Edith in 1943 London did I come to realize that committed relationships, while messy, offered the chance to make a person stronger, not weaker. My days as a misogynistic dog were now far behind me.

Who'da thunk it?

We all have to grow up some time.

"Yes, your sister," BB affirmed. "That was my thought. Somehow she used her magic to keep your soul intact inside that Spell gem, enabling Alex to reintegrate it with your body."

"So ... unless someone just happens to have the spirit of a dead Magician latched on to their soul, there's no coming back?"

BB nodded. "That seems to be the case."

"Bummer. Why tell me?"

He shrugged. "Just thought you might like to know."

Su-u-ure .... I almost believed him. Almost.

"You're trying to soften me up," I accused. BB never said anything unless there was something to gain. He hoarded words like a miser hoards gold.

"Yep."

Damn, I hate being right all the time. "Okay, what's the mission?"

"You're not going to like it." BB stood and moved to the small wet bar near his desk, centered under the picture of the current President.

One snifter, one tumbler, three fingers of alcohol in each. Brandy for him and horrendously expensive vodka for me.

Oh, this was bad; I could feel it in my cells. What was it going to be this time? Zombies? Ghouls? Oh, Lord … hopefully not vampires. I got extra dead by a vampire once and once was enough.

I let the vodka burn its way into my stomach and waited for BB to drop the bomb, which he did after a healthy sip of brandy.

"You're going to take over as director of the BSI for the next few weeks."

Okay, a *really* big bomb. Hiroshima big. Two kilotons and no waiting.

I pretended a cough. "Don't know, boss, my throat feels kinda sore and I'm pretty sure I'm running a fever."

He was not impressed. "This isn't a joke, Kal. I submitted my recommendation to the President and he signed off on it. It's done. I'm off to Switzerland for a while on a summit to discuss the recent Sidhe incursion."

Bleh. The Sidhe. A few months ago they had tried and come damn close to overthrowing mankind. Only after losing most of my team did my best friend, Canton Alsate, and I manage to stop them. I've had some low points in my career, but that was the lowest, despite it being a "successful" op.

Of all the Supernaturals, the Sidhe are the baddest of the bad, the New York Yankees of the World Under, and the fact they were trying to once again muscle their way into the really real world was cause enough to give the most hardened dictator heart palpitations.

"Unless the plan is for everyone to start wearing iron underwear, there's very little anyone can do," I said. *Grind, grind, grind* went my teeth as I counted the ways I wanted to make the members of the Unseelie Court (those Sidhe who hated and wished harm upon mankind) die … in very interesting and prolonged ways. I got to 116 before BB interrupted my pleasant fantasy.

"That's what the directors of the other Bureaus want to discuss," he said between sips of his very expensive brandy, pacing back and forth in front of the President's portrait. POTUS' soft, painted eyes seemed to follow the viewer. Very unnerving behavior from artwork. "We have to prepare ourselves. I personally don't think the Unseelie Court is through with us."

"Neither do I." There was no way they were done with humanity. They hated us *that* much. It didn't help that I gave one of their rulers a major crapburger to eat by kicking his son's ass from here to kingdom come. Said son, Prince Ephelor, was the bastard responsible for all the mess in San Francisco.

Another thing that chapped my patootie was having to give up my little Brownie buddies. Faë can sense other Faë and I couldn't keep the little folk around lest the Sidhe hone in on me. Those wee folk had been the best dry cleaning service ever and now they were housed with an elderly former Agent who was thrilled that his clothes were cleaned and mended overnight, midsummer fresh, all for the price of a bowl of milk.

"You see my dilemma," BB said. "I must go on an all-expense paid trip to Switzerland and someone must run the Bureau in my absence." Long pause and I closed my eyes against what I knew was coming. "And that someone is *you*."

"I need more vodka."

He took the tumbler from my hand and prepared a few more fingers worth of that heavenly fluid. "It's why *I'm* drinking. There's no one else who can do the job half as well as you, but the thought of leaving you with all this," he waved his hand, indicating the office and the desk, "scares me more than that cave of vampires in Texas."

Me too.

"What about Canton?"

"What about him? He's good, he has the respect of most of the Agents, but *everyone* will listen to you. You are the one they fear and respect the most." He lifted the snifter in a toast. "In equal measures."

"That doesn't soothe my nerves any."

Once again I was treated to a near-invisible smile. "My job is not to soothe your nerves. No, you are the man for the job and if you think you have a choice in the matter … think again."

Big dramatic sigh. At least I wasn't off to fight yetis or anything, although as pro tem director, I'd rather face rabid yetis hip deep in a snow drift while blind drunk. "I had a feeling you'd say that, boss."

BB let loose a small chuckle, the kind Hannibal Lector might give over liver and a nice Chianti. It scared the hell out of me. He reached into the top drawer, pulled out a small, oblong case and tossed it to me. I held it as if it were radioactive until I realized it was an eyeglass case.

And what do you know? Inside the case rested a pair of silver wire-rims. Stylish, but useless to me. "My vision is perfect, boss," I said, more than a little puzzled.

BB smiled again and I felt a cold chill slide down my back. I wished he would stop *doing* that. "Didn't you ever wonder why I never had Lasik? Or at least purchased contact lenses?" he asked.

"It crossed my mind." A thousand or so times.

"Put them on."

Shrugging, I did so … and the damndest thing happened. As I looked at BB, readouts appeared around his head: skin temperature, pulse rate, identification, and even pupillary dilation. It was like a HUD, but much smaller. "Holy cats!" I yelled, startled, taking them off.

"Rather nice, eh?"

"What the hell is this?"

"Put them back on."

I did.

BB sat back in his chair and crossed his arms. "I am from a galaxy far, far away."

Instantly a new readout appeared above his head, letters glowing red: FALSEHOOD, PROBABILITY 99.2%.

"A lie detector?"

He nodded. "It's called a Data Retrieval And Forensic Technology unit, or DRAFT. The best in magical/tech, and it is mated to my computer." One slim finger tapped the top of the desk. I looked and saw a glowing virtual keyboard floating a millimeter above the polished wood. "These glasses are the only interface that will work with the desk and you've been given DELTA/ORANGE clearance, above TOP SECRET. As pro tem Director, you now have access to all the files and information I do."

"So this is your dirty little secret, how you've been controlling the BSI, always one step ahead of everybody." My voice was filled with wonder. "And here I thought *I* was the sharp cookie."

The boss lost his air of good humor. "Kal, you have been a royal pain in my ass for the past ten years," he growled. "These glasses are the *only* reason I've been able to keep up. That and Ghost."

I chuckled. Ghost, an entity that was half spirit, half computer code, was the BSI's own *Deus Ex Machina*, its ace-in-the-hole. Navigating the information superhighway with the ease of an Indy car racer taking a Sunday drive, Ghost could cause more havoc in one minute than a terrorist could achieve in twenty years with unlimited funds. It was a near miracle he was on the side of the angels. That said, he did creep me out more than a little.

"So while you're away, I get to play."

BB nodded.

"Why do I feel there is 'however' going to be inserted here somewhere?"

"Because while you're a pain in the butt, you're not an idiot," he said, standing. He carefully adjusted his dark blue H. Huntsman suit. "I leave for Switzerland immediately, and everything you need to know is in the desk, under the 'KAL'S FIRST TIME' directory. Just hit RETURN on the virtual keyboard and the desk will do the rest. Your password is 'BONEHEAD.' " BB slapped my shoulder as he walked past, heading for the exit. "There's an issue in Chicago and I trust you to make the decision on which team to send, or if you want to create a new team. If you need help, Ghost will be around."

Before he could make his getaway, I said, "How do you know I won't screw this up?"

At the office door, BB stopped and threw a stern look my way. "You could screw it up, Kal, but remember … if you do, people will die. Also, it will be your ass if you do." Then he walked out of the office, leaving me feeling three kinds of nervous.

Great.

CHAPTER TWO

———•———

The Desk and I Have a Chat

WITH A SOMEWHAT HEAVY HEART, I sat down behind the desk, the burden of responsibility a crushing weight upon my shoulders. My finger tapped the virtual RETURN key and met no resistance, but a display appeared on the glasses, a for-my-eyes-only monitor. A cursor blinked and I tapped the keys, entering my password. BONEHEAD. Thanks loads, BB.

"Hello, Kal," came a familiar, buzzing voice that seemed to originate from midair.

"Hello, Ghost." I said, smiling. "Haunting BB's desk, are you?"

"This is where I … live, so to speak."

Well, that was just damn peculiar. "I hope the rent is cheap. You here to give me a hand? Or ectoplasmic pseudopod, or whatever."

"Yes, is my duty to walk you through the process of choosing the team to send to Chicago and assist you with the many functions of this desk. I am the 'KAL'S FIRST TIME' directory."

"So what's first?"

Several file headings came into view, the personnel records of all the Agents currently available at Warehouse, what teams they belonged to, plus a list of available Magicians and Receptionists. The latter two made for light reading. Magicians, while never plentiful, became even scarcer when Whitcombe and her turbo-ghouls decimated Special Branch, the Bureau's R&D, but that's another story.

One name did jump out at me. "When did Canton get back?"

Like me, Canton had been on leave, his fiancée, Winch, having lost her life in San Francisco. More accurately, the Farallon Islands. *Beneath* the Farallon Islands. Personally, I thought Canton should've taken more time off.

"Mr. Alsate arrived late last night," buzzed Ghost "Currently he is in COMBAT, training."

"Hmmm." I stared at the names on file. "How do I click an icon? There's no mouse or trackball."

"Much like the virtual keyboard, all you need is a finger."

Neat. I tapped the air where I perceived Canton's name to be and the file opened wide, his whole life laid out—easy to read, clear documents, ready for my perusal.

"Ghost, this is way too cool." I had to figure a way to keep the DRAFT glasses when BB returned.

"Kal, you have two options here. You can either read a file, poring over every word in an effort to ensure that the people or team you pick are right for the job, or you can 'experience' the file."

I heard the quotation marks in his voice. "Experience?"

"One of the more recent breakthroughs. The wearer of the DRAFT glasses can observe a file much like a movie, but more in-depth, like virtual reality. Alex created the Spell Shape after watching *Vanilla Sky* one evening."

Alex was a friend, the leader of Special Branch and possibly the greatest mind of the century, but sometimes what he invented didn't work so well. Such as the bulletproof shirts that had a tendency to explode, or a hyper-advanced ultra nifty handgun that worked erratically at best.

"Has it been tested? I don't want to wind up a puddle of green goo."

A static-y laugh assaulted my ears. "Tested and retested. It has been rated 'SAFE', Kal." There was a pause. "May I suggest you click on the 'CHICAGO' file first, so you can see what attracted the attention of the BSI?"

"Sure … how do I do that observe thingy?"

"The glasses and the desk are coded to your voice and your DNA. Tap the file and say, 'VR.' "

Sounded simple enough. Of course, in my experience the most incredibly dangerous things sounded pretty damn simple.

Taking a deep breath, I tapped the CHICAGO icon and said, "VR."

The office, my whole universe, disappeared.

***

Officers Trent Polanski and Jim Bressler parked their cruiser in a lot on the corner of Lake and Canal Streets, just a stone's throw from the river, which smelled like a combination of rotting vegetation and sweaty armpits. Less than a block away, the EL made a godawful noise as it clattered past.

Polanski removed his cap and wiped the sweat from his wide forehead. Not that it was hot, but the bulletproof vest he wore coupled with a good dose of acid indigestion from his lunch of Vietnamese pho made for one sweaty cop.

"Where did they say those kids saw that thing?" asked Bressler, a big African-American veteran of fifteen years whose love of lasagna kept him in size 40 pants. He cast a worrying glance at his partner.

"By the water," huffed Polanski. He belched and acid burned the back of his throat.

"Lovely. Smells like wet ass out here."

"Don't say that! God, my guts hurt." Polanski wiped away more sweat. A former football player with wide shoulders and hips, he looked like a walking blue brick. A very damp blue brick.

Bressler smiled. "I ate at the same place as you, so how come I ain't sick?"

"'Cause you got guts make of cast iron," came the reply as the two crossed railroad tracks, heading for the sparse trees edging the Chicago River. A block south, the glass and steel tower of Garver International loomed over the area like a shining sentinel.

"Well, keep your guts in. I don't need to hear or see you blow chunks." Bressler kept smiling, clearly enjoying his partner's discomfort.

The two men split up as they approached the trees, the only stretch of green for a couple hundred yards in either direction. Dispatch had radioed that some kids farting around next to the river had spotted human remains. The Chicago River was no stranger to floaters, having housed thousands since the city was founded. To the police, it was business as usual. Albeit disgusting business.

Bressler was the first to reach the river, the wide expanse of muddy green that flowed through the city and thanks to the heat and humidity, did indeed smell like 'wet ass,' as he so colorfully put it. The olfactory assault was enough to start his lunch rumbling.

A few dozen yards up and downriver and no body, nothing on the bank, nothing in the water, only trees swaying gently in the late spring breeze.

Rubbing his big gut through his vest, he was about to call out to Polanski when he heard the unmistakable sounds of puking. With a sigh, he began a fast trot toward the source of the noise.

He was brought up short by the sight of his partner on all fours, a thin trail of puke-coated saliva dribbling from his lips to the bleached gravel near the railroad tracks. The big man's normally pale complexion had a grayish tinge as he threw up until not an ounce of pho was left in him. Then he began to gag, as dry-heaves racked his body.

"Jesus, can't be that bad, can it?" Even as the question left his mouth, his eyes darted to and fro, as if he feared the answer.

Polanksi pointed toward the river, to a clump of long grass on the bank, then leaned forward again and heaved.

Brassler took a look at the spot his partner had indicated. Within moments his own lunch reappeared.

***

LIEUTENANT KEVIN BEINFORT STEPPED UP to the scene, his shiny brown Italian leather shoes crunching on gravel. The area around the grass clump had been cordoned off with bright yellow police tape, and half–a-dozen officers stood around, backs to the water, keeping an eye out for reporters and looky-loos.

No one acknowledged him as he gingerly stepped over the tape and crouched next to the clump. Reaching into the pocket of his light brown Bottega Veneta suit, he pulled out a pair of purple latex gloves. The buzz of flies came thickly from the clump, a droning accompaniment for the dead.

"Nice to see you mingle with the rest of us … sir," said a somewhat sardonic female voice from behind.

Lieutenant Beinfort grinned toothily as he snapped the gloves into place. "Always like to see how the other half live, Sergeant."

Sergeant Sara Mills stepped over the yellow tape and crouched next to the Lieutenant, her JCPenny's business suit and flats a far cry from her superior's $5,000 getup. "You drive a crap car, but you dress like an oil baron," she said. "You spend so much money on clothes that you can't even afford basic cable, so what makes you think I'm part of this 'other half'?" Her voice held a wealth of disdain.

Beinfort's smile grew wider as he considered the grass, his boyish face seeming lit from within. "I may be poor, but I look *good*."

In that he wasn't wrong. Beinfort did look good, and his attitude said he knew it. Tall, slim and athletic, he was close to forty, yet his jet-black hair remained untouched by gray. He seemed to be the type of guy mothers warned their daughters about.

From beyond Beinfort's line of sight, Mills stuck her tongue out at him. Younger than Beinfort, she was too burly for most, and her short, curly red hair had already started to turn gray. She looked as if she could out-wrestle Beinfort four out of five falls.

"Let's see what all the fuss is about," muttered the Lieutenant, parting the long grass and disturbing a cloud of flies that buzzed around the scene. The two detectives stared.

Mills's normally milky skin went greenish. "Oh, that's so wrong …."

Beinfort nodded, his smile long gone. "Damn."

In the center of the clump of long grass were bones, a good sized mound of them—grayish white and stripped of flesh, not a single shred remaining, not even the pale white of ligaments. Bare and stinking, they lay as if carefully, almost reverently, placed there with the skull on top grinning at the two cops. But what made the scene grisly was not the bones themselves, but what had been done to them. Each one had been gnawed clean and then broken so that the marrow could be extracted. Even the skull had teeth marks. The swirling black cloud of flies hovered over the mass, as if angry at the intrusion.

"What kind of animal does this?" asked Beinfort.

Mills stood abruptly and walked away, blundering through and tearing the yellow police tape. The Lieutenant rushed after.

"Sara, Sara! Wait!"

"Damn, Kevin ... damn," moaned the tall woman, scrubbing her face with her gloved hands.

Beinfort grabbed her by the shoulder and spun her around. "Damnit, Sara, get a grip. What is it?"

Between gulps of air, Mills said, "You know my husband is a dentist, right?"

Beinfort nodded.

"So I recognize those tooth marks," she continued. "They're *human*."

He blanched. "Oh, damn ...."

***

I CAME BACK TO MYSELF in a rush, the crime scene dissolving into the furnishings of the office around me. It took a few moments for the disorientation to fade.

"That was disturbing ... and cool." I shook my head to clear the residual images. The whole thing had been so *real*, as if I had stood on the holodeck in *The Next Generation's* Enterprise. The drama had unfolded around me, every sensation engaged in the moment.

"I am given to understand the experience is ... intense." Ghost sounded amused. "Perhaps you wondered why so much effort went into debriefs? Every iota of data that could be collected has been. It allows Special Branch to render the VR simulations as real as possible. Only the last forty years have been rendered into VR.

However, there is one file from before the forty year limit we have been able to convert and it is Alex's hope that next year, all those earlier files with enough data will be part of the VR system."

"That's pretty damn nifty. As for 'intense,' that isn't the word I'd use," I replied, settling back in the chair. "Mind wobbling, brain-hammering … those are the right words. This beats the Hollywood 3D craze cold and my glasses are so much nicer." Although I could see how someone might become addicted to the experience. "Are all the files like that?"

"Most of them. Some files do not have enough data for the Spell to construct a virtual environment. Perhaps someday we will be able to make up for what's missing, but not now."

Time to get back to the Chicago business. "Did BB say what kind of Supernatural ate the victim?"

"No, he trusted your vast knowledge of the various Supernaturals. What do *you* think killed the victim? Who, by the way, has been identified by dental records as one Oliver Kowalski."

Only two cannibalistic Supernaturals came to mind, well … actually, several if you counted B-movie horror flicks, but I was dealing with the real things—not poorly made cinema. First on the list were ghouls: hyper strong undead with a penchant for long pig. I'd had enough of those horrible things during a recent mission in Denver, which ended in the death of so many good Agents. However, ghouls were not fussy eaters, not the type to pile the bones like that, and the teeth marks didn't match. Ghouls had sharp, long needle teeth, not the normal human dentate.

The answer had to be the second creature on my list: the Windigo, a cannibalistic spirit that possesses a human and uses the host to snack on the nearest neighbor, lowering property values considerably. The first humans to encounter the savage Windigo were the Algonquian people who inhabited what is now the northern United States and southern Canada. The Algonquian shamans managed to halt the spread of the Windigo, but not before thousands had become snack packs.

I related my hypothesis to Ghost.

"That fits the data," he buzzed softly. "Now to pick the correct team to handle the matter."

Right … the *correct* team. "Any suggestions?"

Staticky laughter assaulted me. "BB said you would ask and told me to tell you 'Nice try.' "

Great.

Once again shouldering the burden of responsibility, I tapped three files and they grew large in the DRAFT. After a few minutes of scrolling through the teams (Alpha through Kappa, minus a couple of letters), I realized I'd already made my choice. Not a team, per se, but three names, people I thought would be perfect for a mission in the Windy City: Canton Alsate, Dove Jacobs, and Matthew Alba.

Dove Jacobs was as tough as they came, hard as titanium and with a chip on her shoulder so large I'm surprised she didn't collapse under the weight. She might be difficult to work with, but there was no one better in a scrap. At four-foot ten inches and 105 pounds soaking wet, she was a bundle of dynamite in a small package. Ready mayhem on tap.

Matt Alba I had met during the Denver mission… solid, dependable, with a head harder than basalt. He was boulder-firm and could weather almost anything the World Under could vomit forth.

And then there was Canton.

As I pulled his file up, Ghost asked, "Why Mr. Alsate, Kal? He has just returned from bereavement leave."

I asked myself that and the answer fell easily from my lips. "Best man with a blade I've ever seen. Never had a shot at leadership, though Lord knows he deserves one. I think he needs a test of his mettle and leading a team ought to take his mind off of Winch. Back in the saddle and all that." I hoped I was right, or it would be cruelty disguised as a kindness. However, Canton was much like me, a man of action, and junior needed to *do* something or feel that he was moving backwards.

"There are currently seven teams here. Why not one of them?" asked Ghost.

Life in the Bureau is not just about policing the Supernaturals ….

It's also about constant testing. Every Agent, every day, is being tested one way or another, be it tests of strength, endurance, dexterity, intelligence, or character. It is the one constant in a job that can come to an abrupt and messy end. Frequent testing keeps an Agent alive when the odds are stacked against him. Ten years had honed my ability to sense when I was being tested, and Ghost's question, asked perhaps a little too casually, put a blip on my radar. I wished that Ghost had a body so I could look him in the eye and give him the old raised eyebrow trick. Doesn't work on a flow of sentient electrons, however.

"I think Canton is the man for the job," I stated, keeping my voice neutral. "Most of the other teams are chockful of Green Peas I wouldn't trust with a potato gun, much less one involving a cannibalistic spirit possessing people, assuming that's what it is. If I'm sending Green Peas out, they are going to be led by veterans like Canton, Dove, and Matt." I took a deep breath. "Besides, Canton needs this and I trust him more than anyone to get the job done." My only worries were the unfilled slots on the team. Who would I send and would I be signing their death warrants?

Ghost kept his opinion to himself, which I took to be a passing grade. Already I wished that BB would waltz back into his office and kick me out. This pro tem director's job was for the birds.

"So now what, Ghost?"

"Click on the Agents you wish to send and either experience their files in VR or just read them."

Before I could press a virtual file, he added, "Kal, because of the massive amount of information absorbed while in VR, you should limit the amount of files you experience in one day. Too much VR can lead to headaches, confusion, temporary loss of coordination, and blurred vision."

At least he didn't mention anal leakage. I considered my options for a moment, then grinned. Why not? What did I have to lose besides my mind?

"That it?"

"No," Ghost replied. "If you wish to terminate the simulation,

CHAPTER THREE

———•———

The Warrior to Be

simply say 'End VR.' "

My finger stabbed at a file and I said, "VR."

THE TALL MAN DROVE HIS 1974 green Ford Gran Torino far too fast and narrowly avoided t-boning a station wagon sporting simulated wood panels as it sped through a red light. Car horns blared, tires squealed and didn't stop until the Torino hit the parking lot of St. Sebastian's hospital, a three-story building that looked like a mishmash pile of mauve adobe. The Torino stopped in front of the glass doors that led to the Emergency Room, and the tall man exited.

A white-clad orderly burst through the doors. "You can't park that there!" he thundered.

The tall man tossed the keys to the orderly. "You park it then." He ran past and into the hospital without a backward glance.

At the admission counter, the nurse was startled to see a tall and rangy copper-skinned man in faded Levis and a gray t-shirt with the letters USMC barrel toward her at unsafe speeds. His snakeskin boots skidded across the slick linoleum and he would have fallen had not the immense admissions desk stopped his headlong progress.

"Ooof!" said the man as he folded over the Formica-coated obstruction.

The nurse let slip a small grin. She had seen worse. "You all right, honey?" she asked blandly, tapping her lower lip with a pencil.

"Jenna Alsate," he said, wiping at the sweat that streamed from his face. Dark patches stained his gray t-shirt at the armpits and collar. "My wife. Where is she?"

The nurse checked her charts. "She's been taken to L&D, third floor. Let me call and inform the doctor you are here, Mr. Alsate." She looked up to see the empty space where Emilio Alsate had been.

Bypassing the elevators, Emilio took the stairs three at a time, long legs straining. Up three flights without slowing down, the son of Marcus Alsate (or Nantan Lupan, *Gray Wolf*, as he was known to his people) burst into L&D gulping air.

Another nurse was waiting for him.

"Mr. Alsate, everything is fine," said the big-boned woman wearing a tight, white uniform, barely containing a smile as the tall Native American stood bent nearly double, panting and sweating. "Follow me. I'll take you to your family."

"My ... wife," wheezed Emilio as he slowly straightened. "She's okay?"

"Your wife and baby are well and waiting for you."

Big brown eyes flew open wide. "My baby? Already?" A smile tried to form on his face, but the worry there forced it away.

"Yes, sir. A healthy baby. Healthy as they get."

"Boy or girl?" Emilio asked hesitantly.

The nurse smiled, revealing slightly crooked teeth. "Why don't you come with me and find out for yourself, sir?"

The two quickly walked down the hall to Recovery where his family waited.

JENNA ALSATE WAS GORGEOUS BY anyone's standards. Tall, sleek as a panther, the woman of the Pueblo people had high cheekbones and generous lips along with long, lustrous black hair. That hair lay matted and sweat-soaked around her head as she cradled her newborn son to her chest, his small form wrapped in a blue blanket. Dark half-moons shadowed her soft brown eyes, which were focused on the sleeping baby.

"Hon?" Emilio entered the room almost hesitantly, unable to take his eyes from the bundle in her arms.

Jenna tossed her head, flinging long locks of sweat matted hair out of her face. "About time, slowpoke," she said softly, with a tired smile.

"Is … is it …."

She laughed quietly. "Our son is strong. And sleeping, so be quiet."

Immediately he dialed down the volume to a whisper. "A son? We have a son?" he asked reverently.

"Yes, all seven pounds, ten ounces of him."

Like the sun breaking through clouds, a magnificent smile appeared on Emilio's face. With uncommon grace, he moved forward quietly and knelt at his wife's side.

"He's so beautiful," whispered the proud father. The child's skin was slightly purple and a blue knit cap covered his cone-shaped head.

Jenna kissed her husband's cheek. "Yes he is." She held the baby up so her husband could take a good look.

"He's … kinda purple," said Emilio. "And his head is pointy."

"That's normal, silly. Actually, he's a little jaundiced, which is very common when the parents have different blood types. A few hours in the sun every day and he'll be fine." Her smile was soft and radiant. "His head will reform and be as round as his father's soon."

Emilio lifted a big hand and gently stroked the baby's cheek with a finger. "So soft."

"You should call your father. He'll want to see his grandson."

The tall man lifted his head and looked to the open doorway. "That won't be necessary … right, Dad?"

Through the doorway strode a medium-sized man packed solid with hard muscle and whose features were starting to see the first seams of middle age. Face broad, with skin like burnished copper, it broke into a wide smile at the sight of the small family. Hair black as a crow's feathers hung to his waist in a long, thick braid. Clad in jeans over scuffed cowboy boots and a blue-striped white button down shirt, he too moved with unusual grace, the silky strides of a predator.

"Hello, Pueblo Woman," he said quietly to Jenna, staring at the sleeping boy. "You done good."

She nodded to her father-in-law. "Thank you, Nantan Lupan. Would you like to hold your grandson?"

"Nothing would make me happier," he replied, eyes glistening with moisture. The older Alsate reached for the bundle she extended to him. With sure movements, he held the infant to his chest and rocked him slowly. "He's a strong boy, I can tell. A fine addition to the Mescalero Apache."

Jenna grinned. "He's half Pueblo."

"I won't hold that against him," Marcus Alsate replied with a wink.

"When did you arrive, Dad?" Emilio asked, moving to stand next to his father and newborn boy.

Marcus didn't bother to look at his son; his eyes were only for the baby in his arms. "A few minutes ago," he whispered. "It is a long drive from Ruidoso."

"You knew."

"I knew. I knew last night when Pueblo Woman here started having contractions."

Jenna settled herself deeper into the bed, obviously tired. "Nantan Lupan, will you See what the world has in store for my son?"

For a brief instant, Marcus's impassive face became pensive. "To See the future of a person is easy, but often that future does not come to pass. Those Spells are tricky, you know, and the Creator doesn't reveal all that will happen. Time is like a trail with many forks: you never know where a person will ride, only the most likely course."

"Please?" she asked, eyes wide.

Marcus sighed and nodded.

The elder Alsate gently placed a callused palm on the small boy's forehead and, closing his eyes, began to hum. It was a low, thrumming noise, the sound an electrical transformer would make, deep and resonant. The vibration reached deep into the flesh. After a few seconds, he began to rock gently on his heels, the hum becoming more rhythmic and soon after, a low chant emerged from his throat. It carried the same electric quality of the hum and circled the room in a flurry of throbbing noise.

Emilio felt the small hairs on his arms rise as magic prickled against his skin and quickly closed the door to the room before returning to his wife. Jenna clasped her hands tight in front of her, eyes wide in a mixture of fear and anticipation. The midafternoon light streaming through the window seemed to dim somewhat as the power of the elder Alsate's magic spun faster and faster throughout the room.

Marcus' head fell back and his eyes opened wide, no iris or pupil to be found; only a dead whiteness that shone with a slight oily sheen. Words in a language older than the Apache people, older than man, tumbled from his lips, dropping like stones into the thick, magic-laden air. Blue/green worms of light twisted around his fingers and over the child, seeping into the infant's skin. Incredibly, the child slept through the din and the streams of blue/green light illuminated the delicate tracery of veins beneath his skin.

As if a switch was thrown, the magic departed and Marcus slumped, holding the baby closer to his chest, sweat running in rivulets off his face to drip, drip, drip onto the floor. "I have Seen, my son," he panted, eyes closed, lips barely moving.

"What have you Seen, Nantan Lupan?" Jenna asked, face creased in worry and doubt.

The older man didn't bother to look up when he answered. "This one may be a great warrior. Greater than his father, greater than his grandfather, but warrior or no, he will be the rock others break against, treading a path few can walk and fewer survive." With that said, he turned to the anxious Jenna and gently returned his grandson. Jenna clutched the boy tight to her breast. Her face was troubled and it seemed she regretted the desire for divination.

Marcus sat heavily in a worn steel and cloth chair, blew out a great sigh and rubbed his temples. "What name will you give him, son?"

Emilio looked at the child and kissed his wife. "I thought we should name him after a good friend of mine, one who saved my life more than once. His name was Canton."

"Canton Alsate. Hmm, that is a *good* name." Marcus smiled tiredly at Jenna, who was still rattled by the old man's prophecy. He stroked the sleeping child's cheek. "You are Canton Alsate, but you are also Itza-chu, the *Great Hawk*, for you will fly higher than us all."

I SNAPPED BACK TO MYSELF, a little sweaty, a little thirsty, but feeling fine. Pretty damn good, actually.

"Whoa … that was groovy." I checked the blinking icon in the DRAFT. The heading read that I had experienced only eighteen percent of the entire file.

"Are you okay, Kal?"

"Yeah, Ghost, just hunky-dory." I shook my head to clear away the cobwebs. "Why didn't I experience the other eighty-two percent of the file?"

"All VR experiences come with limiters that prevent the user from experiencing too much lest the download damage the brain. A fifteen minute break and you will be able to continue."

"Why create this … system of viewing the first place? I kinda feel like a voyeur."

"The director said you would ask that. His response is, 'You can't get a true measure of a person and what they've been through unless you've been there.' He said you would know what he meant."

Yeah, I did. Reading a dossier is all well and good, but how many nuances are lost in dry files? In a position where one must pick the right team to handle an ugly situation, all data is vital. They say one picture equals a thousand words, so how many words did I just see? A million?

"It's surprising that Canton's file starts with his birth," I said.

Ghost's drone became somber. "That is because Canton's father, Emilio, is a former Bureau Agent, as was his grandfather Marcus. He is third-generation Bureau and as such has been under scrutiny for his entire life. As for Jenna, she had been a Bureau Receptionist for six years. It is where his parents met."

Wow … the mind boggles. He never mentioned that aspect of his past. Of course, we rarely delved into such deep issues as family. Our lives were heavy enough without digging into history like that. It did explain, however, the magic Marcus used. Considering that magic-sensing devices weren't invented until the late '90s, it wasn't surprising that Marcus was able to cast Spells with little fear of reprisal.

That thought raised another question. "How long was I in VR?"

"Six minutes."

It felt like hours. I was seriously impressed. A minute of searching the desktop revealed a small virtual button labeled INTERCOM. I gave it a nudge and waited.

"Yes, Director?" Andrea's voice emerged from that same patch of thin air as Ghost's. Those glasses were way too cool.

"Uh, call me Kal. How do I get a bottle of Tommyknocker cream soda and a bowl of Lucky Charms?"

"I'll put the order in for you." She sounded faintly disapproving. "May I suggest Shredded Wheat or All Bran? Something healthy?"

Philistine. "Have you ever *had* Lucky Charms?"

"No."

"Then don't judge. They're phenom-freaking-enal. And don't underestimate the nutritional value of marshmallow hearts, moons, and clovers."

Was that a disdainful sniff? Surely not! Not at the director pro tem who held the fate of the BSI in his hands.

Whatever.

I considered a slug of vodka, but quashed the impulse. Ever since the San Francisco mission I had scaled back on the alcohol consumption. Now that I was in a relationship, and a monogamous one at that, cirrhosis of the liver seemed like a Bad Idea.

Before my will could weaken (the wet bar was looking *that* good), the DRAFT gave a chime and Andrea entered the office pushing a small cart. Her knee-high black dress gave me a nice view of a well-turned calf. A bottle of Tommyknocker cream soda, dark brown glass sweating, and a large bowl of Lucky Charms rested on the stainless steel surface. I felt my stomach rumble in anticipation.

Awesome.

"You didn't have to bring those here," I said when she came into hollering distance.

"One of the perks of being the director is office-service. One of the perks of being the director's Receptionist is that I get to leave my post and stretch my legs a bit." She smiled. Smiled! The shock of it nearly gave me a heart attack.

After she set the bowl and bottle on the desk, I thanked her and offered her a taste of the cereal. "You don't know what you're missing."

She made a face. "*Gross*. All that sugar …. I don't think so. Too sweet for me."

I pointed to the spoon. "One bite. Try something new. I dare you." When she didn't respond, I smiled wide and mean. "I Double-Dog Dare ya."

Not one to shun a Double-Dog Dare, she sighed and took a healthy spoonful of marshmallow ambrosia and chewed. Then took another just to be sure. She carefully set the utensil on the desk and crossed her arms.

"I hate you. Sir."

My smile nearly split my face in half. "Told you."

Walking away, I heard her mutter, "That is *so* going to my thighs."

Chuckling, I tucked into my eats and pondered on what I had learned. Canton's grandfather, Marcus, or Nantan Lupan, was a Magician. In 1975, he cast a Spell to divine the future of his grandson and even under the best of conditions such a Spell fails more often than not.

That time was one of the 'nots.' Calling Canton a great warrior would be damning with faint praise.

After one last sip of my cream soda, on a hunch, I typed in the names of Marcus and Emilio Alsate. Their files popped up immediately, thick and detailed.

Looked like the Alsates had made Bureau work a family tradition. Instead of heading into VR, I decided to skim the files. This is what I learned:

Marcus (nickname: Wolf) Alsate, 1946-1950. Recruited out of the Army after WWII. Magician on active duty in the field. Personally responsible for the elimination of an Afrit (sort of like a genie, but not like the cartoon one in Disney's *Aladdin*—more like a psychotic fiery humanoid with no sense of humor and an attitude problem) in the desert west of Odessa, TX. Commendations for bravery and was given Distinguished Service Award upon retirement after serving four years. Well liked, no black marks, no reprimands. In the Straight world he purchased a successful ski resort in southern New Mexico and was responsible for the creation of a casino on the Mescalero Apache reservation outside of Ruidoso. It seemed that everything he touched turned to gold. Or at least poker chips.

Emilio Alsate (nickname: Razor). 1969-72. United States Marine Corps, 1965-68. One tour in Vietnam where he was awarded the Bronze Star for bravery above and beyond the call of duty. Upon his return the then BSI Director scooped him up. Marcus Alsate had been such a valuable asset that it was supposed his son might be as well.

After SEAL training, he joined Gamma Team, which a year later he would lead. In his tenure as team leader, he amassed a short but impressive list of Supernatural threats eliminated: a Cyclops in Pennsylvania, a pesky poltergeist in Barstow, a Will O' Wisp in the Everglades and a mated pair of Griffins in Maine. All in all, a career marked by intelligence and fine leadership. After retirement he used the large sums of money from the Bureau to start a construction company in Long Island and, with Jenna's help, it became one of the largest on the eastern seaboard. Subsequently, the couple split their time between New York and New Mexico, spending time with Marcus and Jenna's family.

As for Jenna Alsate (nee Baca), United States Marie Corps, 1963-1966, she was one of the first women in the Corps to serve under hostile fire. Awarded a Purple Heart in 1965. Recruited into the Bureau in 1966 and served until 1972 when her second contract expired. Married Emilio Alsate two weeks after her retirement.

Had Canton's family covertly steered him toward the Bureau?

There was only one way to find out.

"Ghost, has there been enough time since my last VR session?"

The specter's electronic hum filled my ears. "Plenty of time, Kal."

"Thank you." I touched the file icon and said, "VR."

CHAPTER FOUR

———•———

A Boy's Life

A SEVEN-YEAR-OLD BOY SPUN AND leapt, the eight-inch stick in his hand a blur. Tall for his age, he had large hands and feet, a promise of greater height to come.

Emilio Alsate, who blocked a thrust and lashed out with his own stick, barely missed tapping the boy on the cheek. Serpent-quick, his left hand struck and slapped the boy on the chest. It wasn't hard, but it did unbalance him. With a wail, the boy landed heavily on the summer grass.

High noon on Long Island in early summer and the air was heavy with moisture but not so warm as to be uncomfortable. The front lawn where the father and son sparred had been mowed to an inch of its life, razor perfect, the envy of any golf course. Trees surrounded the large house at the property line, providing a windbreak and a measure of privacy at the same time.

"You're getting faster, son," Emilio remarked, wiping the sweat from his eyes. Even though the day was mild, his tank top was soaked.

Young Canton leapt to his feet, all elbows and knees, and gave his father a fierce hug. "Thanks, Dad."

"Go shower, son," said his father. "You're sticky. Then go see your grandfather. He wants to spend some time with you before he goes back home."

"Why can't Nantan Lupan stay with us?" Canton asked.

A big hand swatted the boy lightly on the butt. "Your grandfather has responsibility on the Rez. As Tribal Chief, it's his job to make sure the ski resort and the casino are running well."

"Why can't we live with him?"

Emilio knelt and took his son by the shoulders. "Daddy's job is in Long Island, so I can't just leave it anytime. I have people whose livelihoods depend on me. Running a construction company is how we can afford to live a good life. You like your school and the town, don't you?" The boy nodded reluctantly. Emilio took a deep breath and tried on a comforting smile. "But at the end of summer, before school starts, we can take a month and visit your grandfather. Would you like that?"

With the unconditional love of a child, Canton wrapped his skinny arms around his father's neck and said quietly, "Yaaay!"

"There's a good boy," Emilio said proudly, ruffling his son's midnight hair. "Now go shower and find Nantan Lupan."

Canton practically flew out of his father's arms, racing into the almost palatial colonial-style home on the edge of small village of Southampton, New York. So far the summer had been a gentle to the people of Long Island. The grass was soft, green and almost postcard perfect, while the air held the just the right amount of Atlantic Ocean scent.

Marcus Alsate lay dozing on a hammock slung low between two trees. Seven years had not aged him any except for a dozen or so strands of gray in his otherwise tar-black long hair. His aspect retained the sandstone quality that gave him an implacable air. He had the face of a man who could weather any storm.

Fresh from the shower, Canton ran out the back door toward his dozing grandfather, moving at speeds most track stars would envy.

Before the running boy could jump onto his grandfather's belly, the older Alsate nimbly rolled off the hammock and onto his feet, arms spread wide to catch his grandson, his face alight with joy.

The two met in a furious hug and Marcus swung the boy round and round while Canton squealed in delight.

"You run so fast, my Itza-chu!" Marcus exclaimed. "Faster than the eagles can fly!"

The boy whooped his glee.

Marcus set young Canton down carefully. The boy was scrubbed clean and looked fresh as a daisy in his denim shorts and new green t-shirt. "Join me, Itza-chu. One last talk before I leave." Marcus sat on the hammock and patted the fabric next to him.

Canton sat next to and snuggled against his grandfather, the older man's hand on his shoulder. "I wish you didn't have to go, Nantan Lupan."

"I have responsibilities, my hawk."

"That's what Daddy said."

"He knows. He has responsibilities, too… to his employees in that big company of his, to Pueblo Woman, to you." Marcus's eyes twinkled. "And to your little sister."

Canton's eyes grew wide. "But I don't have a little sister."

"Not yet, but you will. Seven months from now. She will be a feisty one, like her mother. Beautiful, too."

Although only seven, young Canton knew better than to disagree with Marcus Alsate. If he said something would happen, then it was a given.

"Wow. A sister. That's so cool! Do you know what her name will be?"

Marcus shook his head. "My vision isn't that sharp, little hawk, but because she will be more beautiful than even the Pueblo Woman, I will call her Sonsee-array, Morning Star Takes Away Clouds." He stared into the sky. "Yes. I think that will be perfect."

"Sonsee-array," Canton whispered.

"Do you know why your father trains you in knife fighting?"

Canton shook his head.

Marcus slapped at a mosquito that landed on his knee then wiped the squashed bug on his shorts. "When you were born, all purple and wrinkled, I Saw that you could be a great warrior, Itza-chu, and a great warrior needs training."

"But what if I don't want to be a great warrior?"

"That is fine, too," Marcus said gently. "You can be whatever you want, but it doesn't hurt to be prepared."

The boy said nothing, but his eyes were wide and trusting.

"Itza-chu, I have Seen more. In my dreams I See you grown into a big man. Not as tall as your father, but wider at the shoulders and stronger. I've Seen you fight and even the rattlesnake will not match your speed. The knife is your fang, one you will use with great skill. No one will best you as long as you have a knife clenched firmly in your fist."

"Who will I fight?" Canton's voice was filled with curiosity and acceptance, but no fear.

"I cannot tell you who will fight, or why. A great magic prevents my tongue from saying such things. I only know it is likely you will fight."

"Dad tells me of magic and of the customs of the Apache, and Mom tells me of the magic of her people, the Pueblo. Is your magic like that?"

"Yes, like the magic of the Pueblo, the Apache, the Navajo, Hopi, Pawnee and all the other tribes of the wide land. There is magic everywhere, in all the peoples of the wide world. There is magic in all things: the rocks, the trees and even the sky. You just have to know where to look."

"Even the white people?"

Marcus laughed loud and hard, slapping his knee in delight. "Yes, my great hawk, even the white people have magic, although most of them don't believe, or don't want to. However, their magic is not like the People's magic and it confuses them." His deep, dark eyes filled with an unreadable emotion. "And that touches on something I want to talk about ... the white people."

"What about them?'

"There is a man among them who you will come to know, a warrior like yourself. I Saw him very clearly, a man whose people live in a distant land. He will be very tall and strong with hair like summer wheat. He will be your friend."

Canton shook his head. "I'm never going to be friends with a white man. I hate them! The white boys at school are *mean* and they call me names."

Marcus cocked his head. "Never say never, my hawk. I think you will be friends with this white man."

The boy considered this for a moment. "If we are friends, maybe he won't be mean to me. Who is he?"

Marcus shook his head. "I don't know, but what I do know is that he is like you—tough, resourceful, and smart. The name I have given him is Jlin-Litzoque, *Yellow Horse,* because of his yellow hair."

"You've Seen us fight together?"

"In my dreams." Marcus nodded. His face lost its earlier joy. "He is a big man, but he is filled with hurt. There is so much sorrow and loss in Jlin-Litzoque that it consumes him and there is no balance in his heart. He is strong, but even the strongest rocks can break."

"That sounds sad. How did he get filled with hurt?"

"It is … a terrible thing. We all suffer in our lives. We lose people, we see things that are too awful to speak of, and often must do things that hurt the spirit. Perhaps you will be his friend and help him restore the balance in his heart. Perhaps you can help heal his hurt."

"How will I recognize this man, Nantan Lupan?"

"I don't know," Marcus said softly. "Trust yourself and you will find him because he will be a true brother to you and true brothers always find each other. It will be a friendship that helps define your lives."

"So I will be friends with him, maybe brothers. That is going to happen no matter what?"

Marcus Alsate stared at his grandson for a minute before whispering, "No, but for both your sakes, I hope it will."

***

FIFTEEN-YEAR-OLD CANTON ALSATE CIRCLED HIS father, an eight-inch stick in his hand. His father was older—a trace of gray at his temples—but still looked the same, lean and formidable with hard, ropy muscle. He, too, carried a stick in one hand.

Once again the scene was set in the summer and the sun shone directly above. It was 1990, the beginning of the end for the Soviet Union. In the Alsate's Southampton home, everything looked the same; the only markers for time were Canton's growth spurts.

Both teenager and man wore matching white t-shirts, black athletic shorts, and white Nikes. Both were sweating as they jabbed and slashed, neither finding the advantage. Canton's dark, dark eyes were empty, as if the life had been sucked from them. They matched his father's dispassionate orbs.

There was a flurry of motion as Emilio darted forward, empty hand stiff, trying for a ridge-hand strike, but Canton moved too fast, a copper-colored blur that left only an empty space where he once stood. Emilio recovered quickly and jumped back, ready for a counterattack.

Emilio moved again and again, his hands and feet striking at his son, but no joy. Canton was never in one place long enough to engage the older man and, after a while, it wore on Emilio. When the sweat began to sting his eyes and his breath began to labor, that is when the young man struck, moving faster than most people could follow. The stick in his hand slashed against Emilio's upper left arm, then the inside of his right. A tap to the older man's thigh and the fight was over.

"Gotcha, Dad," Canton said, backing away across the grass and panting lightly. The white leather of his Nikes was striped with green from the freshly mowed lawn.

Emilio threw his stick away and rushed his son, grabbing him up in a huge bear hug. "Good job, boy!" he yelled. "I couldn't be prouder."

"So I'm a great warrior now?" gasped the young man.

Emilio dropped his son back onto the ground, where he stumbled and fell hard onto his butt.

"Ow!" yelled the younger Alsate.

"A great warrior? Hardly, boy. It takes more than some fancy moves to make a great warrior." Emilio helped his son to his feet and thumped him in the chest with a knuckle as hard as teak. "A great warrior is in here," a tap to the head, "and here. It's not about skill with a blade, but skill with your heart and head."

Canton rubbed his temple where his father had tapped him. "But I still won."

"Smart aleck. Yeah, you still won. You have talent, and a lot of it, more than any I've ever known, but talent only gets you so far, then it gets you dead. You haven't fought, you haven't bled, and you haven't had to hold the person you fought alongside in your arms and watch the light fade from their eyes. All that talent, and you haven't earned the right to sit at the table with all the other great warriors of the past. Only when you've really fought, shed your own blood and stood shoulder to shoulder with your comrades, willing to trade your life for theirs, will you be on the path to becoming a great warrior." Emilio ruffled his son's hair to remove the sting of his words. "Now, follow me."

Father and son entered the house and ambled across oak flooring, past the large kitchen stuffed with stainless steel appliances and into Emilio's home office, a twenty-by-twenty-five foot room decorated in the same understated opulence as the Oval Office. Dark wood bookshelves lined one wall and a turn of the century settee graced the middle of the room on top of a meticulously well-maintained Persian rug. Dominating the far end of the room was a redwood desk that showed signs of great age—faded and worn lacquer, small scuffs and scars coated with the grit and grime of decades and hand-carved ornamentation on the legs that modern carpenters fail to create, but antiquarians adore. Opposite the desk, next to the door, hung an original Manet, purchased from a German businessman back in '79. It was worth more than the house and its entire furnishings.

Emilio opened a desk drawer and removed a long object rolled in a white cotton cloth and secured with a piece of twine. "This was mine when I worked for … the government. It's yours now." He handed the object to his son.

Canton untied the twine and removed the cloth. "Wow."

What he had unwrapped was a slim hunting knife … five inches of pale bone handle and six inches of blade wrapped in worn blond leather. He unsheathed the weapon, revealing metal that gleamed with silvery malice, so sharp it seemed to sever the very air that surrounded it.

"Tungsten carbide steel plated in 99.99% pure silver." Emilio patted his son the back. "Never use it unless it is a matter of life or death. You will have a permit to carry a concealed weapon, so wear it always." He gently pulled his son's chin, forcing Canton's gaze from the knife. "Promise me."

Canton Alsate nodded, eyes wide. "Yeah, Dad. I promise."

***

WHOA. BACK IN THE OFFICE and my head was beginning to pound. I checked the desk drawers and found what I felt had to be there … ibuprofen. BB must have suffered from his own overload of VR.

"Are you okay, Kal?" Solicitous as ever, that electronic eidolon.

"Yeah, Ghost. I'm fine." The cream soda was still cold. I hadn't been under for too long and it tasted *so* good, even when gulping painkillers.

"May I suggest a break? Although I suspect you will not listen to me."

"See, you know me so well."

"At least rest a bit longer …. Wait for the ibuprofen to work."

"I will, mother Ghost. I will."

Jlin-Litzoque. Yellow Horse. Me, had to be. Canton and I had taken to each other with a steady friendship that helped, as Marcus had said, define us both. The first time I met him, as we sat down for breakfast that first morning at the Bureau, it was natural, comfortable and I knew then that our friendship would be forever. It was a metric crap-ton of a surprise to me that Marcus Alsate foresaw the relationship.

He even gave me a cool Native American name … Jlin-Litzoque. I liked it very much. Maybe even enough to have it monogrammed on my underwear.

Canton's past fascinated me, but I felt a little bit guilty. Oh, all the information was on file, but the re-creation was amazing … stunning, in fact. Now, if I could work out a way around the headaches.

"I almost feel like a Peeping Tom," I said, stroking my chin. "Like I'm watching through the windows."

There was no answer.

"Ghost?"

Still no answer.

What was wrong? "Was it something I said?'

When Ghost's voice emerged, it contained a kind of wistful sadness I'd never heard before. The fact that his droning buzz could express such emotion perplexed those who didn't know him as well as I. "Why a peeping Tom, Kal?"

"Because it's as if I can see too much and I'm on the outside looking in."

"That is … very much how I feel all the time, Kal. Always on the outside looking in."

Bowl me over with a feather. "I-I never considered that before, Ghost."

"Remember, I used to be human. I used to be a slave to my hormones, used to play videogames all night long, and I used to laugh and have fun with friends, drink beer and worry about my mid-term grades. Now I am a disembodied spirit floating in cyberspace, freewheeling past firewalls and riffling through more data than the human mind can process, but I am all alone in here. A stupid, childish dream of downloading my mind into the Internet worked too well and now I cannot even talk to my parents, not ever see them again.

"Kal, I just want to go *home*."

That was the saddest, loneliest goddamn thing I'd ever heard in all my life. Ghost was such an unnerving entity, so proper and reliable that I'd forgotten he used to be a normal Jewish kid named Casey who'd gone to MIT, had friends, had a *life*.

What do you say to a homesick ghost? He was stuck riding the information superhighway and had to watch as the authorities told his parents that their brilliant, creative son had 'disappeared' under mysterious circumstances. Where was his closure? Where was the closure for his parents?

"Damn, I'm sorry, Ghost. I never thought of it that way." It was enough to break your heart. "Always thought you were living the dream, you know, cruising the Internet with nothing to stop you."

"I think you are aware that if I turn against the Bureau and America, BB has failsafes to insure that my treason would be short-lived."

Yeah, I figured as much and told him so.

"My world is the Bureau now and I have limited interaction. I can talk, but not feel. Look, but not touch, the ultimate peeping Tom. While the world of the Internet is continuously fascinating, I would shuck it all to be able to eat a cheeseburger. I'd be willing to die just to feel a woman's skin against mine.

"I am lonely as hell, Kal, and I envy you so much."

It had been a long time since Ghost and I had a heart-to-heart. 1943, to be exact, when I had traveled back into the past and was trying to save my teammate, Mouth. I felt like three kinds of asswipe for not catching on to his angst.

Some friend I was.

"Why don't you take the out?" I asked in a small voice. "Get exorcised, walk into the light?"

"Because I am scared as hell, Kal. I do not know what is waiting for me. Heaven? The fires of Perdition? My view on the afterlife has been radically changed ever since I altered my state."

Understandable. "When you were … translated into cyberspace, what happened to your body?"

"I do not know. Perhaps it was translated into the computer world with me. All I know is that currently I am running a flesh deficit."

Couldn't help myself, I laughed. I laughed until my sides hitched with pain and my stomach muscles started to protest and, from the strange buzzing sound that rattled around in my ears, Ghost was laughing too.

"Damn, Ghost, I think that's the first time I've heard you crack a joke." I wiped the moisture from the corners of my eyes.

"I think it was my first since I came here."

"Tell you what, buddy. If I can ever figure out a way to get you back into a real live body, I'll do it."

A long pause. "You promise?"

At his plaintive question all mirth faded. "Yeah, Casey, I promise."

I sat there for a good long while wondering how I could keep such a promise. Didn't matter, really ... if there was a way, I'd find it. Maybe Alex could give me a hand.

Back to business. "Ghost, is the input of information to the brain the only reason for this VR headache?" It seemed far-fetched that a few minutes of data-download would do that.

"No. The Spell and the program—which I helped create—does the bulk of the VR recreation, but it is the human mind, the mind of the person experiencing the VR, that fills in the tiny details. No computer or Spell out there can handle that much data. So it is the effort of your own brain to help fill in the pieces of the VR recreation that causes the headaches."

"Doesn't seem like much info to me, actually."

"Consider the lines of code necessary for a computer program to create a virtual ... motorcycle, for example. The cracks in the leather seat, the shine of steel, the sheen of oil, and the reflections off of shiny chrome. All the tiny things that are needed to fully realize the image. Thousands upon thousands, but you say 'Harley Davidson motorcycle' to someone and an image forms instantly in their minds. The human brain has far more computational ability than a mere supercomputer. The Spell uses the human mind to augment and finish all the details. The polish on the wood, so to speak."

Wow. This is your brain. This is your brain on VR .... See the difference?

I waited a full half hour, shortly after my headache faded into nothingness, to dive back in.

CHAPTER FIVE

———•———

Bad Roommate! No Biscuit!

G EORGETOWN UNIVERSITY, WASHINGTON D.C., AUTUMN 1996. Canton Alsate drove his red Honda Civic from the campus to the house he shared with three other undergraduates. Most people who looked at the young man thought he must have received an athletic scholarship to the prestigious school, but they were wrong.

Canton had graduated Valedictorian from Southampton High School and easily rocked his SATs, scoring so high that most schools gave him one hell of a look. However, Georgetown had been the first university to which he had applied, and they snapped him up before he could change his mind.

His father paid most of the ancillary educational expenses but refused to lavish his first-born son (besides his sister Angela, Canton now had a younger brother, Eduardo, who was showing signs of becoming a world-class athlete) with an abundance of money that could cause him to become a self-indulgent ass. Canton didn't care; he was more than happy attending such a prestigious university. He knew how good he had it and didn't take it for granted. Weekends he would tend bar, and the tips were enough to keep him stocked in burgers and fries.

It was his junior year and he had all but forgotten about being a great warrior, although he still practiced knife fighting on weekends and with his father on the occasional visit home. Summers were spent with Marcus, learning the culture of his people and how to lead without seeming to, although he didn't care for the leadership role. Even after six years, he still wore the silver hunting knife, tucked away out of sight. It was like wearing a watch, or a ring, but with lethal possibilities.

At twenty-one, he had broad shoulders and long arms filled with powerful muscle, a body that was trim and lean. He looked every inch the warrior his grandfather and father prepared him to become. Black, shaggy hair hung below his shoulders in a thick mass, framing a face more charismatic than handsome with its broad nose and strong chin under wide cheekbones and eyes so dark they were almost black.

Cathy Anseki, his girlfriend, rode shotgun. Short, slightly chubby, with curly dark brown hair worn long to complement her round face. She smiled at Canton, her teeth very white against her olive skin. "Your roomies going to be home?" A red-nailed finger traced a pattern on his arm. Those roomies were Charlie Portrey, Nolan McManagle, and Eddie Kostwich. Four healthy college men crammed into a small, three-bedroom house with only bathroom. It made for an awkward date night.

His normally copper skin became scarlet as he blushed. "Yeah. I guess we'll have to be quiet."

"Mmmm. That's no fun."

He drove faster. "Trust me, it will be."

She made a face. "As long as I don't have to talk to that creepy Eddie. He makes my skin crawl."

Canton's Goth roommate made most people's skin crawl with his almost slavish devotion to the occult and love of piercings. So many arguments had been started over whether the *Necronomicon* was a real or fictional text and whether magic was real and could be used of summon the demons from the deep places between worlds. Eddie Kostwich, small, pale and sallow, was convinced of the existence of not only that mystic tome, but also of Cthulu, Yog-Sothoth, Abdul Alhazred, and Klingons.

More than once Canton argued with Kostwich, mostly because of the smells coming from the smaller man's room and his unwillingness to explain their origins. It never went beyond words because not only did the other three need Eddie's money for rent, they actually felt sorry for the little nerd.

"He don't make me feel none too comfortable, girl. I get the itchies sometimes just looking at him."

"Heh. Why is it that whenever you try to put me at ease, you pull out that silly drawl and try to sound all hick-like?"

"Well now, it's just my country-boy charm an' all."

"Country boy, my ass. You were raised in New York, the Hamptons of all places, so don't try your tricks on me."

"Already did, girl. You're goin' out with me, aren'tcha? Besides, spent many a long summer in the backwoods of New Mexico."

Cathy giggled. "If you call your grandfather's huge spread 'the backwoods,' that doesn't count and I'm going out with you because you're cute *and* rich." The kiss she bestowed on his cheek held a promise of more to come.

"Sarky wench."

"You better believe it," she purred.

The Civic pulled into the driveway behind Portrey's little green Rio, which had seen better days.

"Hello?" Only faint echoes replied Canton as he entered the front door. "Charlie, I know you're here. I parked behind your car."

No answer.

"Maybe he has a girl in *his* room," Cathy said, snuggling close.

"Hmm. That would be a first." They went through the tiny living room and down the hall to his bedroom, a ten by ten affair that had enough space for a twin bed, a desk with a PC, and little else.

Lips met in a fevered kiss that grew in intensity with every passing second, while hands roamed, clutching and kneading. Eyes bright with anticipation, Cathy broke off the kiss to tear at her boyfriend's shirt. Buttons flew, exposing a wide expanse of smooth, muscular, coppery flesh. With great relish and a teasing smile, she licked a quickly hardening nipple, teeth nipping gently at his skin.

"You are a bad girl," Canton panted, darting in close to kiss and lick her neck.

"Don't I know it," she said, arching her neck and exposing her throat to his hungry mouth. As his tongue tasted the salt of her skin, she began to unbutton her cotton blouse, eager to feel the breadth of his skin next to hers.

As their clothes began to hit the floor, a rising, howling shriek cut through the house like a scalpel through flesh, vibrating the walls.

Canton, clad only in his boxers, grabbed the silver hunting knife where it lay with the rest of his clothes, eyes wide in alarm. "What the *hell*?"

"What's going on?" Cathy cried, hastily re-hooking her bra with shaking hands.

Canton held up a hand. "Stay here."

Cathy nodded and sat on the edge of the bed, her normally dusky skin sallow with fear.

"Nolan? Charlie?" The hall rang with his shout, but no one answered. An electric tension filled the air like humidity and the hair on the back of Canton's arms began to rise. "What's going on, guys?"

His eyes widened in fear as blue-green sparks briefly flicked around the arm hair that now stood on end, each spark living for a brief moment before fading into nothing. The silver knife glowed softly, swirling with aqua light.

"What is this?" he whispered, watching the edge of the hunting knife glow with curious energies. Marcus had told him of magic and he never doubted his grandfather, not once. His belief was a diamond surety in his soul. "What the hell is this?" He licked his lips. "Eddie, what have you done?"

A peculiar sort of grunt came from Nolan's room at the end of the hall. On the door there was a sign depicting a canine Dirty Harry, .44 Magnum pointed at the viewer with the legend BEWARE OF DOG, PUNK! in big red letters.

Canton held the knife in front of him, eyes wide and sweat beading his forehead. "Nolan? You in there man?"

Thump.

"Jesus!" Canton swore, jumping back a foot.

Thump. The noise sounded like someone had hit a side of beef with a wooden mallet.

Gathering his courage, he grabbed the brass-colored doorknob and pushed the door inward.

Something black, with far too many teeth to believe, rushed out in a blur of fur and knocked him headlong down the hall. He hit the hardwood of the floor and flipped, once, twice, three times. The last thing he heard before he lost consciousness was a woman screaming.

Canton came to with a throbbing headache and to the sound of weeping. Probing fingers revealed a half-clotted cut to the back of the head that was still seeping red onto the floor. Even the tiniest poke with a fingertip produced needle-like jabs of pain.

"Oh, damn," he groaned. "What the hell is going on?" Sitting up was an effort that made his head swim, but he managed it without falling over, even though the world didn't want to steady for him.

A plaintive voice, filled with sorrow and self-loathing, drifted down the hall. "Canton?"

The young Native American rubbed his eyes. "Eddie? Where are you? What's going on?"

There came a snuffle and a rattly cough. "You okay?"

"Well, my head feels like there's a cement truck parked on it, but otherwise I'm fine."

"Dude, I am *so* sorry!"

"Where are you, Eddie?"

The little Goth began to cry. *Sob.* "In your room." *Sob. Sob.*

Standing took more effort than he thought possible, but once his feet were on the bottom and his head was at the top, he felt much better. Except for the warm stickiness oozing down his back, that is. Placing one foot in front of the other, he took the five hesitant steps necessary to reach his door.

What met his eyes would have unhinged an older, more jaded man, but for Canton Alsate, it was too far out of his realm of experience to register fully.

Splotches and splatters, streaks and smears of gore festooned the walls, not a surface untouched. Coppery smelling dark chunks lay in heaps on the floor. Some of the bits were identifiable—a kidney, pieces of rib bone—and some were mere shredded tatters of flesh rendered to a pulp.

Three bodies, almost unrecognizable … almost. Charlie Portrey stared at the ceiling from the floor in surprise, as if shocked at the state of his body, of which there was precious little left. Nolan McManagle lay in a heap of ripped flesh in the corner, as if he were a piece dirty laundry carelessly tossed aside. His blue eyes had been torn from their sockets and tears of blood streaked his shredded cheeks.

What was left of Cathy lay on the bed. Canton knew it was her because her face was intact, while the rest of her had been torn apart. One leg, one perfect leg, had been … eaten, a great chunk taken out of the thigh muscle to the bone, which looked gnawed upon.

Eddie stood in the center of the small room, bloodied face streaked with tears. Not a stitch of clothing remained on his skinny, pale body and it looked as if he had literally been dipped in blood. From his long, matted hair to his small feet, Eddie was drenched in a crimson stain. But other than the coating of blood, there wasn't a mark on the man. No gaping wounds, bullet holes … nothing. He turned to Canton, mouth coughing up broken sobs. Whatever used to be Eddie Kostwich had gone, leaving a broken *thing* in his place.

"What the hell, Eddie?" Canton breathed in shock, hands trembling.

Kostwich spread his slender arms wide. "I tried for one of the Old Ones, dude," he moaned in a sort of crazed mixture of joy and sorrow. "Like Nyarlathotep or Shub-Nigurath, a being that would give me power. Real power." His blasted eyes stared past his roommate, past the carnage and into a realm only he could see.

"It was my ticket, my way to prove that the Old Ones existed, so everyone would stop laughing at me." Something moved slowly behind the flesh of Eddie's face, as if his bones were constructed of writhing worms.

One person in a million has a reaction time swift enough to border on the magical. History has given those people names—Doc Holiday, Charlemagne, Jeanne d'Arc, and Jim Thorpe, to name a few. People of such exceptional ability and athletic prowess that they are all but guaranteed a certain level of immortality.

Canton Alsate was one of those people.

As soon as the bones of Eddie's face began their subtle undulations, adrenaline rushed through his veins, heightening strength and perception and chasing away all fear and nausea. Thanks to his body's chemical cocktail, a crystalline clarity possessed him and he was in motion, eyes searching for the one thing that could give him a chance. Nolan and Charlie had been big boys, but soft. For Canton, being in shape was a full-time job. But excellent physical condition wasn't going to save him. He needed a weapon.

The knife. It was lying in the hall not more than two feet from where he stood, gleaming on the polished hardwood of the floor. Within a second, it was in his hand and a second later he beheld what Kostwich was becoming.

A rare few have these uncanny reflexes, the ability to switch their conscious minds off, allowing their training to take over, to turn them into living, breathing mechanized weapons. This allows them to be unaffected by horror and dismay during combat situations. Odysseus, Audie Murphy, Bruce Lee, Seth Bullock.

And Canton Alsate.

Eddie Kostwich's body was no longer there. Something horrible had taken its place, an enormous creature with long arms ending in human-like hands and three-inch-long black talons. Its skin was dark, the hair covering it coarse, dense, wiry, and black as the pits of hell. A wolf-like head, shaggy and drooling, grinned at him with a mouthful of ochre daggers, teeth so sharp they could effortlessly slice flesh to the bone. It crouched in the middle of the carnage, its multi-jointed legs drawing beneath its great mass in preparation for pouncing on the mortal it beheld.

Shining opal eyes narrowed in anticipation of an easy kill and a phlegmy hiss emerged from the thing's wet jaws. As its flesh rippled and writhed, completing its awful transformation, Canton leapt forward, slashing with the silvery knife, scoring a deep slash on a muscular forearm that gushed viscous red blood and gray smoke that smelled like gasoline and sulphur.

The Kostwich thing screamed, a ripping, guttural sound that tore through Canton's eardrums like razors of ice. As the creature jumped, Canton dropped to all fours, a talon narrowly missing his scalp. A few fine black hairs floated free and drifted slowly to the floor.

The creature flew through the doorway, its vast bulk crashing through the opposite wall and into the bedroom beyond. Canton jumped to his feet, mind clicking along like a supercomputer, weighing every angle, calculating the monster's speed and relative size and strength. In less than a second he knew what he had to do.

Before the monster could emerge from its shattered pile of drywall and two-by-fours, Canton was at the end of the hall at the entrance to the living room. Running away was not an option; the creature had proved too fast. The only choice was to stay and fight, and that was something he knew very well how to do.

"C'mon, you ole broke dog," he drawled, his face flushed with battle lust. "Let's play fetch."

As if summoned, the Kostwich thing burst back into the hall and looked around, its mother-of-pearl gaze finding and locking onto the crouching Canton. Snarling, front talons raking deep scars into the hardwood floors, it sprang.

Canton whirled to the side, knife flashing, silver blade once again scoring a deep gash, this time along the creature's side. Crimson droplets flew and the beast shrieked again. This time, however, it landed on its feet, momentum partially blunted by the students' old blue corduroy couch. It twisted around to face its opponent, a little more wary as gray smoke and blood oozed from both gashes. Its lips pulled back in a buzzsaw snarl-hiss as it eyed Canton then took a slow, slouching step to one side.

A warm trickle and a sudden sharp pain shot along Canton's right bicep. He risked a quick glance down at a five-inch slice, absently noting that it leaked, not spurted, and discounted the wound. He hadn't felt the diamond sharp talon slice his flesh. If the wound wasn't going to kill him, it didn't matter. The only thing that mattered was staying alive and the only way to do that was by killing the monster that spat and hissed in front of him.

With a flash of ebony limbs, the monster lunged, claws grasping, attempting to grapple instead of going for a straight headlong rush. It looked bestial, but it seemed to retain some of Kostwich's intelligence. Its long arm swept forward with terrible speed, but Canton wasn't there to meet it, and the fearsome claws snagged cotton, not skin.

The knife flashed again and again. The ebony skin parted to the silver blade and more foul smelling gray smoke met the air. Another howl and another attack that found no target, only more pain and parted flesh. Again and again the creature whirled, claws flashing, talons reaching for tender skin, but Canton used his greater speed, letting the monster commit to each attack before responding. Each cut in and of itself was no great wound, but on the whole they began to tell on the creature.

Seven long slashes, and the creature leaked life and smoke. The air was becoming redolent with the gassy stench as the gray smoke gathered in dense clouds. The monster shook its lupine head in frustration, pain and blood loss weakening its immense body. An arm swiped at the young Native American and was snatched back bearing a long furrow that bared bone.

It began to whine, a deep penetrating steam whistle keen, but still the creature attacked with talon and tooth until the opening Canton had been waiting for arrived. The creature overextended by the tiniest amount, dagger teeth closing with a loud *crack* on air, but it was unbalanced, and it wasted a split second to gather its great muscles to pull its bulk back from the blindingly fast human.

The hunting knife descended with horrific speed, the tip piercing skin and burrowing through bone to bury itself deep into the beast's brain. The monster spasmed, claws piercing through the hardwood floor. Canton placed his other hand on the hilt of the knife and wrenched, snapping the blade in two, leaving nothing exposed. The Eddie beast died without a sound, its black body slumping to the floor. Within seconds, it was no longer the shaggy, humped creature, but a skinny runt of a human with waxy, wan skin and bushy, blood-matted hair.

Canton stood there, panting and sweating for a few long moments before his broken weapon dropped from nerveless fingers.

"Awwww ... Eddie." A hiccupping sob escaped his chest. "You stupid son-of-a-bitch. Look what you've gone and done." Tears coursed down his cheeks as he picked up the receiver of a white princess phone mounted on the wall. It took him a few tries to punch in the number; post-adrenaline shakes convulsed his body.

"Hello? Dad ... I think I just killed a Skinwalker."

"IT'S NOT A SKINWALKER, AT least, not like out of legend." The older Alsate had taken the company jet and landed at Bolling Field. Just as he pulled up in front of the house in a rented Ford Taurus, several black Crown Victorias arrived. Three tough-looking women in no-nonsense suits and two equally tough-looking men in matching garb exited. All carried briefcases and all had pushed past Canton (very politely), beginning a thorough walk-through of the premises. Before his disbelieving eyes, they opened their briefcases and removed heavy, black bolts of cloth, which they hung on the windows. Once all the windows had been effectively blocked, they moved all the human remains into Canton's room.

One of the women—a tall brunette with twin parallel scars on her left cheek—removed a silvery vial from an inside suit pocket. She smiled at Canton—an expression conveying very little pleasure—and said, "Please wait outside, Mr. Alsate." Before he could object, the two men (one huge linebacker with acne-scarred cheeks, the other short and stocky with a grip like iron) ushered him gently but firmly out the door, where his father was waiting. The other two women were escorting neighbors back to their homes, concocting a story of an outbreak of extremely contagious Tuberculosis.

Canton turned to his father, who was clinically observing the black-clad Agents. "What's going on, Dad?" he asked.

Emilio's eyes glittered in the streetlights. "You will find out soon enough."

Within a few moments the house gave a creaking groan and the front door opened to reveal the scarred woman. She smiled thinly, something like respect flashing in her hazel eyes. "All done. You can bring him in now. Make sure he doesn't go into his bedroom; it isn't safe." She left to assist with crowd control.

"What do you mean 'it's not a Skinwalker,' Dad?" Canton whispered, the first threads of panic lacing his voice as they entered the house. The adrenaline was long gone and emotions were beginning to run rampant. "I saw him change right before my eyes." He was having a hard time holding himself together.

The only clean glasses Emilio had found in the kitchen were a quartet of small jelly-jars. He plucked two from their cupboard and started pawing through the other cabinets. "Not for me to say, son. There will be someone here soon who will tell you what you need to know."

Canton rested his head in his hands, elbows on the small kitchen table. "Who?"

The older man found a bottle of Tanqueray. He poured three fingers worth into two of the jars and handed one to his son. "A government man. Just wait. Be patient."

"I broke the knife you gave me, Dad," Canton said quietly, staring into the glass.

"How?"

"Snapped it off in the Skinwalker's skull."

Emilio winced. "Then I don't care. It did what it was supposed to do. There are plenty of knives, but only one Canton Alsate."

At that moment a short, swarthy man entered the kitchen. He had a wrestler's build and a wide, round face and his suit was expensive without being ostentatious. "Hello," he said amiably, dropping a grayish quartz crystal on the table. "My name is David Merced. You must be Canton." He extended a thick hand to the young man.

Canton grasped the proffered hand. It was like gripping marble clothed in flesh. He felt a momentary dizziness as he stared into Merced's eyes, but it passed, leaving him feeling as if a weight had been placed on his shoulders. "Yeah, I must be. And you must be the government fellah Dad said would explain things."

"I must be," Merced replied and turned to Emilio giving the older man's hand a vigorous shake. "It is an honor to finally meet you, sir." His grin lit his round face like a lantern. "They still tell stories about you."

Emilio nodded. "Exaggerated, of course."

"Hardly. I read the file." Merced turned back to the young man and sat opposite. "I have been authorized by my director to inform you of the Bureau I work for and to answer your questions. First, tell me everything that happened. Omit no detail."

Canton sighed, a tear forming at the corner of his eye. One deep breath, then two, and he was ready. "I drove back here with my girlfriend, Cathy Anseki …."

It took Canton a half-hour and three more snorts of gin before his tale was told. Merced interrupted every now and then to ask for clarification. His carefully worded questions relaxed and drew more detail from the exhausted student. His manner reminded Canton of a particularly attentive doctor.

Eventually Merced spoke of the Bureau.

And offered him a job.

CHAPTER SIX

———◆———

Green Pea

VR CRACKED AND FRAGMENTED, LEAVING me smack dab back in the really real world. I noted dimly that my skin was covered in a cold sweat.

A werewolf. An honest-to-goodness werewolf, a 'my, what big teeth you have grandma and please don't eat me' kind of bad news you never want to meet. *Ever*. The fact that Canton—the greenest of Green Peas—survived the encounter without being bitten or turned into Purina Werewolf Chow was a bloody miracle and a half.

It was obvious to me that Eddie must have had some magical ability that he'd used to try to summon one of the fictional 'Old Ones' from the Lovecraft mythos. That in itself should have made him the winner of the 1996 Darwin Award and the teeny tiny fact that there *are* no such things as Old Ones (not as Lovecraft portrayed) would have made him an absolute shoe-in. While no one knows what the mechanics of a lycanthrope curse are, current theory states that a malignant spirit, or demon, possesses the victim and the magic of the full moon releases it from the psychic bonds the possessed keeps it under. I reckoned that because Eddie had willingly allowed the spirit to enter his flesh, it was under no psychic constraints whatsoever. It would explain why Eddie could change form in an instant and why that change was beyond his control. Poor dumb son-of-a-bitch became the hellish version of a roach motel—demons check in, but they don't check out.

I knew Canton was good with a blade; I just never knew *how* good. Most of the time we used guns, and that was enough. Not even watching him slice and dice Sidhe warriors during the San Francisco op prepared me for what I saw. He was like a deadly ballet dancer.

"How long was I under, Ghost?" I asked, removing the DRAFT and wiping my face.

"Eight minutes, thirty-two seconds," came the specter's drone.

"You think BB will let me keep this DRAFT?"

"Each pair is worth more than a Republican Super PAC. Best guess, you may keep them when you take over the position of director on a permanent basis."

Oh, hell *no*. I had enough headaches in my life without dealing with the heads of the other alphabet agencies, the Joint Chiefs and—*shudder*—politicians.

"That's a fate worse than taxes," I said, eyeing the wet bar. Perhaps if I became *very* drunk on the job BB would fire me. A little extreme, but I'd rather star in an S&M porno with Lord Voldemort than be director of the BSI.

Ghost's chuckle was, well … ghostly. "Who else could do the job? Face it, Kal, if and when BB retires, you are most likely to be appointed."

Oh, the *horror*. "Matt Alba is as solid as they get; then there's Canton." Probably not, he'd probably run screaming for the hills first. "Also Lindsay Michaels, she's a good three-year Agent—"

"Face it," he said. "It is *you*. Learn to deal with the reality."

"You really know how to pee on my parade, don'tcha, you cybernetic spook."

"Illuminating the terrain on which you find yourself deployed is one of the small pleasures I look forward to, Kal." Ghost gave off an electric hum that lasted a few moments, then said, "Now, what are your other choices for the team?"

I took a deep breath. "Not done with the file yet, Ghost."

His surprise manifested itself in a tinny electric squawk that skittered across my nerves. "What? Have you not seen enough? Canton is your friend and with what you have just witnessed, you should know if he is ready for a team leader position by now."

"Yeah, if I was perfect, I'd be one hundred percent sure, but I'm not." I took a deep and shaky breath. "These decisions have to be made without emotion, completely dispassionately. Unfortunately, I can't be dispassionate because he *is* my friend and that scares the hell out of me. If I make a decision based on what I 'feel' and it's the wrong one …." My laughter was a bitter thing. "Then it's all on me, my screw up that kills people and that isn't going to happen."

"Kal—"

"No," I interrupted, stomach in three different kinds of knots. "I'm ninety-nine percent sure and in this business, ninety-nine percent isn't near good enough. It's a hundred or nothing, you know that."

"So what will it take for you to become one hundred percent sure of your choice of Canton as team leader?"

I just witnessed young Canton kill a werewolf, moving like liquid death, so what could tell me more about his leadership qualities that I hadn't already seen? The answer came immediately.

"His first mission for the Bureau." I smiled. Yeah, that felt right. My finger stabbed Canton's file.

"VR."

***

Three weeks since Canton had arrived at Warehouse and he had been left completely alone. Of course he met the director, and several of the teams, but all in all, he was given more space than he was used to.

"Fifty-five, fifty-six, fifty-seven," he grunted, arms pistoning his body up and down, up and down. For an hour he had been in COMBAT, training with knife and hatchet, fists and feet. Then came squat-thrusts, chin-ups, and push-ups as he worked his body to the bone. Although he had been in great shape to begin with, thirty-three weeks in the crucible of Coronado had taken his iron and transformed it into steel. He had become leaner, more defined, and now looked far more dangerous than he ever had.

"Green Pea." The voice was deep, an echo from a basement.

Canton stood, wiping the sweat from his forehead. He missed his shaggy hair, but the buzzcut he now wore kept his scalp cool. "Sir," he said.

The man in front of him dwarfed all others in the training room—tall and wide with a round face, roughened skin, and an oft-broken nose. A monolith in a tight polo shirt and a bad attitude.

"Come with me."

"Don't you want me to change?" Canton asked, indicating his sweat-stained gray t-shirt and shorts.

"You'll have time enough to change," rumbled the monolith. He turned away. "Follow."

The big man led Canton through Warehouse to RECORDS, to a meeting room decorated in earth tones, smelling of lemon furniture polish. Three people awaited, sitting in plush leather chairs surrounding a large oak table.

One of the men, short, wide shoulders with receding black hair, stood. "Hello Agent Alsate, I am Benjamin Bauer, leader of Team Epsilon. Like the others, you may call me BB or boss." He pointed to a severe looking but pretty redhead, built long and lean. Something about the set of her thin mouth gave him a cold shiver. "This is our Magician, Winnie Keener."

"Yo," said the redhead, slouched back deep in her chair and looking bored.

"And this is Will, our sniper." A medium-sized surfer type with spiky blond air waved lazily. "You've met Thomas Mace. You are now a member of Team Epsilon, taking the place of Cheryl Washington, who retired once her two-year contract expired. Normally there would be one other, Bill Mortimer, but he is on compassionate leave, so it will be the four of us plus Ms. Keener, who, as our Magician, normally operates in a support capacity. Now, sit please."

Mace and Canton took their seats.

Canton noted that the wall behind the team leader, instead of paint over sheetrock, was made of some satiny material. Before he could say anything, the material came to life in a riot of color, forming a picture of the corpse. Or, more specifically, what was left of one.

Although the scale could not be judged (the corpse was lying upon a stretch of dun-colored, sandy earth), the body looked to be of a large man with brown hair, clothes and skin shredded to ribbons, body partially dismembered by scavengers with intestines strewn across the sand. "This, obviously, is our victim, one Nathan Sokrek. Our next objective: a Supernatural that kills and partially consumes its victims."

Winnie raised her hand. "Looks like an animal attack. Perhaps a great cat."

BB nodded. "Yes, yes it does. Perhaps a mountain lion killed Mr. Sokrek and ate his liver, leaving the rest of the body to rot in the harsh earth outside of Las Vegas, Nevada. That might indeed be the case, but there *are* no mountain lions just outside of Las Vegas." She raised her hand again, but BB cut her off. "No, no escapes from zoos or private collections."

Winnie shook her head. "Nuts." She considered the photo for a moment. "Any alerts from those fancy new sensors?"

"No. But that's not surprising. There are many places in the desert outside of Las Vegas that offer no cell towers and no cell coverage. A Magician or magic-wielding Supernatural could cast Spells to their heart's content and we wouldn't know."

"So what are we looking at, boss?" Will drawled, eyes at half-mast. He looked sleepy, but he was drinking in every word.

"That's what I want to know," said BB. "Why was Mr. Sokrek, a pit boss at the Bellagio, out in the middle of the desert near a seldom traveled road? Why was his car found in Henderson? Why were the only other tracks that of a great cat and why did they disappear? Can someone tell me of a Supernatural that can do all this?"

Canton sighed. "Skinwalker," he said with absolute certainty. "That's why I'm on your team. You wanted someone who fought a Skinwalker before."

BB gave him a slight smile. "Exactly. We had an opening on the team and you have experience at the kind of mission we are about to undertake."

"Okay, we're dealing with some sort of lycanthrope—" Will began.

"No," said BB. "Skinwalker. Lycanthropes assume the aspect of one creature while a Skinwalker can assume the form of many creatures."

Will's brow furrowed in puzzlement. "What makes you think it's a Skinwalker, not a were-panther or were-mountain lion?"

"Because Mr. Sokrek wasn't the first victim," BB answered. "Five days previous, Simon Ellenbrucker, a blackjack dealer at Mandalay Bay, was found in the desert, apparently mauled by a large animal." He waited a moment for that to sink in. "A bear, according to the teeth marks … and his liver was eaten."

Silence.

"The Navajo had the most legends and stories involving Skinwalkers," Canton said finally. All eyes turned to the Native American as he steepled his fingers and stared off into the distance. "A Skinwalker was called *yee naaldlooshii,* or 'with it, he goes on all fours.' Assuming that this isn't a curse and it is a Skinwalker like in the legends, then it could be one who practices the Witchery Way. A witch, or Magician, who becomes so powerful they can assume animal form. These were the most evil of all the Navajo, usually having to kill a family member to attain their full power." He paused for a moment. "Or it could be a witch who uses the skin of animals to assume their form. Assuming the witch has several skins, then he or she could transform into several different animals. Either way, if the legends are true, this witch is going to be one mean hombre." Everyone was staring. "What?"

"You're smarter than you look," said Mace with a frown.

Will laughed. "That ain't too damn difficult."

BB held up both hands and the pic behind him morphed into the remains of a young woman in the tattered, blood-soaked remnants of a cocktail dress. "Pipe down, everyone." He turned to the pic. "This is our most recent victim, Rina Martin, found two days ago. The body was dumped north of the city near a small road in the middle of nowhere. Like the other two, as you can see, her liver is gone …

well, *most* of her is gone, actually, picked through by scavengers. All the victims had their liver *eaten* out of their bodies. Total count is three victims and no motive and before you ask, we checked with the casinos and accessed their recordings. Whoever our killer is—whether it is a Skinwalker, lycanthrope, or serial killer with an animal fetish—we can't find them through the recordings." BB turned back to the team. "Someone or something is using the Mojave Desert as a dumping ground. I want them found fast. This is going to be an op with a lot of legwork: searching the crime scenes, grilling the local LEOs, and interviewing and re-interviewing the staff of all three casinos."

"Boss?" Will held up his hand.

"Yes, Will, you can gamble as long it is on your own time, but no drinking."

The blond sniper leaned back in his chair, smiling beatifically. "God, I love my job."

THE SYDNEY OPERA HOUSE CASINO was the newest multi-million dollar attraction on the Las Vegas strip and one of the busiest.

Constructed to a seven-tenths scale to the original in Australia, the 'shells' used to make up the structure, like the original, were composed of sections of a sphere, each made of precast concrete and set on a large podium. This main structure housed the casino, three restaurants, an amphitheater, a movie theater, a spa, and a gymnasium. Behind the famous 'shell' structures were two thirty story towers, the hotel proper—1,200 rooms, all suites, all with jetted tubs, hand-cut Italian marble tiles for the bathrooms, large screen televisions, and wet bars. The top three floors, however, were even more opulent—$3,000 a night suites that gave new meaning to the word *opulence*. Those suites were meant for the high rollers, the ultra-rich and heads-of-state.

And the Bureau. At a much-discounted rate, of course.

The Grand Australian Suite was 3,600 feet of Italian marble, a silk-carpeted wonder consisting of five bedrooms and an outside wall constructed of double-reinforced tempered glass that overlooked the strip. Each member of Epsilon, except for Canton, had a room. As the Green Pea, the young Native American was stuck with the couch, but that was hardly an inconvenience. The suede couch was bigger than his old Honda Civic and more comfortable than his bed back in the Hamptons.

"You like the Bureau life, eh, Green Pea?"

Canton, draped bonelessly on his impromptu bed, opened one eye and stared up at the looming Thomas Mace.

"It sure does have its advantages, bud," he drawled. "I could get used to this."

"Go get us dinner, Pea, I'm hungry."

Canton sniffed, closing his eyes. "Go blow it out your ass," he said pleasantly.

Everyone in the suite came to a dead standstill. Had mice actually had the temerity to exist within its walls, they would have halted as well.

"What did you say?" growled the big man.

Without moving or seeming to care at all, the Green Pea said, "Listen up, Buttercup …. I've been in Warehouse long enough to hear all the Green Pea stories, and let me tell you, pard', I ain't impressed by a long patch. Don't get me wrong, I will take what punishment comes my way if I do wrong—that's only right—but there ain't no way in this godforsaken chicksquat outfit I'm going to be somebody's bitch boy because I happen to be the newest stallion in the herd." Finally Canton's lids opened, his normally warm brown eyes cold as arctic iron. "Don't have the desire to be gelded, neither. You got a problem with that?" Suddenly, he didn't seem like a sleepy young man, more like a coiled steel spring ready to unleash its potential energy with devastating consequences.

Mace stared as if his gaze would bore a hole in the smaller man. "It's all part of Green Pea hazing," he said slowly, as if addressing a particularly dimwitted child.

"Not this Green Pea. Order room service your own damn self."

One long minute passed without a word, almost without a breath. Will took a tentative step forward, but BB quickly grabbed his arm, face turned to the tableau in the middle of the room.

Finally, Thomas Mace bent at the knees until he was crouched at the Native American's side. "You got guts, kid," he said quietly. "And that will do." A fist the size of bowling ball punched the other man lightly on the shoulder.

Everyone exhaled and life went back to normal. That is, until Winnie stuck her head out of her room. "Boss, State Police just reported a body found out in the desert."

THE CORPSE LAY IN THE sand among stunted sage-colored scrub like a bag of trash thrown carelessly from a speeding car. Not much was left. The flesh had been savaged, both face and torso. It lay on its back, empty sockets staring at the noon sky, but there was enough left of the body to identify her as a woman. She was half-concealed by a blanket of black flies and parts of her body were scattered around the area, testament to the scavengers that still roamed the dry land near the city.

Canton looked around. Fifty feet to the west lay a track that could barely be called a road, almost wide enough for a car. The land sloped gently upward toward the mountains to the north, blasted and dry like an alien world. It was inhospitable to strangers, except its inhabitants—the coyotes, vultures, scorpions, and burrowing insects—who bided their time waiting for encroaching man to succumb to the relentless heat.

He knew this was the land of the Paiute, and not too far off, the Navajo. He wondered if this location, this particular spot of the Mojave, was important to the killer. Was the Skinwalker hoping the denizens of the desert would dispose of the bodies? Did he or she even care?

State police had reluctantly bowed to the authority of the team's FBI badges, although two cruisers were still parked eighty feet away next to the Coroner's van, which was a good forty feet from the team's twin black Crown Vics. Four Staties, including Chief Bendorf—a tall, rawboned man with ginger hair and a lantern jaw—stood next to the vehicles and watched impassively.

The team had arrived at the same time as the Coroner's van and was met with suspicion as they exited their air-conditioned vehicles. Chief Bendorf had crossed thick arms over his wide chest when he inspected the FBI IDs the team used and hawked a ribbon of tobacco onto the sand, narrowly missing Mace's mirror-polished black shoes. The two men regarded each other warily, one from behind jet-black Oakleys, the other from behind mirrored shades. Although Mace topped Bendorf by a head, the smaller man held himself with the total confidence of an Apex predator. Fortunately, BB intervened smoothly, preventing a jurisdictional pissing contest by offering the FBI team's services in a support capacity. The tough State trooper kept his mouth shut, but graced the team leader with a terse nod.

Winnie's voice came through the earwigs the team members wore. "*BB, I've been cross checking all the missing persons going back ten years.*" Her voice was clear as a bell despite her being in a small office building south of the Strip that served as the BSI field office. "*Do y'all know how many casino workers go missing every year? I could fill a football stadium with ten years' worth. It would take two weeks to sort the data. Hold on. Frida wants to say something.*"

Frida, the Receptionist, came on line. "*Boss, I've got a hunch.*"

BB, hardly sweating at all despite the cheap, black suit he wore (much to the envy of everyone there) subvocaled, "*Go ahead.*"

"*All three victims were Caucasian, so maybe that's the common thread. I'll eliminate all non-Caucasians from the list and see where that will lead us.*"

"*Good job, Frida. Let me know.*"

"*Check, boss.*"

"How did we miss that, boss?" Will asked, wiping his brow.

"Couldn't see the forest 'cause the trees were in the way," Canton said drily. "Boss, think we better wrap it up quick or that Chief is liable to bust in on our little sideshow here."

BB nodded. "Mace, what does it look like?"

The big man grunted from where he was crouched next to the body. "Dunno, BB. This heat, all the critters that have been at the body ... sure looks like our perp did this, though. Liver is gone, but that could have been due to coyotes rather than the Skinwalker. Best guess, the woman's been dead for about two days."

"It was the Skinwalker." Canton's voice was emotionless.

Mace squinted at the young man. "What makes you think so, Pea?"

The Native American pointed at the hard ground. "Faint tracks. Looks like mountain lion and coyote and vulture. By the look of the torso—how shredded it is—I'm gonna guess that was our killer, the mountain lion. The coyote and vulture came after for an easy meal.

"Over here." He took a few measured steps. "The mountain lion went off this way, leaving some faint tracks, but they disappear." Canton stared at the hot, pewter sky, a frown on his face. "I think we have a real Skinwalker, a Navajo shaman who took the Witchy Way and became evil to the bone. He or she lures the victims out to the desert, maybe with magic. How sensitive are those newfangled sensors you have?"

"Not very," BB said with a shake of his head. "Still working on tweaking their range and sensitivity."

"One of the legends attributed to the Skinwalkers is their ability to charm and put fear into their victims. So my guess is that our bad boy casts a Spell, controlling the victim and bringing them out here to their deaths." Canton went subvocal. *"Winnie, would a charm Spell trip one of them sensors?"*

"I don't think so," she replied. *"Current ratings are for 200 megamerlins. You could turn someone's brains into tapioca with less than 200 megamerlins. Only reason we're using them now is to catch the really big mojo. Unless there was another Magician in the area to sense the Spell, it would pass unnoticed."*

Canton began to walk in a circle, head down and eyes half shut as he began to speak, his words tumbling forth faster and faster with every step. "The Skinwalker has them under control. He makes them drive out to remote locations where they can be killed without anyone hearing the screams." Faster and faster, his leather shoes were kicking up clouds of dust. "The Skinwalker then uses one of the several skins he or she possesses to morph into an animal, kills the victim, and turns into a bird, which is why the tracks disappear. The bird flies back to the road and changes back into the Skinwalker, who drives away in the victim's car. It is abandoned in the city, perhaps with the doors unlocked or keys left in the ignition so it will be stolen. By the time anyone files a missing person's report, the car is in a few thousand pieces."

Eyes still half-closed, he continued to circle and rubbed his temples as if trying to massage his thoughts into order. *"Winnie, Frida, can either of you tell me if Mr. Sokrek's car had the keys in the ignition?"*

"That's a roger," said Frida. *"Police were surprised."*

"That's it, that's how the perp is bringing the victims to the desert and getting away," he said out loud. To Frida, *"Cross reference missing white people with cars left abandoned, and I'll bet you dollars to donuts that you'll find a few."*

"No bet. Good work." Winnie sounded impressed.

"And I wouldn't go back farther than a year or two. If this is a real Skinwalker, and I think it is, then it wouldn't take long for the evil in its soul to rot the mind. My guess is that this witch hasn't been doing this too terribly long."

"BB?"

"Listen to the man," the team leader said. "I think he's onto something here."

"Check, boss."

"How do you know so much about Navajo lore?" Will asked, raising an eyebrow.

"Anthropology classes at Georgetown with a focus on Native American Culture." Canton stopped his circling. "Far more interesting than European history and customs."

BB walked over until he came almost uncomfortably close to the younger man, invading his personal space. "You know, I might have to take you off Green Pea status after this mission."

Canton's sweat-streaked face stretched into a grin. "Why not now?"

"Oh, you have to survive first."

"Okay, Mr. Smart Guy, why the kills?" Mace stood, brushing his hands together. "We know he or she is devolving, killing more often, but why kill in the first place? Why eat the liver?"

Canton walked slowly over to the bigger man. "The Skinwalker took evil into its soul. It's a creature of malice and hate and everything negative in this universe, so I don't think it *needs* a reason to murder, it wants to."

"*Canton?*"

"*Yes, Winnie?*"

"*You said it uses the skin of animals to become those animals?*"

"*Yeah, a necessary component to the magic is the skin.*"

"*How does the Skinwalker obtain the pelts? Go to a taxidermist? What?*"

"*Well, one of the lesser known Navajo legends states that the Skinwalker must kill the animal and prepare the skins through some arcane ritual that has never been documented.*"

"*Y'all are one strange hombre, you know that?*" Winnie said. "*Don't bother answering .... I think I know why that Skinwalker might be killin' all them folks.*"

"*We, as they say, are all ears.*" Somehow, even subvocally, BB managed to sound dry as the desert surrounding them.

"*Okay, big boss man, riddle me this. Notice that all the victims have been placed on their backs? Do me a little favor, turn the victim over.*"

Mace grimaced, but complied, donning latex gloves and flipping the corpse easily on what was left of its front.

Putrescine and cadaverine gasses filled the still air as its back was revealed, a mass of exposed muscle, fat, dried, black blood and bone. A neat incision had been run laterally up both sides of the back, horizontally above the shoulder blades and six inches above the waist. The section of skin removed made a tidy rectangle of raw meat, a work of geometric precision measured in horror and dismay.

"What the ever-loving ...." Will began, his fair skin turning a shade of pale green.

"*I take it y'all are seeing what the pathologist missed, but yours truly did not. Although, to be fair, the bodies were in a severe state of disarticulation and decay, not to mention torn to shreds by the critters munchin' on them.*"

"We're seeing it," Mace said, shooing away flies from his face. "Just a little sickened."

"*Yup. So, Mr. Injun, what do you make of this?*" asked Winnie.

Canton stared at the dirty, gory wound that Mace exposed to the air, trying not to gag at the smell. "I think our Skinwalker wants to use their skins to become them …. He or she wants to shape-change into other humans."

His brown eyes focused on the Staties, no longer waiting by their vehicles. "Here comes the Chief. I think he's a mite angry that we're messing with the body, Boss."

BB looked over to where Bendorf was striding purposefully toward the team. "It's always something," he said.

CHAPTER SEVEN

———•———

In the Dark

AND BACK TO THE PRESENT with a splitting, hammer-to-the-back-of-the-skull headache that threatened to pop my eyeballs out on springs like in a *Looney Tunes* cartoon.

"Kal ...."

I clapped hands over my ears. "Hush, Ghost, I know, I know, leave off, please."

I didn't want a digitized apparition trying to mother me, no matter how necessary. Head pounding like a kettledrum, I stood and went to the far eastern corner of the office where BB had his private lavatory.

Hallelujah! A shower, and a nice one at that. Huge, marble tile and multiple showerheads placed on the ceiling and walls. He had everything but a valet standing in the corner handing out toiletries. Yeah, just what Dr. Hakala ordered.

Forty-five minutes later, feeling clean and less like warmed-over crap, I sat back down at the desk and put the DRAFT on. Ghost was kind enough to keep his spectral trap firmly shut.

"VR."

***

WINNIE WAS WAITING IN COMMS when they returned from the desert after Chief Bendorf silently, but firmly, escorted them from the crime scene.

"Why did you let that Chief bull us around some, boss?" Canton asked as they placed their palms on the Receptionist's desk. Frida stared at them with dead eyes while her Mac and the silver Spell Shapes embedded in the Formica assessed their identities.

"One thing I learned about working with the locals, Canton," said the team leader as he waited for the others to pass the scans, "is that it is easier to go with the flow than to fight the current. Let the Chief have his way. We'll still do things ours."

Once everyone was seated in Coms, Winnie started the show. "While y'all were coming back from looking at dead people, we found something I think is pretty darn interesting." A wide smile lit her severe face and her short, red hair practically crackled with the energy of her excitement. "Six missing people had cars that were reported as abandoned. And get this: all the people were casino employees, and all were white."

"What does this Supernatural want with white casino employees?" Will asked.

Canton scratched his head. "Maybe killing tourists would attract too much attention. Make the casinos tighten security and bring the law down that much faster. The only reason Vegas exists is because of the traffic from gambling."

Will shook his head. "Could be, dude, but you have to admit it's pretty damn freaky."

BB pursed his lips. "I think the question we should ask ourselves is, why these *particular* employees?"

"Can't be money," Canton said, holding up a Slate and displaying a document on its glassy surface. "According to the report, they didn't have much. Oh, they made a good living but weren't well off enough to attract attention."

The team sat there for a while, studying the reports on their Slates, trying to figure out the killer's angle. Eventually Frida left to order dinner and take position at her desk while the rest continued to brainstorm.

Dinner came and everyone broke out chopsticks and dug into cheap Thai delivery.

Mace took a long drink from his can of cola and belched. "The Skinwalker can't be thinking about robbing a casino; even magic would be just about useless for that." He turned to BB. "Boss, you might want to think about retasking a satellite and having Otto keep an eye out for vehicles moving on the back roads who stop on deserted stretches for more than a minute. We might get lucky."

BB nodded. "Good idea." He tapped a section of the large meeting table and it became transparent, revealing a touch-screen monitor and keyboard. He began typing furiously.

"Who's Otto?" Canton asked.

"Not a who, but a what," Winnie replied, without bothering to look up from her Slate. "Automated Program, Otto for short, a first generation pseudo-artificial intelligence. Not very good yet, but soon someone will figure out a way to make it *really* think."

"Wow, this is getting into some serious science fiction stuff."

"Welcome to the Bureau."

Will wiped his mouth, swallowing the last of his tofu platter. "You know, been thinking about the victims. The Skinwalker is going all *Silence of the Lambs* Jame Gumb on these people to use their skins so it can turn into them, I get that, and we been trying to figure out why. I think it *is* about money."

Everyone stopped what they were doing and swiveled their heads toward the spiky-haired sniper. "You see," he continued. "I think it's not about the money they have now, but the money they're *gonna* have.

"Think about it … this person, this Skinwalker, he or she is taken to the cleaners gambling, or is done dirty by a casino. The Skinwalker wants revenge, wants to stick to the white man … you know, assuming that's it's a Native American. So, it uses its charm magic to find out who stands to inherit a lot of dough, then, one by one, it kills daddy, or auntie, or grandma, so it can pose as a sweet grandson or whatever and inherit the wealth."

"Y'all figured out all that by yourself?" Winnie asked.

Will smiled winningly. "I ain't just a pretty face." The smile slowly disappeared. "Besides, money is an awful big motivation when it comes to murder. It's always about the money."

"It would have to be an inheritance that wouldn't be hung up in probate or contested by other relatives," Mace said slowly. "Something the Skinwalker can liquidate or utilize almost immediately."

BB stood. "Winnie, have Otto check to see if any of the victims have rich relatives."

"And see if any of the suspected past victims had relatives who died recently." Canton took another bite of rice. "The Skinwalker has to act fast; he can't fart around just waiting. If they do have relatives who passed recently, find out the manner of their deaths."

"Good thinking," BB said.

It was nearly an hour later when they received an answer. "Boss, two of the suspected vics from the last four months had relatives who passed away." The silvery screen that comprised the eight-by-fifteen wall behind BB came to life, showing two photos: a young woman and an older man of perhaps fifty. "Melanie Shaw's grandmother, Amy Meriweather, was attacked and savaged by a dog in Detroit. She was eighty-seven years old and, although the wounds weren't fatal, her heart gave out while she was under sedation. She left her only grandchild antique jewelry worth an estimated $175,000.

"The second person, Abel Rassmussen, had a brother, Arthur, who died of a fall while rock climbing in Colorado. Arthur left his brother, his only surviving relative, over half-a-million dollars."

Canton raised his hand. "Let me guess …. Both relatives showed up at the reading of the will to collect their inheritance?"

"Yep."

"That's all well and good. We got motive." The newest member of Team Epsilon stood and stretched tired muscles. "But it won't catch us a Skinwalker, not soon. It seems to me that the kills are coming faster and faster." He stared off into the middle distance. "Thing is, I don't think it's devolving, I'm thinking it's going to be leaving soon. It probably realizes that it's attracted attention. Hell, I bet it has a police scanner and is monitoring the situation and knows the jig is up. Skinwalkers may be five kinds of crazy, but crazy don't mean dumb. This thing is gonna go for one, perhaps two more victims, then head for the horizon."

Mace shook his head. "How can you be so sure?"

"If you were the Skinwalker, what would you do?"

No answer, only the pressure of eight gazes against his skin.

"Exactly. It's crazy and crazy smart. We can stake out our victims' relatives, but that's not going to save the last one or two victims and I *know* that sick bastard isn't done with killing here yet. I can feel it."

"What do you suggest," asked BB around a mouthful of sticky rice.

Canton smiled. "I do have an idea."

"NOT MY IDEA OF FUN, Green Pea." Will sounded less than amused.

Canton replied, "You're just angry because you don't get to gamble tonight."

"Damn skippy, Pea."

"Just think, if this doesn't work we can start casing relatives of our victims and our suspected victims."

"Oh, be still my beating heart."

"I guess the bloom is off the Bureau rose for you, huh?"

"*Let's pipe down. Communications only when absolutely necessary,*" BB subvocaled.

"*Check, boss.*"

"*Check.*"

Past midnight and four brand-new black Crown Vics cruised the Cardinal points outside of Las Vegas. One Agent per Vic, with Winnie at the office coordinating using satellite data and ready to assist magically if necessary. Light pollution spilled into the sky from the city, but miles out into the desert the stars shone through in a spectacle of galactic glory.

The team had been out driving since 10 p.m., slowly tooling around desert roads, leaving grit and dust in their wake. On the passenger seat of each car was a steely disk the size of a silver dollar lying on a Slate—the flat-panel touch-screen mini-computer assigned to each Agent. Each disk was able to sense magical energy (called merlins) starting at 200 megamerlins. It was Canton's idea to turn each Crown Vic into a mobile sensing unit.

With nightvision glasses (a combination of tech and magic that was far superior to its bulky military counterpart), the team was able to drive the near abandoned roads without headlights, the darkness broken into black and white and all the shades of gray in-between.

Also as part of their gear for the nighttime excursion, each team member had four Spell eggs, two pistols, and a fully automatic weapon of their choice. In Canton's case, it was an AR 15 armed with 5.56 NATO rounds—not the most reliable weapon but hellishly accurate. For personal protection, they wore black Kevlar/titanium body armor. It looked like a mad conglomeration of hockey pads and a catcher's chest protector. It was bulky, but light, and could stop any round up to and including 20mm. It was the best armor available, but a hit from a 20mm could still shatter bone.

"If it is a Navajo Skinwalker," he'd said to the team earlier, "a real one, not just some Magician playing around with Navajo magic, then I reckon it's keeping its magic place out in the desert somewhere."

"What do you mean, magic place?" Winnie asked.

"It has to turn those skins into artifacts that allow it to shape-shift. It takes a magic ritual to do that and no self-respecting, white-man hating Navajo shaman would perform that ritual in a city built by Caucasians." He shook his head. "No, this Skinwalker will do it out in the desert or on a mountain where it can be alone and undisturbed."

BB nodded, fingers steepled beneath his chin. "It's worth a try."

"Got one question, Pea," Mace rumbled softly from deep within his chest.

"What?"

"I'm no expert on Native Americans, but aren't these Paiute and Shoshone lands? The Navajo have reservations in New Mexico, Arizona, and Utah, right? So what is a Navajo Skinwalker doing near Vegas?"

Canton stared at the big man. "I don't know," he said pensively, "but thinking geographically like that isn't going to help us find the thing. My guess is it picked Vegas because there are a lot of loners and gypsy workers who wouldn't be missed much."

So the team obtained four sensors from four different cell towers and hit the road. Canton headed north, BB east, Mace west, and Will south, in hope that the Skinwalker would use enough magic to sound the alarm.

12:45 A.M.

"*East checking in. Neg signs so far.*"

"*West checking in. Negative.*"

"*North checking in. Negative.*"

"*South checking in. Negative.*"

"*Winnie, any movement on the roads besides us?*"

"*Negative, just the usual traffic around the city and things are looking pretty darn quiet. We have four more hours of satellite time left, boss, then we have to relinquish control to Commander, Submarine Forces Atlantic. Seems the bird is needed for some 'urgent matter' off of Norfolk and COMSUBLANT is an entity I have no desire to irritate.*"

"*Roger. I don't want to keep the Vice Admiral waiting too long.*"

Listening to team talk, Canton smiled, amazed at the power the Bureau held. To commandeer an armed forces satellite at a moment's notice was nothing short of incredible. Not to mention scary as hell.

Legs beginning to cramp from sitting in on position for too long, he pulled the car over to the meager shoulder. "*North taking a short walkabout. My legs are killing me.*"

"*Understood, North. I think that's a grand idea. Everyone take five and stretch your legs. Keep your eyes peeled, though.*"

Muscles protesting, the young Native American left the car and stretched, grunting and straining as his muscles protested the workout. He scratched his head and stared at the lone vulture winging its way west. He unzipped and let flow a long stream of urine that used to be several cups of coffee. The relief was almost orgasmic. When he was done he began to stretch to work the kinks out of his muscles.

"I could sure use a drink right about now," he muttered, stretching his left arm overhead and bending to the right. "But noooooooooo …. I had to have the brilliant idea to drive around all goldarned night. Should have remembered rule number one: never volunteer. Nantan Lupan woulda kicked my ass for opening my big fat mouth like that."

Bending forward, he tried to touch his toes, but the bulky armor wouldn't let him. "Damn, this thing looks ridiculous. *I* look ridiculous. If Mom could see me now …. Of course, she can't see me because it's nighttime and …." His voice trailed off. A couple of seconds passed, then he swiveled his head to the west, eyes frantically searching the sky. "Oh, damn …."

"*West, you read?*" he subvocaled frantically.

"*Of course I read you. What is it, North?*"

"*Skinwalker heading your way!*"

BB cut in. "*You sure, North?*"

"*Yeah, big ass vulture heading west/northwest at a good clip.*"

There were a few seconds of silence while BB mulled that over. "*What makes you think a vulture is the Skinwalker?*"

Canton bared his teeth, more of a snarl than a smile. "*Because vultures don't fly at night.*"

Minutes later, Canton was on the 157 heading west while Will and BB burned rubber to catch up. By the time he rendezvoused with Mace, the vulture had passed and was heading toward Mt. Charleston.

"*Don't lose it, Mace,*" BB said. "*I'm almost to you.*"

"*I'm no amateur, boss. I have a bead on our target. Want Will to take it out?*" The blond man had the only sniper rifle in the team, a .50 cal.

"*Negative. Let's find out where it's going. Winnie, you think the silver ingots sewn into our armor will stop a Spell from an angry Skinwalker?*"

"*It's rated for up to a gigamerlin before it needs to cool, so it should do you. I cast a 300 megamerlin Spell and I need a rest like something fierce. I'd recommend a top-of-the-line Faraday coat, but you'd sweat your cajones off.*" Even at night it felt hot enough to bake bread. "*I think they'll do fine.*"

"*Copy that. Has Otto zeroed in on the vulture's heat signature?*"

"*Yep. With this satellite, I can tell you the temperature of a baby's bottom and see if it needs to be changed as well.*"

"*Let us know where it goes.*"

"*Check, boss.*"

"*How come it's out here?*" asked Will. "*Sure didn't kill anyone or the sensors would've gone crazy.*"

"*Vultures have excellent vision, so it spotted us,*" replied Canton. "*Probably spooked it.*"

"*Not as much as it spooks me.*"

"*Hush, you two,*" BB sent. "*Care to join us, Winnie? We could use a Magician of your caliber out here.*"

"*Oh, gosh boss. Thanks SO much for the invite, but I just washed my hair.*"

Winnie's reluctance was greeted by subvocal laughter.

TWENTY-FIVE MINUTES LATER FOUND THE team walking along a twisty trail up the north slope of Mt. Charleston, the Crown Vics parked a half-mile back on the 157. At the higher altitude, it was cooler, and they had stopped sweating in their bulky gear, though the air was becoming thin enough that the men were beginning to pant.

"*Any lead on where it is?*" BB asked, staying subvocal despite their close proximity.

Winnie's voice was chagrined. "*Sorry, boss. Last known location was about a couple hundred yards from your position, just below the snow line. Like I said, it landed and disappeared.*"

"*Damn,*" he said.

Mace, on point, stopped, bringing the others up short. "*Split up, boss?*"

BB looked around, the black and white world of carbonate cliffs, deep, narrow canyons, ponderosa pine giving way to even more rugged terrain dotted with bristlecone pine and short, tough grass. "*Not sure. Look at this area. One misstep and your body is broken at the bottom of one of those canyons.*"

"*My vote is we give it a try,*" Canton said. "*We stay within line of sight and in constant communication. We have our Slates and our sensors. Sure, the Skinwalker has magic, but we have this silver-loaded armor and lots of firepower."*

"*Sounds like plan to me, boss.*" Will hefted his .50 cal. "*I can hang back, keep an eye out and shoot anything that comes for us.*" He flashed a nasty smile.

"*All right. Canton, go left. Mace, stay on point and I'll flank right. Will, keep an eye out and watch our six.*"

The sniper grunted. "*I always got your back, boss.*"

"*Okay, move out.*"

The four split up and Canton made his way to the edge of a steep ravine, a jagged, gray gash in the side of the mountain, fifty feet deep. Mace was clearly in sight and BB a dark flitter through the white ash a hundred feet away.

Will stalked slowly around scrub brush and over the corpses of trees, one eye looking through the scope of his .50 cal. No movement except for the extraordinarily quiet rustlings of his teammates, their SEAL training rendering them ghosts in the night.

"Where are you?" he whispered almost inaudibly. "I know you're out there, Mr. Skinwalker. You may be sly, but so am I."

The cool air at 7,000 feet brushed against his cheek, bringing the scent of dust, pitch, and pine needles that tickled his nostrils. He scratched his nose absently, clenching his jaw, stifling a sneeze.

A rustling—faint, directionless, nearby—and Will spun, bringing his rifle to bear but seeing nothing. Perhaps a chipmunk?

Pain, disorientation. The .50 cal fell from nerveless fingers and the ground swallowed him whole.

"*BOSS!*" WINNIE'S VOICE WAS FRANTIC. "*Will's gone! Was on your six, then nothing. The satellite is picking up no thermal readings from his position, nothing larger than a squirrel.*"

"*Damn!*" BB swore. "*Ambush! Canton, back on Mace. Mace, you sta—*"

Silence.

"*BB?*" Canton felt the small hairs on the back of his neck rise.

"*Boss!*" cried Winnie.

"*Eyes sharp, Green Pea.*" Thomas Mace was all business, cold, brutal and lethal. "*Winnie, do you see BB anywhere?*"

"*He disappeared as well, as if he was erased from the monitor. What the hell is going on, Mace?*" Her voice cracked.

"*Hush now, hold it together. Check?*"

A moment of silence, then, "*Check.*"

Mace spun in a slow circle. "*Green Pea, make your way to my position, slow and careful. Keep your eyes peeled. Check?*"

Canton looked around, eyes alert for danger in a world rendered black and white. "*Check,*" he said absently.

Some sense, some instinct warned him a split second before he felt a steel band around his ankle. The band lifted, taking his leg with it and he found himself airborne. The first bounce knocked the breath from his lungs and broke a rib, agony shooting through his chest. The second bounce brought with it a white-hot sickening pain along his left arm along with a harsh *snap*.

He didn't feel the third bounce.

CHAPTER EIGHT

———•———

Down at the Bottom

THE WORLD WAS A CACOPHONY of pain and rue. Searing agony on one half of his body tearing at his nerves, cold aching soreness on the other. One swollen eyelid, bloated and colored in purple, slowly forced its way open, dried blood cracking and flaking off. It felt hot and tender and Canton groaned in misery.

Stars. Blackness. A dark expanse above him. More pain.

"BB! Mace! Come in, ya'll! Repeat, BB … Mace … Canton, are you there? I am on my way, ETA ten minutes." Winnie sounded scared.

Through a shuddering haze of pain and dizziness, Canton managed to lift his right arm and tap the throat mic. *"Maintain … radio … silence until … I tell … you. Until then … fix on my … location."* Even subvocal communication hurt. He took a deep breath and needles of agony shot through his torso.

From the Crown Vic, Frida drove like a NASCAR racer on crack along the 157, lights off and nightvision glasses on. Winnie let out an explosive sigh of relief, noting Canton's position from the satellite feed to her Slate. *"Check,"* she replied to the wounded Green Pea.

The Native American breathed a sigh of relief, a tear coming loose from his eye to roll across his temple as he stared at the sky. Help was coming and he could relax. It was time to assess his situation.

Ribs broken, he wasn't sure how many, but they were on the left side of his torso. No blood coughing explosively from his mouth, so no punctured lung. A mind-numbing throbbing from his left arm told him that it was broken and broken badly and he could smell freshly spilled blood. He tried to move his head to see the damage, but when he did, the world spun at crazy angles, causing his stomach to rebel. Concussion, he reckoned, if the nausea was any indication. He tried to move his legs, but his right knee hurt abysmally and was too swollen, while his left seemed fine, albeit bruised.

Using his right arm, he moved his hand across his chest armor, finding the Kevlar torn and several of the titanium plates bent and twisted. Eyes now fully open, he looked up, trying to pierce the darkness (his nightvision glasses long gone) and noted the fall he had taken. A steep slope of gray stone, jagged outcroppings here and there, outcroppings he must have hit on his way down, breaking his bones like matchsticks.

With his good arm he reached around, wincing as every movement brought nails of pain, his gloved hand probing the ground around his head. Dirt, scree, tough, scrabbly brush, but no large rocks. He stopped, his breath ragged as he gingerly sipped at the cool air. It hurt too much to breathe deeply or continue exploration.

Time moved so slowly and sensory overload—so many aches, so many pains—all blended into a solid mass of nauseating agony that strobed through his body from head to toe. It was a hot mass that ate at his muscles and tore at his guts with blunt barbs. He knew a goodly amount of time must have passed, but it was too fluid, too greasy … like oiled snakes, it slithered through his grasp. One moment bled into the next and the next and the next in a meaningless blur.

Pebbles clattered down the small cliff of the ravine, pocking the ground around Canton's head, and every nerve and muscle in his body came alive, sending a fresh wave of agony to the back of his skull. Dimly he heard a sniffing, a snuffling, as if someone or something was testing the air, trying to catch an elusive scent. This went on for a minute, then came a curious sound, like that of a sheet ripping, followed by the flap of wings.

Thud. The sound of ruffling feathers. Canton slowed his shallow breathing and closed his swollen eyelids, leaving only the thinnest of slits to peer through.

Again the sheet-tearing sound, but from very close by, almost close enough to touch. It was right there and he knew he was in danger because Winnie would've announced herself. It had to be that the Skinwalker, and it was only a few short feet away, ready to skin his back like all those poor victims left to rot in the Mojave. Even though agony pulsed through his body with every beat of his heart, he held himself still, knowing that death was coming ever closer. Through the narrow slits of his eyes, he saw a form blotting out the stars.

"Well, well, well … what have we here?" A deep voice, masculine, throaty with a harsh rasp. Callused hands gently touched his skull. "A man of the People given over to the great, white Enemy. That is a shame and I am sorry to have killed you, but know this, my brother, your skin will live on. Oh yes it will."

It was too dark to see the Skinwalker features, but it leaned in close and through the slits of his eyes Canton saw the edge of a knife gleam in the pale moonlight. He could feel the other man's foul breath on his face and knew that he only had moments before the evil witch would start to flay him alive.

Fear drove his arm, fear that pumped adrenaline through his body, turning the broken mechanism into a potent force, if only for a moment or two.

A moment was all he needed.

His right arm—the good arm—shot up, fingers straight and hard, hard like steel, hard with all the fear and resolve and anger and hate that invigorated him at that moment and the pain was gone, the terrible barbs that had been tormenting him, his broken arm, his battered and bruised body, his splintered ribs, all of it negated by the desperate, adamantine will to live and overcome all threats. Those hard fingers glanced off a jawbone and into flesh, springy, tough flesh and something *gave* way to his steely fingers, something that emitted a soft *crunch*. The Skinwalker fell away and the pain returned with a vengeance, with such magnificent force that it stopped the breath in his lungs.

It was worse, far worse than before and it tore through his body, causing it to buck and arch convulsively. His arm, his ribs, all were flensed with blades of electric agony. The world was gone, the team was gone, and the only thing that existed was the agony that robbed him of reason, reducing him to a reactive *thing* that gibbered and mewled.

From the back of his mind where a spark of sanity still resided, Canton was still able to observe the outside world, although at that moment interaction was impossible. He heard the sound of flesh slapping stone and a horrid, wet gurgling that went on and on. Dimly seen through the haze of pain was the glint of moonlight on metal and a dark form that thrashed in and out of his sight; then there were two wet slaps and warm fluid splashed his face. The form disappeared, followed by a dull *thud*.

"Oh, Jesus Canton, y'all got yourself messed up something pretty, didn't you?"

Winnie's voice never sounded so good.

Warm hands touched his face and a strange lassitude overcame his body, removing the involuntary spasms that racked him. The pain slowly receded, the dull barbs withdrawing from his guts, his side and his arm.

When Winnie's voice came again, it sounded tinny and far, far away, as if she were speaking from deep within a cave. "Frida, give me a hand here. Take his hand …. There, now he ain't gonna feel a thing, so don't be shy in pulling when I tell y'all to pull. Got me?"

"Got you." A soft, feminine voice. It reminded him of feathers on the wind.

Two heartbeats, then three. "Okay now … pull."

Crack!

She was right, it didn't hurt. Canton felt a wrenching pressure in his left arm and the slide of bone through flesh, but the lassitude didn't let him care and when the warmth came it was *wonderful*. Liquid and yet not, it flowed up through his fingers, past his elbow, and wrapped his upper arm in a honeyed heat that sunk into flesh and bone and brought a sleepy kind of joy.

"Oh, yeah," he slurred, "that's the stuff."

"Hold on a moment, Canton," Frida said in her feathery tones. "Winnie will set you to rights. Just a little while longer."

"S-she can take all the time she wants if it keeps feeling this good."

The warm, honeyed heat flared again around his bicep, traveled up to his shoulder, and flowed into his face, where it set up shop. A pair of callused hands probed his cheek and the bone *twisted*, snapping back into place. Canton almost laughed. He had no idea his face had taken such a pummeling. Apparently the damage to his arm trumped the hurt inflicted on his face.

After the magic was done, it traveled to his chest and began to mend his broken ribs.

"Deep breath, Canton," said Winnie in a voice like steel.

He almost laughed, ready to tell her to go take a flying leap, but the honey warmth urged him to follow her advice. As he breathed in, his chest expanding, he felt ribs pop back into place, settling together like LEGOS. Before the air could leave his lungs, the warmth knit together cracked and broken bone and once again he could breathe without pain.

From there the slow warmth spread over to the lesser indignities his body had suffered, healing them, removing hematomas and repairing tender flesh.

When she was done, Winnie sat down heavily next to him. "I ain't doin' that again anytime soon," she said, her west Texas dialect thick as molasses.

Canton slowly sat up, probing his face and body with his fingertips. "That is freaking amazing," he marveled. "I'm completely healed."

"And I'm completely wiped, y'all."

With a grunt, the Native American stood, marveling at how *good* he felt. "Man, that should come in six-packs." His .45 ACP had fortuitously landed next to him. He checked the weapon in the dim light of the moon. The tough pistol had weathered the fall better than he had.

Frida handed Winnie—decked out in her own set of black, bulky armor—a canteen and said, "When you disappeared, I alerted Warehouse. The Director has sent Team Alpha. They'll be on the ground in less than two hours."

"Then head back to the office. They'll be expecting you there." He stared at her for a moment. She was an attractive woman, African-American with flawless skin and a trim figure, evident from her lack of armor. "Why are you out here anyway? You aren't mission-rated yet. We can't leave the Armory unprotected."

Frida stood and Canton nearly took a step back. Although she was a good inch shorter than he, she radiated power and fierce determination.

"I go where I'm needed." The feathery voice turned to granite.

He held up his hands. "Right. Check that." He cleared his throat. "Please go back to the office and wait for Alpha."

A small nod, barely a dip of the head. "Now that you ask so nice, I will," she said, the granite softening somewhat.

Canton helped the Magician to her feet. She was a bit wobbly, but able to stand unaided. As he steadied her, he noticed a body on the ground not five feet away. If his nightvision glasses hadn't been in a million pieces, he would've seen the corpse earlier.

"Can I borrow your nightvision a sec?"

Wordlessly, the Magician handed them over, revealing eyes like chips of dark ice. Winnie might have healed him, but anything soft and caring in that angular face had been burned away ages ago. He suppressed a shudder and turned to the corpse.

It was a powerfully built Native American male, naked, wide-shouldered, with midnight-black hair that reached to his waist. Paint or makeup had been applied in an oval stretching from temple to temple, and a wide black band encircled the forehead. Two black, diagonal slashes had been painted across each cheek, while a whitish line ran under the right eye with three short lines radiating downward to the black slashes on the right cheek.

Frida pointed to the decoration. "Is that war paint?"

"The Navajo, or Diné (the People) as they call themselves, didn't really fight wars," Canton said. "They raided, took slaves from people like the Paiute and defended themselves from other tribes, but no real war." He pointed to a trio of holes in the man's broad chest. "What happened? I know I musta crushed his windpipe."

Winnie nodded. "He looked to be dying, but he also was set on taking you with him. Had a knife, so I shot him." She held up a matte-black Baretta 9mm. It was standard practice on a mission to use magically Silenced weapons. Winnie used the pistol to point at the dead man's hand, the fingers of which were curled around a brutal looking short knife.

Canton pried the fingers loose and examined the object. Six-inch curved bone handle with a four-inch obsidian blade. Sinew had been used to cement the incredibly sharp glass to the bone. "A skinning knife," he said. "Probably what he used to peel his victims. Works just as well for slitting throats."

"Ugh. That's nasty."

"Question is," he said, "where are the skins he uses to shapeshift?" Looking at the body, he considered the problem for a minute before reaching out and rolling the corpse onto its stomach.

There, in a small depression that had been concealed by the Skinwalker's body, was a rumpled mass of fur and feathers.

"Lookee here," said Canton, using the skinning knife to hold up a piece of hide about two feet long and a foot wide, covered in tawny fur. "Skins. Smaller than I thought they would be. Maybe that's all he needed." He tossed it to the Magician. "What can you tell me about it?"

Winnie held the hide with two fingers, away from her body as if it carried disease. A look of disgust twisted her face. "Ugh, I don't know about y'all, but this thing makes me feel like I got ants crawling on my skin." She dropped it and spat. "It reeks of death magic, nasty. Necromancy. This is wrong, Canton. Powerful wrong."

Frida shuddered. "Man, that is *so* gross."

"Here's how he was able to fly." Canton carefully held up a rectangle of skin dotted with vulture feathers. The artifact had a worn, mangy look, but the greasy-looking feathers moved and fluttered despite the absence of wind in the ravine. He considered the grisly artifact for a moment, stroking his chin. A few moments later, realization dawned on his broad face. "The son-of-a-bitch led us here," he said, eyes glittering with anger. "This was an ambush. Question is, how did he know and how did he overcome four highly trained Agents who could see in the dark?"

The other two remained silent, trading uneasy looks.

"Here." The feathered skin was handed to Frida, who took it reluctantly. "Grab the other one and take them to the office. Put them under lock and key. Special Branch will want to examine them."

She nodded, clearly unhappy with her charge.

The young Native American turned to the Magician. "Winnie, can you walk?"

"I'll walk straight the hell outta here."

"Well, let's get out of this ravine. I'll need you at the cars while Frida takes hers back to office."

The redheaded Magician raised an eyebrow. "I stay behind enemy lines, don't do any of that Agent stuff."

"You took your training in Coronado, didn't you?"

"Yeah, but only the sixteen weeks we field Magicians get, not the thirty-three standard for Agents."

Canton crossed his arms and gave Winnie a good, hard stare. "That's good enough," he sighed. "Listen, I appreciate the healing, but I need you out here, next to the cars, keeping an eye on my six while I go looking for the rest of our team, got it?"

Winnie seemed to wilt under the force of his gaze. "Got it."

"Good. Look at it this way. If I disappear, you can send in Team Alpha when they arrive. Now, let's get out of this ravine."

LEAVING FRIDA TO LEAD WINNIE back to the Vics, Canton retraced Mace's steps, wearing the Magician's nightvision glasses. He had almost reached the spot where Mace had vanished when his earwig squawked with static.

"*Yeah*?" he sent.

"*Back at the car. Frida's gone back to the office to report to the director.*"

"*Good.*"

"*The Satellite feed on my Slate shows no thermal activity in your area. Wherever BB and the others are, they ain't near you. Our time is up. I have to turn the bird over to the Navy.*"

"*Check that.*"

A difference in shades of gray caught his eye, a straight edge where, in nature, straight edges don't exist. He moved to the anomaly, careful not to make a sound, knife in one hand, .45 ACP in the other. As he moved closer, he noted the edge turned at a right angle, then another, and another, forming a rectangle. Grass and sandy dirt covered the area. Had the rectangle been moved to the right another couple of inches, it would have been near invisible.

"*Well, I'll be damned …. Just found out how we didn't see our ambusher and why the satellite didn't pick him up.*"

"*What?*"

Canton slipped the tip of the knife under the anomalous edge and lifted, exposing a three-by-two foot hole in the hard dirt of the mountain. Propped on the knife's tip was a piece of half-inch plywood, the surface covered in grass and sandy soil, camouflage for a tunnel that ran into the mountain. He relayed the information to the Magician.

"*It's a trick as old as the prairie and I feel three kinds of stupid for not thinking about it earlier. The tunnel looks to be kinda rough, man-made, but not with modern tools … far too crude.*"

"*What the hell? There're no caves of note on the mountain, nor any mines. Mt. Charleston is a campground on National Forest land. That tunnel should not exist.*"

"*I have no idea why it exists, but Will, BB, and Mace are at the end of this tunnel and I aim to get them out of there.*"

"*Canton, wait!*"

"*What?*"

"*Don't get dead.*"

He smiled grimly. "*That's the plan,*" he said and entered the tunnel.

CHAPTER NINE

―――・―――

Magic, Sand, and Skinwalkers

ENTERING THE TUNNEL WAS THE easy part, but continuing proved to be much harder than Canton anticipated because the ceiling sloped down until it was only four feet high, forcing him to duck-walk.

The walls, floor, and ceiling were tightly compacted dry, sandy soil and every dozen or so feet wooden braces and crossbeams shored up the tunnel. Some looked to be brand-new, factory-milled two-by-fours, while a few were made of old, dry wood, insect-riddled and gnawed by dry rot.

"*Winnie, it looks like these tunnels are far older than I thought. Old shorings updated with new wood. The tunnel is crudely dug, like something from the nineteenth century. I think our Skinwalker found this place or inherited it.*"

"*And I care why?*"

"*Just making conversation. This place is creepy, like the set of a slasher flick.*"

"*In situations like this, I think of what Shakespeare said.*"

"*Which was?*"

"*'Better you than me.'*"

"*Har-de-har.*"

"*Just find our boys and bring them back safe. Skip the commentary. I'm way too tired for what passes for sparkling conversation these days.*"

He grinned. "*Check that.*"

Heading onward, he traveled at least fifty steps before the tunnel forked, splitting into three. Peering into each branch, he noted the left-hand tunnel sloped at a noticeable angle before veering toward the right and out of sight. Without hesitation, he went left.

Down, down, down he went, thighs burning from the strain of the awkward slouching gait and gritty dirt tickling his nose. Sand lined his teeth and his spit tasted like soil and bug crap, but he kept going, ignoring the fire in his muscles, the cramps attacking his back as he stepped-skidded down the sloping tunnel. Sweat streamed into his eyes and his breath became more labored, echoing in his ears. His team was down there somewhere, in the dark, dank mountain depths and he refused to let them go. What was discomfort and minor pain compared to the lives of his comrades?

"Nantan Lupan," he panted. "Did you ever have to do this during your time?"

Crunch! Something gave beneath his foot.

Cursing, he snatched a broken egg-shaped piece of polystyrene from the floor. A small pebble fell into his hand. Behind the nightvision glasses his eyes grew round. In the monochromatic gloom of his vision he beheld a Spell gem, lusterless in the lack of light. From one of the many pockets on his belt he produced a glow stick, breaking the glass vial beneath the polymer casing and shaking a green phosphorescent light into existence. Taking off his glasses, he held the gem to his eyes, its sudden sparkle dazzling him.

A diamond. Examining the container, he pulled the tape free from the underside. The word LARCHFIG was typed in bold letters on the adhesive and on the case was a pictogram of audio waves moving toward a human ear. Canton knew right away what it meant.

Sonic grenade.

One of the first lessons after joining the Bureau was the care and handling of Spell gems. Spell gems were able to hold Spell energy commensurate with their quality and value. Diamonds could hold the most magical energy of all the gems and thus harbored the Spell shapes that utilized great amounts of energy and spells of great complexity. Semi-precious stones like amethyst and certain quartz held the least amount of energy, so they housed less complicated Spell Shapes.

Spell gems held Spells that required a predetermined action or vocalization to activate the Spell, like an 'if/then' statement in a line of computer code. The most common action used to cast a Spell from a gem was a word, but not just any word. Someone holding the gem certainly didn't want it to go off accidently, so the word was never a simple one like *pie* or *shoe*. The Magician who created the Spell Shape within the gem often used a compound word that would never come up in normal conversation, hence LARCHFIG.

The Native American knew that the gem and the polystyrene case that it had rested in had not fallen out of a pocket or been carelessly dropped. It was a clue from one of his teammates, a breadcrumb that told him he was on the right path.

Grinning, he tossed the glowstick behind him and donned his glasses, continuing his shuffle-walk down the tunnel.

Along the way, the transition subtle, soil became stone and the wooden supports vanished, leaving unbroken rock. Gradually the ceiling rose until he could walk only slightly hunched over. The relief to his aching muscles was enormous.

The tunnel took a turn to the left and he found himself facing light that flickered softly off the walls. He slowed, stepping carefully, ghost silent. Sweat trickled down his sides under the stifling armor, itching abominably, but he savagely crushed the desire to scratch.

Closer, closer …. An opening lit by soft yellow stood before him— an entrance into a wider space beyond—but with the light came only silence, broken by his soft breath and the beating of his heart. Profound and deep, that silence spoke to him, as clear as words.

Weapon ready, he swiftly reached the opening and saw a cave. What he beheld took his breath away.

It wasn't the cave—a roughly circular space twenty feet across—

that captured his attention, but what lay on the floor next to a softly glowing electric lantern.

"*Winnie, you still there?*"

"*Still here. Where else am I gonna go?*" She sounded bored and a little tired.

"*You should really be seeing what I'm seeing.*"

Suddenly, she no longer sounded bored and tired. "*Tell me.*"

Canton edged toward the light and the object on the ground. "From what I can tell, a three foot by three foot piece section of hide, probably deerskin, is laid out on the floor. There's a painting on the skin made with multicolored sand. Black, ochre, red and white."

"*A dry painting, like the Buddhist monks make?*"

"*More like what a Navajo Hitalii, a medicine man, would make.*"

"*So? What's the big deal? Dry-painting is practiced all over the world. Even in Australia, the Aborigines practice the technique. Ain't no big thing.*"

"*Yeah? Well, I'm looking a painting showing a stylized bear dragging a man clad all in black by the ankle. The man in black looks an awful like BB.*"

"*Holy crap!*"

"*That's not all, Win, not by a long patch. The images are moving.*"

And they were. The bear, rendered in black sand or coal dust, dragged the flailing stick man across the scene toward another stick figure that waited patiently at the far end of the painting. The figure had eagle feathers draped from its arms and wore stylized leather garments. As for the stick man in black, he was in bulky armor rendered crudely by the artist, but his face was the pale white of crushed gypsum. Despite the crudity, Canton recognized the leader of team Epsilon. Along the edges of the painting were stick figures representing hunters. They also moved, in a bizarre sort of shuffling dance that repeated every ten seconds or so when the scene reset.

"*Do … do y'all see any Spell Shapes?*"

Canton snorted. "*I wouldn't know a Spell Shape if it came up and bit me on the ass.*"

"*Do y'all see any Shapes that are hard to look at, kinda confusing to the eye?*"

"*No, all I see are stick figures and a big black bear dragging BB across the painting. When it reaches the far end, the whole scene resets and starts over again, like a faulty recording.*"

"*See any precious stones, or silver? Is the sand composed of crushed gems?*"

Canton knelt and examined the painting. "*Nuh-uh. Looks like red sandstone, maybe charcoal and gypsum and some yellow stuff.*"

"*Ochre.*"

"*Oh damn!*"

"*What? What's happening?*" Winnie's voice rose an octave in fear.

"*Oh, nothing bad … sorry.*" Canton couldn't tear his eyes from the painting. "*I didn't notice it before, but when the bear reaches the end of the sand painting and it resets, it's dragging a different man behind it.*" He took a deep breath. "*I think this one is supposed to be Will. The bear must be the Skinwalker, but we didn't find a bear pelt with the one you killed.*"

"*Which means there might be more than one.*"

Canton sighed. "*It's always something.*"

"*Damn, you have any idea how that sand painting works without precious metals or gems?*"

"*Not my department, I just shoot or stab things until they stop moving. I'll let you know if I see something else.*"

"*Check.*"

At the far end of the cave, where it narrowed to the width of a man's shoulders, the tunnel continued, rough and level, deep into the belly of the mountain.

Before he could complete his first step toward the exit, Canton saw a flash of black from the corner of his eye and something like a pillow with a core of iron slammed him in back of the thighs. The Native American flipped, gun flying from his hand, and landed hard on his stomach.

A rough growl cut through the ringing in his ears and pierced the fog of shock that gripped his torso. Another blow, this time to the hip, hurled him across the uneven floor of the cave like a hockey puck, slamming him into a wall.

Gasping and choking, Canton levered himself to his hands and knees, trying to shake the red and yellow stars that shot across his vision. From the corner of his eye he caught a glimpse of what had hit him.

Humping and slouching out of the sand painting was an enormous bear, black as pitch. It seemed to drink in the light from the lantern, sucking it in. Fangs as long and as sharp as daggers gleamed whitely from a slavering maw, shockingly white against the backdrop of such infinite darkness. Its head was the size of a pony keg, easily over a hundred pounds in and of itself. The black sand of the painting flowed *into* the beast's form, adding to its massive bulk. Each grain seemed to melt into the giant creature and with each grain the creature drew farther and farther out of the painting.

Four-inch claws pawed at the cavern floor, carving shallow scars into stone as the creature tried to work itself free, its foul breath stinging Canton's nose. It didn't roar, or growl, and its silence was more frightening than any cry of bestial anger. Black eyes like polished obsidian stared with uncanny intelligence at Canton, who hastily scrambled to his feet, drawing his secondary weapon, a Sig Sauer.

Two shots from the Silenced weapon, then four more dead solid center between the beast's beady eyes.

The rounds disappeared into the bear's black mass and emerged from the back of its head in sprays of charcoal sand. It bared its fangs, an ursine smile of malice.

"Damn," he cursed, holstering the weapon.

Silently the beast broke free of the painting, like a cork bursting from a champagne bottle. It charged and Canton barely ducked aside as an enormous paw that would have torn his head off flashed millimeters from his scalp. He scrambled off toward the cave entrance, but the bear was too fast, blocking the way before he could get there. Once again the bear took a swipe at him, its claws *hissssing* through the air. Two claws sheared through the Kevlar on his chest piece, but were deflected by the titanium under-layer. It was the titanium that protected him thus far, but he knew there would be spectacular bruises come morning.

Another swipe and Canton felt like he'd been hit by a truck, the force of the blow knocking him backward into the wall. He rebounded and leapt over the beast in a bid to maneuver. Bouncing off the back of the bear, he landed on his hands and knees and scrambled to his feet, just in time to avoid another slash of claws.

A stone the size of a robin's egg turned his ankle, and he fell to the floor directly in front of the attacking animal. The stone skittered across the floor and onto the painting.

For the first time the bear made a sound—a hissing, whistling cry of pain that raised the hair on the back of Canton's neck and caused goose bumps to pebble his skin. Canton's eyes fell to treacherous stone lying in the middle of the painting. Colored sand swirled sluggishly around the obstruction while the bear shook its great head in pain and confusion.

Not wasting an instant in thought, Canton scrambled on hands and knees over to the painting, grabbed the edge of the deer hide base, and *pulled.*

Colored sand flew into the air in a spray of ochre, rust, and black and white, raising a multi-hued cloud that momentarily obscured the lantern's light.

As the particles began to settle, Canton saw the bear swaying side-to-side, grunting and snuffling dazedly. Its great head rose and those all-too intelligent eyes met his, expressing a wealth of evil and hate. With a last grunt and groan, it fell apart into a heap of blacker than black sand.

"Damn, that's was spooky," Canton whispered while he painfully rose to his feet. "*Winnie, you should have seen what just happened.*"

Nothing.

"*Winnie? Winnie?*" He tapped his throat mic. Nothing. "Well, damn …."

Sighing and shaking his head, he left.

The other tunnel led farther into the mountain, this one wide and high and well cut into the bedrock, the product of more modern tools. His footfalls echoed slightly, so he slowed, stepping carefully across stone with almost no sound, a flitting black-clad ghost that burrowed into the deeps. His back hurt, his newly healed ribs groaned with every step, and what felt like a bruise the size of a dinner plate was forming on his hip, but he ghosted on, weapons in hand, heart hardened against the misery of his body.

***

SWEAT TRICKLED DOWN BB'S NECK and streamed from his armpits, soaking the thin black shirt that used to lie beneath his bulky, black armor. His wrist bones were beginning to creak alarmingly and his fingers had just gone numb from the rawhide used to bind his hands together behind his back. The situation looked grim and he hadn't a clue what to do.

On the mountainside there had been a moment of pain, then nothing. When he woke he found himself in a large irregular cavern lit by several electric lamps, hands and feet bound so securely he could scarcely wiggle his fingers. He had been stripped of his armor and placed between Mace and Will, both unconscious and stripped of armor as well.

A thirty-something woman in a plain white t-shirt and faded blue jeans had been staring at him, her brown eyes so dark they almost seemed black. She had a broad forehead and high cheekbones and her coppery skin glowed in the lamplight. Acne scars marred her cheeks. Her mad smile was full of yellowed and rotting teeth.

"So the government man wakes," she'd said in a fluting voice, tossing her head like a horse, long black hair flying. "The man who would kill us."

BB, a bit woozy, asked, "Us?"

She snorted in distain. "Government men, so stupid."

Too late he realized his mistake. "We have to bring you and your accomplice in, young lady. Surrender now and no one needs to get hurt."

Suddenly she was right in his face, sniffing his skin, one hand clamped cruelly on his jaw. A wet, pink tongue flicked from between her liver-colored lips and licked sweat from his temple. BB remained perfectly still, only a slight twist of his lips indicating his disgust.

"Stupid government man knows nothing," she hissed softly. "Government man brings more government men into an ambush. Stupid, stupid, stupid."

"Killing only white people who worked at casinos was smart," he said quietly, staring into her dark eyes. "Gypsies, who had a habit of changing jobs frequently. Your only mistake was trusting the Mojave to get rid of the bodies for you."

"Stupid man. Stupid government man. Stupid *white* government man. There was never a worry about bodies. Bodies don't matter, stupid white government man."

"Show him, Dezba," came a hoarse, gravelly voice, sounding choked with sandy phlegm.

The woman, Dezba, let go of BB's chin and stood back, revealing an old man sitting at the far end of the cave near one of the several tunnels that dotted the walls, his feet propped up on a large stone. Native American with long gray hair, he was dressed like the woman—no shoes, faded jeans and a white t-shirt. Soles thick with dark calluses protected him better than boots. The wide smile on his seamed face showed more gum than tooth, but conveyed more danger than a mouthful of dagger fangs.

"Look, stupid white government man," she sneered. "Look at the floor."

BB looked.

In front of his feet lay five sand paintings, all shining and glimmering, shimmering and gleaming with soft opalescent light, three round and two rectangular masterpieces of magic. Each painting showed a scene and those scenes *moved*. From his vantage point, BB could only see one painting clearly, slightly below his position and to the right on the irregular floor.

A stylized airplane landed on a runway made of powdered gray rock, disgorging five people. Somehow, as he stared, the stick figures, crude and slightly blurry, resolved into recognizable people.

The team. *His* team. He didn't know how he knew—there were no details—but a sense of identity clung to each stick figure like an odor.

"Jesus God," he whispered in horror.

"Your Jesus God can't help you now, enemy," the old man rasped. "We are *yee naaldlooshii*, and cannot be beaten." Dry laughter skittered across BB's ears. "I can See your thoughts and I know who you are, despite the spider that spins its web in your mind, the one what keeps you from divulging the secrets of your Bureau." More horrible, hacking laughter.

Dezba cackled, not even remotely in the same zip code as sanity.

"We knew you were coming," the old man continued. "The Witchy Way gives us powers you whites can't even *imagine*. Don't you understand? No white man can stop us. We have you three and Hok'Ee is disposing of the last of your Team Epsilon lingering on the mountain."

BB lashed out—not at the woman, who was too far away, but at the one sand painting he could see clearly. Heels struck the edge of the deer hide base, sending sand flying. The artifact flared brightly for a moment before fading, reduced to no more than a couple of pounds of pigments, sand, and leather.

Dezba screamed and leapt, the ball of her foot catching BB in the gut, driving the air from his chest. While he gasped, she began to beat him, fists pistoning into his face, shrieking and swearing, spit flying from her lips.

"Enough." The word was iron.

The crazed woman stopped and stood, blood dripping from her knuckles. "Stupid white government man."

"Who are you people?" BB's torn and bloodied lips could barely form the words.

The old man, far from bent or frail, stood and stared with eyes like chips of glistening black hate. "We are the Skinwalkers, the workers of the Witchy Way, and we have been here for centuries. We work the magic of the People, a kind of magic you white men have no knowledge of. It is *strong*, stronger than you know, stronger than white man magic, but most of the People don't want anything to do with it. I have used the Witchy Way to keep us safe." He raised his arms, indicating the cavern with its many exits. "But I have come to realize, in this new age of machines and free information, that hiding in the Witchy Way will not keep us safe. No … *money* will keep us safe."

Drawing an obsidian knife, the old man began to walk slowly to the bound BB, the feral light of madness shining from his eyes. "Of course we know of your Bureau. Our magic has revealed all your secrets. You are not the first of their Agents to wander into the path of the *yee naaldlooshii*. You will, however, be the last." At this the woman cackled. "It means that we must move, but there are many places for us to hide, and with the money we will collect, we can hide very well."

He moved closer, the obsidian knife glinting evilly. "I wanted to look in your eyes as I scalp you." The tone was conversational and some thought stopped him in his tracks. He cocked his head to one side and smiled. "I do so love the old customs, though I do not think you will enjoy them." Nasty laughter filled the cave.

"There's an old custom I like, too," said Canton, emerging out of one of the many tunnels leading from the cavern, pistols filling both hands. His armor was battered and torn with titanium bits sticking out here and there, but he looked healthy and extremely dangerous. "That's shooting the bad guys. Though I don't think either of you will enjoy it." He bared his teeth in a travesty of a smile.

"How do you live?" screamed the woman, fingers curling into claws. "Where is Hok 'Ee?"

"You mean the naked guy with the bad attitude? He won't be joining us for the rest of forever."

Dezba's mouth opened and closed a few times before she leapt at Canton, taloned fingernails first.

Calmly, almost nonchalantly, he emptied the .45 into her torso, saving one round for her head. She fell to the cavern floor in a heap of broken bones, blood, and brains.

"What have you done?" yelled the old man, dropping his knife. The blade shattered into a thousand black, glinting fragments. "You, who are like us, siding with the whites. We are your people!"

"I ain't like you at all and my 'people' are the ones trussed up on the ground behind you and the Mescalero Apache. You … you ain't anything to me but dead." With that he fired one shot from the Sig that took the old man on the bridge of the nose. The bullet exited the back of his head in a gory spray.

As if in slow motion, the old man collapsed, landing face-first onto unyielding stone.

"You didn't have to kill him," BB slurred through his mashed lips. Blood coated his chin like a red goatee. "We could have questioned him, learned from him."

Canton reloaded, not bothering to remove his gaze from the corpses leaking blood onto the floor. "The only thing we needed to learn from those assbags is how dead they can get." He sighed. "Besides, they wouldn't have told us a goddamn thing."

BB sighed and shook his head. "Would you mind so terribly much untying us?"

Canton smiled and drew a knife from his hip sheath. Shaking his head, he tossed a diamond onto the floor. "Got your message, by the way."

Thomas Mace cracked an eyelid. "Took you long enough … Agent."

"So, how was your first debriefing?"

Canton leaned back in the plush leather recliner, a heavy sigh whistling past his lips. "I never had to answer so many damn questions in all my livin' life."

BB chuckled. "Yeah, Special Branch knows how to scrape the bottom for details, but you never know what might be useful. Besides, the director told me that all that information assists with team assessments."

"Whatever, dude."

"I have one question."

A black eyebrow rose. "Just one, boss?"

BB leaned forward in his own plush recliner. "Yes, smartass, just one. While you continue to impress, I was surprised at your ability to kill two people so quickly, efficiently, and without remorse. Why is that?"

Canton considered for a long moment. "Once you've seen your possessed Goth roommate change into a werewolf and munch on all your friends, then you have to stab him over and over with a silver knife so he won't chew on you as well …. Let's just say I didn't sweat it at all."

"So you don't mind acting as judge, jury, and executioner?" BB's eyes were intent and his tone was deceptively soft.

"After looking at what my roommate Eddie did …." Canton's voice trailed off for a moment. A few seconds passed before he shook his head firmly. "And what those Skinwalkers did to those casino employees … well, being *Judge Dredd* is by far the lesser of evils."

"Thus endeth the lesson."

CHAPTER TEN

———•———

I Dream of Jeanie

THAT LAST EPISODE THOROUGHLY PUT to bed any doubts I might have had about Canton leading a team. In my experience he had always played second fiddle to the other team members, never showing much assertiveness. It was sure nice to see that he could and would take control if necessary.

The Chicago mission would be in capable hands. I was one hundred percent sure.

I took the DRAFT off and gently set it down on the desk and rubbed my eyes. Fatigue washed through me as well as the beginnings of a diamond-splinter headache behind my eyes.

"Satisfied?"

Was I? Of course. "Yeah, Ghost. I am. The only question I have is why he never took the position of team leader."

"According to the director's notes in Canton's file, BB offered him the position several times, but he turned them all down."

"Turned them down? I didn't know that was an option." If I had, I might have turned down several … dozen.

"Of course you did not. The previous director made it known that Agents could refuse the position of team leader, but BB has been … less forthcoming, although he has never rescinded the policy."

Outrage began to chase my headache away. "He always said I had no choice in the matter."

"He lied."

"He. Lied." Damn, I needed a drink. "He freaking lied to me?"

"Of course he did. As have you ... several times. You are the best, and most troublesome, Agent in the Bureau. There is no way he was going to let you off the leadership hook. Not if there was something he could do about it. Consider it his attempt at asserting a measure of control over a troublesome asset."

That sonofa—! All these years he'd been hornswoggling me. Rat bastard. I let Ghost know exactly how I felt in no uncertain terms, which included anatomical impossibilities, BB's possible canine origins, and his likely destination upon his sudden and most likely imminent demise.

"Oh, please," said Ghost when I finally wound down. "You are not satisfied with someone else leading a team. You never have been; you are far too much of a control freak. So BB's little charade is merely the excuse you need to step forward and take a leadership position—a position for which you are eminently qualified."

"Hmph."

"That is your rejoinder? 'Hmph'?"

"Best I've got." What could I say? Any argument I might have come up with would sound petulant. Not every day you get dressed down by an Internet haunting spirit.

There was a moment of static, which I took to be amusement, then, "What about the rest of the team?"

"Once the team leader has been chosen, choosing the rest is a piece of cake."

"Shall I make suggestions?"

"Not necessary," I said. "I have some ideas. But first I need a rest. VR takes a lot out of a body."

A half hour later, after another cream soda, I donned the DRAFT and began to manipulate icons, flipping through the files of Henry Johansen, Nancy Mason, Michael Dufresne, Kaleb Portner, Adda Freeman and William Stockton. The first three were Green Pea

Agents, the latter two Magicians, also Green Peas fresh from training at Coronado. I had run Mason, Dufresne, and Portner to the ground on more than one occasion in an effort to toughen them up and they were all about equal in my book. Picking two of the three would come down to careful, calculating consideration and a thorough examination of what they had to offer as Agents.

"Eeny, meeny, miny, moe …."

Portner and Mason it was.

"Really, Kal?"

"Don't bug me, Ghost, I'm carefully constructing a team here."

"How are you going to choose a team Magician? One potato, two potato?"

"Now you're just being silly." My eyes were glued on the files of the two Green Pea Magicians. "However, I don't think either of Freeman and Stockton are quite ready for something this big."

"Then who?"

"Don't know. Would love to send Alex, but BB would tear my hide off in strips if I did. The files on Freeman and Stockton are so thin that I don't need VR to tell me about their qualifications; they're far too fresh off the farm. They need to start small, not with something like a cannibalistic spirit—more like The Giant Hamster of the Apocalypse." Another sip of cream soda. "I have to send *someone.* This case is practically begging for a Magician."

"May I make a suggestion?"

"Can I stop you?"

"Cute. You could almost cut cheese with that wit."

Did Ghost just sass me? Was there real wit in that conglomeration of electrons? I suppressed a grin. There was hope for the old spook yet. "All right, go ahead."

"There is one Magician who is available. One you haven't considered."

A cold and slimy thing twisted in my guts. "She's with Team Alpha. Carla won't let her go."

"There are no other missions currently and if you ask nicely, Carla won't raise a fuss. She practically worships you."

Many other, less scrupulous men wouldn't mind a little hero worship from Alpha Team Leader Carla Menendez. She was a whole lot of woman with everything put in the right places in generous dollops. Most men would stare, drool and howl at the moon, but for me it raised my discomfort levels through the roof. I consider myself a reformed philanderer and I already had a girlfriend who was a damn sight more than most men could handle. Plus she could probably turn me into something you could pour into a pitcher if I stepped out on her, which can really put a damper on your day.

"She belongs to a team, Ghost. I just can't go in busting it up." It was a poor excuse, weak as circus lemonade.

And Ghost knew it. His silence spoke volumes.

"Awww ... dammit."

"There is always Rat or Tweezer," he said.

Bleh. Those two Magicians were the prize idiots of the Bureau. One was the biggest pervert known to man—enough to make a hooker blush—while the other .... Well, let's just say I was damn surprised his own team hadn't killed him.

"You know you must consider her, Kal." Ghost's voice was as gentle as a droning buzz could be. "It is part and parcel of being the director, even if it is temporary."

Great. "Yeah. I guess."

"You guess?"

"I *know*, dammit! Why the prodding?"

"It is a rare thing for me to be able to push your buttons, Kal. Usually the reverse is true. Now, just wait a second .... I need to savor the moment."

Mumble, mumble, grumble, grumble. Being on the crap side of stick really sucked.

A few minutes passed while I stared at three files. Three Magicians, all fairly powerful, all capable, no doubt, of handling some of the more basic jobs the BSI encounters. Two green as fresh-picked bananas, one from MI-7 who entered the Bureau without the requisite training at Coronado.

Jeanie had been a big deal in 1943 and she'd saved my life from Dr.

Mengele (long story, filled with Nazis and other sundry bad guys). She had out-Spelled that powerful necromancer and kept him from turning me into Kal-kebabs, so I knew it wasn't a matter of magical ability, more an issue of the rough-and-tumble. While Bureau Magicians generally stayed back and provided support, having them join the brouhaha was common enough that they *had* to receive much of the same training as an Agent. If they didn't want to head out into the big bad world, there was plenty of work in Special Branch to keep them busy.

"You do not think she is qualified, or you do not want to be responsible for sending your girlfriend into harm's way?"

Damn. Hearing that out loud really made me feel like a total heel. "A little of both." My guts began to twist and turn.

"I see. Then I suggest you experience her file in VR."

"Jesus! I can't do that. It'd be too voyeuristic."

"It was okay for you to experience Canton's life, but when you think of viewing Jeanie, you become squeamish?"

"Canton's not my girlfriend."

"That is a matter of opinion."

Wow, two in a row ... the sarky specter was on a roll. "Har-har."

"Seriously, though. There is no difference between viewing Canton's life, dismissing any doubts you might have had and viewing Jeanie's. Read the file or slip into VR, but you have to make a choice. Will the Magician for Canton's team be Jeanie or one of the other two? It is your decision; you know what you must do."

Yeah. I knew. With a heavy heart I tapped the file icon and Jeanie's life appeared in all its digital glory. Parsing through the first few pages, I found dry commentary about an extraordinary woman, as if all she is could be squeezed and distilled down into a dull thesis extract.

By the time I finished the fifth page, my eyes were beginning to cross. Whoever had debriefed my girlfriend had no hand for prose.

"Crap." Snagging a bottle of Fiji water from the wet bar, I considered the file. Ghost's presence was an itch I couldn't scratch because he was assessing me for BB. Everything's a test in the BSI and always would be and even after eleven years it still remained the bitterest pill. Intellectually, I knew the reasons for the constant testing: we Agents wielded awesome powers and had the ability to command and commandeer vast recourses from law enforcement and the military. If an Agent became a serious whackadoodle, he or she could cause some major mayhem.

What would I find in VR? What subtle nuances did Special Branch bring to the VR file? Why was I so afraid?

Maybe I was afraid she wouldn't live up to my expectations.

For whatever reason, Jeanie had followed me from the past and had chosen me to be her love bunny and that was plenty fine by mama Hakala's baby boy. I didn't *want* to know more about her. The thrill of discovery still existed between us and I didn't want that to be damaged by a damn personnel file.

Candy bars. I needed sugar. Fortunately, BB was addicted to Snickers and I had a good idea where he kept his stash. Disguised as a cupboard under the wet bar was a fridge and in the small freezer were a half-dozen of the tasty little treats. Yum.

Ghost had the good taste to keep his big … electrons shut and leave me alone. Frozen Snickers should be enjoyed in silence.

Three sweet treats, a diabetic overload, plus a bottle of water later, and I was fairly good to go, having finally worked up the courage to check the file, to see if the woman I loved was ready for the big leagues.

Not that I had doubts. No, not me ….

Crap.

"VR."

CHAPTER ELEVEN

———•———

London, January 1941

THE THIRTY-YEAR-OLD WOMAN RAN THROUGH the cold, dark streets of London's East End, her stiff leather shoes *slap, slap, slapping* against pavement. Silver light streaming from the half moon did little to illuminate her way and the streetlights had been extinguished for fear of the Luftwaffe. She was fast, despite the threadbare dress she wore, her legs blurred as her lungs pumped huge quantities of air, but her pursuers were young, fit, and relentless. They also had the advantage of wearing pants.

Even as a young girl, Jeanie had been striking, with large, dark eyes and perfect skin the color of roasted chestnuts. A hard life had done nothing to dim her beauty. In fact, suffering had defined it, bringing the strength of character to her features. She had the grace, bearing, quiet dignity and charisma associated with heads-of-state.

The daughter of a Senagalese mother and a father from Sierra Leone, she grew up in a loving, albeit poor, home in London's East End. Life as a dark-skinned woman in WWII Great Britain was difficult, almost impossible, but her parents had worked hard to give their only child a decent home and education.

When she turned twenty-five, she caught the eye of one Desmond Morrow, a factory worker with large, scarred hands and slightly battered features that gave him a ferocious aspect. She could tell, however, that under that harsh exterior lay the soul of gentle man, a poet. Their courtship was quick and furiously passionate. A month after they met, they were married.

Slap, slap, slap. Her footfalls echoed off the uncaring buildings and her lungs began to burn.

"You gots to learn how to fight, luv," he would say every time he held out the nine-inch knife for her to take. "Ain't no one gonna give you nofin' and plenty out there who wants to take what you got."

She took the knife and, in the privacy of the tiny apartment not more than a stone's throw from where her parents lived, he would teach her how to fight.

"Don't aim for the ribs. The knife'll get stuck in bone. Soft targets only. Throat, guts, and groin. Even the thigh meat." His gentle eyes became chips of obsidian, sharp and cold. "Soft targets … remember that, luv."

Desmond was a kind, attentive husband, but a despot when training. He would not allow her to be anything less than absolutely lethal. Perfection meant survival and he honed her like the knife she sparred with, transforming her already quick reflexes to lightning, teaching her to watch for the subtlest changes in her opponent's stance, the set of his shoulders, or facial expression that could warn of an attack or shift in tactics. Within a few months his new bride qualified as a weapon herself, deadly and hard.

Theirs was a marriage of love in a time of segregation and suspicion. It hurt her soul that her husband felt it necessary to teach his wife how to kill efficiently, but she'd seen too many of her friends raped, murdered, or both to kick up much of a fuss. She hated that her husband had to fight in bare-knuckle matches in the basement of the local pub to bring in enough money for groceries. But, despite having to brave the fear and the hatred in the eyes of many of the whites in the neighborhood, it was a grand time for her.

Three years later an accident at the factory where Desmond worked took his life and four of his co-workers. Jeanie received £100 as recompense and was left with a broken heart and an empty apartment. Days later she moved back in with her parents, who were more than happy to have her back home. That is, until the Germans decided to bomb London into the Stone Age in preparation for invasion.

On September 7, 1940, a cool, wet evening, her parents and most of the block ceased to exist thanks to a 1000 kilogram *Spengbombe Cylindrich* dropped by the Luftwaffe, the beginning of the Blitz and the end to what fragile happiness she had found, as well as that of thousands of her fellow Brits.

Slap, slap, slap. Fire etched her lungs and she tasted coppery spit at the back of her throat. A painful little stitch pinched her side and she cursed her worn leather shoes. They were almost worse than going barefoot, but her soles would be cut to ribbons by debris if she removed them.

When the first raid hit Jeanie had been across town, working as part of the kitchen staff for Mr. and Mrs. Howard Stanton, an elderly society couple whose wealth was matched only by their eccentricities and desire to throw lavish parties. At the sound of the air-raid sirens, the couple and their two-dozen or so guests, along with the staff, absconded to the basement. After two terrifying hours, Jeanie arrived home to an alien landscape of blasted, burned wood, shattered brick and the wails of the grieving and injured. What was found of her mother and father, and most of the neighbors, could have fit into a coffee tin. Ever since then she had been on her own, a lone black girl smack dab in the middle of a male-dominated white world.

That night, the night of running and fear and hate, she had stayed late, cleaning up after a particularly extravagant gathering. The Stantons seemed to believe that if they threw the best parties, and enough of them, the Germans would not have the heart to bomb their lovely home. The fact that they were still alive seemed to prove their point.

Jeanie had walked toward the run-down flat she'd recently begun to share with a young woman from Haiti. Isobel's broken English was on a par with her atrocious French. Isobel and Jeanie seldom saw eye-to-eye, but they had no one else, so differences were put aside.

Necessity was often the mother of compromise as well as invention.

She was more than a dozen blocks from home when she heard the footsteps behind, more than one set. A quick glance showed four young men shadowing her less than fifty feet away, so she did what was prudent for a woman in her situation .... She ran like hell.

The men behind would normally never have caught her, not in a million years. She was *that* fast, even in worn leather shoes wearing thin at the soles.

Jeanie ran and ran, lungs burning, putting her pursuers to shame as her long legs chewed up the distance. That is, until two more appeared less than half a block in front of her. She swiftly calculated the odds of running across the street and dismissed the idea as too risky. With a whirl of skirts, she took a left into an alley between two buildings slightly less ancient than the river Thames.

It led to a twelve-foot-tall brick wall covered in glittering frost and slime.

Coarse laughter drifted down the alley after her, filled with dark anticipation and malice.

"Welcome to our trap, darkie girl." The voice was deep and hateful, youngish, too young to be so well acquainted with the evil that stained it. Six forms swaggered slowly toward her, taking their own sweet time, drawing the moment out in delicious cruelty.

"Stay away," Jeanie warned, arching her back like a cat. Six men. No, six young men, barely older than boys, dressed in the shabby and careworn clothes of the down-on-their-luck working class. Three were mid-sized, but the other three were tall—the tallest towering nearly a foot over her five-eleven-inch form and muscled like a bear. Dirty and rough with almost bestial features, he moved slightly ahead of the other five—the Alpha Male who would have first crack at the prize. She knew that if he were to die first, the others might lose their nerve.

"Oooo-hoo!" chortled one of the smaller three, a youth with a shaggy mop of black hair. "We have a feisty one here, we do! That's going to make this so much sweeter, ain't it?"

As a single beautiful black woman growing up in the hard end of town, Jeanie had learned a few tricks before she met Desmond, most of them dirty. Keeping her eyes on the menacing forms drawing ever nearer, she slid a hand through a slit in her dress, turning her body slightly to the side. A snarl of anger turned her lovely face into a mask of loathing.

"C'mon, you bastards." Her voice was as cold and hard as iron. She widened her stance, just as Desmond had taught her, and braced for the attack. "Come on and die."

And they did, rushing all at once.

Her hand emerged, filled with eight inches of sharp steel that flashed toward the biggest youth as his large hands grabbed at her shoulders. *Not too deep in the gut,* Desmond's voice echoed in her mind. *Don't let it catch on bone. Shallow and long.*

Shallow and long and intestines spilled onto the filthy cobblestones with a hard *splat*, mixing with garbage and feces.

The big youth wailed, a terrifying sound of despair and heartbreak before falling to his knees, clutching futilely at the greasy, bloody loops of gut.

Jeanie took a punch to the jaw from one of the smaller youths that set her world spinning, but she swung wildly with the knife, slicing across a tender throat. Blood fountained in the cold air, steaming as it sprayed across her face and chest. Cries of anger like the howls of wolves echoed through the alley.

Before she could swing again, one of her assailants grabbed her wrist and with his other hand wrenched the knife free. Two attackers lay dying while the other four made ready for awful sport.

Fists flew, breaking her nose, her ribs and her jaw, and through the white pain she imagined she saw her assailants' faces, leering and filled with terrible lust. She knew then that she would die, and not quickly. Oh no, not near quickly enough.

The dress was torn from her body and rough, pitiless hands ripped at her undergarments while a horrible *pressure* began to build up behind her eyes. She fancied she could feel the front of her skull slowly detach from the back and a looping whorl, a dipping twist, a crazed set of patterns began to form in her mind as her vision began to fail. That crazy spider's web of lines began to pulse with the beat of her heart—gold, green, red, and aqua—each flashing and flaring with greater and greater intensity as a *pressure* threatened to pop her eyes from their sockets. Her legs were forced open wide. The pattern, the shape, began to flare as dreadful energies built up, and she wanted it out, out of her, out of her skull, her skin and her brain. She wanted it *out*. As she felt the first violator begin his assault down *there*, she *pushed* the pattern, the shape, out and away, away toward those who hurt her. She felt a draining then, as if her very life departed along with the shape that flared and vanished from her mind.

Actinic blue-white light filled the alley, brighter than the sun, and flesh and bone proved to be no barrier. She imagined she could hear cries like the lost souls of the damned.

Then she was gone … and the alley was silent again.

"WELCOME BACK TO THE WORLD of the living, young lady." The voice was smooth, like soft butter and silk against her ears.

Jeanie clung to that voice while luxuriating in cottony warmth.

"You are safe. No worries. Please, open your eyes."

That voice … cultured, rich. Was that a hint of a Scottish accent?

"Considering the magic you tossed about yesterday, it is quite amazing that you are in the peak of health."

Eyes cracked open, a slight crust of sleep sand at the corners fractured and crumbled. Slowly, carefully, she wiped it away. "Where am I?" she asked, staring at olive drab paint on corrugated steel. The room was rectangular with curved steel walls that arched over her head. A corrugated cylinder cut in half and set flat side down.

"You're in hospital."

The lie was so blatant she quickly cranked her head to the left where the speaker sat not more than three feet away smoking a cigarette in a thin black holder. The sharp movement sent a rill of pain down her spine.

"Oh, not the kind of hospital most are acquainted with, mind you." The speaker was a well-dressed blond man with a long, horsey, slightly acne-scarred face. Smoke dribbled from his lips as he smiled fondly at her. His teeth were even and slightly yellowed from nicotine.

"Who are you?" Her voice was dry, raspy. She blinked rapidly as her eyes stung.

The man offered her a blue enameled cup, which she carefully accepted. Water. Tepid, metallic and delicious. The wonderful liquid was gone in an instant.

"I am Fleming. Ian Fleming. If you will have it, your employer."

Her ears must have been playing tricks. "My what?" she asked dubiously.

Shrewd blue eyes bored into hers. "What do you remember about the night you were assaulted?"

"N-not much." Her face became fierce. "No, that's wrong. I remember now. There were six of them, right bastards all. I gutted one, I did, and cut a throat ... after that not much. Blue light." A shock ran through her. "Did they ... did they *do* something ....?"

Fleming shook his head. "No, lass, you were not raped." A drag on the cigarette holder and a puff of smoky breath. "Tell me about the blue light. Tell me everything you can remember."

Jeanie squinted at the man. Trim and slim, he seemed the ultimate British aristocrat, except for the implacable hardness around his pale blue eyes. These eyes had seen too much of the world, seen things that would strip a soul of all humanity. "I barely remember," she said. "Although ... I think there was a line, all squiggly and twisty, and it had depth and breadth. It came into my head and I forced it out of my mind before the blue light knocked me out."

A flash of yellowed teeth. Fleming grabbed a file folder from Jeanie's bedside table and withdrew a glossy sheet. Mutely, he handed it to her.

It was a photograph of the alley, starkly lit and sharply lined, every edge and crack defined in black and white. It took her a moment, but she finally realized there was no rubbish in the alley. Instead, a fine layer of gray ash coated the cobbles and brick as if the substance and been sprinkled down from the sky.

"That, my dear girl, is the result of your magic. Most of that ash is the remains of your attackers. Your burst of magic was so powerful that even the weakest Magician could feel it across town. It led us to you."

At the mention of magic, she looked incredulously at the dapper Fleming but held her tongue as he told her the tale of His Majesty's Supernatural Services and how it protected the British Empire from all otherworldly menaces.

It took a long time and a lot of convincing, but when he was finished, she was a believer. The blue light and the ashy remains, the odd shape or pattern that flashed behind her eyes … it all made sense, no matter how incredible. Besides, she *felt* it was true. Deep down in the hidden places of her soul, she knew it to be real. "Why hasn't it made the papers or radio? We would've seen or heard of something by now. People talk."

More puffing on the cigarette holder. "In 1779, the Director of the Committee of Unnatural Affairs, the American version of the HMSS, commissioned the most brilliant and powerful Magician of that century—perhaps of all time—to create a Spell. This Spell, when cast properly, prevents people from communicating, *in any way*, the existence of the Committee or the Supernatural world it deals with, except to those who have also had the Spell placed on them. The director, you see, realized that the everyday man was not ready to accept the existence of a supernatural world and all the creatures that it birthed. He felt that in the Age of Reason, mankind would be better off leaving the fantastic behind. He shared the Spell, which was dubbed 'Interdiction', with all like-minded nations. Ever since then, there have been many, many brushes with the Otherworld, which the Americans call the World Under, but no one has been able to let the cat out of the bag, so to speak. There are hundreds, perhaps thousands, who know about it, but the Spell effectively keeps the Otherworld a secret, as well as the government agencies that police the threat it poses."

Jeanie clutched at her warm blanket and bit her lip. "What, you mean nobody can talk about it? Then how come you can chat away pretty as you please about such things?"

"Members of the HMSS can speak freely amongst themselves.

Also, certain key phrases allow us to identify members of other agencies under Interdiction and communicate freely with them. It is possibly the most elegant and complex Spell ever created."

"So, you going to cast it on me, then?"

His eyes sparkled like sapphires. "It's already been done."

"What? Already?" Her hands moved to her temples.

"Now, now," he said, patting her hand in an effort to soothe her. "It doesn't hurt and it keeps this conversation rather private. There are no ill effects."

"This American bloke, the best Magician of his day … what was his name?"

"Benjamin Franklin."

Her laughter died at the utterly serious look on his face.

Jeanie gave what she had been told some consideration before speaking again. "You said you're my employer if I agree. What you want me to do?"

"Well, unless you have been hiding in a cupboard somewhere, you must know we are at war with the Hun and they have their own agency chockablock full of Magicians called the VGG. Now, normally HMSS would stay in Great Britain and deal with the Otherworld on our own shores, but these VGG chaps are rather bad news, practicing necromancy … death magic."

At her questioning look he snorted. "There is a Spell, a rather simple one, that manages to capture the life energy of a person as he is murdered. That life energy equates to a large amount of magic, which can be harnessed. That is what the Nazis and their minions in the VGG are up to, the use of death magic." Fleming leaned in close, his voice dropping to a whisper. "The heinous crimes those unholy bastards are committing right now upon their own people would cause even the heartiest warrior to faint dead way. Thank goodness His Majesty has decided that the best way to counter those VGG blighters is to use the Supernatural Services against them, foil the bastards at every turn." He smiled like a fox. "That should give old Hitler what-for."

With a smile that had more than a hint of anger in it, Jeanie said,

"You want me to kill some Jerries?"

"Quite."

"Well, why didn't you say so in the first place, guv? I'm the lady for the job."

"Brilliant," Fleming said, regarding her with unabashed joy. "First things first. We must bring you up to snuff with some intensive training in magic so you don't accidently turn yourself into something nasty, and then you must receive the best in combat training." A long pause as he took a drag from the cigarette. "After that, you will join a team. I have just the one in mind. They are in dire need of a Magician, which are in short supply thanks to the Blitz."

Fleming leaned back and crossed his arms, studying her carefully with sparkling eyes as blue as the summer sky. Jeanie opened and closed her mouth several times, but kept her peace, certain that he had more to say.

And he did. "You must realize that it will be especially difficult for you, this training. As a woman, you will be seen as a threat to the male dominated profession of Agent in the Supernatural Services. It will be brutal and I will not be able to shield you. Once training begins, you will be on your own. The question is: will you be able to handle it?"

For a second she was tempted to come at him with bravado and righteous indignation, but a small, sensible part of her saw a tightening at the corners of his eyes. She realized he expected her to react hotly, with blind anger and indignation, and that this whole meeting, her being in this sham of a hospital with him by her side was a test. A test, perhaps, of her ability to remain calm, to tolerate condescension or of her fortitude, she wasn't sure, but she damn well knew that the next words out of her mouth were going to be the most important of her life.

"Not a problem," she said, expression placid as calm waters. "Sir."

When he smiled, she knew she'd been right. "Well said, Mrs. Morrow." Fleming removed the burned stub of the cigarette from the holder and inserted a fresh fag. "Well said."

It was a full minute before Jeanie spoke again, slowly rising to a sitting position and grateful to be wearing anything, even a hospital gown. "I got a couple of questions, Mr. Employer, before I agree to join this organization."

He nodded. "Fair enough."

"How much do I get paid?

He grinned. "More than you can possibly believe."

"Oh, you'd be surprised how much I can believe. I believe in magic, don't I?"

"True. What's your other question?"

"Once I finish this training, I don't get a bunch of men telling me what to do, do I?"

"The only people you take orders from are His Majesty, the Colonel and your team leader, in whom I have the utmost faith."

"So if some bloke tries to push me about a bit, I can tell him to go stuff himself?"

His laughter was warm molasses and soft nights. "Yes, you most certainly can."

***

VOMIT CHOKED THE BACK OF my throat and threatened to spew out my nostrils. The DRAFT was perched on the end of my nose, wobbling there, ready to fall off. I removed the glasses and set them down gingerly.

"Kal, are you all right? Kal!"

"Yeah, Ghost." *Gack ... gag ... cough.* "I'm fine. How long have I been out?" It was there, at the back of my mind, the desire to rage, to lash out and give vent to the anger flooding my brain. Adrenaline fizzed in my muscles and they twitched with the need for some very drastic and intemperate action.

"Four minutes. I terminated the VR. You were screaming and damaging the desk."

I looked down and saw small cracks on the smooth, polished surface of BB's ultra-sleek desk and groaned. "He's going to kill me. Hope I didn't break his computer."

"You only cracked the veneer. It would take much more to damage the titanium housing."

"What?"

"The entire desk is the computer, Kal. A thin layer of wood has been placed over the surface."

Now that was too cool ... a desk-shaped computer. A bit different from the earlier models, to which computers had been attached with the hard drives underneath, slotted carefully out of sight. If I hadn't felt like ten miles of bad road, I would've been impressed. Time to face the elephant in the room.

"Man, Ghost, it hurt so much to experience that. I'm so friggin' *angry*." Cruel faces in the dark alley, the freezing cobbles on Jeanie's skin and those rough, hard hands. Once again I felt bile rise. "Much more so than when Canton fought the werewolf."

Ghost buzzed quietly before answering. "You have been on multiple missions with Canton, not to mention your foray into Las Vegas a few months ago, and you are aware of his capabilities. However, your relationship with Jeanie coupled with your uncertainty concerning her training made you vulnerable to reacting more deeply to her experiences on that cold night in 1941."

"So you're saying I should forgo entering VR today?"

"It might be best."

Thought so. If I witnessed any more of Jeanie's trauma, I might go nuts suppressing the futile desire to protect her. Not so evolved after all, eh? Just a big ol' cave man grunting and growling at the saber tooth tigers sniffing around his family.

I rubbed my face. "They talked about the Colonel ... same one, I suppose, we met back in '43?"

"Yes. He took over the position in 1938."

The Colonel ... the name for the head of the Supernatural Services in the 1940s and the rank for one of its most famous leaders, John Ronald Reuel Tolkien. I'd met the man briefly and had been impressed by the sheer force of his personality and the depth of his wisdom.

Ghost continued, "I understand your worry, Kal, but you have to realize that she killed all her assailants with a single Spell in one of the greatest explosions of magic from a Magician ever recorded. Needless to say, Sir Ian Fleming was very impressed and, as you saw, attended her personally during her recovery. She was very possibly one of the most powerful Magicians of her day and finding her was a great coup for the Supernatural Services."

Sir Ian Lancaster Fleming. Most people recognized him as the author of the original James Bond novels and a member of British Naval Intelligence. He assisted in the planning of operations Mincemeat and Golden Eye. He also was involved in the planning and oversight of two intelligence units: T-Force and 30 Assault Unit. I guess you could call him the James Bond of his day, but what was known only to a select few was his two-year stint as Special Training and Recruitment Officer for His Majesty's Supernatural Services, later known as MI-7.

A few months ago I'd traveled back in time—not as fun as it sounds, trust me—in an effort to save a good friend and fellow Agent, Rebecca McTavish, aka Mouth. She decided to stay back in the past, in war-torn England, to be with the dashing brother of Sir Ian: Richard Fleming. She chose love over the comforts of the twenty-first century, and I can't say that I blamed her. She went on to become the Grand Matriarch for the Fleming clan. On certain nights when I'm feeling melancholy, I think of her and wonder what would have happened if she had returned with me to the present. We almost had a thing, she and I, and it might have been good.

Who am I kidding? With Mouth it would have been good, very good in fact, but with Jeanie it was *great*.

"The expenditure of that much magical energy nearly killed her," Ghost continued. "So the first thing MI-7 did was train her to keep her from accidently draining herself like that again. By the time her magical training was complete—which took just four months, an amazingly brief span of time—the VGG had neutralized three MI-7 teams in France. Sir Ian lobbied for her inclusion on a combat mission and Great Britain was running short on Magicians. Crown could not afford to be picky about gender and realized it was better to be color-blind."

I nodded. The Blitz had killed thousands while thousands more were dying on the battlefield. One of England's greatest Magicians, Patrick Reid, had been captured by the Germans—who had no clue he was a Magician or they would have executed him on the spot—and held in Colditz Castle. He didn't manage to escape until 1942.

Amazing how lack of manpower can turn a society much more tolerant.

"Okay, I guess I didn't need to see the whole file, just the bits that relate to her competency in the field."

Ghost gave an electric chuckle, which sounded like a cat throwing up a radio. "Kal, she is a black woman who worked covertly in Nazi-occupied France for nearly a year. Are you really worried about her competency?"

Ouch. Score another one for the spook.

I decided on a break and went to DORMS to eat some lunch. Andrea gave me a startled look as I strode by with a wave and a smile. One steak sandwich later, feeling much better and totally headache-free, I sat back down at BB's desk. My desk.

During lunch I'd come to a decision. I had to know more. I had to. Not knowing more ate at me and I realized that BB would've gone through Jeanie's file with a fine-toothed comb. Without a word, I donned the DRAFT and flipped through the file until I found the section I was looking for. "VR."

CHAPTER TWELVE

———•———

Hot and Cold

"I AM SERGEANT DONNELL MACTEAGUE!" screamed the little man, standing ramrod straight in front of six terrified recruits. "You do not address me as 'sir,' you call me Sergeant! I hear a 'sir' flung my way and by His Majesty's testicles, I will tear you a new arsehole! Do you understand me?"

"YES, SERGEANT!" yelled all six, bodies at rigid attention.

The Scotsman was typical of his kind—short, ginger hair, ginger moustache, pale skin with a smattering of freckles, and a pug nose that looked like it had been on the wrong end of a fist more than once. Everything about the man was meticulous, from the creases in his uniform to the precise angle of the cap on his head. Even his moustache looked like it had been trimmed using a ruler.

For Jeanie Morrow, fresh from her training in magic, the man wasn't only a Sergeant, but the devil himself.

When she had arrived at the tiny camp in the Scottish Highlands, the wind scraping her face like frigid sandpaper, MacTeague was there, standing next to the dirt tracks laughingly referred to as a road. He stared with his washed-out eyes as the six descended from the covered truck, marking each one on some sadistic mental tally board. When those soulless eyes touched hers, she *felt* the hate there, the condemnation. *Outsider,* those eyes said. *You don't belong in the company of men.*

She squared her shoulders and stood with the others, determined to prove him wrong at all costs.

"What a worthless bunch of incompetent arseholes! I swear His Majesty must be playing a joke on a poor Scotsman. I have no idea where the Empire scraped up such disgusting pieces of rotten, maggot-ridden dung. Perhaps you useless gits are all French?" His eyes swept over the group and Jeanie could swear the temperature dropped another fifteen degrees.

MacTeague strutted up and down the line, sneering at their rumpled sweaters and stained pants. Never mind that it had been an incredibly uncomfortable five-hour ride by transport truck over the dirt tracks that were more goat trails than proper roads, never mind that it was colder than a witch's heart in winter, it was perfectly clear that their appearance offended his delicate sensibilities.

He stopped in front of a largish, lanky man with a blond hair and bad skin. "Name, you piece of gobshite!"

"Fawkkes, Sergeant!" barked the man, obviously scared out of his wits.

"No, that is *not* your name. Not anymore. Since you are entering my beloved HMSS and have come to me for training to be a real man, your name is now Fork until I say different! Do you understand me, Fork?"

"Yes Sergeant!"

It went on like that with all the recruits: Hutchinson became Hopeless, Eddington—Enema, Bowles—Bowels, McMann—McWorthless. Then MacTeague reached Jeanie.

"Well, well, well. What's all this, then? His Majesty sure must have a stiff one in his drawers for me to receive such a one as you, little lady." The furnace of his eyes became cold and terrible and his pale, freckled face was suffused with blood to the extent that it clashed with his olive drab uniform. "You offend me," he said softly. "Oh, not your skin color. I know plenty of darkies, good blokes all." She could smell the mint on his breath as he leaned in. "It's the fact you're a woman.

You should be spreading your legs for a husband, not fighting with the lads. Who are you what upsets the natural balance of things?"

Anger like acid burned through her veins and black spots appeared at the edge of her vision, but she quashed the desire to punch the detestable man in the face.

He's trying to goad you, luv, Desmond's voice said, echoing from the past. Instead of longing, his voice brought comfort, like a warm blanket on a cold night. *He wants you to fail and he thinks you can't do nofin', can't fight. Wants to make you angry so you'll take a swing. Gives him a bloody good reason to send you packing.* The voice became stronger. *Prove him wrong, luv.*

"I'm no one, Sergeant!" she screamed in his face, spittle hitting the corner of one of his pale, pale eyes.

MacTeague didn't bother to wipe the saliva from his face. "And that's who you are," he said, honeyed malice coating his voice. "No One. That's your name. Understand?"

"Yes, Sergeant!" Her yell carried none of the hate she felt.

It went downhill from there.

If MacTeague was hard on the five men, he was doubly so with Jeanie, never letting her rest more than four hours, always choosing her when demonstrating hand-to-hand combat techniques. She never voiced a complaint, never once showed the little Sergeant anything but the absolute respect and fear that was his due.

Bruises became her badges of honor, aching muscles a gift from God. Every night she stored a little more hate for the man down deep in her soul while Desmond's voice whispered, *Wait, wait.*

Five weeks of hell, five weeks of learning how to fire a weapon, how to fight barehanded or with a knife (not that she needed much instruction) and five weeks of brutality under the hands of the most sadistic man in the universe.

Not once did she cry …. Tears were for those who could afford to spill them. Sorrow was for those who had room in their souls. She had room only for hate and an overwhelming desire to prove she was the best.

At the end of five weeks of training in the amazingly cold and brittle air of the Scottish Highlands, MacTeague had them flown into Hell via the incredibly cramped interior of an Armstrong Whitworth Abermarle. Originally designed as a twin-engine medium bomber, the plane entered the war as a transport vehicle instead. Inferior to other aircraft already in service, Jeanie discovered with every jarring bump and poorly placed weld that it was also inferior as a troop plane.

After several hours of flight and one refueling stop, the ungainly aircraft finally landed and, as the hatch opened, the six recruits felt the first wave of the discomfort to come. It was a hot, dry wind that carried dust and sand to coat the teeth and threatened to melt bone and flesh into greasy puddles.

"Welcome to Egypt, my lovelies," MacTeague purred, smiling wide. The little Sergeant stood on a tarmac so heat-worn that it looked like the surface of an alien world. He spread his arms wide as they descended. "RAF Station Kabrit." There was a melodramatic pause. "Your new home for the next few weeks."

"Why Egypt, Sergeant?" Fawkkes asked as his booted feet hit the runway. The tall recruit was already sweating profusely.

"Because, Fork, it has been decided and so it shall be done!" barked MacTeague, face contorted in a rictus of hate and dark joy. Jeanie noted that not a drop of sweat dotted the sadistic sergeant's face, confirmation that he was part hellspawn or that he could make his sweat glands heed his will. "For such a poncey stupid question, you may now run around the base twice in full gear and when you're done we'll see if you have anything further to ask of your beloved sergeant. GO!"

Blanching, Fawkkes belted out a quick, "Yes, Sergeant," and headed out at a trot, his forty pound pack jostling up and down with each footfall.

"Now my lovelies, does anyone *else* have something they care to ask while I am in such a generous and loving mood?"

No one did.

MacTeague's smile was beatific. "Wonderful. Let's grab some chow and a drink of water. They tell me tomorrow is going to be *really* hot."

With a chuckle, he led them toward their housing.

Three weeks passed in a haze of heat and exhaustion. More training, more hand-to-hand with every conceivable weapon from knives, to swords, to shovels. Anything and everything that could be used as a weapon was eventually employed and mastered. Jeanie discovered that while the Highlands were brutal in winter, Egypt was as close as she would come to the surface of the sun.

After weapons training came the basics of survival in the wilderness. MacTeague took special joy in having the recruits sample a variety of edibles, from Australian witchetty grubs to oven baked tarantulas, and woe to the recruit who balked. Even more woe to those who threw up. Punishment ranged from running laps around the camp in full gear, to latrine duty, to two days without showering. It was this last punishment that really motivated the six to suck it up and chew it down. Jeanie grew to like the taste of fire-roasted grasshoppers.

Eventually they reached a point where they could eat (and keep down) items that would make a goat gag. After that, no one ever again turned their nose up at haggis or boiled beef tongue.

THE STREAM OF HEAT THAT passed for a breeze slid over Jeanie's skin like the scorched air from a blast furnace, and the meager moisture from Lake Elmorrah did nothing to alleviate her discomfort. As soon as sweat beaded on her skin, it evaporated, leaving her sticky and grubby.

The men to the left and right of her were uncomfortable as well, perhaps even more so. What made the experience nearly intolerable was MacTeague, marching up and down the line of soldiers … dry as a bone in his uniform. The crisp brown material lay against his ruddy skin as if impervious to the encroachment of bodily fluids.

"I don't believe it!" screamed the little Sergeant in his raspy brogue, strutting to and fro, his back ruler straight. "You miserable lot of worthless maggots managed to make it this far. Not a single wash-out. I have trained sheep who handled themselves better, yet somehow you lot managed to survive everything I've been able to throw at you." Every passing second his face became more and more flushed. "It's enough to make a soul believe in divine intervention, it is!"

The six dared not smile, dared not even let the smallest hint of satisfaction slip because they knew it would only lead to punishments that would make Satan blanch.

As Jeanie stared out into the harsh, dun-colored Egyptian landscape, her mind floated back in time a few days to when Ian Fleming had suddenly showed up at Kabrit wearing a tailored suit, seemingly unaffected by the heat.

"Good to see that you made it this far, Mrs. Morrow," he said as they sat in what was laughingly referred to as the *lounge*, the ten-by-ten tent. The sole purpose of the flimsy, sand-colored structure was to house the recruits' meager supply of water. It was strategically located next to the even smaller tent that was their latrine. Fleming pulled a flask from his duffel and offered her a sip.

"Cheers." The liquid hit her throat like a velvet covered freight train and detonated with pleasant warmth in her stomach. "Smooth," she grunted.

Fleming laughed. "That's eighteen-year-old Scotch, lass. You don't gulp it, you sip it."

"Now you tell me." The fire in her stomach reached her eyes and they began to water. She handed the flask back.

"I don't have time for chitchat," Fleming said after a tiny sip. "The big test is coming up. Are you ready?"

She nodded. "Yes."

"You don't seem nervous."

"I've been through worse."

His piercing blue eyes regarded her gravely. "I need you to finish this, Mrs. Morrow. There's an expedition heading into France that I want you to join. The Supernatural Services doesn't have another Magician to spare. We have lost so many in the past few months."

Tell him, luv. Tell him what you really want.

Jeanie bit her lip. "Oh, I'll pass the test, but there's something I need when I do."

"A demand?" Fleming's voice became dangerously soft.

"A request."

"Go on."

"When I pass, when you're ready to take me out of this hellhole and drop me into a new one, I want Sergeant MacTeague to face me square and salute me proper."

The man from HMSS began to chuckle. Within seconds it became a full belly laugh.

"WHAT ARE YOU STARING AT, Miss No One?" screamed the Scotsman, spit spraying from his lips. A drop smacked Jeanie in the eye. "You want to be somewhere else? Is that a smile on your black face?"

"NO, SERGEANT!" she bellowed at the top of her lungs. No other volume was tolerated when he asked a question. It took a great deal of willpower not to blink the spit from her eye.

MacTeague stared at her as he would an insect, then nodded slightly. She let out the tiniest sigh of relief as he walked down the line.

"We are gonna fly you to the middle of Egypt's own ruddy evil desert with a canteen of water and a knife," he barked at the recruits standing at attention under the merciless sun. Weeks of burning air and constant training had trimmed what fat they might have had and leeched away excess water weight. All six looked lean and mean, with leathery skin over iron muscles. "It's up to you to reach the camp within three days. If you can't do it, then tell me now, and it's off with you back to merry old England. No one will think the worse of you. There's a lot you've accomplished what you should be proud of and I'll be the first to admit it. Any takers?" MacTeague waited ten long seconds while the six sweated bullets. Finally he went on, "If you don't make it back in three days and you are not dead with your flesh slowly drying into leather half buried in the sand, I will kick your buttocks out of Egypt and send you home. If you do die, know that I will personally write the letter to your next-of-kin telling them that you gave your life in defense of King and country. My money says I'll be writing letters for most of you sorry, miserable lot.

"However, my lovelies, if you do pass this last and greatest test, you will become a member of the most elite, the most dangerous, and the most honored service in British history. You will become HMSS Agents and warriors for the Empire. Every day will be a holiday and every paycheck a ruddy fortune. You will know more joy than you can imagine and do things no one will believe. Trust me, there is no greater honor and, by God, that is the *truth*!"

MacTeague gave each of the six a good long glare that had wilted lesser men. "That is all. Grab your kits. We are wheels up in ten minutes."

ONCE AGAIN THE ARMSTRONG WHITWORTH Abermarle was pressed into service, flying with its precious human cargo twelve thousand feet over the Egyptian desert. The recruits sat in uncomfortable silence, dressed in tan uniforms. Each of the six sported a single canteen and a knife long enough to qualify as a short sword. Each wore a parachute and an anxious expression.

"Oy, Jeanie!" Fawkkes shouted over the roar of the twin Bristol Hercules XI engines. The big Brit smiled nervously, the acne scars on his cheeks standing out in stark relief. "Buy me a pint when we get back?"

She smiled and all five men smiled back. Weeks of shared hardship and a collective hatred of MacTeague had forged bonds stronger than steel. "Ha! You buy me one, you cheap wanker."

Fawkkes extended a hand. "Deal." They shook.

"You two want to get married?" MacTeague screamed at the pair from the cockpit.

"NO, SERGEANT!" they chorused.

"Then get ready to jump, you poncey pair of useless wags." His granite gaze turned to the other men. "The lot of you get ready or feel my boot up your arses."

"YES, SERGEANT!"

The Avro had taken off that morning at false dawn and flown for several hours. Every now and then the engines emitted a gurgling sort of stutter that made Jeanie and the men nervous, but cramped quarters and righteous fear of the Sergeant kept them in their seats.

MacTeague gestured to the starboard opening. "Fork, you bastard son of a Welsh goat, you! Go! Go! Go!"

Fawkkes got, hopping through the drop hole in the rear fuselage. Every two minutes thereafter to the second he would beckon to another recruit. Soon, only the Sergeant and Jeanie were left.

The Scotsman leaned toward the taller woman. "Listen up, girl, and you listen up right good now." He kept his washed out eyes dead level with hers and slitted thin. "I'm a right bastard, I know that. It's me job, to be the kind of bastard to mold useless gits into HMSS Agents because if you die because I was a slackjack, then that's my mistake. For ten years now that's been the job His Majesty has seen fit to give me and I will be double-dipped in shite if I don't do it to the best of my ability. I know you hate me, girl, and I don't begrudge your feelings, but there are a couple things you should know.

"Mr. Fleming himself told me to push you and to keep pushing you until I found your limits, girl." MacTeague paused as if gathering his thoughts and he actually relaxed, looking almost human. Jeanie felt faint, but kept her face impassive. "And so far I ain't found 'em. So don't you go failing this test because I've told Mr. Fleming that you'll make it. Don't you dare show me to be a liar."

Jeanie stared at him impassively, a strange feeling roiling around in her gut.

"You're the best of this lot, girl," he continued, face grave. "The best I've ever seen, God's truth to that, and if you don't beat those idiots to the camp, I will personally gut you like a fish. You got me?"

"YES, SERGEANT!" she bellowed. It dawned on her that there might be more to the little sergeant than she thought.

"Too right, you great wallowing slag!" he screamed in her face, full of rage and lunacy.

Then again, maybe he was just a nutter.

"Go! Go! Go!"

Jeanie went, arms and legs splayed as she fell toward the tan sand of the desert. Even at twelve thousand feet the air felt like it would bake her skin from her bones. She counted to five, then deployed her 'chute.

The ground came at her faster than she expected. The shock of landing sent a wave of prickly pain up her long legs as sand flew from around her boots.

She quickly buried the 'chute and checked her canteen. A quick look at her compass told her where the camp lay.

"All alone, Des," she whispered, shading her eyes as she stared out at miles of heat-blasted sand. "I can use all the help I can get here."

No worries, luv. Just follow your feet.

The sun beat down on her skin as she began a measured pace across the dunes. "Easier said than done, my love."

Trust yourself.

"Just don't leave me, Des."

There was laughter in the still, dark corners of her mind. *No matter what happens, luv, I ain't never leaving you.*

"HERE COMES THE FIRST ONE."

Commander Ian Lancaster Fleming of His Majesty's Supernatural Services shaded his eyes with one slim hand, noting the lone figure stumbling toward the camp, partially obscured by heat shimmer. He smiled wolfishly, his long, homely face reddening under the Egyptian sun.

"Is it her, sir?" MacTeague asked, shading his eyes as well. Standing under the large umbrella with Fleming, the little sergeant stared at the dim figure, body almost thrumming with anticipation.

Fleming shook his blond head. "I can't tell."

"I don't suppose you could do us a cooling Spell, sir?"

"You know I hate to toss magic about, Sergeant. In a place like Egypt, so steeped in enchantment and legend, you never know who or what might notice."

MacTeague rubbed his eyes. Sweat drip, drip, dripped from his pointed chin. "Those quartz Spell crystals you gave me weeks ago are all used up, sir, and I swear I've lost three stone already. I hate sweating, I do."

Fleming sighed and dug into a pocket, handing the sergeant a small, grayish stone. "It will last only an hour. Don't waste it."

"Word, sir?"

Fleming handed him a slip of paper. "Here is your activation word, sergeant. I swear, the men must think you're the devil himself for surviving such brutal heat without breaking a sweat." He chuckled—a thin, mean sound.

MacTeague looked at the paper, which read JERRYBUGGER, and laughed.

The two stood at the edge of the camp, a large umbrella, the exact hue of the sand that surrounded them, provided limited protection from the sun and almost none from the heat. Behind them lay a pair of folding camp chairs and a small table on which rested a sweating glass pitcher of lemonade and several glasses, a treat for the recruits who would arrive on that third and final day of testing.

Fleming raised his voice. "Khalid." A young boy of ten, wearing only a pair of worn khaki shorts on his rail thin brown body, ran forward.

"Yes, sir?" he asked.

"Please bring a glass to yon recruit. I am sure he or she bears a terrible thirst."

The boy, face browned to walnut by the sun, smiled, revealing very white teeth. "Yes, Mr. Fleming, sir! Right away!" He poured a glass and ran off into the shimmer.

"It better be her, sir," The Scotsman said darkly. "When you told me to train her, I was sure you'd gone mental." He shook his head. "I ain't never seen her like, sir. She's got steel in her that runs for miles. That's a fact."

"A sight more steel than Eddington and McMann," said Fleming. Egyptian auxiliaries, in case of failure, had shadowed all the recruits. Eddington and McMann had both given up the second day, surrendering their will to succeed. The auxiliaries had rescued the two recruits in the nick of time and at that moment they were in the Medic's tent resting and rehydrating. "Where the devil is that woman?"

Slowly, almost painfully, the distant, blurry form resolved itself into Fletcher Bowles, Khalid at his side. The tall, robust Englishman was sipping at his glass of lemonade while he staggered along, his wide-brimmed hat shading a sunburned face. He smiled as his tired eyes caught sight of the two men standing under the fading sun. He stopped ten feet away and gave the Commander a crisp salute. "Sir!" His voice was cracked, drawing the word out to three syllables.

"At ease." Fleming said. "Have you seen any of the others?"

"No, sir. Am I the first?"

The Commander started and MacTeague smiled as a melodious voice floated out on the scant breeze. "Don't be silly, Bowles." Jeanie emerged from behind the umbrella, the sun at her back and a smile on her face. "What took you so long? I've been waiting for bloody *forever.*"

ONE WEEK LATER, IN AN underground bunker that served as the Supernatural Service's headquarters, the Colonel (the head of HMSS) lifted a glass filled with an inch of amber liquid and gave a toast. "To a job well done," he said, his thin lips parting in a smile of genuine pleasure. J.R.R. Tolkien was a man of medium height with a long, slightly bent nose and thin lips whose intense blue eyes revealed the inferno of his intellect. Jeanie could hardly look away.

"I'll second that, sir," Fleming said, raising his own glass.

"To His Majesty's Supernatural Services," said the newest member of HMSS.

"Cheers," the three chorused and downed their drinks.

"Now, down to business," said the Colonel as he sat. The head of HMSS handed Jeanie the olive drab file folder, which she opened carefully. Inside was a detailed map of France.

"Sir?" she asked.

"You will be part of a team heading into France, to a place called Natzweiler. It's a village on the French/German border. There is a small German base we would like you to investigate. Your team will rendezvous with the French Resistance and they will guide you through the area. Something is happening there and we do not know what, but anything that hampers the Jerries is a result for us."

"Where is my team now, sir?"

The Colonel steepled his fingers. "They are here. Your team leader is Mr. Richard Fleming."

"My brother," said Ian with a warm smile. "Do be careful with him. He is rather fragile. The baby of the family, you know."

She grinned. "Yes, Commander."

As Jeanie made her way to the meeting room where her new team awaited. Desmond's voice came to her softly. *Good job, luv. I knew you could do it. Just be careful.*

"Just don't leave me, Des. I wouldn't be able to take it."

I'm here when you need me, my love.

***

"Does that dispel your fears, Kal?"

I placed the DRAFT on the desk and rubbed my face. Dispel my fears? Not hardly. No matter what, I would be fearful as long as Jeanie was in danger, especially since it would be *me* who placed her in harm's way. BB sending her out with a team to tackle truculent werewolves was one thing; if she died he would be able to emotionally handle the fact. Me ... well, it would break me in half. "Had to know, Ghost. For me ... I just had to know." Did she still talk to Desmond? Was he still the voice in her head that kept her on the straight path? Was I jealous of the ghost of her long-dead husband? Surely it wasn't that thought which made the acid in my stomach erupt, causing cramps? Could I get over it?

Damn BB. He knew I'd face this decision. Tests, tests, and more tests.

"You have your team, then," said Ghost.

Yeah. Big whoopie. I had a team and I felt like three kinds of crap for spying on my girlfriend, no matter how justified. My one consolation was that she would be with the one man I trusted most in the world, apart from my father, that is.

As for Jeanie talking to her dead husband, who was I to judge? I had my own issues to deal with. The fact was, I was action-packed with personal problems, enough to make any psychologist's career.

Donning the DRAFT, I pushed a virtual button. "Andrea, get me Canton Alsate."

CANTON

CHAPTER THIRTEEN

———·———

Back in the Saddle Again

IT HAD BEEN TWO MONTHS, six days and four hours since Winch died when I got the call from Andrea. *"The Director wishes to see you, Mr. Alsate."*

What did BB want? Not that I cared so dang much. Since that day at the Farallon Islands everything tasted like ashes and dust. Still, I was back at Warehouse and had to do what the devil directed, follow his awful will, even if my heart wasn't much into the task.

I went through all the tomfoolery that had been installed after that dustup with the rogue Agent, the one who took a chunk out of the Bureau's butt. Coyote himself couldn't get though all the safeguards (both magical and technical) in place and I reckoned that if anyone did, they deserved to kick some ass.

The Spell Shapes in Andrea's desk tingled against the palms of my hands as they did whatever the heck they were meant to do. During that time I caught Andrea's look of compassion, which she quickly masked. I'd been getting that a lot lately and it was beginning to wear somewhat thin.

"Go ahead, Agent Alsate," she said, removing her hand from the shotgun mounted under the desk. "The Director will see you now."

"Thanks." I hit the door and entered BB's office, expecting a pep talk or some such nonsense.

Kal.

What the heck was he doing there sitting behind the boss' desk? And wearing a goofy pair of specs at that … something a guy with his excellent vision didn't need at all. Didn't fit … sort of like an elevator in an outhouse.

I couldn't help myself, I laughed. He looked like a complete doofus in those wire-rims. "What is with the eyewear, white boy?"

He gave me that big silly grin he thinks is so charming. "The better to see you with, my dear."

"A laugh riot, you are." I draped myself in the chair and tried to keep a straight face. It was a patch of work. "Where's the boss?"

"Off doing some director-y type stuff. He put me in charge for a couple of weeks."

Really? "There goes the neighborhood."

" 'A laugh riot' right back at'cha."

Damn, it felt good to be with my friend. I almost felt normal again. "You didn't call my happy ass in here to show off, didya?"

Kal stood and strode to the wet bar. For some reason he was in his exercise outfit, a look incongruous with his surroundings "You ready for one?"

"No thanks." Why did I get the feeling he was pussyfooting around? "Just skip the foreplay, white boy, I don't have the patience."

He sighed and rubbed the bridge of his nose. He looked tired, big pouches under his eyes and signs of strain on his long face. Even his blond locks were in disarray. "You want out in the field?"

"A mission? Sure." Didn't have anything else to do except train and mope. "Why me, though? Why not one of the teams here? I figure Three Toes on Gamma is due."

"She came back from a mission two weeks ago. It's you. You're due."

"Sure. Who's the leader? What team?"

"New team now that we have enough Agents. Epsilon as a matter of fact." He showed me his pearly whites again. "You're team leader."

"You want me in charge of this rodeo?"

"Yep."

"Are you nuts?"

"Like I said, you're due. Besides, you're third generation Bureau—thank you *so* much for never telling me by the way—and I can't think of anyone better for the job."

"I refuse." There, that ought to do it."

He shook his head solemnly. "I refuse your refusal."

"Aw, c'mon!" The situation was starting to spin out of my control. "I said I refuse and that's that, white boy. You can't make me."

"You sound like a twelve-year-old," he said. "You know that?"

Didn't care. "Don't care."

Those big blue eyes became all serious-like and his face became grave. "You have to. Jeanie's on the team and you're the only one I trust to keep her safe."

That dirty— "No fair, white boy. No fair at all."

"Then you're in?" His smile told me he knew my answer.

What could I say? "Yeah, I'm in." Winch died sacrificing herself for Kal and I know deep down that he would've gladly traded places with her, given the chance. Besides, he was my friend. My best friend. I *had* to do what I could to keep Jeanie safe so he didn't feel the loss I was feeling. Sneaky bastard.

"Thanks, Canton. I appreciate it."

Me in charge … wasn't sure what to think of that. The thought of others looking to me to make a decision, to be responsible, turned my stomach a touch. I never wanted to be the guy to have to make the lousy call that put Agents in harm's way. "It ain't a big deal, white boy." Actually it was a pretty big deal, but no one was going make me admit it. "What's the op?"

Kal smiled that infuriating smile of his that has the women set to swooning and the men wanting to hit him with a wet shovel. He's too clever by half—the only guy I know who can tie his own brain into a Gordian Knot—and one day that's gonna get him into a pile of trouble. He tapped the desk like BB does when he's thinking and chuckled like it was all some sort of big joke.

"Andrea is making arrangements for the office and living

quarters," he said. "You will also be the first team in months to have a Receptionist, a new woman named Jo Essex. She's tougher than an anvil and pricklier than a bag of nails. Perfect for the job. Now, go to the research lab and check out RediPad 106. It contains a full debrief."

"What about the new YJ200? Those make a RediPad look like an old Atari game system." The newest in tablet/computer tech, the YJ looked like silvery eight-inch metal cylinder, but touch the button on one end and an ultra-thin polymer touch screen unspooled from the side. The screen was held rigid by a small electric current and retracted when the tablet was powered down. I'd attended a briefing on the new tech before the San Francisco op and they looked to be the next Big Thing.

Kal shook his head. "One thing about blending in, buddy, is not to have the kind of tech that would be noticed. You think the other feds have access to a YJ200?"

Oh. Damn, that made sense. Still, I felt let down. "What about the armory, what do I take?"

"Take what you want. You know my motto concerning weapons."

" 'Less isn't more,' " I quoted.

"'More is more,'" he finished with a grin.

"Who do I get?"

"Your other team members are Dove Jacobs, Kaleb Portner, Matt Alba, and Nancy Mason."

"And Jeanie."

His face sagged. "And Jeanie."

We stared at each other in mutual understanding. It was a testament to his faith in me that he trusted me with her safety.

"I'll bring her back, you know that, white boy."

His lips drooped at the edges and I could practically see the worry crawling inside him like a burrowing insect. "I know that."

I stood and offered my hand, thinking that a hug would not befit an acting director. Kal seemed to sense this and shook mine hard. "Good luck, *Itza-chu*."

Looked like he'd read my entire file. The smile that tugged at my mug felt genuine. Been a long time since one crawled on there. "You too, *Jlin-Litzoque*."

"WHAT IF IT'S JUST SOME person who went Hannibal Lector on the vic?" Dove Jacobs crossed her massive arms over ample breasts, as if she was afraid I'd stare at them instead of paying attention to her question.

The DisplayWall behind me held a pic of the bones, all chewed to hell and gone, pink and gray and stacked neatly. The Agents of Team Epsilon had been assembled and were back in action. Felt almost like coming home. Everyone seemed like solid types, even the Peas, although you could reach out and touch the humongous chip on Jacobs' shoulder. She was a taciturn, short, pretty blonde with one of them pageboy bob haircuts and shoulders like a linebacker. She looked more like a pro wrestler than an Agent. Cold marble under soft flesh. Word was she once took on a hippogriff all by her lonesome and twisted its head 'round a full 360 degrees before biting its throat out. Outrageous, obviously exaggerated, but I believed it.

"If it is a *Silence of the Lambs* scenario," I drawled, "then we give it to the Feebs and get on with life. Until then, it's a windigo, or something similar." I swept my gaze around the long, oak table of the conference room. "Anyone else have an idea what it could be besides a windigo?"

"How about a werewolf?" asked Portner, a balding man with a big chin and jug ears.

I winced. Not my favorite subject, werewolves. Visions of dead Eddie came to mind. Stupid twerp. "The teethmarks, Portner; they're human. A werewolf would leave fang marks, natch. Next?"

No one answered. The fact was, there weren't many things it could be. A windigo fit the bill just fine … only, it didn't feel right to me. I couldn't for the life of me figure out what was wrong. I even checked the database at The Place and the first answer the computer spat back at me was *windigo*.

Matt Alba, a bald, solid Latino with a ready smile and a good head full of brains, said, "Doesn't matter. We load up, fly to Chicago, do some proper recon, then kill the damn thing. End of story."

Jeanie lifted her RediPad. "It says here a windigo is a spirit that possesses a human, eats other humans and grows bigger every time it feeds. Sort of like a zombie from *The Walking Dead,* but with intelligence. If it's a spirit, then we might need an exorcism or it might come back, won't it?"

I had the answer to that one. "There are several legends concerning the windigo. Some say it is a creature of flesh and bones, which means it should die just like most of the Supernaturals we fight. If it's a spirit, well … Agent Portner there is an ordained Inter-Faith Minister. I reckon he could whip up a banishment if need be."

Portner nodded in agreement, his eyes hooded.

Nancy, a thin brunette with a pug nose, said, "Let's hurry this op up. I wanna get back in time to watch *Undercover Boss.*"

I rolled my eyes. Did Kal ever have to deal with twits like this? Scratch that, of course he did.

WE WERE OVER OHIO IN one of the Bureau's Gulfstreams when my RediPad beeped and a message icon appeared on its surface. I tapped the icon and a memo flashed in front of my eyes. Another body, or more accurately, pile of bones, had been found near the Chicago River, not far from where the first set had been discovered.

A photo was included, a gift from Ghost. Another pile chewed and gnawed by what looked to be human teeth, most broken and the marrow sucked out. No fangs, in fact the bite radius wasn't large at all. It could have been a cannibalistic serial killer; at least I hoped that was the case. Gross as that may sound, it would mean that we could go back to Warehouse, safe and sound, and call it a win.

But a part of me wanted it to be a Supernatural just so I could get around to a good dose of killing, to plunge my bowie knife over and over until the icy anger inside of me was sated. Winch was gone and her absence infuriated me. Most people thought I was in mourning, inconsolable over the loss of the woman I loved. That couldn't be further from the truth. I was pissed off as hell and ready to do some serious damage, to cover myself in the blood of my enemies and scream my victory at the winking stars.

Some people cried at the death of a loved one …. I just wanted to kill something.

Kal knew. He could see it in my eyes. He was Jlin-Litzoque, Yellow Horse, the other half of my soul. I knew it the moment I clapped eyes on him eleven years ago. I knew it in my blood, my flesh, my bones. His pain was mine, and vice versa, and he understood what I felt was not only anguish, but anger and hate. It was why he was sending me on this mission; so I could bleed out all the bile in my soul. It was simple and elegant and just what I needed, even though I didn't want to be team leader. Nantan Lupan would approve.

I could feel it in me, seething. All that poison bubbling inside. When I thought of Black Shuck ripping into Winch, I saw the world through a haze of blood and violence and death. I wanted to take something, someone, and kill them with my bare hands. I could feel my flesh tremble with the sick lust of it.

Sorrow? Too many people in my life had died for me to feel much of that particular emotion. The capacity for it was scourged from my soul early on in my career. Friends, family, colleagues. Especially colleagues. I had seen so many good Agents and Magicians die in ways no human should. Dying like dogs, screaming, crying, pissing themselves, crapping their pants. The last moments they had on earth had been filled with abject terror and horrendous pain.

I was numb to sorrow. Now there was only the violence inside of me.

I really, *really*, hoped it was a Supernatural we flew to, not a Straight, a damaged human being unable to control himself. The palms of my hands itched for the feel of my bowie knife slicing deep.

There came another ding from the RediPad … everything was ready on the ground, our HQ secured.

I sat there staring at nothing, wondering why a Supernatural would dump two sets of bones in the same location. Was the windigo staking out its territory? If so, finding it wouldn't be too damn hard.

At O'Hare one large, black GMC SUV and a truck met us for the Armory. We transferred our lethal cargo quickly and took off, the on-board navigation system already programmed with the coordinates of our office.

The Washington Heights district on the southwest side of the city proved to be our destination, a part of Chicago that had seen better times. Central Chicago was too congested to place the office there. No matter how great the Bureau's tech, gridlock is still gridlock and fighting through rush hour is hell in a SUV.

When the market went bust in 2008 and unemployment started to increase exponentially, it was the older neighborhoods in the big cities that seemed to suffer the most. In the late nineteen century Washington Heights had been a bedroom community, comprised of Irish and German families. By the '70s the residents were primarily African-American. Little had changed since then, except for an increase in vacant houses. Empty and reproachful reminders of an economy gone bad.

We pulled into a small parking lot occupied by a tiny, neutral-looking, single-story building constructed of pale brick. Blinds covered the windows and the only entrance was a steel door that bore the name CHAMBERS AUDITING SERVICE. Not the kind of name to arouse curiosity, a Bureau specialty. The mere mention of an audit would have most people hightailing like jackrabbits.

Inside was a small lobby done up in puke-yellow carpeting and wallpaper. There were no obvious doors to the rest of the building.

A pretty brunette with hair cut close to her scalp smiled at us from her cheap Formica coated desk, hands out of sight. "Welcome, Agent Alsate. Identity verification, please."

I placed my hands on the desk, letting the Spell Shapes embedded beneath the Formica do their thing, and stated my name all flat and emotionless. A warm tingle skittered across my palms as the Spells confirmed my identity. If I weren't Canton Alsate, Jo the Receptionist would cut me in two with the shotgun mounted under the desk and not even blink an eye.

After the ID checks, we unloaded the Armory and Jo opened the hidden door to our offices.

Every Bureau field office has been set up the same way for as far back as anyone can remember. An office for each Agent, a lounge for eating and relaxation, Comms to stay in touch with the boss, and the Armory for lethal alternatives. Stocking the Armory took the better part of an hour, along with sorting Spell eggs (Spell gems in egg-shaped polystyrene containers), racking the various automatic and semi-automatic weapons, and storing our armor.

When the detail work was done, I asked Jeanie to follow me to my office.

"What can I do for you, Canton?" she asked as we settled into large leather chairs.

I fished a small object from the pocket of my jeans and tossed it to the Magician. She caught it one-handed and held it up to the light.

"What is it?" The object sparkled and fractured the light into rainbow sprays.

"A vial."

"I can see that, but why does it sparkle like a diamond?"

"Because it's one big, man-made diamond. It's called a spirit bottle. If the Supernatural doesn't have a physical body and Portner can't exorcize it back to the World Under, I'll need you to Spell the critter in there."

She made a face. "Will that work?"

I smiled, not in a nice way. "There are over five hundred other vials like that stored away in a vault buried deep in the middle of the Sonoran Desert that tell me it should work." From the front pocket of my jeans I handed her a folded slip of paper. "This is the Spell Shape that should do the trick. Should be a piece of cake for you to learn."

Jeanie grinned and once again I realized how beautiful she was. I mean beautiful in a Halle Berry/Vivica Fox/Helen of Troy sort of way. If that wasn't a face that could launch a thousand ships, then the rest of the male population was seriously short of testosterone. Kal sure was a lucky guy, luckier than most men. I quickly quashed a surge of envy. "Go, and tell the others to dress up in their cheap suits. We're going to scout out the area where they found the bones. Bring ICE identification."

"Will do ... boss." With a saucy grin, she sashayed off.

Boss. I was a boss. That really ... stunk. I didn't want to be a boss. Sounded like far too much responsibility.

Sighing, I unholstered my phone from my belt and made a call.

"Hello?" came a voice after the third ring.

"Nantan Lupan, how are you?"

"Itza-chu! It is good to hear your voice. It would be better if you were here."

I couldn't help but smile. Nantan Lupan knew I was back in the Bureau, but he still wanted me to drop everything and hare off down to New Mexico. "No can do, Grandfather. I'm on the job."

"Of course, but you should have come. It is good to be with family in a time of loss."

"You sound more like Mom every time we talk."

"You should be so lucky. For one born of the Pueblo, she has the soul of an Apache." His laughter was the rasp of dry leaves.

I could picture him in his overstuffed leather chair, easing back with a glass of tea on the side table next to him. His long hair a bar of braided gray that ran down to his knees, his face a mass of wrinkles etched into soft coppery stone.

"This job ...." I paused, feeling the vise-like grip of the Interdiction in my mind. Talking about work over an open line had the Spell stirring in its nest. "Turns out I'm the foreman."

"Mmm. How do you like the responsibility?"

Like a hot lead enema, but I didn't say it. "Not much, but Jlin-Litzoque seems to think I'll do okay."

"Then listen to him. Your yellow-haired friend is smart ... for a white man."

"Thanks, Grandfather." Despite the words of encouragement, I still felt uneasy.

"Now that that's out of the way, when can you visit?"

"Really, I call and all you want to talk about is visiting?"

"Yes. So now what?"

I had to laugh. "After the job is done, is that okay?"

"Good."

"Thank you, Nantan Lupan. I needed a good chuckle."

"All right, Itza-chu, go do what you have to do. You will be fine."
The line went dead a second later.

Oddly enough, I felt better. Talking to Nantan Lupan did that for
me every time.

Time to go and face the bones. In the middle of donning my cheap
black suit and dreading the drive through Chicago traffic, I had an
idea.

"Jo," I subvocaled.

"Here, boss."

"Here's what I want you to do ...."

CHAPTER FOURTEEN

———◆———

Oh Where, Oh Where?

A LITTLE MORE THAN AN hour later, the five of us were at the site where the first and second set of bones had been discovered and a recon of the area showed us nothing new. The heavy, wet-rot smell of the river assaulted my nose almost as much as the humidity.

"*Boss, I've double and triple checked the police files,*" Jeanie said through the receiver behind my ear. "*No escaped mental patients, no other unusual activity. The remains found don't match the pattern of any known serial killers roaming the Midwest.*"

That was not entirely unexpected. "*How many known predators are there?*" I shot back.

"*Currently there are at least forty-five of the sickos at large today and active in the U.S. Thirteen are believed to operate in the Midwest. The closest I can find to a serious cannibal is the person the press is calling 'The Nibbler.' He or she shoots the victims with a .25 caliber pistol, then bites off their earlobes.*"

I really didn't need to hear that. "*Check Interpol ... hell, check everywhere. I want to know if maybe we inherited this sociopath from another country. If we did, we can give the info to the Feebs and head home.*"

"*Check, boss. On it. I'll have Jo help.*"

Despite Jeanie's throaty British accent, she was starting to sound more American with every passing day. I wasn't sure if that was a good thing.

Although the bones had been discovered next to the river amid trees and tall grass, it surprised me that there were no witnesses. After all, we were a block away from a high rise and several businesses and less than a hundred feet from a busy parking lot. Even though trees lined the lot, they didn't obscure the sightline to the river. It wasn't as if someone could stroll on up with a Santa sack full of bones and commence playing Jenga with them.

At the warehouse a short ways yonder was the newest crime scene. We checked it out quick and came up with nada, not even footprints. Whoever placed the bones had some serious sneaky skills.

I tugged at my tie, uncomfortable in my cheap black suit and black leather shoes. "Jacobs, why is it that no one saw the perp dump the bones?" I asked the muscular blonde.

She stared at me from behind her Oakleys. "Done at night?"

"Could be." I mopped the sweat from my forehead. "Take Portner and look for bums. The police may have talked to the business owners but neglected the homeless." A nod at the buildings not so far away. "But if the bones were dumped at night, there might have been indigents around." It was a long shot, but one worth exploring.

She nodded and gathered Portner, who looked as uncomfortable as I felt.

"What's on your mind, Canton?" Nancy asked, staring at the water. She was a tall woman with mid-length brown hair and a hard look to her eyes. They looked like chips of gray flint set deep into her round face.

I pointed. "Bones were dumped next to the water in an industrial area, right near the EL, in front of God and everyone, and nobody sees anything?" A couple of taps on the RediPad and a video appeared on screen. "The ME's report says that the bones were left here no more than a day before they were discovered, give or take a few hours. I've gone through the footage of the local traffic cams. See, the dump site is on the edge of the frame here, but I haven't seen anyone approach the scene."

After a few minutes of watching the video, her finger tracing back and forth along the fast forward and rewind icons, she shook her head, almost dislodging the two bone needles holding her hair in a bun tight at the back of her head. "Maybe the water. From this angle, you wouldn't be able to see the … Supernatural emerge from the river."

I nodded. "Yeah. I figured that. Could be this isn't a windigo."

Matt, who had been watching over her shoulder, said, "Just up north is the Holiday Inn Chicago Mart Plaza. They have external cameras that might have a shot of the river."

"Damn," I swore, angry with myself for not seeing it sooner. "Good call. Didn't think of that. Go check it out."

When Matt Alba made himself scarce, I walked away, staring at the river. Already I felt like a loser. Kal would have had the recording from Plaza in his possession before he even arrived. My first day and I was already working up a powerful streak of incompetent, but I couldn't let my anger show. Nothing tears a team down faster than a leader perceived as weak.

Nancy wasn't going to let me go so easily. "What's wrong?"

I shook my head.

"You're doing fine."

Damn, I hated being transparent. "Don't feel it. I'm missing something. *That* I can feel."

"Is this normal for the Bureau? Checking the lay of the land, detective work?"

The Chicago River glinted an impossible green in the midday sun. "Only in the big cities and then only sometimes. If a Supernatural is in a big city and the Straights have no clue, then the critter knows how to hide. That makes it even more dangerous. Give me a good old-fashioned haunting any day, or a misplaced yeti or a lonely sasquatch. Easy to deal with."

She frowned. "You think those are easy?"

"Yeah, easy. San Francisco was hard." Once again I felt the bile in my guts and closed my eyes against the ugliness I felt inside. "Please don't say you're sorry. I'm sick of people saying that. I may punch the next person who does."

She backed off, a troubled look on her face. "Okay, boss."

There I go, upsetting the Green Pea. I had to hold it together, or at least act like I could. We stood in uncomfortable silence, the heat and humidity of the day washing over us. I continued to stare at the water, wondering if a strange sort of cannibal mermaid could have committed the crimes. Before I could continue that train of thought, Jacobs and Portner returned with an update.

"We talked to some employees at the rent-a-car place across Canal Street," Jacobs huffed, face bright red from the heat. "There's a few winos around every night, but they come and go, no rhyme or reason."

I nodded, staring at the tall glass and steel buildings across the river. "Anyone else?"

"Cops queried all the locals, including the people in the apartments next door. Nada."

Nada, nada, nada tostada … darn. I wasn't surprised, just a little disappointed. Sometimes things get overlooked; sometimes all it takes is one tired or lazy cop to miss one small detail. Kal always said the devil is in the details.

What was I missing? What detail had escaped me?

"We'll come back tonight," I said suddenly. "Whoever is doing this is not going to be taking care of business in broad daylight. Also, we may find some indigents later who aren't here now." Wasn't much of a plan, but we didn't have much to go on.

Alba returned sooner than expected with a RediPad full of data from the Plaza's security cameras. Seeing the mess of gigabytes of information, I wished for Ghost's help. He could have siphoned through those images in a second.

"Let's head back."

A HOARD OF IMAGES FLASHED on the DisplayWall, a week's worth of digital recording from the Plaza. We all sat in Comms, eating popcorn and drinking heavily caffeinated sodas, trying to find the proverbial needle in the haystack. A very dark haystack. Four hours had passed and nothing, not a clue. The far bank from the Plaza had been undisturbed. Not even a rowboat or a floating corpse marred the scene of the silently moving rivers. It was as if the dark water wanted to keep its secrets.

"Any chance our dumper could be invisible, boss?" Nancy asked, rubbing tired eyes.

My own eyes were beginning to burn from the strain. "Jeanie?"

The Magician took a long drink from her Mountain Dew. How she could drink liters of that sugary stuff every day not gain 800 pounds was a mystery. Magic? And all that caffeine .... Her heart should've been ready to explode out of her chest. "As far as I know, true invisibility is impossible. In 1943 I used a camouflage Spell on Kal when he was sneaking up on the Jerries, but true invisibility ... no way." Her face became troubled. "Unless it's a natural ability, not a Spell."

"As far as I know, windigos can't vanish." I stifled a yawn. "Okay, people, *think*. We have a perp dumping bones for whatever reason and he's unseen. We've searched this footage for the past four hours frame by frame. Nobody came up out of the water, so where did the bones come from? How did he or she put them there and how the hell can I keep doing this nonsense without eating? Someone order Chinese."

They all made yummy noises, especially Jeanie, for whom Chinese food was new and exciting. I didn't have the heart to tell her about MSG. Kaleb took our orders and trotted off to buy the food. One constant in an inconstant world was the Chinese restaurant and they sprouted up on the urban landscape like weeds. Even in a recession they still flourished, if the food was halfway decent ... real beef, no cat or dog. Low food cost and free delivery made a good business model.

"Okay folks, let's rest our eyes, eat some dinner, and then go back to the river. Maybe we'll have some luck tonight." There were mumbled assents as the team made for the lounge to relax and ready themselves for some Lo Mein.

As for me, there's no rest for the wicked … or the wretched. I settled in for a little cramming. While I had a good grasp of the windigo from my Native American studies at Georgetown, more information was needed. A quick search turned up quite a few hits on the subject.

Turns out that the windigo—or wendigo, wetiko, windago, windikouk, there were many variations—legends are as diverse as their spellings. The one thing each legend has in common is the creature's monstrous appetite. A windigo is the epitome of gluttony and greed, never happy to kill and eat just one person; they are the Corgis of the Supernatural world, always snacking.

One of the legends states that if a human turns cannibal, as a matter of survival or due to madness, then the windigo spirit visits while the host sleeps and possesses them. Then comes a feeding frenzy for the possessed, who kills and kills until they are in turn killed by violence or magic.

On the other hand, if the windigo is not a spirit, but an actual being of flesh and bones, then it is yet another Supernatural that slipped through the cracks between worlds to invade ours. These windigos are thought to be giants, gaunt and grotesque, with gray skin stretched tight over skeletal structure and sores covering their tattered flesh. Not the kind of picture that invokes thoughts of gluttony.

I sighed with frustration…. I wanted answers, not more speculation. Whatever kind of critter this thing was, it needed to be dealt with in an abrupt and violent manner. The desire for bloodshed was so intense that my palms were twitchy, and I wanted to draw my bowie knife and slice anything that annoyed me.

To keep my hands busy, I pulled a whetstone and oil can from the left-hand drawer of my desk and began to sharpen the bowie as I read.

Shhhhhkkk, shhhhkkk ….

The Algonquin medicine men had a ceremony to banish the

windigo called a *wiindigookaanzhimowin*, which was an Ojibwe word.

Shhhhhkkk, shhhhkkk ....

It was comforting, the soft hiss of the heavy steel blade over oiled stone. Kal had given me the knife, or, more accurately, his father had, at Kal's request. Formed from an industrial file, it had a six-inch grip and a blade long enough to count as a short sword. One side still had the coarse grooves from its former incarnation.

Shhhhhkkk, shhhhkkk ....

Blood splashed on the grass of my mind. Sidhe blood, the blood of Prince Ephelor of the Unseelie Court (those Sidhe who hated us human types), the sonofabitch. It was his tiny figurine of a dog that transformed into Black Shuck, a demonic hound the size of a Clydesdale, killing Winch in its powerful jaws. If it hadn't been for her, Kal might have died. Me, too, and then we wouldn't have stopped the Sidhe from destroying mankind.

Shhhhhkkk, shhhhkkk ....

Princess Uloeth of the Seelie Court (those Sidhe who thought mankind was swell enough to live) had taken her body to Faërie, that part of the World Under where the Sidhe lived. There she was laid to rest in a place called the Grotto of the Fallen, the resting place for heroes.

Shhhhhkkk, shhhhkkk ....

I suppose it was a great honor to be buried alongside the greats, who in ancient times had been worshipped as gods. I suppose I should feel grateful that Uloeth would do that for her—place her among such august company—but I felt no sense of closure, no peace that she rested with heroes. It just hurt like an open sore on my heart that she wasn't in my life anymore.

Shhhhhkkk, shhhhkkk ....

Winch died saving Kal's life, putting herself in the path of that monster hound, and I'd give my left one to have her back. Some would think that I'd be angry at Kal, but that's stupidity on the hoof. It wasn't his damn fault and it was her decision and there was no way

I would challenge that. It would be an insult to her bravery. Still, that bravery got her killed.

Shhhhhkkk, shhhhkkk ....

Damn, I was becoming maudlin, like a broke-down old dog. A few hours of anger would serve me well, but I had no direction for it, no purpose without a target.

Really needed to kill something.

Soon.

Shhhhhkkk, shhhhkkk ....

Jo's voice came through the bone induction receiver behind my ear. "*Boss?*"

"*Go ahead.*"

"*The DNA came back from the lab on our two victims. Ghost lent a ... hand ... with the search, but no hits on any database. Whoever they were, they weren't criminals, armed forces or government employees.*"

I guess a result was too much to hope for. "*Okay. Anything else?*" I sent.

"*Yeah, Ghost also helped with like MOs on the killings ... nothing. Nothing in the U.S. and nothing in any other country. It's either a Supernatural or a brand new serial killer on a serious spree.*"

"*Okay. Thanks.*"

"*Check, boss.*"

Boss. I hated that word when directed at me.

Shhhhhkkk, shhhhkkk ....

Knock, knock.

It never rained, it poured. "Come in."

Jeanie stuck her head in. "You busy, boss?"

I used a clean cloth to wipe the bowie and stowed the oil and whetstone in a drawer. "Come on in. Have a seat."

She sat, crossing her blue-jean covered legs. They sure looked shapely under all that denim. "Boss, I need a favor."

I smiled. "We're a lot less formal than MI-7, Jeanie. In private you can call me Canton." Informal to the point of chaos—that was the norm in the Bureau. When you have so many highly skilled and bullheaded individuals, a rigid system would strangle their operational creativity. In a world where Supernaturals walk among the Straights, being creative was a survival trait. The only thing the Bureau demanded was absolute obedience to team leaders and, more importantly, the Director. Obey them like you would obey the word of God and you were hunky dory as far as far as The Man was concerned.

She smiled and I marveled how even and white her teeth were. In 1943 Great Britain, good dental hygiene was a rarity. Maybe she just had fabulous dental genes.

"What's the favor?" I asked, leaning back in my chair and crossing my arms.

"Tonight I want to go out with the team to the river to investigate," she said in a rush.

My head was shaking before she finished. "No can do. You have to stay behind and coordinate our efforts."

Her smile vanished. "Jo can do that."

True, but I wasn't going to admit it. "Standard protocol is we recon the site, then bring in the Magician. We can't risk losing you."

Ever had a strong woman stare a hole through you? Personally, I'd rather face a slavering chimera. She was doing her level best to stare a hole through me with brown orbs turned diamond hard.

"Hey, don't look at me," I said defensively. "It's protocol."

"Protocol hell," she grated with a glare. "You are the team leader and can do as you like within reason." Long pause. "Kal told you to protect me." It wasn't a question.

There exists among comrades in arms an unspoken promise when it comes to loved ones. They will be taken care of. Kal had entrusted Jeanie to my care and it was my duty, it was upon my honor, to see that she came back from this mission in one piece.

Looking into her large, brown eyes, noting the anger and determination, I realized a very important thing … to hell with honor. I didn't want this scary lady angry with me. She looked like she was fixing to be madder than a wet hen.

"Jeez Louise … fine. You're in, but if you die, don't come running to me."

And there was that smile that so captivated my friend's heart.

Lucky dude, that's all I can say about that.

"I have a question, if you don't mind," she said, settling deeper into the chair. From the look on her face I knew the conversation was going to head on out into interesting destinations. Just my luck.

"Go ahead."

"Ever since I followed Kal through the time portal to this marvelous new century, I've been studying. History, sociology, politics, everything that could help me become accustomed to this time."

I had a feeling that this was could be a long and drawn out chin-wag, so I motioned her to speed it along.

"All right," she said. If she was annoyed at my impatience, she sure hid it well. "Over the past few months I've noticed that there are very few Magicians in the Bureau, even though, with the current population of the U.S., there should be several hundred if not several thousand underfoot. My question is, where are they all?"

"*That's* what you wanted to know?" I asked incredulously. Here I thought she was gonna grill me like a salmon about Kal or something.

She stared at me for a few moments. "What?" Bright teeth shone as she laughed. "You thought I was going to ask about Kal!" she accused.

"Well ... yeah."

Jeanie crossed her arms and shook her head. "I know all I need to know about Kalevi Hakala, thank you very much."

I seriously doubted that and told her so.

"I know that he is broken," she said after a long, pregnant pause. "Knew it the first time I laid eyes on him in France when he cut through those VGG bastards like a razor."

After he returned through a greasy-looking pillar of unnatural light that was the time portal from 1943, Kal told me the story. In the village of Natzweiler he encountered the VGG, the Nazi version of the Bureau who used Necromancy to achieve their magical ends. They made the Gestapo look like the Vienna Boys Choir. He had to kill them all in order to save Mouth, Jeanie, Richard Fleming and members of the French Resistance, but not before they put the hurt on one of the locals. Good riddance to bad rubbish was my view on the whole matter.

"You know what he faced when he was a kid," I said softly. "The Class Five that killed his sister and nearly broke his mind into a billion pieces."

"It seems to me that you're worried that I'll break his heart." Her voice was as quiet as mine and slid through the air like blades of ice. Anger and violence were dragged along with those words. She was offended that I'd think such a thing.

"He's my friend." My best friend. Jlin-Litzoque, the Yellow Horse who was my other half.

Jeanie shook her head slightly. "I think I know him better than you, so I trust you will keep your nose out of something that isn't your concern."

Okay, enough was enough. I had to speak my peace or blow a gasket. "Of course you've got it all back asswards thinking that Kal's *just* my friend. He's more than that." I took a deep breath. "He's family. There's nothing I wouldn't do for him, just like there's nothing I wouldn't do for my flesh and blood brother and sister, so you'll just have to smooth pardon my damn nosiness. I will keep my big honker in your relationship with him just like he kept his in mine before it went to hell and gone." By the time I was done with my speechifying, I was seeing red, as if I was ready to hop into one of those rages Kal was famous for.

Knock me over with a feather …. She was grinning, teeth sparkling from ear to ear. I about felt my heart skip a beat or three as she began to laugh, full and throaty. "You cast iron bitch," I blurted, stunned. "This was a test, a damned test! I get enough tests from the Bureau, I don't need them from you. Trying to give me a heart-attack?"

It took a moment for her laughter to die out, but eventually it did and I sat there fuming while she wiped her eyes. "I love him," she said, half-wheezing from her bout of mirth. After wiping her eyes, she became grave. "I love him so much it hurts, it does, and I see how much you mean to him. Every time he's confronted by a difficult decision, I can practically hear him think 'What would Canton do?'

and it scares me. He loves you like the brother he never had and I don't know you. I had to know, you see? I had to know that you felt the same way.

"I know Kal is broken," she went on. "I can see it in his eyes, the way he interacts with the world using sarcasm as a shield against deeper emotions." Jeanie's voice cracked slightly. "Even with me, but I think he's healing. However, there's a fear he might break before he heals—he's *that* fragile—and even the smallest thing, the tiniest betrayal, can shatter him."

She's scared, I thought. *Scared out of her everlovin' mind.* Damn … she was really in love with the big galoot. Head-over-heels in deep up to the chin love and she thought he might break at any moment. Well, she might love him, but she sure didn't know him very well.

"He's stronger than you think," I said slowly. "Stronger than anyone thinks. Sure, Kal is a bit off his rocker, who wouldn't be doing this job? But he can hack it. He's the strongest man I know." Long pause. "He's the best of us."

Profound emotions were hidden behind the shield of her features. "You think so?"

"Yeah, I do."

Jeanie let out a long sigh through her lovely lips and stood. "Thank you for that, luv," she said in her thickest English accent. "I needed that, I guess."

I was still hopping mad that she went ahead and tested me like that, but fear makes people do crazy things. Fear robs reason, steals certainty, and makes a pauper out of all of us, so cutting her some slack was the right thing to do. Besides, that anger brought me outta my deep blue funk. "Good night, Jeanie."

As the door shut gently behind her, she said, "Good night, boss."

Minutes later I realized I'd never answered her question.

CHAPTER FIFTEEN

———•———

A Bite in the Dark

JUST AFTER SUNDOWN, NEAR THE river where the bones had been dumped. Instead of our cheap black suits we were outfitted in Faraday coats—thick leather trench coats lined with silver or platinum mesh, designed to absorb magic energy—over NewTanium/Kevlar armor. The whole ensemble was done up in black. I thought we looked pretty bad-ass.

Everyone was hidden, watching the area through nightvision contact lenses, weapons at the ready. Maybe we could catch the bone dumper in the act, maybe not, but at that point, with no leads, I was willing to piss on a spark plug to get a result.

First hour: nothing. Cars came and went, as did pedestrians, but not so much as to give a crowded feel to the area. I was beginning to see why the dumper chose the place.

Second hour: same as the first, but with less traffic. It was chilly, but the coats kept us warm enough.

In the third hour we began to move and shift our positions, knees creaking and muscles sore. I hated stakeouts because they were so *boring*. Give me a giant insect or a manticore to shoot with extreme prejudice any day.

"*Boss, this blows.*" Jacobs. Even through the bone induction mics she sounded riled.

"*You got that right.*" Portner.

"*Check that.*" Mason.

"*Stow it.*" Me, more than a little pissed at their unprofessional attitude. "*Anyone else want to complain? If so, do it after you brief your replacement. Until then, 86 the chatter!*"

Portner and Mason were the first to apologize. It took some uncomfortable silence for Jacobs to finally chime in. She'd be a top-flight Agent once she manhandled the chip off her shoulder and lost the screw-you attitude.

In the fourth hour a black Taurus arrived, and a tall, square-jawed Asian-American exited, looking all kinds of lean and mean. The man began to walk toward the river.

"*Who the hell is that?*" asked Jacobs.

"*One sec,*" I replied. From a belt pouch I withdrew a half-inch thick rectangle of what appeared to be slightly tinted blue glass the size of a cellphone edged in black plastic. I tapped a corner and the glass sparked to life, several icons appearing on the shiny surface. Putting the rectangle to my eyes, I tapped one of the icons, and immediately my vision zoomed in on the Asian-American man. Conservative, off-the-rack clothes, not cheap, but not expensive. Probably JCPenney. Leather shoes, rubber-soled and a haircut that came from a chain barbershop rather than a privately owned salon. It didn't take a genius to figure out who the dude was.

"*Cop,*" I subvocaled. "*Fed, not local.*"

"*How do you know?*" Mason asked.

"*Cop shoes, cop clothes, cop car. Easy. Dresses like every fed I've ever met.*"

Alba cut in. "*Boss, another car.*"

And so it was. It seemed there was a cop convention that night because a black Crown Vic cruised up next to the Taurus and stopped. This time two people emerged from the vehicle, a burly redheaded woman in a no-nonsense business suit and a slender man who walked and dressed like a wannabe James Bond. He was good looking in a dashing sort of way, and by his strut, he knew it.

"Everybody stay where you are," I sent. *"Keep your eyes peeled. I'm going in. Matt, man the .50 cal."* Agent Alba was stationed on the roof of an office building over a hundred yards away—our safety net should we get into a situation that required serious firepower. With the TAC®-50 McMillan loaded with 7.62 NATO rounds, I knew he could shoot the earrings off the redheaded cop's lobes from over a thousand yards without much effort.

"Check, boss."

A plan began to form. *"Jo, I'll need you to access the Immigration and Customs Enforcement database. Keep listening and stay ready."*

"Check, boss."

The armor and the Faraday coat didn't allow any other clothes besides undergarments, so I flitted from shadow to shadow back to our SUV, which was parked a block away on Fulton. In the back was everything we needed in case of such incidents. For me the disguise consisted of a white button-down, tan slacks and loafers. Along with the appropriate ID, of course, making me top cop in case of jurisdictional pissing matches.

Using the rectangular lens (dubbed a MagniGlass by Special Branch) I kept an eye on the three newcomers. The two cops were talking to the Fed cop with plenty of animated gesticulating and head bobbing. It looked intense, intense enough that I was able to walk a block, cross the railroad tracks and get within a few yards before the Fed caught sight of me.

"Stop right here!" he warned, hand moving to the weapon holstered under his suit jacket.

"Two fingers," I said, holding up said digits and using them to pull my wallet from my back pocket. My ID shone in the parking lot halogens. "Special Agent Daniel Westmore, Immigrations and Customs Enforcement."

The dapper cop made a face. I could smell his cologne. Expensive, but he used far too much of it. "What the hell is ICE doing here?"

I smirked, replaced my wallet, and gave him a good hard look. Up close he was even better looking than I thought. Expensive salon cut hair to go along with his hideously expensive suit, which he wore far too well. A superior air coated his features like thick makeup. I'd known guys like that in high school, idiots who used to call me derogatory names because of my race. Perhaps he was different, but I wasn't going to place any bets.

The Fed checked my ID. "Okay, Westmore," he said in a curiously high, fluting voice. He passed the wallet back. "What are you doing here?"

I held out a hand. "I showed you mine; now show me yours." My smile wasn't seconded by my voice, which carried a definite edge. Alpha dogs sniffing each other, right?

The three offered their badges. "Right. Kevin Beinfort and Sara Mills of the Chicago PD and Special Agent Wesley Ng of the FBI. Good to meet you."

Ng stared impassively, patient as a boulder, while Mills waited on Beinfort. It didn't take long for the James Bond wannabe to ask, "Mind telling us why ICE is interested in Chicago PD and FBI business?"

"Manny Garces."

"Who the hell is Manny Garces, Boss?" Jacobs sent.

Beinfort echoed the question.

"Manny Garces," I began, warming up to the BS story I'd concocted while changing clothes, "is a former enforcer for the Gallegos Cartel in Mexico. Escaped from a mental institution three weeks ago and is believed to have fled north."

"You think Garces is our doer?" Ng asked. "That he dumped those bones by the river and in the warehouse?"

I nodded. "Everything fits his MO, although stacking them all nice and tidy is new. This guy used to eat his enemies and leave their bones for their families to find. To say he's a nut-job is to damn with faint praise. He is so far around the bend he can't even *see* the bend anymore. I heard about the bones by the river and knew it had to be him."

"*Okay, Boss,*" Jo sent. "*Got all that in the ICE database. As far as anyone is concerned, Manny Garces is a real, ex-Cartel, at-large cannibal in the U.S."*

Gotta love the Bureau, we have all the coolest toys and access to all the Alphabet Agencies.

"Why wasn't the FBI informed?" Ng didn't sound angry and by the look of it, he could teach rocks about inscrutability, but there was the slightest edge to his voice that spoke of great restraint.

"It's what I'm doing now, isn't it? The question is, what are you three doing out here in the middle of the night?" That's what really fried my bacon. Why wouldn't they meet in a nice office somewhere?

It was Ng who answered. "I asked them to."

I waited.

He sighed. "Something about this case bothers me and I wanted to come here firsthand, pick their brains, get the lay of the land. Being at the scene helps me focus."

"Which has me wondering," Beinfort cut in. "Since this case *hasn't* been turned over to the Feds, why all the interest?" His glare encompassed both Ng and myself equally. Mills merely stood by patiently, a small smile on her homely face. "This case belongs to Chicago PD, not FBI or ICE."

Before Ng could answer, Beinfort raised his voice, staring over my shoulder. "Mister, go on now. There's nothing here that concerns you."

I swiveled my head in time to see an indigent—a short, stubby man with a graying, bushy beard and filthy clothes—walk toward us along the tracks. A bottle encased in a paper bag was clenched in one grimy fist and I could see, thanks to the nightvision, that his lips were parted in a smile of glee or madness. The rest of his face was obscured by a battered and grimy Cubs hat. Hmph … the Cubs. No accounting for taste.

"I done seen what shouldn't be seen," the bum crooned, his teeth surprisingly white. "I seen what no one shoulda seen." He gave an odd little twirl as he moved closer. His black Converse sneakers were torn and tattered to the point I could see his long, black toenails and the weeping sores on his feet.

Ng held up a hand, palm outward. "That's close enough, sir. Turn around and go back where you came from, sir."

"Back where I came from? Back where I came from?" gabbled the bum, dancing a jig on the rails with remarkable grace. "Tra-la-la! There is no back home for me! I is home right here, right now. Life is good, life is sweet, life is best with fresh meat!"

"Great, another rum bum," muttered Beinfort, stepping toward the dancing indigent. "Listen, pal," he said loudly. "This is police business. Move along."

"What do you think I is doing? I is moving right along. Tee-hee! Fresh meat, so sweet, puts you right on your seat!"

"Jesus, pal. Get outta here!"

The bum was only a couple yards from the dapper Beinfort. "But I just got here! I think I'll stay. Because the meat is so sweet!"

And the suddenly the bum was *there*, in Beinfort's face, teeth flashing, mouth opening impossibly wide and arms, freakishly long arms, arms that extended so much farther than the sleeves on his filthy jacket, wrapped around the Lieutenant and there was a *crunch* and a slurping sound that reminded me of inhaling soup from a spoon and Beinfort *screamed* long and loud, a wail filled with anguish and rage. Blood, slick and black in my nightvision, sprayed into the air, an arterial spurt that coated the gobbling bum in coppery fluid.

I was already in motion before the first dark drops of Beinfort's blood hit the gravel, bowie in fist, other hand reaching for the grappling pair. Alba didn't have a shot, not without risking hitting the Lieutenant. My grasping hand knocked the grimy ball cap aside as I grabbed a hank of long, greasy, gray hair.

Steel flashed and soft flesh parted, the bowie cleaving clean and straight and with scalpel-like ease. The bum's second mouth, rimmed with crusted dirt, parted like the lips of a lover and exposed quivering, severed muscles and the tough cartilage of his throat.

What should have resulted in arterial spray produced nothing but a dry hiss, as if hair, not blood, filled the man's veins. I stabbed with the bowie, burying it hilt deep in the bum, but he merely laughed at me around a mouthful of bloody gobbets.

Almost lazily, those impossibly long arms dropped Beinfort, who had long since stopped screaming. Spider quick, the bum hit me in the chest, knocking me head over heels across the railroad track, where I bounced off the rails. For a brief moment everything went darker than dark and the world went away.

Well, maybe not, but there was a lot of pain, more than I'd felt in a long time. A sticky wetness flowed from the back of my head. My brains had been bounced off the inside of my skull like a ping-pong ball. Who had done that?

Oh yeah, the bum.

Popcorn popping. No, that's not right, the sound resonated more, had a sharper tone. It took a second but I realized it was the welcome noise of gunfire. Yeah, shoot the bum and I would lie there and play 'possum for a spell.

No good … 'Possum was never a game I played well.

One eye cracked open. My vision swam, blurred this way and that, but eventually the scene came into focus. The bum continued his dancing—no, that's not right, either. He was juddering and shuddering as bullets tore gobs of flesh and cloth from his stout frame. Finally, the cops were there when I needed them.

If I lived, I promised never again to crack another cop/donut joke.

The bum laughed. A real, deep-throated, demonic laugh that started at his belly and traveled up his torso. It spat out air from the gaping, flapping hole in his throat before moving up and out his mouth through teeth jammed with shreds of meat. The result was a peculiar whistle followed by a basso blast—a car horn from Hell.

Crack.

The top of the bum's skull broke free and flew off into the dark, leaving his face to end at an inch above his eyebrows. Matt and his .50 cal, God bless him.

Only, the bum didn't fall. In fact, he kept on laughing, all the while dancing to the tune of bullets hitting his body. Mills and Ng emptied their weapons and reloaded while Matt Alba blew more chunks out of the bum, who laughed and laughed and laughed.

That was scarier than I could ever have imagined.

Alba continued to fire and the thing that used to be a bum continued to lose big chunks of itself, not that it cared. By the time the .50 cal took one of the freakishly long arms off at the elbow, Mills was shrieking and cursing up a storm, a look of wild desperation and insanity on her face as she emptied a clip into the bum's torso.

"*Cease fire, Matt*," I subvocaled, rising painfully to my feet. The world was all wibbly-wobbly, but I stayed upright. Oddly enough, my right hand still clutched the bowie, which was excellent because there was no way I was capable of bending over to pluck it from the ground.

"Stay back, Westmore," shouted Ng, firing while Mills reloaded her big .44. The bum continued to laugh and laugh and laugh. I wanted to shove my fingers into my ears and rip out my eardrums so I didn't have to listen to the creature's horrible mirth.

It took another step toward the two cops, freed from the damage of Matt's sniping. I was going to give it a little damage of my own.

Three long strides and the world titled sideways, but I kept on moving on, both hands clamped to the hilt of the bowie. Another step and my stomach told me in no uncertain terms that I was a mule-headed idiot for falling back into the fray.

Screw it, I thought. You only live once, right?

Three more strides, taken much faster. My right foot landed on a rail and I used every erg of energy I had in my leg to launch myself into the air, swinging the bowie in a deadly arc.

Thunk! The bowie's razor edge impacted upon the bum's neck with all my strength, all my weight behind it. It came to me that I should have yelled for a cease fire—it would be a damn shame if I got plugged in the gut by a terrified Straight—but I didn't have time to worry about it. I was too busy swinging for all I was worth.

The bum's skull made a hollow, wooden sound as it bounced off a rail, while its body folded at the knees and fell to the gravel.

"What the hell?" Mills moaned, gun trembling in unsteady hands, eyes round and terrified. "What the hell was that thing?"

I gave the two shocked cops the patented Kalevi Hakala raised eyebrow that never seems to work and said, "There can be only one."

"Boss, you okay?" Jeanie's subvocal voice was tinny with concern.

"Just my head, kid," I shot back. *"Wasn't using it much, anyway."* And then it all came up—dinner, lunch, and breakfast spewing forth as I bent over, my stomach clenching and shuddering in rebellion. One, two, three, four times I retched while my head pounded to the beat of my heart.

A crunch of gravel, several footsteps, and I turned my head to see the team converging, Faraday coats flapping and their fists full of ICE badges. "They're with me," I croaked, sitting heavily next to the pile of stinking puke. My head swam and little black spots began to flicker in my vision. The pain was becoming worse, eclipsing my ability to reason.

"Boss?"

Pretty sure that was my designation, but I was broken inside. I couldn't respond. My spirit was disentangling itself from my flesh and I experienced a peculiar sense of dislocation. I found myself looking down at the scene, where I sat on the tracks. Jeanie was there, long fingers running over my scalp. I wanted to say something, tell her it was all right, but my mouth wouldn't work; it had been disabled for the duration and that was fine by me because I was one tired hombre and needed some much deserved rest. Spit ran down my chin and spattered my once-clean oxford button-down shirt.

Jacobs and Mason had secured the body of the bum while Alba, solid, dependable Alba, was keeping Ng and Mills occupied, quietly taking command of the situation, his .50 cal stowed away. He'd made good time from his sniper's perch. From the look on Mills face, she didn't like taking orders one bit and Ng looked as impassive as ever, stoic and calm. I bet he was riled up something fierce on the inside though. What he had just witnessed would have half the people on the planet locked up in a room with nice, cushy walls.

I began to recede, moving away from the scene, from grasping, quarreling humanity and it was okay, I felt peace. No more fighting, no more having to watch friends and colleagues die in horrible, painful ways. I could let go of the fleshy world and perhaps find a place that offered a modicum of rest.

That would be nice.

My peaceful departure was interrupted by a sharp tug that traveled through my navel and up my throat, into my head. It hurt like glass on exposed flesh and I would have screamed if I'd had a tongue or mouth, but I didn't. All I could do was flail against the insistent pull that had me returning to the body I'd just left.

I thrashed, I pulled back, but nothing happened. My return was as inevitable as the tides and relentless as gravity.

Like a hand slipping into a soft, worn, glove, I was back … tired and logy, but back in the cage of my flesh.

Damn.

"You okay, boss?" Jeanie asked, wiping my brow.

My eyes opened. "Define 'okay,' " I said wearily.

"As in 'not dead' and 'still able to walk while not being very dead.' "

"Oh, then 'okay.' " Body check time. Everything attached? Yep. Good, I would surely hate to be missing something I could use later on. "Yeah, I'm mostly okay." Except the feeling of peaceful rest was gone, chased away by crude reality. That really reeked because I was sure I was close to some impressive revelation, one that would shake me down to the core of my soul. Oh well, I guess I'd find out eventually.

"Good. You were nearly gone there. Your skull had a nice knock-about—a fracture, actually—and it took quite a bit of power to bring you back. Mucking about with a severe head injury is a quick way to find the afterlife. I'm surprised you were able to stand, much less fight."

"Swell. Thanks for the healing," I grumbled, slowly levering myself to my feet. The earth remained steady, just how I liked it. "You know your Interdiction Shape?"

Jeanie treated me to the kind of look only women can master. The kind that said, *Aren't you just an idiot male.* My mom had that same look down pat—she could teach lessons—but Jeanie's was pretty damn good, too.

"Of course, foolish of me to ask."

She nodded. "I agree." With one last, almost pitying glance, she left to Interdict the two Straights.

"Boss!" It was Mason, looking like she swallowed a frog. Her homely face was all big eyes like one of them Anime cartoons. Dragonball Bureau Agent or some such.

"Yeah?"

"The bum!"

"What about him?"

"He's staring at me!"

Now what? I tottered over to where Mason was standing above the shattered remains of the skull and pulled up short. The head, skull obliterated above the brows, stared malevolently, accusation and hate boiling from its eyes. They gave a slow blink and continued staring while it grimaced with a mouthful of blood-slicked teeth.

I rubbed my temples. "You don't see that every day."

"No kidding." Mason looked ready to throw up. "What do you want to do?"

"Put it in a bag and take it with us."

"I was afraid you were gonna say that."

"Well, you know what they say."

"What?"

"Better you than me."

She made a face. "How do I get outta this chicken-squat outfit?"

"That's easy … die."

CHAPTER SIXTEEN

———•———

A Surprise Visit

A LAS, POOR YORICK, I KNEW him … blah, blah, blah.
Never did like *Hamlet*, but despite my objections, the team
decided to dub the bum's half-skull after the one made famous by
Shakespeare, although that one was whole. Ours was still alive and
trying to talk, also a bit fleshier than the one ol' Willie S. wrote about.
How's that for gross?

And that wasn't the worst. What happened to Beinfort I wouldn't
wish on my worst enemy.

Portner and Jeanie had been keeping the looky-loos from
disturbing the scene. Him with gentle persuasion, her with Spell
craft … not anything that would affect their minds—the human
brain being a tricky little conglomeration of organs; mess with one
part and another might shut down entirely in response—but with
gentle magic that would induce a near overwhelming lassitude. By
the time they were done, any who had been alerted by the sound of
gunfire found themselves politely persuaded to leave or too tired to
give a damn.

Mason had stuffed the glaring skull into a plastic bag. Alba had
Ng in deep conversation while Mills had knelt by her Lieutenant's
side, weeping softly, while Jacobs stood by looking uncomfortable.

Everything seemed as normal as it ever is on this job after a Supernatural incident.

Beinfort hadn't a chance. The bum's scalpel-sharp fangs had ripped right through skin and muscle to sever his carotid. Pink, shredded flaps lay about his neck while the exposed cricoid cartilage glistened in the dim light from faraway halogens. His death must have been painful but quick. I gave his body a quick glance, noting the blood fanning out from his neck down his expensive suit like a wet bib, and was ready to turn away when his eyes opened.

In the milliseconds that followed, my perceptions kicked into a higher gear while the world shifted into slow motion. I saw that Beinfort's eyes were dead black, the soulless black of a shark, glistening with a thin veil of transparent ooze. My hand found the hilt of my bowie as the creature smiled wide and horrible, a cartoon clown grin filled with ancient malice.

Mills gasped. Jacobs drew her weapon, but I was faster in spite of my fatigue, my blood singing in my veins. Once again I leaped, this time knocking Mills to the side and landing knee-first on Beinfort's chest. Ribs snapped under the impact, but his smile only grew wider, lips nearly touching his ears.

The next thing I knew, long arms—incredibly, spiderishly long—wrapped around my shoulders, pulling me into an obscene embrace, but I was ready. The bowie flashed downward, its keen edge finishing the job begun by the bum's teeth and with a few brisk sawing motions, I cut through cartilage and bone, severing the tall man's head. Had anything been left in my stomach, I would've thrown up again.

As I lifted the head by the hair, Beinfort's eyes stared balefully at me, the light of madness shining hard within. Behind me I heard a gasp, then a deep, throaty retching.

"Jeanie!" I shouted, stomach flopping something terrible as I stared into those hateful eyes. "Get over here."

"Damn," she muttered as she knelt next to me, staring at Beinfort's lifeless body and his all-too lively head.

"Any ideas how to put this poor bastard to rest?"

Ng chose that moment to join us, Alba at his side. "I suppose you will explain?" he asked, voice hoarse.

I nodded. "Suppose so."

Meanwhile, Jeanie relieved me of my grisly burden, holding Beinfort's skull by the ears and staring intently into his eyes. We all watched in hushed expectation for at least a minute as her will battered against the thing that inhabited the head.

Finally, she lowered the skull to the ground and took a deep, shuddering breath. "Whatever's in there has bound itself permanently to the flesh with chains of magic." Jeanie shook her head. "The magic needs to be broken somehow before the … spirit or whatever it is can be released."

"Did you say magic?" Ng's stress-roughened voice was so matter-of-fact he might as well have been talking about the weather.

I gave the FBI agent a close look. He seemed to be handling things well, but I knew that could change in a damn hurry. "Yeah, magic and immortal cannibals. Go figure." To Jeanie, "What can we do?"

"I can't break the malignant spirit free magically. It shrugs off whatever Spells I throw at it like water off a raincoat."

Hmm. "Anyone packing silver bullets?"

It took a second, but Jeanie got it. "That could work," she mused.

Matt pulled a clip from a thigh pouch and handed it over. "9mm," he said.

"Perfect, thanks." I loaded the silver into my Glock and shot Beinfort between the eyes. The silence Spell held true. Not a whisper from the expanding gasses reached our ears.

The bullet carved through Beinfort's skull and exited out the back, spraying reddish gore out onto the gravel. The thing he had become was finally dead.

Mills made more retching sounds. Although a homicide cop, such things were far outside her realm of experience, while Ng continued to look on impassively. It was a little scary how he remained so stoic. So it came as no surprise that he took the news of the existence of magic, the Bureau, and the World Under pretty damn well. Better than I would have. As for Mills, well, she looked to be about two steps away from uncontrollable drooling, so I had Jacobs take her under his wing in an attempt to talk her off the ledge and onto solid ground.

To keep things tidy, I had Jo arrange things so, to the Straight world, the pair would be seconded to ICE for the foreseeable future, then had her arrange a quick flight to points far the hell away from Chicago, escorted by Portner to O'Hare, where he would personally ensure they boarded the plane. When they returned, there would be a commendation listed in their file, a pat on the back from Uncle Sam and the Bureau, and no way to talk about the strange and unusual world beneath the world they had just experienced.

"WHAT ARE YOU TRYING TO say, Yorick?" I asked the half-skull. The eyes, dead and black, merely stared while the lips moved soundlessly as if trying to whisper terrible secrets. It didn't take a grip of intelligence to figure out that its silent words weren't complimentary.

"Yeah, you too, buster." The damn thing was a grotesque horror, shattered pink/gray bone surrounding the bowl that housed torn brains above a pair of black-as-sin eyes. I half expected it to start leaking all over my desk, but no, no cerebrospinal fluid, no blood. It was as if the bum had been freshly drained for our convenience.

A knock at the door disturbed my reverie. "Come in."

Matt stuck his head in. There were dark circles under his eyes and his normally ruddy skin had a sallow, washed out hue. "Going to the apartment, boss. You coming?"

"Nah. You go on ahead. I'll be there later."

He stared for a moment, eyes narrowed, before entering. He'd changed out of his armor and Faraday coat and now wore a plain white t-shirt and jeans. A pair of Air Jordans encased his feet. "Permission to speak freely, boss?"

Oh lord, why me? "Sure." I waved him to a chair. "Take a load off and stop with the formalities. This 'permission to speak' stuff ain't my bag. You know that."

His full lips quirked in a half-smile as he sat. "I like the formalities. Comforts me."

"Well, hell ... far be it for me to transport you outside your range of comfort, Mr. Alba."

"Thanks." Matt scratched his head. "You need sleep like the rest of us, so why don't you come with me to the crib? You gotta bunk down, boss."

Fatigue pulled at me and I battled a yawn. "I'm okay, Matt. It's just that I have work to do."

"What? Talking to a busted skull? Not sure if you noticed, boss, but it ain't in no condition to hold a lively conversation. Put a silver bullet in what's left of it and call it a night."

I shook my head. "I need to figure out a way to interrogate it."

"Why?"

"Because I'm stumped," I growled, giving voice to my frustration. "This thing has answers."

"Request help from Special Branch."

"First thing I did."

"Then get outta here, boss. Get some sleep."

"I can't."

"Why?"

"Because I'm missing something. There's some detail that's slipped through my grasp and I need to figure out what it is."

"You should sleep on it, then."

"Kal wouldn't." The words were out of my mouth before I realized I'd said them. Damn.

Matt Alba's dark eyes reflected the light of the fluorescent tubes overhead, giving them a shiny, gemlike quality. He let out a slight sigh. "Boss, there ain't no one like Agent Hakala. He's got a mind so twisty-turny that he can beat the Devil at chess while blindfolded."

I had to laugh. "You worked with him in Denver, didn't you?"

He nodded.

"Impression?"

"He's messed up, boss," Matt said carefully. "He don't act like it where one can see, but he's screwed up just the same." He held up his hand before I could object. "Oh, he's better now than he was. Ms. Morrow has been good for him, but he still isn't quite right in the head."

Why did talk always seem to turn to Kal? Perhaps because he's done so much in his seemingly never-ending quest against the World Under. When he first came to the Bureau and was assigned to BB's team, I knew he'd been through the wringer. Facing a Class Five Supernatural (a being of Mythic or Deific proportions) can take a chunk out of your sanity in a hurry, but he was still the best I'd ever seen.

"Point is, boss," Matt continued. "You can't be like Agent Hakala, just like you can't be like me. You gotta be like yourself, figure crap out your own way."

"What are you Alba, twenty-four? Twenty-five?"

"Twenty-seven, boss, last month."

"How'd you get so smart?"

He flashed a set of large, even teeth. "My mama always had a word or two for me. I'm just paraphrasing what she said."

"Paraphrasing?"

"The words she used were a little more blue."

We shared a laugh and it felt good. Laughter was a rare commodity on a mission and when you work in the Bureau, seeing all the horror the World Under can offer, your sense of humor turns a little … peculiar.

"You know he's the best," I said. "Kal, I mean. There's been no one better."

Matt shook his head. "No, I think he's been lucky. Audie Murphy and Jim Thorpe were better. Between them they accumulated over thirty-three missions. Thorpe lost two men while Murphy lost none. All that was done before the age of the microchip."

I couldn't help but smile. Matt was so wise and dependable that I forgot how young he was. "Listen, kid, both of them were great Agents, no arguments there, but they never faced what Kal has. Eleven years, sixty-eight missions, think about *that*! And don't forget, luck is always part of the equation."

THE LAND FLASHED BELOW ME, dry and stark, filled with life as harsh and remorseless as the terrain. My eyes, so sharp, picked out the scurrying of small mammals, movements so fast no human could register them accurately.

I was the lord of the air, the ruler of the skies and my shadow brought fear to those below. There was no kindness in my reign, only the rule of beak and talon and I was an absolute despot.

A slower, more languid movement caught my attention and the familiar pattern of a rattlesnake met my gaze.

I dove.

Legs outstretched, my wings unfurled long enough to slow my descent and my talons curled around the branch-thick body of the snake. There was a slight snapping as bones broke and I flapped, rising into the sky with my prize.

The meat was sweet and I tore off large chunks, swallowing them whole. Eventually I was sated, so I left the torn remains of the carcass on the flat rock I'd perched on and once again took to the sky.

Thermals lifted me higher, caressing my wings with their heat. Higher and higher still and I was free, no longer tied to the earth, forced to travel upon a pair of stalks that were oddly jointed. Here there was only predator and prey. Life was cruel but understandable. You lived, you died and that was it, no take-backs, no do-overs.

A gentle caress against my face.

"Wake."

It was a command, but I chose to ignore it. I was the despot of the sky, the ruler of what my eyes could spy.

A gentle poke.

"Wake."

No! This is where I belong! I am Itza-chu and I—

POKE!

"Wake."

I woke, and not well. Before my conscious mind was aware of it, the bowie filled my fist and my arm was swinging. Pain, sharp as scalpel, shot through my neck. I had fallen asleep at my desk and the crick in my neck shot shards of agony to the base of my skull. I could feel drool drying on my cheek.

A familiar sight stopped me stone cold dead, bringing an icy sweat to my skin and halting the knife in mid-air. A stick the length of my forearm was pointed between my eyes a few inches from my nose and the sight of it terrified me something awful.

Made of pale wood, there were curving and looping black lines, thread thin, buried organically amongst the fine grain. The pattern formed by the lines confused the eye, tricked the senses and generally conveyed more menace than they should have. It was an artifact of almost incalculable power and in the right hands, could instantly render a body into dust. I'd seen such a stick before. On my last mission.

San Francisco.

Where Winch died.

One of those innocuous sticks had enough raw magical power to overcome the absorption capacity of a Faraday coat in an instant, turning the mesh lining the garment into superheated plasma. That was how the Magician Ilena died, cooked to ash in less than five seconds. I remembered her flying straight up into the air as her coat exploded in flames, washing my upturned face with heat, scouring my skin. She didn't even have time to scream before she was rendered into fine particles that rained down upon my team. All that damage done by one little, innocuous stick. It was frightening.

And what carried that stick scared me even more.

"Do not move, please," said the kid who pointed the stick in a high, fluting voice.

I had no intention of doing so. While some might laugh a riot at 'assault with a deadly twig,' they had no goldarned clue what that kid was.

You see, the kid was a puca, a kind of Sidhe (or Faë or Fairy, whatever your preference) that was the inspiration for Robin Goodfellow, or Puck, in Shakespeare's *A Midsummer Night's Dream*. Although if old Will had actually met a puca, he would've burned the play and scattered the ashes before hiding under his bed and crying for his mamma.

This puca wore a red Lady Gaga concert t-shirt with blue jeans and red Keds. He looked kind of normal except for his shoulder-length blond hair, the ends of which seemed to fade into a distant nothingness, and his eyes. Emerald, chartreuse, shamrock … think of all the synonyms for green and then think of some more. Looking into them evoked images of teeming, sweltering jungles, peaceful mountain glens and the depthless reaches of the ocean. They sucked you in by the soul and wrapped you in chains of hopelessness.

I calculated the odds and didn't like them one inch—even though the cold iron in my fist was anathema to Sidhe, able to melt his body into a pile of black goo in under a minute. I'd killed one of his brethren, pinning the little puca creep through the throat and embedding my bowie in a hardwood floor. It died quickly and not pleasantly.

It hadn't bothered me one bit. The little dude had been trying to suck Kal's soul out through his eyes. It was as scary as it sounds.

"What do you want?" I whispered, unable to take my eyes off the stick.

Those cat-pupiled emerald eyes stared at me until I began to squirm. "You are not the Hakala. He should have been here."

"N-no. I'm here in his place."

The puca swore, sounding like a cat drinking a quart of oil. "I had hoped it would be him. We need the Hakala."

"We?"

He took two steps back and lowered the stick. "Yes, the Seelie Court has need of him."

I let out a startled curse, relief robbing me of strength. The best news ever … the Seelie Court, the association of Sidhe who viewed humanity as allies rather than enemies.

"Christ! You scared the life outta me!" I hollered.

He merely stared, unblinking.

"How did you get in here?"

Finally a smile, albeit a small one. "There is no place a puca cannot get into." The smile quickly disappeared as his eyes wandered to the grisly trophy on my desk. "Why is that *ollphéist* here?"

I hooked a thumb over my shoulder at the skull, trying for casual, but failing miserably. "What? Yorick? He's an old pal and here at my invitation."

"It is evil! Can you not *feel* it?"

Actually, no. I glanced back at poor old Yorick and felt my blood freeze solid in my veins.

Where there had been a big nothing above the bum's eyes, revealing the slurried leftover of brain, there was now the smooth gray and white of bone. The ripped flesh around the regrown skull had healed as well and had started creeping up the bone.

"You don't see that every day," I muttered in shock. You'd think I'd be used to such things by now. It's always something.

The puca hissed like a snake. "Destroy it."

"Nope, I'm becoming rather attached to the old skull."

Yorick continued to stare balefully and mouth obscenities. To put the little puca at ease, I dropped the head into the desk file drawer and locked it.

"There. Out of sight, out of mind."

From the look on his face, the puca wasn't buying it, but he shrugged and sat cross-legged on the floor, still gripping that wicked stick.

"Now that we're alone," I began working the sleep-crick out of my neck. "Why are you looking for Kal?"

"It is imperative that I speak to the Kal Hakala," he intoned gravely. I shook my head. "You'll have to settle for the Canton Alsate."

The forest green eyes grew round. "You are the mate to the Winch?"

My stomach roiled with acid. I nodded as the vision of Black Shuck ripping his teeth through Winch's armor crossed behind my eyes. I shook my head violently to clear it of the awful memory.

"You are the one they call the Apache, the savage one who defeated renowned Olludir?" There was real respect in the puca's voice.

Once again I nodded. Olludir the Sidhe warrior, encased in runic obsidian armor that shone with magic which rendered the glassy plate near invulnerable. Only cold iron was able to cancel the magic of Sidhe runes. The Sidhe looked human only through the grace of magic. Without their illusions, they looked … different. Not horrible, not ugly, per se, but plum alien. As if a drunk extra-terrestrial had constructed the bones of their skull, having only a vague knowledge of what human anatomy. I remember the hard planes of their cheeks, the square-ish foreheads and the disturbing angle of Sidhe jaw lines.

Olludir had been better than me at knife fighting—he'd had centuries to hone his craft killing humans and Sidhe alike—but he wasn't as fast, nor as stubborn as I. I won through sheer cussedness, speed, my steel knife and a whole plateful of luck. "Yeah, that's me," I said woodenly.

He stared so long that his regard began to wear thin and I was just about to give him a helping or two of my thoughts when he spoke. "Your beloved was brave, facing a Shuck, sacrificing herself for the Kal Hakala. In her name, I will tell you why I have brought you to this stinking place." His nose wrinkled at that last, and I had to agree— Chicago definitely had an odor. But hey, at least it wasn't New Jersey.

If my brain hadn't been parked in neutral due to being plumb-tuckered, I might have caught on sooner, but the few brain cells I had left managed to rub together to generate the heat of realization.

"It was you! You stacked those bones by the river!"

He nodded.

"That was your way of summoning Kal, playing Pick-Up-Stix with skeletons? What made you think it would be Kal who would come?"

"I had hoped. Windigo are a plague like no other and who better to send than the Kal Hakala?"

"Oh, I don't know … me, perhaps?"

He gave me a blank look. I guess they didn't have sarcasm in the World Under. "So it seems," he said while parking his butt in the other chair. "But to understand the urgency, I must start by relating my story."

Three in the morning, an exhausted Apache with a human head in a desk drawer, no booze and a huge need to pee. "Hit me, big guy."

CHAPTER SEVENTEEN

———•———

The Puca and a Tale of Two Sidhe-ies

I AM OTHIL OF THE Seelie Court, born of the wild places the tall Sidhe dare not tread, but that is a tale left for happier times.

To understand what has happened, you must know about the Courts. The Seelie and Unseelie. The history of the Courts is filled with blood, magic and woe.

There are several intelligent races in Faërie, all labeled the Faë, but mightiest are known as the Sidhe, while the lesser are simply consigned to a single category of Faë. These include such beings as goblins, hobs, brownies, sprites, pixies and others almost without number. As for the puca, the Sidhe counts us as members of their Courts even though we are creatures of the wild magic that existed before time, before the tall Sidhe and the lesser Faë. This I make known to you to forestall foolish questions that would only serve to irritate.

Millennia ago this was our world, green and verdant, not yet covered in cold iron, cruel glass and harsh concrete. Yet all was not idyllic because the Sidhe were warlike and, absent enemies, all Faë became target to their boundless ferocity. Even the beasts of the field fled before the dread steeds of the Sidhe and the very earth became saturated in the lifeblood of all living creatures.

Like pebbles on the beach, the Faë are of shape and visage uncounted. Tall, short, fair and foul, straight and bent, we are legion, but the warlike nature of the Sidhe cut short our numbers. Had it not been for the timely arrival of humanity, the Faë, including the Sidhe, would be but a memory.

Mankind offered us sport, servitude, and worship and we were happy for it, reveling in their adoration and crude gifts. Though they bred like animals and their numbers eclipsed ours, their weapons were simple; bone and wood, flint and obsidian. To us, such things are the pricking of nettles, offering no lasting hurt. We laughed at their feeble attempts at war and even took the place of the gods they worshipped. On the fields of Troy we enjoyed their sweating, thrusting and dying as we observed, cloaked by the magic that protected us, and we were sated by the sport offered there. Man's nature amused us no end.

Then came the true working of iron, the downfall for all the Faë. Once mankind knew of its effect on us we ceased to be gods, we ceased to be the rulers of this world and instead became victims. Mankind's rage at our deception became a torrent we could not stand against and slowly, regretfully, we began our centuries-long exodus to Faërie, a small portion of the land you call the World Under.

It was during our long and reluctant retreat that the Noble Sidhe— the most powerful, those Faë whose limbs were proud and straight, with no animal taint to their features—split into two groups: the Seelie and the Unseelie, two Courts, two very different philosophies: those who would ally with Mankind and those who would march to war against man in an effort to annihilate.

The rift was a bitter one, with many duels fought and assassinations ordered, neither side gaining advantage. Eventually, as the last of us crossed the barrier between worlds, a truce was called and this green world that had housed us for countless years was forever lost to a race without the beauty of magic.

***

"WAIT A MINUTE," I SAID, interrupting the musical flow of words that painted bright and horrific images in my mind. It was as if the runt was able to thrust M. Escher paintings directly into my brain with words alone. Eerie and disturbing as all get out. "Humans have magic. My grandfather is a Magician."

Othil tossed me a look of distain. Obviously the irritation had begun. "Humans have magic because they lay with the Sidhe. Mongrel children were born, weak and mortal, but carrying the seed for magic's use."

Oh. So, if I heard the runt correctly, some time about the Stone Age, there had been a Sidhe in the woodpile. That didn't sit well.

The puca cleared his throat. "May I continue?" he asked archly.

I nodded.

***

So few of us survived the crossing. Both Courts had been mercilessly savaged. The Seelie were much reduced by the Unseelie, who in turned suffered grievous losses at the hands of Man and cold iron. To ward off extinction, a truce was called and both sides sought healing, retreating to the heart of their new kingdoms.

Know that centuries passed here in the First World, the world of our birth. Our numbers slowly swelled, thanks to that uneasy peace. We are not a fertile people—the price paid for immortality—but our women still bore children, enough so that our population has reached its former glory of millennia past.

Now, once again after countless years of licking horrid wounds, we are at war.

I see this offers no surprise. This is where my story begins in earnest.

Let us start with the most important matter first. Me. We puca are creatures of forest and glen, groves and grottoes, born of the wild places and creatures of wild magic. Beings of root, branch, leaf, fur and teeth. We are the get of Nature and Magic, bound yet not constrained. Not for us towering castles of crimson glass or deep caverns of amethyst and quartz. Our roof is the sky and the earth our floor and has been since the beginnings of beginning. Although creatures of the wildest magics and therefore superior to all other living things, we do yearn to belong, to be part of something other than ourselves. It is a desire so deep and abiding it consumes those puca who remain aloof. If left unfulfilled, it often brings madness, so when we offer loyalty to the Court we believe is worthy, that loyalty is unshakable and to the death. A puca's word is rock and root. This does not mean we are chattel or servants. Our bond is that those we are loyal to may *ask* boons—not demand, cajole, or command. We may refuse any directive should we choose. To force a puca to bended knee brings sorrow and calamity to those who would do so. Many a Noble Sidhe has found this lesson more than a little costly. Loyalty does not mean servitude.

I tell you this so you may know the import of my presence here.

When the call came from Duke Mileendar of the Shadowed Hills—he to whom I had pledged my loyalty—I was sleeping on boughs of fragrant pine, surrounded by the quiet drone of insects and the rose sky of Faërie above.

Othil. The voice was a sweet, soft belling in my mind.

My eyes opened and I felt the discomfort of the calling. Sighing, I turned to my side and tried again to discover blessed sleep.

Othil, please.

Oh, by the forest, I thought. What does he want?

Othil, I call upon you. The mental voice caused unintended discomfort. The one to whom I gave loyalty had strength much envied among the Sidhe.

Sleep would not come, not with Mileendar's insistent calling echoing in the chamber of my skull. Lightly, soundlessly, I dropped the several Sidhe-lengths from my perch to the piney floor of the forest and began to lope toward Castle Inwyn, the Duke's home.

A Sidhe castle bears as much resemblance to Man's as an eagle resembles the sparrow. Crafted of multi-hued glass, the towers twist and turn at angles no human can discern. Each footfall brings a chime too deep and subtle for human ears but is a symphony to Sidhe senses. These castles are grown, not built—their glass a living organism as delicate as fog, more durable than mere stone.

It was toward the cyan and scarlet castle of Duke Mileendar I sped, trees flashing by in a blur as I bounded across the leafy floor. No creature can best a puca for travel in the wild, for we are most at home surrounded by the comforts of nature, and the untamed world aids us in our speed. Other Sidhe have magic; the puca *are* magic, wild and deep.

Before the cobalt sun could travel more than a finger's width, I came to the Duke's lands, to the thinning of the trees, the border of Tame and Wild. I will allow you to use your limited intellect to conclude where I belong the most.

Holding true to the fashion of the nobility, the Duke had set a pavilion to welcome me, though I disdain such niceties, preferring the simplicity of nature.

On the edge of the great wood stood the pavilion, burgundy spidersilk awning rippling gently in the breeze. A half-dozen lesser Faë servants (those tiny beings who sported such things as rabbit ears or squirrel tails) plied the Duke with wine and food, tending to his every need as he took his ease on a crimson cushion.

Mileendar, tall even by Sidhe standards, wore a soft smile, glassine cup held languidly in hand. Dress among the Sidhe is casual by human standards, most clothing consisting of tunics and simple wraps. It is not the style of the cloth, but the cloth itself that determines status and wealth. The finest garments, those worn by the Kings and Queens of the Courts, are created of Dream Spider silk and unicorn hair, while the lesser Sidhe make do with baser materials such as satin and velvet. The Duke wore simple breeches of ochre and jet, crafted from the mane of a Pegasus, which shimmered softly in the shade of the pavilion.

As I approached, still hidden among the trees, long leaves of green and purple flew through the air to drape themselves upon my skin. While puca care nothing for clothing, preferring the wild state to which we were born, my loyalty to the Duke included the desire not to cause him discomfort at seeing me ungarbed. Within moments I was clothed in a breechclout of soft leaves that rustled softly with every step.

"There you are, Othil," the Duke said with a smile, standing to his full height. "Thank you for dressing." His tone displayed only pleasure and gratitude for my consideration.

I entered the cool shade of the pavilion, luxuriating in the feel of the short grass beneath my feet. "My lord," I replied with hand to heart, a gesture of respect.

"Drink?"

"Have you lavender wine, my lord?"

He smiled, revealing long, even, and slightly pointed teeth. The teeth of a predator. "Of course."

One of the lesser Faë, a goblin with a vole's face, handed me a blue glassine cup of spiced lavender wine, a drink for which I have a certain fondness. At his urging, I sat upon the grass, distaining the use of a cushion. All puca relish their connection with the natural world and feel discomfort when severed from it—as when clothed in base fabric and footwear. I stared at the seven spires of the Duke's castle and to my ears the towers hummed a melody that spoke of peaceful things. The castle rested upon a tall hill, surrounded on all sides by harsh splinters of gray and black rock—jagged, sharp, and foreboding. There was one path, and one path only, to the gates, a narrow track through the treacherous, ankle-snaring rocks. The Sidhe had been at peace for centuries, but the Duke favored preparation. I believe the human phrase is 'It is not paranoia if they are really out to get you.'

Still smiling, the Duke made himself comfortable on his scarlet cushion and took a long drink from his cup. The Sidhe are most fond of their wines, although their vintages are too potent for mere mortals to bear.

"My lord has summoned me for more than lavender wine, I think."

His glistening purple eyes narrowed, but his smile never wavered. "I have some unfortunate news," he said after a few seconds.

"Is it news that affects the puca?"

"All of us, I should think."

Such was the gravity in his voice that I instantly became wary. "Yes, my lord?"

"Have you heard about the incursion into the human world, the attempt to destroy all that is iron?"

Sidhe plots mean nothing, save that they involve puca. News of such a scheme was known only because the Unseelie Court sent *two* of my brethren to facilitate their undertaking. Surely with the aid of two of my kind, mankind's days were drawing to a close, although I bore mortals no ill will. Their impact upon me was measured only by how it would affect the Duke. I nodded curtly, sipping the sweet wine.

"It has failed. Both of your brethren fell."

This news was more than shocking. Geógh, the puca whose loyalty lay with Prince Ephelor of the Unseelie Court, was a creature millennia older than I and his magic was far more potent. The thought that a human could cause his death strained credibility. My breast stung with the news.

"How did such a thing occur?" I asked.

The Duke shook his head, his shoulder-length black hair flowing about him like water. "It was the Kal Hakala."

The Kal Hakala! That name conjured a vision of fierce claws sheathed in terrible iron, of steel teeth and great muscles wrapped in plate armor. If the people of Faërie have a Boogeyman (in reality, the Boogeyman is a kindly gnoll who has never eaten a child, only scared a few by accident during the period you call the Dark Ages), it would be the Kal Hakala. A giant of a human with the ability to summon fearsome strength and speed, dispatching his foes through sheer brutality and low cunning. Although a mortal, he had killed or banished many creatures mightier than even the Sidhe. Even the dread being named Iku-Turso was not invulnerable when faced with this terrible human's wrath. Ironically, the Kal Hakala had succored a family of minor Faë, a trio of brownies he treated with both respect and affection. The fact that those timid, reclusive folk allowed a fearsome human like the Kal Hakala to care for them was a source of great puzzlement for all.

Duke Mileendar continued, "The Seelie Court agreed to allow the incursion with the proviso that we send one of our own. Princess

Uloeth was chosen as hostage, to prevent any treachery on the part of our rival Court."

The comings and goings of nobility meant nothing, except, of course, for the Duke. "And?"

"And she lives, bringing with her a fascinating story of the Kal Hakala." He then proceeded to spin a tale of an angry ghost and how the Kal Hakala managed, with his teammates, to kill most of those participating in the Unseelie Sidhe scheme and foil a plan that had been years in the devising. It was a story to chill the bone, for with the help of his friends, the Kal Hakala had slain a Black Shuck artifact, a statuette of a dog that when activated becomes the full likeness and lethality of a true Black Shuck. Such was their valor that one of the fallen, a human female named Winch who sacrificed her life for the Kal Hakala, was awarded a resting place in the Grotto of the Fallen, where lie only the most heroic.

I knew the Duke well enough that the smallest movement in his face, the shifting of his eyes and even the cadence of his breath spoke more clearly than the words that passed his lips. "Tricksy and twisty, troubled and true, all those scents flow about you."

***

"REALLY? VERSE?"

The little dude gave me a sour look and lifted his stick, pointing it directly between my eyes. "I have often wondered if it were possible to transform a human into a garden slug," he said quietly.

I raised my hands slowly, skin prickling all up and down my arms. "Okay, shutting up now."

He smiled, showing me some impressive chompers. "Good."

***

THE DUKE'S LAUGHTER SHOOK THE burgundy fabric of the pavilion. "Yes, my friend, you know me so well. My hands are not clean in this affair; I had been working with Uloeth the entire time. While observing the Unseelie Court's schemes, young Uloeth informed me of a human man, a very large human man, who called himself

Thomas Mace. She said he had worked with the Kal Hakala in the mortal's Bureau of Supernatural Investigations. It took much magic, but I entered our former world where Prince Ephelor had his base and arranged for the man to escape. Providing, of course, that he informed the Kal Hakala of our brethren's plans. Naturally he agreed, but Ephelor set the Shuck artifact and a Gargoyle loose upon the man and, 'twixt the two, the human was slain." The Duke took a great draft from his cup and held it out for refilling. The vole-faced Faë filled the cup from an enormous cobalt ewer. "He was more resourceful than I imagined and somehow alerted the Kal Hakala before he plunged to his death. And so, with one small action, I set the Unseelie Court's plans awry."

"Why would you do such a thing, my lord?" Though the Seelie Court held no ill will toward Mankind, they had been indifferent to the happenings of our former world since the exile to Faërie. I could conceive of no reason for such an intercession. Then again, the actions of the Sidhe were always a mystery to me.

Duke Mileendar provided one. "Had the Unseelie Court's scheme been successful, it would have left our former home blighted and poisoned and would take countless millennia to heal. Think of it, a burned-out wreck blanketed in rotting corpses. I have no will to tolerate genocide. The Unseelie Court would have ruled over a land turned dung-heap." His gaze became fixed on a far away point only he could see. "We lost that world because we were prideful and arrogant, offending Danu. She created humans to teach us the error of our ways and set us on a path to this world."

"This is a good place," I said, eating grapes proffered by a goat-headed little goblin. "Dangerous, true, but filled with wonders unimaginable."

"Yet the Unseelie Court is not content with such things, they would rather be rulers of a charred cinder than live side-by-side with the creatures of this one. 'All or nothing' is their creed, regardless of cost to others. This brings me to the second tidbit of news I believe you will find most dire."

"Which is?"

"The Courts are once again at the brink of war."

Dire news indeed. Had I been involved in the daily life of the Sidhe, fear would have been the response, but only concern for the Duke stirred in my breast. The Duke knew of the indifference of the puca to the other races, save those offered loyalty.

"Do you know why they teeter on the edge of conflict?" he asked wryly.

"Boredom?" The Sidhe do not suffer ennui well.

He shook his head. "The Unseelie Court suspect the involvement of the Seelie Court in the disarray of their schemes and prepare to wage war against us so that they may set another plan into motion without interference. This new plan was never meant to be implemented. In fact, I believe it was meant as an alternate exercise should the plan to destroy iron in our old world fail, which it has. It is foolish and, I believe, unwise to conquer our former world before the humans and the Kal Hakala can band together to obstruct further incursions."

It is difficult to surprise a puca, but the duke managed to do just that quite well. "Their new plan is worse than genocide?"

His eyes were hooded as he stared darkly at me. "Yes."

"And you know this ... how, my lord?"

"I have ... ways."

Ways, indeed. I took that to mean he 'persuaded' an enemy Sidhe to divulge the information, a practice at which all Sidhe excelled. He continued his staring, seemingly unaware of the world around. After several minutes, in which I enjoyed many more cups of lavender wine, he shook his head sadly.

"They mean to unleash the Windigo Curse upon the mortals."

A cold wind seemed to wash against my skin, and I shivered. "The Windigo Curse? That is madness of the most horrific sort!" Some things should never be brought to the light of day, and that curse was one. "How is that possible?"

"You've heard of the Lord of Stern Barrowlands, Nuvada?"

I inclined my head. A most infamous Sidhe among a race of infamous Sidhe. One of the Dukes of the Unseelie Court. His enemies among the Unseelie had a disconcerting habit of disappearing.

"He has Fir Bolg gems."

My cup fell from nerveless fingers. "That cannot be," I breathed. "They were destroyed during the Banhaven Crusades, before humans began to beat each other with clubs of bone," I said. Dread objects, the Fir Bolg gems, portals into places far more terrible than any could imagine, where existed fierce and appalling creatures.

The Fir Bolg was among the first races to set their feet upon the world. Giants, they were gentle creatures, preferring harmonious nature magic and peaceful tending to vast fields of fruit-bearing trees and furrows of grain, until they were set upon by the Sidhe, whereupon they became implacable enemies. Once pacifists, they turned their minds to fell potencies and unleashed upon the Sidhe foul beasts from that place you call the World Under. So many battles fought between the two, with grievous harm done on both sides, until the very stones of the land became soaked in the blood of warriors. Despite their ferocity, the Fir Bolg began to lose the war.

In desperation, a lone Fir Bolg of great power designed the gems in an effort to entreat the most horrid of beings to battle the Sidhe. Each gem was a portal and led to ever darker, deeper places, worlds without light, without hope or joy, where lived ever greater powers. The Fir Bolg magus begged those powers for help and received eager replies, but that which he summoned could not be controlled. Leviathans (such as the dreadful Iku-Turso whom the Kal Hakala later banished) of dark majesty were loosed upon the world and rained havoc upon both races, blighting and befouling the land. Scars from their passage still mar the world, places no one dares to stray.

The Fir Bolg master of magic was so horrified by what he had wrought that he took his own life, leaving the world to its fate. Faced with such might, all the races of the world united under the banner of the Sidhe and did battle on what had been released.

Fire consumed continents and the seas boiled. Shining cities that lay scattered like gems upon the land were laid to waste or swallowed by heated waters, and ash covered the sun for centuries beyond counting. At long last the monsters were defeated and forced back into their pits and the land slowly began to heal.

Devastated, the Fir Bolg retreated from the world to places beyond the beyond, leaving the blasted world to the victorious Sidhe, who in turn were much reduced in number. It was thought that the gems were lost or destroyed.

"How Lord Nuvada came to have them is a mystery, save that he uses them now to visit the Curse upon the humans. I would have you help the mortals."

Loyalty I have aplenty. Stupidity … not so much. "You would have me enter a world of iron, where the merest scratch would have my flesh melting into a black puddle? The cause is just, but I did not reach such a height of power among my own kind by indulging in foolish risks. I may be a puca, but I am no fool."

"You will not do this?"

"Lord, by our bond you may command any reasonable service. I find such hazard unreasonable."

There came the smallest quirk to his lips, so faint that even I, whose powers of perception are legendary among the puca, could barely discern its presence. "Not even for rainfire gold?" he asked softly.

Rainfire gold! In all the worlds, in all the lands, only rainfire gold is craved by the puca, so rare and beautiful and so *magical*. Born in the streams of the Shattervale valley, the home of dragons, rainfire gold sparkles like no other. Rainfire gold is desire given form and magic given substance. Duels have been fought over rainfire gold; dragons have razed entire towns in search of it for their hoards. He who controls the rainfire controls Faërie, but fortunately dragons keep the adventurous and greedy Sidhe to a minimum, a sort of Faë population control.

A nugget the size of the nail on your smallest finger is worth more than the Duke's cyan and crimson glass castle. It also contains the power to shatter a mountain.

It is the only metal that can seduce a puca. I have spent countless hours staring at my own private hoard of rainfire, the smallest flake the size of fly's eye, fascinated by its shimmer and basking in the heat of its magic. In that way I am much like an ordinary cat, distracted by bright and shiny objects.

"Rainfire," I moaned.

The Duke knew he had me wrapped in chains of my greed and desire. Only that precious glittery stuff held the power to sway a puca of such legendary prowess as I.

"Indeed," he said. "The size of your thumbnail."

I groaned softly, undone. That is more raw magic in rainfire of that quantity than can be found in all the gemstones hidden in the vaults of the Seelie Court. I should know, for I have been there.

"How did you obtain such an amount of rainfire?" I asked numbly, my lavender wine long forgotten.

The Duke offered me nothing but a mysterious smile.

"Agreed," I sighed.

He held out a hand, which I eagerly grasped.

Sanity returned slowly. "I will need assistance."

***

THE KID'S VOICE FADED AWAY while those strange eyes remained half closed. Dreaming about his rainfire gold, I guessed. The stick in his hand was no longer pointed my way and I was pretty damn happy about that.

His daydreams weren't helping me out, though. "What about the Curse? And those furry bolgy jewel thingies?"

Snapping back to reality, those green cat eyes focused on mine. It was unnerving. "The Curse," he spat. "A windigo is an evil spirit that enters a host, seizing control. Its craving for living flesh is uncontrollable and it will stop at nothing to get it. Precious metals like silver and gold sever the bond between flesh and intruding spirit. The Sidhe have found that cleansing fire also works wonders."

"I get that, but what does that have to do with the furry bolgy jewels?"

"The Fir Bolg gems."

"Yeah, what I said."

Othil snorted. "The gems form a gateway that allows part of the Great Windigo Spirit to access this world. Those fragments of the whole seek out the corrupt and the venal, taking over their bodies,

using them as hosts. They have a lust for living flesh that cannot be
sated because it is part and parcel of their nature. A cursed one's bite
opens a gateway in the bitten that allows another spirit fragment
entry and, even if the bitten has a strong will and a noble heart, he
will undergo the change and become windigo. This can go on and on
and on until all are consumed or transformed."

Yuk on a stick and goldarned nasty, too. "Wait a sec, you said
'gems,' as in plural."

The little dude nodded. "Thirteen gems, thirteen portals into this
world for the windigo to send shards of itself through. Four on this
continent alone."

"Christ!" I exploded. "Now you tell me?"

"My mission here is to be covert," he said, baring teeth that showed
too many points. "To be discreet, lest the Unseelie Court know of the
Duke's involvement. Thus far they have not warred upon him because
of his oft-declared disdain for politics, yet he has secretly worked his
will against them. I am here now, I have warned you, brought you to
this nasty pile of steel, glass and concrete called Chicago to correct
the issue."

There was at least one more question still nagging at me. "How
come all those cameras never recorded you when you dumped those
bones?"

"If a puca wishes not to be seen, then seen he is not."

"Do you know where the windigo, or windigos, are?"

He gave me a pitying look and it grated hard against my nerves. After
a moment, I cursed myself for an addlepated fool. "Underground, in
the sewers." So obvious, not seeing it sooner was a rookie mistake.
The Sidhe loved to do things underground and enough rock, steel
and concrete could easily block the furry bolg gems emanations from
the Bureau's merlin sensors.

His smile did nothing to reassure me. Rising from his seat, he slid
the wand into the waist of his jeans and donned a pair of Wayfarers.

I grabbed my cell. "Which cities besides Chicago are targeted?"

The little dude looked troubled. "That is unknown. Some things
not even the Duke can ascertain. However, you must look to the

south, east, and west. Search for large cities where accesses to vast underground areas are easily found."

Worms of unease turned in my guts. The thought of another major city, Houston perhaps, overrun by Yorick's brothers gave me the ever-loving craps. "Where is the gem in Chicago?"

"I know not. That is for you to discover. Only this I know: the gem needs a goodly space to work its magic, a goodly space that is underground, where your tiny machines cannot detect its vasty magics."

Time to make a call. I began to dial and the little dude moved gracefully to the door, the fading ends of his hair swaying gently to some unfelt wind. "Time for me to depart. Farewell." With that he left, ghosting out the door and the world of men.

I would love to have grilled him some more, but I had places to go, big ol' people-eatin' monsters to kill.

CHAPTER EIGHTEEN

———•———

Down and Down Again

FIVE A.M. AND FALSE DAWN was beginning to color the sky in shades of red. All of us save Jo were once again at the river staring down into the darkness of a sewer. The smell that wafted from the opening put the river to shame.

As I looked into the darkness, all self-doubt fled; all worry and self-consciousness gone, baby, gone. I was cold, icy, below freezing … an absolute zero kind of cold that produced the best in me in times like these. Clarity of vision, clarity of mission, it was all there and I was ready for the fight ahead. It felt good, that coldness, because it scoured fear from my soul.

"On your mark, boss." Alba sounded as determined as I felt. He had faith in me and I knew it wasn't misplaced.

Part of the reason for my newfound clarity was the phone call with Kal. Once I gave him the info on the windigo, he began coordinating with the Bureaus in all countries friendly with US. All the teams in Warehouse, along with Special Branch and a very busy Ghost, were analyzing every scrap of data on the planet, looking for signs of possible windigo infestation. There were three other cities in America that needed scrubbing of the Curse, and I prayed to whatever god or gods there were that my comrades would find them in time.

"You have enough silver rounds?" Kal had asked.

"Seven thousand, and if it ain't enough, white boy, then we will be down to throwing sterling silver flatware and using Spell gems."

"Good. I have everyone scrambled, so don't worry about us, just take care of Chicago."

"Will do, boss."

"And Canton?"

"Yeah?"

"Don't get dead. That's an order."

That was one order I planned on taking right serious. It warmed me to no end that he was worried more about me than my ability to watch out for Jeanie, implying a heap of confidence.

"*Jo*," I subvocaled. "*Did Ghost get the updated sewer schematics to you?*"

"*Already downloaded into everyone's contact lenses, boss.*"

"*Check that. Hold down the fort. You know what to do.*"

"*Check.*"

A flurry of motion, a scuffle and the sound of an armored body hitting the ground. My .45 was in my hand before I knew it, tracking toward the sudden movement in my peripheral vision a microsecond before Ng's face loomed large in my sights.

"What the bloody hell are you doing here?" I grated, noting that Portner was rising unsteadily to his feet.

Portner wiped the blood from his lip. "Sorry, boss. I tried to stop him, but he hit me with some chop–socky and took my weapon."

Ng's normally impassive face was flushed with passion. "This is my city," he said vehemently as he struggled in the iron grips of Alba and Jacobs. "If something's going down here, I'm part of it." Dove looked like she wanted rip off a wing and go for a gizzard. Mason had her own weapon, a Mac-10A, pointed at his face. "And if you must know, that 'chop-socky' was Tae Kwon Do."

"We don't have time for this happy horsehockey," I said tiredly, lowering my weapon.

"Let me stuff him in the trunk of the car, boss," Dove said, her slitted eyes full of violence.

"Ease up there, Hopalong, we ain't hurting anyone." I considered the problem. One FBI guy, a bunch of hair-trigger Green Peas, and a windigo problem that could literally eat the city. Sounded par for the course. Jeanie's quick flash of a smile told me she knew what I was thinking.

"Ng, I'm not even gonna ask how you made it back here and found us. The only thing I need to know is, do you have any military training?"

He nodded. "Regular army."

I gestured to my Agents. "Okay, let him go." Ng stood and straightened his now less-than-immaculate suit. "This is what's gonna happen. Kaleb, you give Ng your armor. He keeps your weapon and most of your ammo, but the Spell gems stay with the group. You'll be fine with your back-up piece. I want you to stay out here and keep watch. As of now, you're our reserve. If you run into anything you can't handle, just run like a stripe-assed ape. Ng, you're with us."

"Aww, boss!" Portner complained as he slowly stripped.

"It's what you get for letting him get the best of you. Be happy it's me and not Kal, 'cause he'd really do you some dirt, kid."

Portner accepted this order with poor grace, handing his Brave Bull auto shotgun to Ng.

"What is this?" asked the FBI agent, staring at the weapon, eyes bright with lust. It was the first real sign of emotion from the man I'd seen.

"Auto shotgun," I replied.

"I know what it is," he replied. "I've used one before, but I've never seen anything like *this*."

"One of our former Agents, an Oglala Sioux named Arthur Black Bear, started a gun manufacturing company about eight years ago," I explained. "Thanks to a government contract, he now produces weapons for the military. That is the latest and greatest in auto shotguns, the Brave Bull. Remember, don't just buy American, buy *Native* American."

That shotgun was a work of art. Matte black, it could fire 350 rounds per minute and was fed by a thirty-eight round drum. Fashioned from lightweight synthetics and steel, it weighed a mere ten pounds fully loaded and had an effective range of 120 feet, making it the lightest and most efficient shotgun available. The Bureau was the first to receive the weapon for use in the field and we took to it like kids in a candy store. Dove wanted two, while the rest of us sported its twin brothers slung across our backs. Although I preferred my pistol and bowie, if things became dicey. Call me old-fashioned.

The rest of the team looked at me as if I were nuts. All except Jeanie, who kept that big grin plastered on her face.

"He's earned the right to be here—God have mercy on his soul—so buck up, cowboys."

Fortunately for Ng, the NewTanium armor could be adjusted for size … somewhat. But, as he was only an inch shorter than Portner, it was easy adjustment to make.

"You wear contacts?" I asked.

Ng nodded, adjusting to the move.

"Check your utility belt, third pocket to the right of the buckle."

His hand came up with a pair of nightvision glasses. Gingerly, as if they were a snake about to bite, he put them on. "Sonofabitch," he breathed as dim light of pre-dawn was rendered into black, white and all the shades of gray in-between.

"Boss, this isn't right," complained Portner. He looked ridiculous in Ng's slightly too-small suit. Dove Jacobs nodded in agreement.

Time to nip that in the bud. I stalked forward until I was nose-to-nose with the startled Portner. "Listen, Green Pea, you let a non-Bureau agent get the drop on you and obtain your weapon. A guy who isn't even a Green Pea and who *should* be on a plane heading out of the city, out of danger, which begs the question, did you personally put him on that plane?" The Green Pea shook his head. Anger I didn't know was in my gut boiled out. "If this was a normal op, you'd be out on your ass, waving goodbye to the Bureau, but since we are in a crisis mode, I'm giving you another chance." A red mist formed in my vision and I turned my attention to Jacobs, including her in the tirade. "Now if anyone else has a problem with how I'm running things, by all means, feel free to speak up. But know this: what we have here, this team, is a dictatorship. I'm the dick and you guys are the taters. Got me?"

Alba was the first to speak. "Got you, boss." His tone let everyone know the consequences of not getting me. Mason joined in quickly and Jeanie laughed.

Dove Jacobs had a mulish look on her face and Portner stood with mouth agape. Before I could do something he might regret, Portner, red-faced, stuttered, "Gotcha, boss."

A few seconds later Jacobs nodded, albeit reluctantly.

Good enough. "Ng, you're last down the rabbit hole. It's your job to watch our six and shoot anything that isn't us."

Ng put on a good face, but the cracks in his inscrutability were starting to show. Had to give it to him, though, he nodded and adjusted his glasses. "These things are cool," was all he said.

"You ain't seen nothing yet." With that, I started down the corroded metal rungs into the darkness of Chicago's own little version of the World Under.

Surprisingly, when my feet splashed to the bottom of the shaft, the circular tunnel was larger than I expected, allowing me to stand almost upright. A thin stream of effluvium ran down the center, bringing with it the smell of decay and human waste. I was greeted by the soft squeak of rats and the noisome skitter of about a billion cockroaches.

Matt Alba alighted next to me. "That's a smell you never get used to. Which way, boss?"

"Schematic, Jo."

A map of the Chicago sewer system rose up before my eyes as Jo activated the information stored in the contact lenses.

"There you go, boss. Standard voice commands. Use the word 'comma' before the command."

"Thanks, Jo."

"Anytime, boss."

Focusing on the schematics, I said, "Comma, show current location." A red dot appeared on the map. "Comma, enhance fifty percent." The image zoomed. Ah, there. I regarded the overlay, then the tunnel as the rest of the team joined me.

"There's no convenient sign stating, 'Here be monsters,' so I'm going to have to guess. Everyone, stay sharp and stay subvocal. Ng, you don't have the equipment, so stay quiet, do what we do and try not to get yourself dead."

"Gotcha," he said.

Which way? Heck with it. *"Come on."* I headed south down the tunnel. Except for the scrim of filthy water, the cockroaches and rats, it was fairly clean. I wondered if frequent storms ran the sewage into Lake Michigan. Wouldn't surprise me one bit if there were an occasional bout of dysentery along the coast.

Let me tell you about hunting bad guys in the sewers; I've done it before and until you catch up with them, it is dreadfully, painfully, mind-numbingly *boring*.

And uncomfortable.

But mostly boring.

After the first few minutes you expect the bad guys to pop out from screen left like in a cheap horror flick, but when that doesn't happen, you begin to relax. The human body isn't built to maintain ultra-high levels of alertness for extended periods. The trick is to keep focusing on your senses while letting the tension bleed from the rest of your body. Not as easy as it sounds.

The sewer branched several times and we stopped to consult the map and check our surroundings, but the area looked empty, with no clue as to where the windigos could be. Heck, they could be on the other side of the city for all I knew. I just hoped that because of the location of the dumped bones and appearance of Yorick, the bad guys were somewhere close by.

"This place is so big they could be anywhere, boss." Jeanie didn't sound apprehensive; she was just stating a fact.

"Understood, but you got anything better to do?"

"You want a list?"

A minute later, a finger gently tapped my elbow. Ng. I nodded at him to speak.

"Agent, you notice something?" he whispered.

I stared, waiting for him to get on with it.

"No roaches. No rats. Haven't been any for the last fifty feet or so."

Sonofabitch. He was right. Gone were the tiny rodent squeaks the soft susurrus of thousands of skittering insect legs. The rest of the team looked around uneasily and it was Jeanie who spotted the anomaly.

"*Canton, over here,*" said Jeanie.

She knelt at the curve of the tunnel, hand brushing a dark and crusty smudge that stood out in stark relief on the pale gray concrete. The smudge, or smear, terminated abruptly.

"*What is it?*"

"*Attempting a diagnostic Spell. One second, please.*" She removed one thin glove and placed her bare fingertips on the stain. A minute, perhaps two, passed before she sighed softly. "*Human DNA, male, Caucasian.*" She stood, slipping the glove back on. "*Blood, Canton. It's blood.*"

Frowning, I removed the MagniGlass from my Bat Belt and held it against the curved wall of the tunnel above the stain. I activated the device and selected an icon, holding it steady while I forcefully tapped the tunnel wall all around with a gloved knuckle.

Thump, thump, thumpity, thump ....

There, an anomalous reading to the left. I moved the MagniGlass a few inches and tapped again. Thump, thump, thump. Another reading to the left and I started the process again. Finally, I was satisfied with what I'd found.

"*There's a cavity right behind this section of wall,*" I sent. "*Big one.*"

"*A hidden door?*"

"*Think so.*"

"*Then I got this.*" Jeanie placed her hand on the section of tunnel wall where the MagniGlass had lain and stared, brows furrowed. After thirty seconds or so, there came a soft click and a seam appeared. Jeanie groaned softly and pulled a candy bar from her Bat Belt, devouring it in large, messy bites.

"*That took more out of me than I expected. I think it was Spell-*

locked," she subvocaled through a mouthful of nougat. "*Give me a moment, please.*"

Mason stepped forward, examining the seam in the tunnel wall. "*Boss, this shouldn't be here,*" she said. "*It's not on the schematics.*"

That I knew. For the past couple of minutes I'd been looking at them myself, more than a little puzzled. "*And?*" I asked.

"*And I think someone got paid. I don't know how they did it, but money got spread around on the sly.*"

"*You know this how?*"

She gave me a wry look. "*My dad is a contractor in Jersey. Believe me, a Ward Boss or Alderman or even the mayor got paid some serious cash, I can feel it in my bones. Unfortunately, it's the way things have always been done.*"

I nodded. Made sense. Graft was an unfortunate side effect of business and politics. Once again I reflected that Kal's hatred for politicians might be justified.

Back to Jeanie. "*You ready, or do you need more time?*"

She stood, taking a deep breath. "*Ready, boss.*"

I motioned everyone down the tunnel a ways and flattened against the tunnel wall. If there was a booby trap, I didn't want anyone else but me to become strawberry jam against the wall. A firm shove and the door opened soundlessly.

A quick peek. Steel stairs covered with a dark, rough-textured polymer. Going down. Way the heck down

"*We ain't in Kansas anymore, hombres,*" I said in awe. The sharply sloping tunnel was as round as the sewer, but there was no sewage runoff. It was as dry as desert sand and had a faint musty/musky smell, like a mummified dog.

"*Looks dangerous, Canton.*" Jeanie's voice was grim. "*You go first.*"

Didn't that warm the heart? Jeanie was learning quality smart-assery from Kal, but that didn't stop me from taking the first tentative step.

Still no booby trap … my foot landed safely without a bang. Nice to know that not all evil villains have traps for the stupidly brave. Gritting my teeth and readying my weapon, I led the team down, down, down into the depths of Chicago, the rank, humid air slithering against my skin. Why did it have to be underground? I always hated the missions that ended up with yards of rock and dirt between me and the sun. Texas, the Farallon Islands, Mt. Charleston and North Dakota, each one more dangerous than the last, each one a gigantic pain in my ass. I lost Winch underground and never saw her again in the light of day. A different sun on a different world shone down on her resting place and maybe someday, when it was my turn to cash in, the Seelie Court would let me rest by her side. It would be an honor to lie next to such a courageous comrade as well as the only woman I ever loved.

Oh, there had been women a-plenty. Like Kal, I ran through my fair share while sowing some very wild oats, but none ever captured my spirit like Winch.

My Diana Pennington.

No, that didn't sound right. That name didn't suit her at all, seemed to be a lesser moniker compared to the nickname she'd earned all those years ago when she hauled all our butts outta trouble in Wichita. There was blood and guts that day … and bullets falling down in sheets as four of us faced down a charge of ogres, ten of them. Brutish humanoids nine feet tall and five wide at the shoulders with corded, muscular arms that could, with no effort, rip a man's head off.

I remember standing there in my armor, firing my AR-16 on full auto, the barrel becoming smoking hot as I emptied clip after clip after clip into the mass of charging flesh. Those rounds barely pierced dense, dark gray skin and it seemed to really piss them off some. Mace stood to my left with his Benelli semi-auto shotgun flinging armor-piercing deer slugs as fast as his finger could pull the trigger. Will stood to my right with his M16, casings from the 5.56mm rounds *plinking* to the ground at our feet. BB stood just beyond, cool as a cucumber, making each shot from his Steyr count. Winnie was unconscious behind us with her cheek resting on asphalt, down for the count, blood streaming from a cut to her temple. Winch (Diana at that time) was in the crow's nest atop a church trying for a bead on the rapidly moving targets with her modified Dragunov sniper rifle, the weapon of choice for lady snipers on the town.

Our magically Silenced weapons spat lead, the only sound the slapping of size twenty feet and the *tink, tink, tink* of shell casings hitting asphalt. The quasi-silent horror of it jarred with our peaceful urban surroundings.

One brute fell, shot through a red eye by Will, who was choosing his targets carefully. It was a miracle hit because the eyes of those giants were so deep set, almost hidden beneath the heavy bones of their enormous, shelf-like supraorbital ridges. The rest came at us with a vengeance—huge, much uglier versions of Neanderthal man holding tree-trunk thick clubs that had once been tree trunks. Their black hair was matted, clotted with drying, decaying blood. We could smell them as well as see them and I knew if they weren't stopped, and stopped within seconds, we would wind up worse than dead.

You see, Ogres are cannibals.

Fifty feet and the leading ogre, a colossal specimen over ten feet tall, suddenly fell, head deforming as if it were a balloon suddenly overfilled with air. The skull exploded, ripping apart in huge chunks of flesh and blood.

Then another died the same way—bone, blood and brain decorating its companions. And another, and another, all dead before they hit the ground as more high velocity rounds tore skulls apart like papier-mâché dolls in the hands of an angry child. By the time they reached us there were four left. Before they could swing their weapons, another died. Then there were three.

I dodged a blow from one wielding an axle from an old truck. It would have splattered me into the pavement had it connected. I fired the AR point blank at the monster's knee, tearing it apart, listening to it roar in agony. Then suddenly the roar was cut off and the ogre fell, empty space above its nose where its skull used to be.

Two.

Mace thrust with a K-bar, the hideously sharp steel blade momentarily stopped by rhino-thick skin, but the big man had a lot of muscle and he used it to drive the blade in and down. If I hadn't seen it, I wouldn't have believed it. Ogre hide was almost as tough as bronze armor, but Mace just tore his blade through it as if the stuff was made of tissue paper. Greenish gray blood spurted and the big beast got to play with its own intestines before it died.

One.

Then none.

Diana had killed eight ogres and used a total of nine 7.62mm high-velocity explosive rounds to do so.

I stood there panting, covered in thick, sludgy blood, staring at the night sky and wondering at my luck. The full moon offered no answers as the cold air seared my lungs. We were fortunate to be alive and the sweet Midwest air seemed to be the best I'd ever tasted.

Diana walked toward us as light spilled across the sky, her long muscular legs looking mighty fine even encased in black Kevlar/Titanium armor. Her hair, as always, was cropped short to an inch from her scalp, which made her slightly slanted eyes look even more exotic.

I stood there, staring at her like a dumb ass while BB prepared the silver Spell vials that would disintegrate all organic matter within a ten-foot radius. Mace was on traffic detail and Will was already tracking potential witnesses. I was sure that if our weapons hadn't been magically silenced, we would've had a sizable crowd.

My eyes locked on hers and I felt something pass between us, a deep connection that had zero to do with camaraderie and everything to do with a sudden heat flushing through my body. I hadn't felt it when she joined the team, but I sure felt it then. It sizzled all the way up from my toes to explode behind my peepers. Both of us averted our eyes as bright blue/white flashes lit the dawn streets. There was nothing left of the ogres. Even the blood had disappeared.

"Thanks," I said, my voice slightly husky. "You hauled us out of that one."

"Well done, Green Pea," BB said, wiping his hands. Back then his hair had just started to thin and turn slightly gray at the temples. "Looks like you did very well indeed. Good enough, in fact, to earn you a new name, something to reflect how well you can haul us out of nasty situation." He treated her to a rare smile. "Welcome to the team … Winch."

After our contracts expired, Winch and I immediately hooked up. At the time, the Bureau forbade any on or off duty romances, so we had to make do with longing looks and a ton of cold showers. I might have set the Bureau record for masturbation.

Our relationship was an off-and-on again romance of fire and ice, passion and a whole lot of steamy sex. We were too stupid to realize what we had, but the fires of youth eventually burn down enough to reveal what's been there all along. Funny, there were years of booty-calls and long weekends in Aspen or Geneva before Kal's private crusade a few months ago cemented our feelings. We finally knew where we stood.

We were in love.

Then the Sidhe took her away from me.

It hurt worse than I could've imagined—a pain that tore into my soul and left a bleeding, festering wound. I finally understood Kal's obsession, his drive to kill the monster that murdered his sister. It was a harsh lesson, but I knew what to do. I would channel all my hate and rage into a diamond pinpoint of lethal focus. No Supernatural would withstand my cold fury.

Chicago offered me the windigo, but it was the Sidhe of the Unseelie Court I really wanted. Those who had taken my love from this world and left ashes in my mouth.

I was coming for them. I vowed to find them … and when I did ….

God help them.

CHAPTER NINETEEN

———◆———

Behind Closed Doors

A FTER SEVERAL DOZEN FEET, THE stairs ended at a door, or, more accurately, a hatch. Four feet wide of shining steel with a large, spoked wheel in the center. A vault door a hundred feet below the streets of Chicago. It was plain surreal.

"*Boss, you all are off visual,*" Jo sent.

"*Check that.*" I ran a finger over the micro cam at my throat disguised as a button. We all had them; it is how Receptionists keep a visual on the team, tracking their movements in the Communications room (Comms for short). However, underground environs tend to interfere with the signal.

Turning back to hatch, I gave the wheel a yank, but it was stuck fast.

"*Jeanie, can you open this one?*"

She placed a bare palm against the steel and closed her eyes. A minute later she shook her head. "*Too big. Too heavy. It would take nearly a gigamerlin of power to open this.*"

Matt stepped forward. "*Acid bomb, boss?*"

I shook my head. "*Too messy and it'll destroy the stairs. Not to mention the time we would waste waiting for the fumes to clear out.*"

"*Then how are we getting through?*"

"*The old fashioned way. We're going to blow it to hell.*"

Jacobs gave a soft chuckle. "*Subtle, boss.*"

"*Sometimes subtlety is overrated.*" I reached into several pockets and started pulling out one-inch square cubes of gray putty wrapped in cellophane wrap. When I was finished, I had a pile of nine cubes and what looked an eighth-inch thick black rectangle of plastic the size of a credit card. I motioned for the others to keep their cubes for later, just in case.

"*Matt, help me place the charges. Keep them as evenly spaced as possible all around the edges of the door. They're not terribly sticky, but make sure your gloves are clean afterwards. You don't want to have any residue on your skin when they go off or you'll never play the piano again.*"

His smile was bright. "*Check that. Although I'm a guitar man.*"

"*Okay, then be careful or you'll be playing 'Freebird' on the guitar with your tongue.*"

Nancy Mason made a face. "*God, I didn't need that image.*"

Slowly, carefully, I set my half the charges on the edges of the vault door. Gently unwrapping one cube after the other, I held the charges with a thin caul of cellophane between skin and explosive. When the charges were finally placed, I centered the plastic rectangle on the door. The magnetic charge adhered it to steel with a small *snickt*.

"*Up the stairs, all the way to the top.*" I sent. When they left, I pressed my thumb to the black plastic. It warmed slightly to the touch and a small, virtual keyboard appeared on the shiny surface. A few taps later and I was hightailing it up the stairs.

"*Care to clue us in, boss?*" Jacobs said wryly.

"*That is a little toy fresh from Special Branch.*"

Soft moans and groans.

"*In theory, it should work.*"

The cubes were a mixture of diamond chips and Semtex with a larger one-carat diamond in the center of each. I didn't know exactly what the chips were for, but I guessed that the larger diamonds contained a very complex Spell Shape that would do something nasty. The black rectangle was a mini computer/detonator. When the timer ran to zero, the plastic card would emit a single Word, the activation Word for the large diamonds. If all went well, there would be devastation galore, perhaps some amazing pyrotechnics. If not … well, anything could happen. Perhaps a fission reaction that would ignite the atmosphere and scour all life on the planet. It would certainly put a brand new spin on global warming.

From far down the stairs I heard an electronic *cheep*. A computer-generated voice said 'GRASSLIPS' and the sewer shook slightly. Suddenly the tunnel was filled with howling wind, as all the air around us decided to head toward the blast area. Our cloaks whipped around our legs as a river of wind rushed down the stairs. A moment later a blast barfed back out of the stairwell, bringing the smell of ozone.

"*What was the hell was that?*" asked Mason.

I grinned. "*Special Branch's version of subtle … a silence Spell activated a moment before detonation, whatever the heck kind of detonation that was. Now follow me.*" I was happy to see that Ng was doing exactly as asked; staying at the rear and keeping his eyes peeled as he followed Jacobs.

We pounded down the stairs as quickly as possible, our boots thudding loudly against polymer-coated steel. I searched for the vault door, the nightvision contacts bringing the dark into crystal-clear, black and white perfection. I expected to see a twisted mass of metal at the bottom.

It wasn't there.

But there was a big hole located … right where the door used to be. A goodly section of concrete tunnel was gone as well, exposing the cracked and blasted bedrock under the city.

It was the smell that hit us first. Rot, mold, sweet things decomposed… a miasma of conflicting odors that had my nose itching furiously. I resisted the urge to upchuck. A couple of the Green Peas gagged. Oh well, if they lived, they would remember this as one of the several different odors associated with horror.

I wondered if I'd ever been that young.

"*Where did the vault door go?*" asked Mason, eyes wide. There was no evidence of the shiny steel door anywhere. "*It should be here. Maybe twisted and broken, but it should be here.*"

"*I find it better not to ask about such things. When Special Branch says things should cease to exist, I take them at their word and keep my trap shut.*" Actually, a Magician named Aashish gave me a convoluted explanation involving extra-dimensional space and such, but he lost me three words in. "*Just think of it as an anti-matter bomb. Not the kind of behavior exhibited by plastic explosive, that's for sure.*" Whatever other Spells were embedded into the plastique, I was quite happy not knowing. Ignorance is bliss and all that horsehockey.

"*Boss, you know what anti-matter is?*" asked Jacobs.

"*Kinda. I've watched enough* Star Trek."

"*Riiight. Let me tell you … squawp!*"

The reason for her surprised *squawp* appeared in front of us as we stepped through the gaping hole. Personally, I was pretty happy it shut her up.

We found ourselves in another tunnel that stretched far into the distance. Unlike the sewers above, this one had a flat floor and walls that arched twenty feet overhead to form the ceiling. Lights were set every ten feet—small circular disks that provided an unflattering illumination. There was enough light that our nightvision contact lenses powered down.

It was the shelving units, however, that captured my attention. Along each curved wall and littered across the floor were thousands of shelves in various states of disarray—bent, warped and torn apart. They were the remains of stand-alone metal shelving you might find in grocery stores or a warehouse. From where we stood just inside the former vault door, the shelves were strewn as far as the eye could see, all the way to the vanishing point.

"*Comma, display schematics.*" They popped into my vision. As I thought, this tunnel wasn't displayed. Somebody had either erased them from city records or spread enough money so they were never filed.

At my feet, a twisted and torn aluminum can. I picked it up. Brownish/orange residue inside, slightly chunky with rot and fuzzy with mold. I gave it a sniff. Just damn nasty.

"I think this was a canned pasta product," I sent. The floor was covered in the corpses of similar cans. This was where the smell came from, the nauseating odor of rot … cans, thousands if not hundreds of thousands of torn, split cans.

Ng spoke softly. "This is a bunker. A storage facility of some kind."

"How come we've never heard of it?" Jacobs asked out loud.

"The Deep Tunnel," Matt answered. Ng nodded.

At Jacob's look of incomprehension, our newest member clarified, "The Deep Tunnel Project. It was commissioned in the '70s to help reduce flooding in the metro area and minimize the harmful effects of dumping raw sewage into Lake Michigan. The tunnels are used to divert sewage and water into temporary holding ponds. Three billion dollars went into creating the tunnels and they will be in full use by 2014."

"To quote a member of my team, 'Someone got paid.' " I stepped over a ripped paper bag that, by the label, contained white rice. "Three billion, huh? I wonder how much to build this section of tunnel?"

No answer.

"Why is this tunnel here? Who made it? Better yet, who had it made?" There was a thread of anger in Ng's voice. It was good to know he experienced human emotions. There was hope for Captain Inscrutable yet.

"Someone wanted to prepare a place with enough supplies to last for years … in case the world came to an end." Matt picked up a piece of shelving and gave it close look. "This appears to have been broken by hand. See how it's all scratched here? Claw marks."

I began to carefully move through the detritus. *"Ladies and gentleman, the real question isn't why or who built this place."* The hairs on the back of my neck were standing on end. I had a good idea who arranged for the massive construction. *"No, the real question is, who ate all the food? Now, follow and be careful where you step. Let's get back to subvocal. I'll continue point."*

Our trek down the tunnel was hampered by the sheer volume of wreckage. Every food that could be canned, bagged, or jarred had been looted and eaten, leaving broken glass and shredded metal to litter the floor. What made matters worse was the piles of dried scat and yellow stains on the concrete that proved to be evaporated urine. They left a faint smell of ammonia and musk both earthy and foul. During our walk down that long tunnel we passed piles and piles of dung, some over five feet tall. Most piles were dry and crumbly, perhaps several weeks or months old. The farther we went, the more fresh and pungent they became. Before we hit the half-mile mark, we found yellow pools that hadn't yet evaporated. As the smell grew stronger and stronger, everyone became edgier and grimmer.

"*Boss!*"

I jumped. Jo's sudden voice over the bone induction pad scared the heck outta me. "*What?*" I asked crossly.

"*Big pulse of magical energy, brief but big. Set off all the sensors in the downtown area.*"

Bingo. "*Triangulate and tell me the source.*"

"*Not sure I have enough data; the pulse was too brief.*"

"*See if you can contact Ghost, and have him figure it out. Damn, put everyone on it. Find me that location!*"

"*Check, boss.*"

"*What do you think, boss?*" From Matt's voice, he had a damn good idea. As did I.

"*I'd bet my last buffalo nickel that whatever or whoever cast the windigo curse just sent a message.*" The team had been fully briefed on my puckish visitor. "*Maybe it's that greater spirit talking to the pieces of itself.*"

"*Boss, when you say that, it sounds so friggin' weird,*" said Mason.

That sounded weird? I had to remind myself that she was a Green Pea and hadn't seen the *really* strange stuff yet. "*You should hear what's in my head.*"

Matt cut in. "*Keep going?*"

"*You got something better you rather be doing?*"

"*What, something better than trudging through a crap and piss laden secret bunker illegally constructed using taxpayer funds a hundred feet beneath the streets of Chicago in the search of infectious evil spirits that like to snack on the on the occasional passerby?"*

I smiled. *"We got a great job or what?"*

Chuckles rang softly in my ears.

"Jeanie?"

"Yes?"

"Back before you joined us, you cast that Spell on Kal that hid him from sight. You still know that Shape?"

She snorted. *"Don't teach your grandmother to suck eggs, boss. Of course I do. But it's a camouflage Spell and it doesn't turn you invisible. It works for a limited time and only if you move slowly."*

That sounded about right. *"Great. Hit me with the big whammy. Everybody, when she's done, stay back fifty yards. I think we're close to something ... bad."*

"How bad, boss?" Alba asked.

"A 'change your underwear' kind of bad, Matt." I shrugged out of my Faraday Coat so it wouldn't soak up the Spell. Handing it to Ng, I nodded to Jeanie. *"Okay, do it."*

The Magician placed her hand on my chest and closed her eyes. I didn't feel a thing—that's true of many Spells—but judging from the harsh, indrawn breaths of my team, it must have looked spectacular.

"I ain't seen anything like that," said Jacobs.

"Pipe down and stay back."

Stepping slowly and carefully around torn pieces of shelving, I left the team behind. I knew from the files on Kal's excursion to 1943 that the camouflage Spell blurred the edges of my form and colored my body in such a way that I blended in with my surroundings. It didn't matter how many people or which angle they looked from, the camouflage was nearly perfect. Only the ripple of my movement gave me away, even though I couldn't see the effects myself. That kind of stunk because I would have no clue when the Spell timed out or dispelled due to unduly quick motion.

After a few hundred more yards, another vault door came into view, the scattered and ripped shelves ending a dozen feet from the tunnel's terminus. The scat and urine here was fresh, the odor nearly overpowering, the piles and puddles still steaming gently. As Kal likes to say, *By the pricking of my thumbs, something wicked this way comes.*

I checked the spoked wheel. It turned easily under my hand. Sweat popped out on my forehead, but I retained the same icy calm felt earlier. Ready to kill, ready for what might be beyond the door. I planned on putting a fair patch of holes on whatever varmints lurked beyond.

"*Ready?*" Naw, my subvocal voice didn't carry a slight tremor, did it?

They nodded.

I sent a prayer that Ng would be as ready as we were for what lay behind the door.

Muscles heaving, I heaved the door inward.

No, we weren't ready for what lay beyond.

Another tunnel like the one we left, stretching into the distance, but instead of shelves … bunks. Thousands of bunks, beds for whoever had this place built and a quite a few close friends. Or maybe an army.

Or two.

Speaking of army, every one of those bunks was occupied. By windigos.

That's a *lot* of cannibals.

Thousands of heads turned my way, tracking the motion of the door with soulless eyes, and I got a very good look at what my death might be like. Yorick had looked somewhat human and so did these save for a few who had progressed farther along the Supernatural scale. Those were gaunt, skeletal, with cadaverous shark eyes and porcupine quills for hair that ran down their backs like a horse's mane. Their flesh was leathery and brown, dry and cracked, oozing a clear fluid.

Men, women, children … all windigos, all wearing normal clothes that hung loose on lean frames. As I stood there, numbed by the vastness of the windigo crisis, I saw arms begin to elongate and long ropes of drool trail from thousands of jaws, spattering the floor in a rain of saliva.

It took a second for me to realize that they could *see* me, despite the Spell. Thousands of dead eyes were focused on my face as I stood there stupidly staring at the cannibal army.

They charged.

I fired. Silver rounds killed instantly as they severed the magical connection between foreign spirit and emaciated body. Some bullets passed clean through ribcages and dry flesh to slam home into the windigo behind, killing them as well. A few rounds grazed flesh, but that was enough and those creatures died as well. Those that died began to change, their bodies slowly morphing back to human form. I backed away, my silenced HK416 throwing a hail of bullets, a blizzard of silver at the monsters. I emptied one 100-round Beta-C magazine and speed-loaded another. The barrel was starting to overheat, but I didn't stop because I was at the choke point, the doorway. Bodies began to pile up, flopping to our side of the tunnel and building steadily as my team rushed to my aid, flooding the narrow space with silver death. The windigos would have to come to us, and we could kill a ton before we had to retreat.

They died by the score, by the hundreds, but still they came, straight on into the line of death we created. Bodies began to pile high, but that didn't stop the creatures. What they couldn't climb, they dismantled, pulling the bodies of their unclean brethren away only to die themselves as we reloaded and began to fire anew.

It wasn't enough. Not nearly enough bullets to save our lives because there were more windigos than bullets. If we carried one bullet for every Supernatural down there, we wouldn't be able to walk. Hell, we wouldn't be able to *move*, there were so many. Still we fired, piling up a wall of corpses.

"Where did they come from?" screamed Jacobs, a look of fear and loathing on her pretty face. "There's so many!"

"Fall back!" I shouted over the crack of gunfire, reloading with my last Beta-C mag. I was happy to see that Ng handled his Brave Bull well, taking his time, making every silver-coated deer slug count.

We started retreating, stumbling through the mass of broken shelving that was now our biggest obstacle. How can you run full out with so much stuff strewn everywhere? Not to mention the great piles of dung that would serve as messy speed-bumps. I didn't join the Bureau to get monster crap on my boots.

I ceased firing and slung my sidearm back into its thigh holster, feeling the heat from the barrel through the NewTanium armor. Snarling, I fumbled for a Spell egg, ripped the paper from the bottom, revealing the activation word, then threw the polystyrene case at the vault door. It landed in the midst of dead and dying windigos.

Out of the corner of my eye I saw Jeanie fire her AR15. She moved with precision and a methodical focus that was as impressive as it was deadly. I made a mental note … she sure didn't need me as a protector. Heck, she might be better off guarding my butt.

"PORKMAT!" I hollered. Special Branch really needed to come up with better activation words.

The Spell egg erupted in gouts of thick, sticky fire that covered the entire area around the vault door from floor to ceiling. Flames burned a deep, fierce blue and even from fifty feet away I could feel the heat against my face. When our Magicians make a napalm Spell, they don't go at it half-assed.

Bodies began to appear through the fire, flesh burning like tinder, only to fall into heaps of charred bones. More and more appeared and more burning piles began to form, bones glowing red from the heat.

"Keep falling back, everyone," I barked. "This isn't going to last long." Already the flames were dying, but dozens of windigos lay scattered in heaps of broken and burnt bones. Teeth crackled and popped like party favors. My weapon clacked softly. Empty. Damn.

We continued our retreat in time to see more windigos burst through the fading flames, a little scorched but unharmed. Instead of heading straight out at us, they swarmed like spiders. Punching yellowed nails into concrete as if it was made of soft cheese, they scrambled up the curved walls and ceiling, spreading out so that we couldn't shoot them all.

Cursing, Alba threw an acid bomb that turned the majority of advancing creatures into piles of black goo. It managed to slow them down somewhat, but more skittered through the door faster than we could shoot.

"*Portner, get a fix on us and start the truck. Meet us topside.*"

"*Got your location, boss. You're off the schematic.*"

"*Understood. Just get ready.*"

"*Check.*"

Matt piped up. "I'm low on silver bullets, boss!"

The rest of the team chimed in with the same news. Ng, however, looked at me and said, "I'm out."

Nodding, I tossed him my backup pistol, a Beretta, and a spare clip. "Okay everyone, keep retreating. Time for Spells." I tossed another egg, a Bouncing Betty that sent blue laser lines in a twelve foot diameter, slicing those windigos close by into itty-bitty bite-sized chunks. I didn't know if I'd managed to kill them, but they couldn't give chase when they were reduced to pieces the size of my hand.

Matt followed with another napalm Spell, while Jacobs and Mason tossed explosive gems. By the time we reached the halfway point, we must have killed over a thousand windigos, yet more boiled through the vault door.

Then it got bad. Real bad.

Skrrrrrreeeeettttcchhhh!! The splitting, rending sound tore into my eardrums and all of us stopped firing as the pain of it damn near split our heads in two.

Tears streamed from Dove Jacob's eyes. "What the f—"

Windigo bodies, both living and dead, exploded outwards from the doorway. With a steam-whistle roar, an enormous windigo at least nine feet tall unfolded from the doorway with the steel hatch gripped tightly in one giant hand. It carried the massive steel door like a shield, holding it between the rapidly failing hail of silver bullets and its leathery flesh.

Foot long quills rippled like seaweed on its head while a strangely hinged mouth opened impossibly wide, exposing a tongue bigger than my size elevens. It hissed—a deep, rattling sound that contained enough hate and malice to blow my hair back. It ducked its head behind the steel door and charged, moving hideously fast, the tangled metal garbage at its oversized, clawed feet flying.

"Jesus God," I whispered. To the others, "Run!"

They didn't have to be told twice. Fear stink replaced the musty scent of old manure as we beat feet as fast as we could. I threw Spell eggs high and low, attempting to erect barriers of flame. The big windigo shrugged off attacks that killed scores of its fellows, wiping them from the walls and ceiling.

I leapt over twisted metal while sneaking glances at the Supernatural chasing us. How that thing was able to carry over a thousand pounds of steel door with one hand I'll never know. Its arms might have been dowels covered in cracked, tan leather and seemed light enough to blow away in a strong breeze. You could have used it for a kite.

As I watched it use the door to swipe away heaps of detritus, I began to form a plan. My stomach dropped. It was a lousy plan, an *extremely* lousy plan, but it was the only one I could think of.

"*This is what … I want … you guys to do ….*" I sent as we ducked and dodged through garbage. We began to pull away from the charging Supernaturals. Though the big windigo merely hammered its way through the debris, it was slowed by that huge steel door and no other dared try to outrun it. Perhaps it was a windigo sign of respect for the Alpha monster.

"*C'mon, boss!*" Jacob's sent when I finished. "*That's nuts.*"

"*Shut it and do what you're told, Agent!*" We didn't have time for arguments; the end of the tunnel was swiftly approaching. Everyone but Ng pawed at their Bat Belts.

As we navigated a nightmare labyrinth of a tunnel filled with broken shelving, crap, and scattered aluminum cans, I tore open cellophane packages, forming a large ball of plastique in my gloved hands. A twisted shard of metal barked against my shin and I nearly fell, stumbling enough for the others to pull ahead. Alba looked back and I urged him to keep going. No need for both of us to wind up on the wrong side of life if my plan went far wrong.

Jo's voice rang in my head. "*Boss, Ghost managed to locate the source of the magical pulse!*"

"*Tell me quick!*"

"*You ain't gonna like it.*"

"*I'm already up to my hips in things I don't like. Spill it!*"

She was right, I didn't like it.

CHAPTER TWENTY

Traffic

"*A*RE YOU KIDDING ME?" I sent. "*Are you goldarned kidding me?*"

"*Sorry, boss, but Ghost says that's where it came from …
under the Sears Tower.*"

Life doesn't throw lemons at BSI Agents; it throws turd sandwiches
and expects you to choke them down with a glass of milk. With extra
hair.

"*Good news though, boss. It's less than a half-mile from where you
entered the sewers.*"

The language I used would've made Nantan Lupan bend me over
his knee for a few stroppings with his belt. He didn't cotton much to
swearing in the presence of a lady. "*Sorry, Jo. Just a little surprised.*"

Tinny laughter tickled my skull. "*Nothing I haven't heard before.
Or said, for that matter.*"

"*Check. Keep us fixed on your RediPad and get ready. I think it's
going to get hairy.*" As if having thousands of cannibal Supernaturals
hot on my ass wasn't hairy enough.

I dodged a dried pile of crap and found a somewhat clear path
ahead. From behind I heard the steady *clang, spang, crump* of the big
windigo as he bulled his way straight through. Looking back, I saw
his black eyes fixed firmly on me like a lion targeting a gazelle on

the Serengeti. Behind it, covering the walls and ceilings like a living carpet, were the smaller windigos clambering along like a spidery entourage.

Spinning around, I drew my sidearm with my right hand while holding the messy ball of plastic explosives in my left. One, two, three shots. Not even bothering to slow, the big windigo lowered the door as I aimed and all three rounds pancaked on steel. It was a lot closer than I'd thought, perhaps only fifty or so yards away. I took another shot, plugging a wall crawler behind and to the left of the big windigo in the face; then I spun back around, not bothering to watch it fall. I holstered my sidearm and continued running.

My team had arrived at the hole where the first vault door had been and was waving at me to hurry up.

"*Go you idiots, find an exit. Portner, wait for Alba's call!*"

"*Check, boss.*"

Alba nodded and ushered the others out while I jinked and juked around piles of junk. I lobbed my second-to-last Spell gem behind

Twenty yards to the exit.

"BLOODGRIME!" I yelled.

Ten yards.

The gem transformed into an enormous ball of sticky, fiery napalm, coating everything in a ten-foot radius in white-hot accelerant. A wall of fire, the heat of which I could feel through my thick armor, obscured the charging windigos. Hopefully that would slow the big nasty down. Heck, I was twenty feet away and already cooked medium rare.

At the doorway, skidding to a halt, my rubber-soled boots sliding along dusty concrete, I pulled another credit card-sized detonator from my Bat Belt and jammed the flat end into the plastic explosive.

A roar sounded from beyond the fire, full of anger and hate. It hurt my ears.

I touched the surface of the detonator. Several icons appeared.

Bodies, dozens of them, were thrown on the fire and began to burn.

Oh my God, I thought, staring in shock as a dozen more soon joined them. Within seconds, a causeway of dead, smoldering windigos had formed, an access way for the big one who began to cross over the bodies, clawed feet punching through ribcages and crushing skulls. I cursed myself for not packing a grip of more powerful Spell gems. A hellfire Spell would have been a ton more helpful. Those windigo bodies would have been cooked to ash before the big monster had time to use them as a bridge. Hindsight and all that.

I selected an icon. Time for my best Nolan Ryan impersonation. I wound up for a left-handed throw and launched the ball of plastic explosives as hard as I could.

For a split second, I feared I might miss and waste a perfectly good ball of technomagic destruction, but it sailed in high arc that nearly connected with the ceiling.

It was an ugly throw and if I'd been a righty, it wouldn't have come anywhere close to the big windigo, but I'm ambidextrous, so it wasn't half bad. I knew it wouldn't hit the creature, but that's not what I was aiming for.

Almost contemptuously, it tried to slap the ball away with the door and the ball stuck with a *splat*. Perhaps it thought I was hurling another Spell. I guess I was, but not one it was expecting.

Four seconds.

It was almost halfway across the bridge of burning corpses. They smelled like roasting pork.

Three.

Two.

It cleared the fire.

One.

Bye-bye.

The detonator said, 'GOLDMUSHROOM' and the charge ignited.

Kal calls Special Branch "a mad misfit gaggle of Technogeeknerds with too much time on their hands and unlimited resources." I finally got an up-close-and-personal look at the results of all that capital and the insane will to create destruction. Have to say that the big guy was right on the money.

When plastic explosive cooks off, there is surprisingly little fire.

Mostly it's an enormous pressure wave at roughly 1,700 feet per second that jellies any living thing within the effective kill radius.

There was enough plastic explosive fixed to the door to turn any living thing within twenty-five feet into strawberry yogurt. Unfortunately for me, thanks to the narrow confines of the tunnel and the ready availability of shrapnel, the pressure wave would be funneled straight toward Kal's favorite Native American, greatly enhancing the kill zone. It would also carry with it enough sharp, broken shelving to julienne my body but good.

I was roughly a little over twenty-five feet from the monster when the activation Word sounded. I prepared my soul for the Land of Ever Summer, the final destination of my people. Assuming what was left of me received a proper burial, of course.

Instead of an expanding pressure wave that would've ricocheted off the tunnel walls and ceiling, pulping my poor body, a basketball sized hole formed. It was filled with utter blackness, a kind of negativity that ate light and shat out a dark radiance that insulted the retinas of my eyes. It was soundless, suppressed by the silence Spell, but its effects were immediate.

The door crumpled like tinfoil and was sucked into that blackness, which grew to the size of a Ford Flathead V8. The giant windigo, whose rail-like yet powerful arm was drawn in with the door, was pulled into the sphere. It howled in dismay, a rumbling roar of pain. It seemed to elongate, becoming spaghetti-thin as it was sucked into the awful vortex, disappearing in an instant. The sphere grew, still sucking in air and whatever happened to be in its radius of effect.

The windigo bodies burning merrily in the fire were sucked in as well, along with the flaming napalm, torn shelving, heaps of dung, aluminum cans and anything else not bolted to the floor. All were drawn to that ever-expanding sphere of deathly quiet annihilation.

That, of course, included me.

My feet left the floor as I was roughly pulled through the air toward the sphere, which had grown to the size of a Camry. I knew this was it—my end had come—and I prayed that my soul would find Winch's.

Before I made it halfway to the sphere, it collapsed on itself, the edges folding inward like origami art from Hell. It pulsed briefly and shrank into a dense, black spot that glowed darkly for a moment. Reality seemed to pulse around it, a corona of warping space and time that flexed suddenly as it disappeared, sending ripples outward in a pulse of distorted reality.

I found myself caught in one of those ripples, pushed by a pressure wave of runaway space/time.

Thumppity, thump, thump. Butt hit concrete, followed by back, shoulders, flip once, then chest and legs. *Ouch.* I wound up face down, kissing concrete, while shards of shelves and the remains of cans dropped all around. The whole event from start to finish had lasted for less than two seconds. Talk about overkill. I vowed to kick some Technogeeknerd butt if I survived.

Okay, that really hurt.

There was road rash on my cheeks and nose, the blood already starting to ooze, and the rest of me felt pretty thoroughly tenderized but in one painful piece. I picked myself up as fast as my battered body would allow because I heard the quickly approaching scrabbling of windigos as they continued their advance. One-track monster minds.

The area where the big windigo had been had been swept clean of … well, everything. Fire, bodies, and garbage all gone into the sucking maw of the sphere, sucked into what I assumed was a stabilized singularity. Special Branch was *way* too well funded with far too little oversight, I realized.

Through the doorway and up the stairs, my long legs pumping, pumping, pumping, while the irritating *scritch, scritch* diamond hard nails on concrete bounced off the walls. I knew they were close— those monsters that wanted to eat me, to *consume* me and spit out my broken bones. That wasn't going to happen, not on my watch, because I was *Itza-chu* and my death wouldn't, *couldn't* come at hands and teeth of monsters like *that*. It was far too insulting.

At the top of the stairs and I looked around and saw a shining star, a glowing point of light off to the right. I blessed Matt's hard-as-nails soul because he had used a Follow-Me, a tiny cube-like device that emits light only those with nightvision lenses can see. It was a trail winding through the tunnel and I followed, splashing through filthy water and other things I didn't care to think about, running half-crouched. I tried to ignore the scuzz from the water that coated my armor, but the smell was enormous, an almost living thing that hated those who would trespass in its dark domain. I could feel it wanting to clog my lungs in foul matter, to snuff the flow of oxygen into my veins and I gagged.

Biting my lip hard brought blood and pain and the crystal-cold clarity I'd lost. The panic that threatened to overwhelm me receded.

"Safe? Are you all safe?" I said, breathing heavily. My legs burned and the taste of copper flooded my mouth, as if I'd licked a penny.

"Yeah, boss," Matt responded. *"You got the trail?"*

"On it."

"Good. Portner will be here in twenty seconds. What about that big sucker?"

Before I could respond, the boiling mass of windigos burst into the tunnel behind me. It took them less than a second to follow and their silent, focused hunger beat at my back, causing the small hairs on the nape of my neck to rise.

Three more Follow-Mes, the last ending at steel rungs leading upward, and my jump cleared nearly a dozen. I scrambled for purchase—heavy, steel-toed boots shoving against the rungs—and I reached, fingers scraped raw. There was an opening above and I had to get there because up top, in the air of the real world, was the world of *Usen* (the Giver-of-Life, the deity of my people) and there I could really *fight*.

Up and out and my ragged breath scored my lungs with shards of glass, but I managed to toss a present into the sewer—a large, glittering gem—just as the first windigo reached the rungs. I bellowed the activation word and shouted for everyone to take cover, to move away. My last gem—the largest at six carats of nearly priceless pink diamond chockablock full of some seriously bad-ass magic. A last ditch, use only in case of extreme emergency gem, the strongest in the Bureau arsenal. Four seconds of scrambling for cover later, an actinic white light shot from the hole to spear into the sky, accompanied by the roar of a thousand blast furnaces at full heat, a sound so profound and deep it reached through muscle and blood, skin and bone, and rattled the core of my soul.

That diamond—a last resort weapon issued to every team leader—and the iron ring that topped the edge of the manhole and the rungs that led down, down, down to Hell glowed white hot for an instant before steaming away into a superheated gas. Even behind parked cars we could feel the heat, and fifteen feet from the spear of light, tires blew out as they caught fire and melted.

The whole street shook, a minor trembling that lasted for less than three seconds, but it brought terror sweat to the skin. All up and down the street, manhole covers glowed cherry red and steamed and hissed before they were blown into the sky, molten missiles of iron that splatted onto the pavement, flinging crimson drops far and wide. Less than a second later, the spear of light and heat that sliced into the heavens faded into nothing, leaving only the brutalized street behind.

And through it all, through the bone-chilling roar, exploding tires, the molten iron and superheated gas, came Portner in a fourteen-foot rent-a-truck, dodging burning cars and the gaping holes into the fiery hell of the sewers. It screeched to a halt not more than five feet from me and the Green Pea exited, M16 at the ready.

"*Boss, another pulse from the Tower. And all over! Ghost is telling me that twelve cities across the globe are putting out magical pulses,*" said Jo, sounding so matter-of-fact.

"*Let's not worry about the other cities right now. I need you to coordinate civil defense. If we don't make it, it's up to you.*"

"*Boss ....*" Uncertain, slightly worried.

"*You got me?*"

"*Check, boss.*" Back to cool and detached. She didn't have time to be a Green Pea Receptionist anymore.

"*Portner, hand out your Spell gems to everyone but Ng. Keep three for yourself. Alba, Jeanie, with me. The rest of you, there's going to be action soon and I need you to defend the Straights. That's priority one.*"

Matt took a step forward. His bald head was dewed with sweat and his face was covered with enough dirt to plant seeds in. *"What's the play, boss?"*

"We three have to take the tower."

He nodded, eyes full of steely resolve. *"I'll clear the way."*

Nodding, I opened the back panels of the cargo truck, revealing five glossy prizes. Black paint and shining chrome, flaring fiberglass and sleek sexiness, BMW S1000RR sport bikes with 999cc inline-4 engines that redlined at 14,200 rpm, hitting a top speed of 188 mph. All were fueled and ready to go. I climbed aboard with a racing heart. I had told Jo to requisition those bikes—those beautiful, fast-as-the-wind bikes—from the dealer. They were the perfect vehicle to negotiate the traffic-clogged streets of Chicago in case of an emergency, and I was pretty sure that current circumstances counted.

Helmet on head, mind filled with deadly purpose, I brought the sleek machine to life. Beside me, Jeanie and Matt, encased in identical black helmets, did the same.

I nodded. *"Ready?"*

Matt grunted. *"Check, boss. Stay behind me. If I fall, don't stop, keep going."*

"I'm beside you all the way, boss." Jeanie's musical voice was hard with intent.

That was why I did what I did, for people like that. What a world we live in that such comrades were made, and such a world was worth saving, even at the cost of my own life. By damn, in the past I'd come a gnat's whisker from death more times than I could count, only to be saved at the last second. I reckoned that if I died that night, doing it stopping the windigo curse and giving the Sidhe high holy hell was as good a reason as any. My voice refused my commands, so I nodded and signaled Matt to go.

With a buzzsaw drone, the BMW leapt forward, flew off the truck, and landed perfectly on both wheels, the stout Latino handling the fractious vehicle with virtuoso skill. I almost envied the grace in that burly body.

My own bike hit the ground with a teeth-rattling *thump*, and I kicked it into the next gear, following Matt's rear wheel.

We hustled west on West Madison Street, zigzagging around traffic that, even in the cold light of dawn, remained heavy. The drivers in their Lexus and Audi sedans obligingly waved one finger at us as we sped along. Onto sidewalks, past startled pedestrians, over the river, then a right turn on Whacker heading south.

It was then that the windigos, those hardy survivors of the tunnel massacre, decided to boil up out of whatever nook and cranny they'd been hiding in. Manhole covers flew open, buildings vomited monsters from their front doors, and the overpass swarmed with even more, climbing from below in an effort to stop us. Without even slowing, Matt raised his pistol and shot one in the face as it leapt at his bike, the silver-coated bullet passing through its teeth and out the back of its head in a red spray.

I could see the tower, a stack of ever thinner, smaller rectangular boxes, pointing at the sky, with a radio antenna bristling from the top. The sight of the massive building almost distracted me enough to miss the woman in red who leapt at me, arms growing in mid-flight, iron claws spiking for my throat. Her jaw unhinged, mouth gaping impossibly wide.

My first shot missed, but not the second. The round hit her shoulder square, shattering bone and her unnatural life.

More windigos appeared, older ones whose hair had long since turned into a mane of spikes. Their suppurating sores decorated leathery skin stretched tight over bone. But the bikes blew past them and I knew we would make it. Sears Tower, or Willis Tower, whatever you wanted to call it, was drawing near and I prayed that someone could please show me where to find that furry bolg gem.

A windigo appeared from out of the sky—perhaps it jumped from one of the several tall buildings lining the street, I didn't know, didn't care because Matt was its target. The monster hit the BMWs front wheel and the bike flipped like a fiberglass and steel omelet, Matt flying over the handlebars, over the windigo, and onto the pavement in a tuck-and-roll that did very little to save his hide from instantly becoming tenderized. I winced as his armor tore.

To give him credit, he made it to his feet in credible time to meet its rush, but I was already past. I wanted to help, but that wasn't the mission and he would've been pissed had I stopped. Especially with Chicago's version of C.H.U.D. on the loose. Unlike the Cannibalistic Humanoid Underground Dwellers in the movie, these bad dudes could grow their arms an extra three feet at a moment's notice and wasn't that a sickening fact? I'd seen a lot of weird Shinola in my day, but that really topped an ugly list.

Another windigo appeared in front of me, mouth gaping, and I knew I couldn't avoid it. Too close and I was going too fast, so I decided I wouldn't even try to swerve the bike. With a snarl, I gripped the front brake lever hard, sending the bike skidding on the front tire and the back slewing into the air in a front-side wheelie. I torqued my body to the right and the bike spun on the front wheel while still skidding forward. The back tire pulped the windigo's chest and sent it flying fifteen feet away.

The bike continued to spin and I held on for dear life as it performed a full 360 before the back tire thudded back to the pavement. I hit the juice and it leapt forward, eager to just *go* and the front tire hit the windigo this time as I drove the bike over its body. It probably wasn't fatal, but it sure put a damper on the monster's day.

That's it, I thought as I sped away, almost to my destination. *Definitely keeping this bike.*

The Willis Tower West Entrance, thick tempered glass strong enough to give a bullet pause. I did what any enterprising Agent would do. I goosed the juice and the bike jumped forward eagerly. I steered around concrete planters and the few pedestrians still out and about ran, screaming, for their lives as rampaging windigos bled out of the woodwork.

Forty feet away, time for another wheelie. This time the back wheel took the weight as I closed in on my objective ... and I was off, legs pumping as the bike—that beautiful, beautiful piece of precision engineering—hit the front door at forty mph and tore through, tempered glass fragments flying. I stumbled after, trying not to fall as I ran, ran so hard through glass shards, over glass shards. Straights—

security guards—were coming at a run, four of them, three drawing down while one talked on a radio, calling re-enforcements. I didn't want to hurt them, but I couldn't stop, had to go on.

My weapon was in my hand and I drew a bead on the closest guard, a portly man who might have been a football player in younger days, but those times of glory were long past. His belly preceded him by a good foot-and-a-half.

Leg, leg, leg, leg, go for the legs. It was part mantra, part prayer and all fervent hope. There, the thigh. Thick, meaty, and if I could just miss the femoral artery, he'd be fine, perhaps walk with a limp, have a nice war story to tell the grandkids and a cool scar. Don't kids like neat stories that involve gratuitous violence? Well, he was about to find out firsthand.

A bright flare, a flashbulb that didn't fade when the picture snapped, instead it burned bright like the heart of the sun. With a wail, the lead guard shot straight back into the guard behind and both hit the floor with bone-crunching force. They rolled, one over the other, and finally coming to rest fifty feet away, very still, but their chests still moved. Alive. My eyes flew wide open as the two others shot into the air twenty feet, heading straight for the curved ceiling of the lobby/atrium, gaining speed, and hitting the glass looking as if they would snap their necks like popsicle sticks, but no …. They fell, screaming, as the floor, that hard, stone floor, rushed to them and *wham*! Two impacts, sledgehammers against a side of beef accompanied by wet, popping and cracking sounds.

They kept screaming, those two, screamed loud and long and it hurt, the sound a nail through the eardrums, but I was glad. They would live. Maybe.

My pistol found its home in the thigh holster of my black, chitinous armor. As I slowed, I passed the remains of my beautiful bike, its fiberglass cowling ripped apart and front wheel assembly a ruin of rubber and steel. For a brief moment I felt a stab off sorrow.

Out of the corner of my eye, I saw the bright flashbulb flare finally fade. There was Jeanie, staring at the diamond in her palm, the source of the flare, now quiescent. She placed it back into a belt pouch.

"Telekinetic Spell," she said. "Allowed me to toss those beggers about a bit. Alex taught me before we left Warehouse." The impassive, insect-like helmet turned toward me. "It required a lot of energy for such fat men. Thank God I have some spare gems to supply the energy because I swear I've never seen so many overweight people. This era should cut down on fast food."

"Thanks for the assist," I said, throat tight.

"I didn't want blood on your hands, Canton. Not if I could help it."

How did I get so damn lucky? Note to self: if Kal is ever stupid enough to break up with this remarkable woman, I'm going for it.

With a backward glance at the wreckage of the bike, I headed deeper into the building. I guess I wasn't keeping the bike after all.

With a quick prayer that the Straights Jeanie just incapacitated would heal without permanent injury, we searched for the stairs. There was only one place the gem could be to mask its presence. Underground, and that meant a basement or a parking garage.

"Jo, I don't know this place worth squat. How many floors are under the tower and what's there?"

"Three, including the U.S. Post Office. Local Guard units should be on scene in fifteen minutes."

Three floors. That was doable. *"Everyone, check in."*

"Matt here. I'm okay. Banged up some."

"Portner here. Me and Ng are in the thick of it, but okay."

"Jacobs. Bad guys everywhere. Civilian casualties high, but I'm okay. Running low on silver bullets."

"Mason here. I'm outside the tower, keeping the bad guys away, but you better hurry. I reckon you have five minutes before I'm overrun."

No time to waste then.

Jeanie found the stairs and we took them three at a time. The first door was locked, but that posed no problem to people motivated by gruesome death and armed with explosives.

Nothing there. Down again.

Same thing.

Third floor was the charm. No door was the first clue; the entirely trashed interior was the second. Walls ripped to shreds, drop-ceiling tiles scattered and broken throughout and all the cosmetic walls torn down. Fluorescent fixtures hung sparking from the torn ceiling, partially obscuring the interior. All furniture, all office equipment, had been removed, leaving only heaps of rubble, crisscross piping along the ceiling and a serious clean-up problem. It was a cave—a dark, square hollow with the oppressive mass of the building above bearing down like a slowly rousing sleeping titan.

In the center of that cavernous space stood a column, perhaps four feet tall and one foot thick, made of red-veined marble. On top of the column, pulsing blackly like a dark heart, was an irregular shaped sphere the size of an avocado pit set in a cage of silvery wire. From the top of the cage, five more silvery wires led, up, up to where they joined in a thick braid before disappearing, piercing the ceiling.

Staring at the black thing in its mesh cage of wire, I could feel its malevolence, the pure essence of evil emanating with every beat of energy that flowed from its core.

"*Doesn't look like a gem,*" Jeanie said, "*but I can feel the magic from here.*"

That was an understatement. "*Looks like a hole. A hole in the universe.*"

We entered cautiously, our boots making the softest of taps as they descended between chunks of rubble. Time was of the essence, but we had to move slowly. Who knew what kind of booby traps lay within the area? We saw nothing. It *looked* clear. My eyes flicked to the furry bolg gem and I had a thought. Would shooting the damn thing work?

I signaled Jeanie to halt and raised my weapon, taking careful aim, and that was when it attacked. We let ourselves get distracted and never looked *up*.

It came down on Jeanie like the spirit of vengeance, a windigo that had been hiding among the piping and ventilation ductwork above our heads. Sores covered its naked body from head to toe, from blazing black eyes to blistered, gnobbly feet. Black porcupine quills grew in a thick mass on its head and continued down its back, ending slightly above its waist. All-too-human teeth snapped at Jeanie as it bore her to the floor, piercing the thin webbing between thumb and forefinger as she attempted to ward it off.

She screamed like a damned soul.

My shot took it though the skull, blowing its brains out on the floor, but it was too late—Jeanie was already in the grip of a convulsion.

The bite on her hand didn't bleed. Instead, it steamed, wisps of grayish green vapor that hovered above the cut in a noxious cloud.

"Oh God," I moaned. It was already happening. The whites of her brown eyes were tinged with gray and I knew in a matter of a few short minutes they would be black. Jeanie would be gone and a hungry *thing* would wear her flesh.

"Hurry, damn you!" she croaked as her teeth slammed together. Greenish foam began to ooze from the corners of her mouth.

She didn't have to tell me twice and the cold, empty feeling in my stomach prodded me toward the column and the gem. I fired. Once, twice, three times. Nothing.

Snarling, I grabbed the wire cage in both hands and ripped it free from the trailing wires above.

A finger touched the gem and it was cold. Colder than despair.

And I went someplace else.

CHAPTER TWENTY-ONE

———•———

Itza-Chu

IT WAS A TORCHED AND dried out husk of world without even the hope or prayer of life. Gray, that color without color, even black, the absence of all colors, was refused admittance in that horridly sterile place. Scoured of hope, it still retained an air of menace, of sharp edges and pointed protrusions that waited to slice and puncture tender flesh and drink of the fluids within. Looking at it tore at the mind and sucked all measure of pleasure from the soul.

This world was a wasteland of tattered nightmares and shrieking denial. There was no light, no sun to lift the heart and warm the skin and if there ever had been a shining orb in the heavens, it had long since burned itself into a dead cinder. No stars graced the blackness above, yet I could see every detail as if illuminated by the harshest bulb … nothing escaped me. Yet despite having perfect clarity, even I couldn't see if life had ever clung to that cracked and powdery soil. The land may have contained a sort of malignant anti-life.

I was a giant bird, judging from the faint shadow I cast on the gnarled, jagged mountains thrusting dead fingers of this world's bones into the sky. Giant protrusions of soured rock that tore at the numb air, these rocks were at once majestic and horrible, monoliths that burst through the skin of the world like ragged nails, born in an orgy of geologic violence.

A desiccated wind buoyed me up, held me aloft over this flat world of hideous torment, and as I flew I could feel the landscape calling out to me: *land, lay down your proud head because there is nothing here for you. All is absent in this place of un-life and I am hungry, so hungry. You will fill me, sustain me. Your warm blood and heart shall be mine and you too shall know such beautiful hunger, the sweet savagery of loss and despair.*

I knew that voice, that horrible, terrible, sweet voice. It was the voice I'd heard every day since Winch's death, whispering in the back of my mind, telling tales of sweet surrender. It was seductive, loving, but it was a lie.

My beak opened and a shriek of defiance rang out, only to be swallowed up by the unliving air in one gulp. It doesn't matter, my scream said, it will never matter what you say because I am Itza-chu, I am the great hawk that flies above and doesn't care what you think or what you want. Itza-chu is the predator here. My soul bears my defiance like a banner, and I will prevail.

And the barren land, in answer to my denial of its seductive embrace, vomited forth a creature of darkness.

It was a windigo. Its claws tore at the soil as it strove to emerge into the cruel, sterile world. And what a windigo it was! Tall, taller than a man, taller than a house, as tall as any building on the surface of Man's world, a colossus of hunger and spite and hate. It ripped the ground asunder as it broke free, rising to its impressive height. The other windigos, the monsters that plagued Chicago, were mere mewling pups compared to the Rottweiler that stood before me as I soared. The windigo's eyeless face had dry, papery gray skin that shifted over bones that bent in ways no human's could or should. Grayish fluid dripped from wide sores and where that thick, gelatinous liquid dropped, the dead soil hissed and steamed. The quills were not those of a porcupine; instead they were blackened spears of crystal that punched through its parchment skin to cut the dead air with needle tips. Its teeth, however, were human, disturbingly so and perfect …

absolutely awful in their perfection. White and sharp, I knew they could slice through my tissues like smoke and gulp down large chunks of my soul.

Millions of flakes of ashy, gray skin drifted away from its body, swirling about in a dermal tornado before disappearing into the black sky overhead. Dandruff of the underworld.

It took a moment for me to realize what I was looking at. Pieces of the giant windigo—pieces that pierced the gelid veil between worlds, pieces that would infect innocent people, turning them into murdering cannibals. The flakes of skin were actually pieces of its nature, tiny flecks of its essence.

I flapped my wings, gaining altitude, and snapped my head forward, my powerful beak slicing through one of the ashy particles.

Dimly, as if from beyond the beyond, I heard a muffled scream. The two halves of skin turned into noxious smoke and vanished.

The windigo giant, the Prime, roared in pain and loss. Talons the size of telephone poles swiped at me.

Pain ... blood ... feathers flew. I fell.

The parched ground grew large in my sight as I plummeted, bleeding from twin slashes across my torso. I spread my wings to catch the barren air and was rewarded with more pain as they caught, slowing my fall, which turned into a sharp bank, then an upward sweep as I worked to gain altitude.

"Now you die!"

The shout was a kettledrum thrum in my mind, pulsing and pounding. The Prime Windigo spread arms longer than its body and swiped at me, but I dodged at the last second, diving down then swooping back up. I caught a glimpse of its hips. It was sexless as a mannequin.

"I will consume your soul and those of your friends," it roared in a world-shattering voice. Anger boiled off it like black vapor.

An ear splitting howl answered the creature. "You leave my grandson alone, unclean beast!"

What?

Appearing out of nowhere, flashing into existence, massive paws raising clouds of foul dust, came an old, grizzled gray wolf the size of a battleship. Scarred, fur patchy from decades of fighting, menacing and hugely muscled, it leapt forward, teeth slashing, taking the windigo in the hamstrings.

The monster bellowed its agony and punched the wolf in the head, sending it sprawling.

"Grandfather!" I yelled. Who else could it be but Nantan Lupan?

"I'm not injured, my brave warrior," the wolf replied, rising slowly to its feet. Blood drooled from its muzzle to land on thirsty earth where unseen things furrowed the ground, seeking the precious fluid. "I knew this time was coming. Sorry I'm late; it took longer than I expected to get here."

"Nantan Lupan, leave while you can."

"Are you kidding? And miss this? Not for all the tea in China, Grandson." Grandfather grinned his wolfy grin and charged the windigo, snarling and snapping, knocking the monster back. I took that opportunity to dive, to attack and I did, talons striking dry, papery flesh, running furrows into the windigo's back all the way to the spine, barely avoiding its steely quills. The monster bled dust and greenish smoke into the air.

Bellowing, it struck both of us at once, knocking Nantan Lupan to the ground and me high into the air, my muscles momentarily paralyzed by pain before my wings once again bit and flapped for altitude.

"You have to call him, Itza-chu. Call your friend the Yellow Horse." The wolf bled into the dust, eyes weeping red as the windigo clawed at his unprotected belly. "Ahhhh! Hurry, it will take all of us to defeat this spirit!"

"But how?" I asked, diving again, distracting the monster from my grandfather. I dodged a talon that would have pierced me through, but it was a near miss.

"Just call, Grandson. You are the Great Hawk. Call and he will answer."

So I did.

My sharp cry rang out once again, this time with a purpose, with a direction in mind. I needed my friend, my brother or we would die, Jeanie would die possessed by a noxious spirit and the world would die, infected by a ravening hunger that knew no end. I called for my friend, *Jlin-litzoque*, the Yellow Horse, the cry shattering through the boundaries of the universe, my heart, my soul put into its sounding.

Only silence greeted me.

The windigo laughed. It was the sound of damned souls and rotted wood splitting in two and the tortured shriek of splintering bones. It raised a gnobbly foot and stamped down hard on Nantan Lupan's belly.

The wolf howled. Then it bit, razor sharp fangs as long as trees, slicing into the monster's ankle. Bones popped thunderously and the wolf worked his massive jaws, grinding, grinding, grinding.

I dove, talons forward, ready to rend, tear, while my beak opened wide to rip Volvo-sized pieces of desiccated flesh from its hideous body. It moved, tearing free from Grandfather's teeth, spinning and flailing at me as my talons scored its shoulder. My beak struck and leathery flesh parted on its face, exposing massive molars that glinted whitely in the un-light of that wretched world.

A hand the size of a semi truck grabbed hold of my midsection, then the other trapped me in a cage of fingers. I pecked and tore at its wrists with talon and raptor beak, but it was too late. The monster *squeezed*.

Hollow bones creaked and a sickening *pressure* filled my body as my organs compressed. Black spots swam in front of my eyes and the ugly world began to fade around the edges. The monstrous windigo brought his hands toward his gaping mouth, ready to bite my head off.

The peal of thunder, the ring of trumpets filled with an incandescent rage rang throughout the land, sending a shiver down my spine. The windigo looked up in time to see an enormous form materialize from the still air, charging it at breakneck speed.

It was a horse. A beautiful, yellow horse taller than a skyscraper, with blazing eyes and a shimmering blond mane that flowed like a pennant from its majestic, arched neck. It was an Arabian, a

Clydesdale, Percheron and more—the best qualities of all breeds combined to form a king of its kind—and it hit the windigo dead solid center, flinging the beast into the air.

I was free, the cage of its fingers no longer constraining me, and I flew.

"Jlin-litzoque," Nantan Lupan howled. "It is good you have come. Thank you."

My shriek tore at the blank heavens as I flapped my wings, gaining altitude. "Kal!"

"You took your sweet time calling, bud. What? You have a death wish? Or did you want to hog all the glory for yourself?" A familiar voice overlaid with a bugling peal. That was the sarcasm I'd been missing for a while.

As I banked, I noticed a rider clinging to the horse's mane. A young girl, thin and coltish, with long blonde hair and a sweet summertime smile. I knew that girl even though we'd never met. She clung to the animal as if it were her lifeline, sharing a bond deeper than flesh. Where her legs touched the barrel of the horse's body, they merged with the equine flesh so the two became one.

Leena.

"Hello Canton," she said, her lips spread in a smile of delight. "It's good to see you again. A giant hawk! You look amazing!"

"How? How are you here?"

Her cornflower blue eyes twinkled. "Because I'm part of Kal, and he is here. I am always with him and I always will be, in one way or another. That is the path we share."

Geez, could she be more cryptic?

She smiled. "This was meant to be. Nantan Lupan has shown me the way."

"A smart one, she is," said Grandfather. "She got the looks and the brains."

"He calls me *Icimanipi-Wihopawin*." Leena leaned from Kal's back and stroked the wolf's fur behind his great ears.

Travels Beautiful Woman? Nice. Nantan Lupan always liked the ladies.

"You all want to jibber-jabber or we going to get down to business?" It was Kal. He reared, bugling his rage at the giant windigo that slowly rose to its feet, towering over us, spiky quills scraping the dark roof of the sky.

"Flesh sacks. Insects. To eat you would be glorious," it said in its ripping, screaming voice.

Kal charged and the windigo set itself, ready to claw the horse into ribbons, but the gray wolf lunged as well, teeth savaging its already damaged ankle. The windigo's howl of pain was that of millions of hungry children wailing in despair. I dove as it began to topple, its ankle torn and shredded by Nantan Lupan's razor teeth, and Kal's front hooves lashed out, catching the beast in the chest. The scream was silenced; instead there was the harsh sound of great logs cracking open wide. Then it was my shot, my turn and my body knew what to do because I was the great hawk and I dove, talons outstretched.

Its throat was there and so were my talons so I dug in, my beak darting forward, carving out great slices of dried meat, exposing dusty bone. I dug and dug and my beak took more flesh, great gobbets, and behind me I heard giant hooves the size of train cars slam down over and over again, shaking the dusty, poison earth. With each strike came the great bass growl of a hungry, angry wolf and we savaged the monster again and again until there was nothing left but flattened, dried scraps of flesh and bone, the rest rendered to swirling dust. The body began to dissolve into gray vapor that hovered over the cracked earth before disappearing.

It was over.

I stood on a pile of torn flesh and regarded our handiwork. The windigo was … dead? Could it ever die? Or was it banished to less hospitable places? If that was possible. Too deep for me. I flapped my wings and went aloft, circling my friends … my family.

The gray grizzled wolf lifted his head and howled. "I must go."

"How did you get here? How is this possible?" I asked.

"I Saw this years ago, grandson, and when you were born, I tethered my spirit to yours. I merely followed the tether to this place."

Kal shook his great head, whipping his long mane to and fro. "How did I get here?"

Leena smiled and stroked his flank. "That would be me, big brother. Nantan Lupan and I have been talking for a while now, ever since you woke me in San Diego last year. He's a very powerful medicine man and spirit walker. He called to me, told me what I had to do. All that was needed was for Canton to call, which was a like a ... beacon, I guess, and I was able to hone in on this place." She looked around. "Can't say I like the décor."

"What a fine Magician she would have made, Jlin-litzoque," the wolf said fondly. "Even in death, her spirit is strong."

Kal tossed his head in agreement, radiating brotherly love and pride.

"But now I have to go," the wolf continued. "My next journey begins."

"Your next journey, grandfather?"

"The one that begins when flesh fails."

I felt a cold chill and I cried in negation. "No! You can't be dead!"

"Of course I can. Don't be silly. My body is in the real world, in the bed I once shared with your grandmother. I look forward to seeing her. It has been a long time. Far too long, let me tell you."

Hawks don't cry, but I gave it a shot anyway. Kal neighed in sympathy.

The wolf shot me a canine grin. "It is time. I am an old man, and the magic used to bring me here has stopped my frail heart. Don't grieve, grandson. Be happy that I lived a better life than most. I am proud of my life, just as I am proud, so very proud, of my grandson."

Hawks don't cry, hawks don't cry, hawks don't cry ....

Damn, but I wished they could.

"As for you, young lady." The wolf padded over and licked Leena's thigh and where his tongue passed, equine and human flesh parted ways. Within a few moments, her legs were free from the yellow horse. "I think it's high time you continued on, don't you?"

She nodded, her smile summer bright, and slid from Kal's back.

"NO!" Jlin-litzoque's shrill cry echoed in pain even in that place of dread hunger and loss.

Leena gave her brother a look mixed with equal parts love and sadness. "It's my time, big brother. I can't leech onto your spirit any longer; it's not my place. You have to let me go."

"I lost you once, I don't want to lose you again," he said forlornly, pawing the ground.

"Silly. You haven't lost me—I'll always be there for you in one way or another—but from now on there'll be a little more distance between us. The only thing is that all this time I've been keeping you healthy with my magic." She shook her head. "As healthy as I could, that is. The scars on your torso …. They should have split and bled long ago, become stiff and sore. I was the one who kept the tissue supple. You'll have to have Jeanie or Alex deal with them now because I won't be able to."

The big horse nuzzled her cheek. "I will. I'll figure something out."

Leena ran a slender hand along her brother's muzzle, caressing the velvety soft skin around his nose and lips. "Back in Finland, when I died, you saw Iku-Turso for what it really was and it broke your mind. When I died and my spirit grafted onto yours, I healed your psyche. I don't know what will happen when I'm gone. The rifts in your mind are wide and poorly healed. You've more scars inside than out and that's saying something. Be careful."

Kal gave a nickering laugh. "I'll be fine, Sis, and I guess I'll be seeing you soon enough. Don't worry."

"I'll be waiting. It's been a fun ride, bro, but I have to go. Stick with Jeanie, I like that one. Very much."

Kal took a few sad steps and nuzzled her cheek. "Love you, sis."

"Love you too, bro."

The wolf howled. "You two boys have a world of work ahead of you. Take care of each other."

"We will," I said.

"You know, Jlin-litzoque, you're okay for a white man. You should've been born Apache." Nantan Lupan's laughter was the yip of a cub.

"Thank you, sir," Kal replied gravely.

The wolf and the girl began walking toward the dark horizon, dust puffing gently behind them. Kal and I watched for a long time, long after they had disappeared to wherever the ghosts of the loved go.

A strange tugging started behind my belly and the desolated world dissolved around me.

"DAMN."

I was back, a wrecked cage of silvery wire in my hands, a lump of what looked like gray glass inside. My insides felt all shaky and shivery and my throat hurt from screaming. Tears covered my cheeks and my eyes felt hot.

"Canton, are you all right?"

I looked up. It was Jeanie, slowly rising to her feet, the bite on her hand bleeding freely. "I could ask the same question. You look … fine." She did. More than fine, actually.

She made a face. "My muscles started cramping after I was bitten and I felt like I was losing control of my body, but it stopped shortly after you picked up that wire thing."

"How long have I been gone?"

"Gone?" She looked puzzled. "You've been here the whole time. Perhaps two or three minutes."

Two or three minutes. It seemed like forever in that sere world. Note to self: never go there again. Ever. *"Team, check in."*

"Matt here … all the bad guys just dropped. Whatever you did worked. But boss, the people who were windigo with the porcupine quills … they're all dead. The ones that still looked like people are still alive, but unconscious."

"Check that. Same here, boss." Mason sounded scared.

"Yeah, here as well," Dove Jacobs said.

Portner was next. *"Ng and I are okay, but … the streets, boss … they're full of bodies. Everywhere."*

"Got it," I sent. *"Everyone, get back to the office. We have to perform some damage control."*

Jeanie stared at her hand and the bite slowly closed, leaving nothing but a memory. "Is it always this bad?" she asked a little too casually.

I took a deep breath. "You remember when you told me about that kid in Natzweiler? The one Mengele sacrificed for life energy?"

Her eyes went dark. "Of course."

"I don't think anything could be worse than that."

"Point taken." She wiped the remains of crusted green foam from the corners of her mouth. "You never answered my question, you know."

"Which one?"

"About why there aren't more Magicians."

I laughed. It felt good. Real joy after such a dog-assed day. *Goodbye Nantan Lupan.* "That's easy. Most Magicians can't cut the mustard in the field and don't want to work directly for the Bureau in Special Branch. You can imagine that the federal government doesn't like that one bit, so they offer those people a different sort of incentive."

She raised an eyebrow, a trick she learned from Kal. "Pray tell?"

"Those that don't want to work for the Bureau are offered a cushy government job in what we call a 'think tank,' where all they have to do is figure out nifty things to do with magic. Lethal and non-lethal."

Jeanie considered that for a moment. "Are they paid as well? Because you Yanks pay very well indeed."

I smiled. "Lady, the United States spends over *one hundred billion* dollars each year combating illegal immigration alone and over fifteen billion on the War on Drugs." Pause for dramatic effect. "The Bureau receives less than a third of what's funded for the DEA and we still rock it better than anyone." I smiled at her shocked expression. "We're just more efficient, and we also have a network of retired Agents who help us with logistics, like my dad. He owns the largest construction company on the eastern seaboard. Whenever there's a mission on the east coast, his company supplies the labor and materials for the offices. At a discount, of course."

She shook her head. "That's rather … efficient."

"A chap from your era came up with the idea of using former Agents to help with logistics. Supply and things like that. He was the second director of the Bureau after General Patton died in Berlin in a

Jeep crash and is considered the best soldier and director we've ever had. Name was Audie Murphy."

She considered that in silence and I left her to ponder while I looked around. After a bit she said, "Maybe I should join one of those 'think tanks,' because it would be much less dangerous than this." Then she broke into a brilliant smile. "But how can I give this up? Most fun I've ever had."

Fun. That's one way of putting it. Still, I understood where she was coming from; the excitement, the thrill of the hunt and the absolute pleasure of making a *difference* in the world. Why the hell did I ever retire in the first place?

I thought about those people above, those who suffered under the Windigo Curse and now lay in heaps like dolls abused by spoiled children and the answer came to mind: sometimes the cost is more than the reward and that weighs heavily on the mind. But, in the end, we Bureau-types do make a difference. We save lives in our war against the forces of darkness. Sometimes it takes a while for that fact to really sink in.

The cage of wire lay in my palms and as I examined the ugly black lump at its center, an idea began to form. I realized that this whole thing wasn't quite over yet. There was someone else I could kill after all.

I placed the cage with its burden on the floor and brought the heel of my boot down hard. Soft metal crumpled and the ugly lump shattered into dust. I guess them furry bolg gems weren't that sturdy after all.

Damn, but that felt good.

CHAPTER TWENTY-TWO

———•———

Butchery

THEY CALLED IT THE CANNIBAL Plague, a virus that affected the brain, causing a rabies-like effect and skin lesions. It was thought that patient zero was Patrice Badeaux, a French arms dealer who traveled the world extensively. The lie was convenient because most people loathe arms dealers and they're easy to pin the blame on. He was found dead on Rue Antoine Arnauld, a victim of the plague he was supposed to have spread.

People believed. The governments and the media the world over spread the story far and wide and proved the point that if you tell a lie often enough, most will accept it as the truth. Although a few conspiracy theory websites concluded that the government created and accidentally released The Zombie Virus, they were not taken seriously.

Chicago, Oakland, Houston, Miami. Those were the four American cities targeted with the curse and, thanks largely to the puca and the Seelie Court's warning, we managed to keep our losses to a minimum. If you can call 83,000-plus dead a minimum.

Kal had taken Miami, while Ayre flew to Houston. Armed with the knowledge of the furry bolg gems and intel coordinated by Ghost, they managed to contain most of the windigos. Apparently Chicago had been the most infected of the American cities, counting for almost half the casualties. Oakland, California, and vicinity suffered the least thanks to the ghost of Emperor Norton, who put paid to the windigos by the droves, his spectral body impervious to their attacks. Several dozen people took pics and videos of him on their smartphones and all around the country people began to believe that the San Francisco area had a Supernatural protector. All that belief must have recharged the old ghost's batteries for centuries to come.

Meanwhile, the death toll across the rest of the globe was substantially higher.

Paris, Moscow, London, Tel Aviv, Johannesburg, Tokyo, Shanghai, New Delhi, and Sydney were all targeted by the Unseelie Court and suffered grave losses. The Curse had spread so widely in India that the government had to use a fuel-air bomb in an attempt to contain the Supernatural attack. The heart of New Delhi became one big charcoal briquette and the resultant firestorm destroyed half the city. The death toll from both bomb and Curse was in the hundreds of thousands. The entire country was in the grip of economic and social convulsions so bad that it was estimated that another million would be dead within six months.

As for the other cities, over two million people all combined lost their lives when Kal, Nantan Lupan and I killed the Prime Windigo. Once the Curse had its hooks in and the porcupine quills started growing, the host was as good as dead. Only the Israelis responded in time and managed to keep their losses to fewer than twenty thousand, although it was a staggering blow to that small country.

Five more of them furry bolg gems were recovered, the rest lost in the heat of battle or buried under tons of rubble. No more portals to distant, dark dimensions to plague mankind. For now.

But it wasn't over.

While I talked to Jeanie in the tower basement, I realized that the unwritten law of the World Under would soon come into play: where there is one incident, there always follows another.

No one knows why those Supernaturals from the World Under follow each other like that—it's a conundrum that's baffled those in the know for centuries—but it's as certain as the sunrise. You could set your watch by it. The real trick is to figure out exactly where and when the next arrival will come.

I had a fair notion of where. When was another matter entirely, but fortunately, I had that kind of time.

"As you see, Mr. Underhill, while the debris and the, ah, fecal remains do present a problem with clean-up, nevertheless they, ah, can be disposed of." The speaker had a voice that reminded me of Mickey Mouse. That is, if the cartoon rodent had asthma and was a chain smoker.

"What is the time frame?" Underhill's voice was a mixture of silk and barbed wire.

"Per your request, we will be using illegals, those people whose families will not report them, ah, missing. With what we offer to pay, they won't ask any questions. The only factor would be the, ah, *disposal* of the remains. I estimate six days to clean the debris field discreetly, another two for the scat. Disinfecting and final cleaning will take another two. This place should, ah, be ready for your people soon enough."

Mr. Underhill, a tall, slender man in a black Armani suit, looked around and smiled thinly, the kind of smile one might see on a serial killer's face before he strikes. "That will be perfect, Mr. Cargill." His handsome features were distorted by cruelty and glee.

The other man, Cargill, stepped over a pile of scat, wrinkling his nose. Short, bald, skeletal, with a pair of wire-rimmed glasses over pale blue eyes, smiled wolfishly. "And payment, sir? If, ah, I may be so bold to discuss such crass affairs."

Underhill barely concealed his distaste. "The agreed upon quantity of diamonds, untraceable, non-Conflict, will be delivered to your offices by secure courier at noon. If the work is completed ahead of schedule, a bonus of one hundred thousand dollars in gold bullion will be paid as well."

Cargill nodded vigorously. "Very well, sir. I, ah, will make every effort to have the job completed in record time."

That was enough. I stepped out from behind a pile of broken shelving, a Desert Eagle in one hand, my bowie knife in the other. "That really won't be necessary," I said evenly.

The little man cringed at the sight of the weapon, but Underhill merely narrowed his eyes and stood very still.

"I was wondering if the Sidhe had help from someone on this side. You never really think that a human would assist in the extinction of his or her own species, but I'm not really surprised. Humans have done worse, I guess." By the time I was done, my voice emerged as a wolfish growl from my throat. Nantan Lupan would've been proud. For a moment my chest constricted with the pain of his loss. The Sidhe had a lot to answer for.

"M-Mr. Underhill is, ah, just a favored client," stammered Cargill. Despite the cool air of the tunnel, he was starting to sweat copiously.

I sneered. "I've been listening long enough." My attention shifted to the motionless Underhill. "So this was your staging area, where the first people were infected with the Windigo Curse. What? Were they the illegals who worked at digging the tunnels? People no one would miss? An elegant way of disposing of the bodies." My attention shifted back to Cargill. "Isn't that right?" The lights from the flat bulbs overhead gave the tunnel a washed-out look and caused a throbbing to begin behind my eyes.

Underhill nodded once, his flat dead eyes betraying nothing.

"Sir," Cargill began. "I'm afraid you don't—*squawk*!" His body shuddered and shook and after a second he fell to the ground in a heap. Cargill twitched and spasmed, gurgly, strangling noises emerging from between his colorless lips. Matt rose from behind another pile of rubble, a Paser stun gun in hand.

"Thanks, Matt. That guy's voice was really starting to grate."

"You want I should do the other one, boss?" Matt's level brown gaze begged me for the opportunity.

I shook my head. "I'm thinking our Unseelie Court friend here is protected from common projectiles."

Underhill nodded once, a bobbing of the head like a bird of prey's. "Indeed." His gaze flickered to the bowie. "Iron, too."

Of course, I expected no less.

"You know what threw me for a loop, Mr. Unseelie Court?" I waited for a response and received none. "Numbers. When we came down here to your staging area three weeks ago, there were thousands upon thousands of windigos waiting in miles and miles of tunnels. It didn't make sense. All those people gone and no one reported missing. But the more I thought about it, I realized that the windigos still had the memories of the people they possessed and could pass for human if they wanted. The ones who hadn't started growing those porcupine quills, that is. My guess is that when the quills started to show, they came here." My smile was brittle and tight. "But the human-looking ones, they went on with their lives until a prearranged time; then they gathered here along with their fully changed fellows in these tunnels. To wait, I suppose. But why?"

I paused for effect, then said, "To wait for you." Those last words emerged low and even. "When your San Francisco scheme failed, you had Chicago as your back-up, your ace-in-the-hole. You prepped both plans and moved ahead with San Francisco because the clean-up from that would be easier than dealing with hundreds of thousands, if not millions, of ravenous windigos."

Underhill didn't bother to deny it. "Impressive," he said, "for a human. Tell me, did the Kal Hakala help you reason this out?"

"Don't get me wrong, buster, I love Kal to tiny, little pieces, but he ain't the only Agent with more brains than sense." I couldn't help myself; I stood a little taller and let tiniest hint of a British accent creep into my voice. "The name's Alsate. Canton Alsate." Matt grinned. "Just so you can tell Satan who sent you."

The Sidhe waved a hand in my direction. "Do you think those platinum-lined coats can protect you from *me*?" His smile was jackal-like.

"Funny you should mention platinum. I've been thinking long and hard on the subject. Silver, gold, platinum. Metals used to store or absorb magic. Metals. Precious metals. Precious for their beauty or perhaps for their uses in magic and who can say which came first, the beauty or the magic?"

"Did you come to bore me to death?" Underhill said. "If so, then I decline the honor."

"Now don't be rude; I'm getting to the point." Perhaps I was savoring the moment too much, but I didn't care. In front of me, not more than twenty feet away stood one of the *things* responsible for Winch's death.

I planned on savoring every delicious second.

"You see, when I fought the Sidhe before, cold iron worked quite well against their obsidian armor. We even had iron bullets. Quite effective A few hits and they were *mine*." I raised the pistol. "But I reckon you thought of that, so I asked myself, 'Self, if silver and gold and such absorbs magic, what happens when a silver, platinum or gold bullet hits a magical shield? Will it absorb the magic?' "

Blam!

The platinum bullet stopped a foot from the Sidhe to hang in mid-air and glow cherry red before exploding like a party popper. Shards of platinum bullet *spanged* off aluminum and steel shelving. I fired a second round, gold this time, and it had the same result. The third bullet was made of silver and it hit Underhill square in the gut. He folded around his midsection, gasping and coughing, a look of stark fear in his eyes.

Underhill's form shimmered briefly and his human illusion disappeared, revealing the true Sidhe beneath. Lavender eyes, strangely hinged jaws, planes and angles of the face that appeared so dang *wrong*. It was beautiful, alien and disturbing as hell.

"Damn," I said conversationally. "That worked better than I expected."

Blam! A plain silver bullet took Underhill in the forehead. The next three were for effect. I saved an iron round for last.

"You killed him!" Cargill shrieked from the floor, still twitching a bit. Fresh urine joined the dried liquid on the tunnel floor.

"Yeah, I did." I took a step forward and took aim.

The little man raised his hands. "You can't kill me! I know my rights! I have rights!"

"You helped plan a genocidal attack on the world," Matt spat, the normally placid Latino livid with rage. "*The* largest terrorist attack ever seen. You are now considered to be an enemy combatant and have no rights." He grabbed the smaller man by the lapels and hauled him upright. "If it were up to me, I'd shoot you through the eye and be done with it, but we need to see what information we can get out of you."

"They'll kill me if I talk!"

Matt brought his face close. "You should be more worried about *me*."

"I'M SURPRISED THAT WORKED," JEANIE said, staring out the porthole at the ground far below.

We were on our way back to Warehouse, a tired group of Agents ready for a vacation. After killing the Sidhe in the tunnels, we stayed around for another two weeks, just to be sure. Better safe than sorry.

Despite the blood and death, the bodies strewn across the streets of Chicago, it was a job well done. All my team, even that bonehead Portner, deserved a pat on the back and a vacation. Ng, the *former* FBI agent, was on his way to Coronado for some training. I hope he passed. That man had ice water in his veins.

We were on our way back and I felt … empty. Tired. Worn out and ready to hit the rack for about a century of really good sleep. Don't get me wrong, I didn't feel bad, but what revenge I extracted from that Sidhe in the tunnel did nothing to make me feel better about the loss of Winch.

On *Star Trek*, there's a saying among the Klingons, "Revenge is a dish best served cold"—or maybe it was the eighteenth-century French diplomat Talleyrand, can't quite remember. Anyhow, that statement doesn't quite ring true. Revenge is a dish best served. Period.

Yeah, that works.

Was it worth it, killing that Sidhe? Placing bullets in his skull, blowing the back of his head out, brains littering the floor? Was it worth it, taking the remainder of his days and rendering them null and void, in effect stealing his future? Was it worth it, that little bit of revenge?

Hell yes it was.

EPILOGUE

———•———

Kal

I'VE NEVER BEEN A HORSE before. Kind of trippy, despite the lack of thumbs and the desire to eat grass. The whole experience in that blasted and dead world was rather uplifting .... I mean, my best friend was a hawk the size of a nuclear submarine! Of course an old gray wolf that could eat a double-decker bus whole was pretty impressive as well, but the windigo, that horrific monstrosity with the hunger of a hundred politicians, really took the taco. That thing could've used King Kong as a hairy suppository.

A few years ago, Canton introduced me to Nantan Lupan. Kind, generous to a fault, ultra cool, he had a slew of stories, tales of his people, which he readily shared with me. He was also very possibly the most stubborn man I have ever met. Must have been part Finnish. Watching him trot off into the distance with Leena nearly tore the heart from my chest.

Leena. My little sister who would never grow up, never meet the right guy, never have kids, and never grow old. No Uncle Kal for me, no Christmases in Minnesota with the nieces and nephews, playing football or sitting around the fire, laughing and carrying on.

I'd lived with her inside me, as a part of me, for so long that her absence was a gaping wound in my soul. It would probably heal and someday, in the hopefully not-so-distant future, it might not hurt so much. But now it was a wound I could live with because she was someplace with old Marcus Alsate. Nantan Lupan, the gray wolf. I couldn't think of a finer escort into the afterlife.

Normal. I was a normal man now without any magical/spiritual augmentation. Along with my sister vanished the rage, the thing that made me more than a man. My scars would start to pull at me and I would feel the rigors of time and abuse. All my extra strength, speed, a certain resistance to magic … all gone and what I had to work with was what other people had.

Humanity.

I hoped I had enough left.

The strange out-of-body experience, the whole turning into a horse thing, happened as we sped toward the Four Seasons Hotel in Miami, the source of the pulsing magic that somehow signaled the windigo to attack. Good thing Dom had been driving or I'd be road pizza. My spirit or whatever had been gone for only a few moments, but it felt like hours. Fortunately I've long since grown used to such oddities. In fact, normal for me would be the most abnormal thing that could happen.

When I returned back to the really real world, most of the windigos were dead. The rest, those possessed for only a short while, were unconscious and would wake with a goodly dose of amnesia, the Curse lifted. Still, thousands were dead. The city was in panic, a nation was in turmoil, and the world teetered in shock.

Alex had a theory. He said that the pieces of the Prime Windigo, those scabby, dandruff-like flakes that floated from its body in that dry world, started to *eat* the souls or the life energy of their victims, and when the quills started to grow, that meant the last remnants of the host's soul was consumed. When the Prime Windigo was killed, the pieces of it died as well, and without their foul energies fueling the engines of their hosts' bodies, those bodies died.

In the end, dead is dead and it was time to clean up.

I rubbed my temples, the beginnings of a headache thrumming through my skull. Reports, reports, reports. Endless reports and videoconferences with the heads of FEMA, the National Guard, the Joint Chiefs, and, of course, with POTUS. All of whom wanted my attention twenty-seven hours a day telling me to "Get something done, damn it, this is your department." I told the Joint Chiefs to shut up and let me do my job, the head of FEMA to shut up and do as I say, and the National Guard to please, please, please, just go where I told you to go and I'll keep you in the loop. As for POTUS, I said I would personally handle the "arms dealer plague carrier" spin and don't worry, everything will be handled quickly and efficiently and allow him to come out smelling like a rose come election day. "Yes, sir, yes, sir, no problemo, sir, Got it covered, no need to worry, have a good afternoon and I will call with a sitrep by the end of the day."

Yadda, yadda, yadda.

Handling those guys was a little like masturbating with a chainsaw—very, very tricky.

INCOMING CALL. The words blinked in my vision, a soft canary yellow.

"Who?" I asked. It had taken a few days, but I had figured out the vocal interface.

INCOMING CALL FROM BENJAMIN BAUER.

Great. BB. Oh, well … why not? "Answer."

BB's face appeared, seeming to float in mid-air thanks to the DRAFT. I knew that mine appeared the same way in his. He looked like hell—eyes underscored with large pouches and skin sallow from lack of sleep. "How are you doing, Kal?" he asked, voice hoarse and hollow. "I trust everything is under control. As much as it can be, considering the circumstances."

I sighed. "If it hadn't been for Ghost running logistics, cloning himself to assist the other teams and acting as a go-between with MI-7 and the like, we would've been hip deep and sinking fast. As it is, what I'm dealing with is trying to calm a population of panicked Straights and stroking the egos of those self-important dickheads in the know."

He rubbed his eyes and sighed. "Tell me you're being at least a little diplomatic."

"If you're worried that I put rusty nails in some politician's Cheerios, you can relax. I've been a good boy."

One of his eyebrows headed for where his hairline used to be. "Is that why you told the director of FEMA to ... wait a minute." He looked down off camera. "I wrote it down so I wouldn't forget ... yes, here it is. You told him to 'Shut your fat gob, get off the stick, and do what I say, or I'll send the one hundred-eleventh Airborne down your chimney to feed you your socks'? Sound familiar?" He sounded less than pleased.

One of my finer moments, if I do say so myself, even if I'd ripped the line off from *Letterman*. "Hey, BB, the guy is a major D-bag. Tried to tell me how to do my job and refused to submit to Bureau authority as mandated under the Global Supernatural Threat Act of 1989. If it had been in person, I wouldn't have resorted to such crude words."

"Meaning?"

"I would've hogtied him and left him in the nearest janitor's closet with his head inside a mop bucket."

The look he shot me spoke volumes, but I returned his icy stare with one of my own.

He broke the silence first. "It's at this point where you apologize for being a horse's ass."

Funny he would mention a horse. I shook my head. "Nope."

"And why not?" The Arctic Circle was warmer than his tone.

"Because you put me in charge and I will run the BSI as I see fit. Within reason, of course. If you don't like it, fire me when you get back. Until then, please get off my back."

BB's eyes flew wide. "What did you just say?"

"At least I said 'please.' "

"You tread dangerous ground, Kal," he growled.

"So, you're not going to fire me?"

The muscles at the corners of his jaws bunched. "No."

"Damn. I could've used the down time after the crapstorm I've been weathering."

One minute, then two passed before he spoke again. "Okay. I'll leave you be, but will you please try to be more pleasant to others? Even if they *are* idiots."

Well that didn't sound like fun at all. "Okay, BB." Conceding the point sucked, but he *was* the boss, even if he was a few thousand miles away.

"All right, Kal, now that that's out of the way, back to the business at hand. Give me the *Reader's Digest* version of events."

"I've already prepared the report from the various debriefs. I can have it there in a few seconds."

He shook his head. "Negative. I want it from the horse's mouth."

Again with the horse metaphor. Did he know about my otherworldly adventure with Canton? "Okay, BB. The nest of windigos in the Chicago Deep Tunnel complex appears to be the largest, with Houston and Miami running a close second and third. Once the windigos started coming out of the woodwork in Oakland, Norton took care of them rather sharpish. Those accounted for roughly fifteen thousand of the total dead.

"Chicago, being the largest, was probably targeted after most of the drilling and blasting for the Deep Tunnel project was completed in 2005. It is believed to be the first major nexus of the infiltration. It is unknown how long ago the first person was turned, but taking into account that the windigo could mimic their human hosts, the miles of foodstuffs underground, the size of the complex, and coordination needed, it is estimated that the contamination has been in process for at least two years. Perhaps it even started prior to the Unseelie Court's San Francisco campaign. However, according to Canton's puckish informant, the Windigo Curse was a sort of Plan B in case the San Francisco Plot didn't pan out. Or perhaps if the San Francisco plot *had* worked and rendered all iron on the planet to dust, thereby triggering a global catastrophe that would have decimated mankind, the Sidhe might have unleashed the Windigo Curse to mop up whatever remained of human civilization. A cleanup operation."

I took a deep breath; the sheer scope and complexity of the plot staggered me. "Initial projections show that if the Primary Windigo spirit had not be terminated by Canton, Marcus Alsate, and myself, the Curse would have spread all throughout the United States and Canada in a matter of fifteen days and would have claimed the farthest reaches of South America within a month. Had we failed to kill the Prime Windigo spirit …." Deep breath, take it easy, Kal. Just facts and figures. My fists were white with fury as I read the words scrolling across the DRAFT. "There would have been little or nothing we could have done to halt the spread.

"We have to consider the intel brought to us via the puca. The two Courts of the Sidhe are close to war and the cause is uncertain. It may be that the Seelie Court learned about the windigo attack and the Unseelie ramped up hostilities. Whatever the reason, the import is this: the Unseelie Court had been implementing a many-layered plan against humanity for years and we have to assume, we *must* assume, that we have foiled only the second stage of that plan.

"There may not be another attack, but until we receive intel that states otherwise, we must assume there will be. For all we know, it may be underway even as we speak." There, I said it and the thought made my stomach churn.

BB remained silent for a few moments, considering my words. "You sure, Kal?" he said softly.

"Hell no."

He sighed. "Very well. Tomorrow is the last day of the Directors' meeting here. Send the report. I will relay it to the other directors. I will relay some further information on the tensions between the Courts when I return, so until then, good job, Kal."

I shook my head. "It wasn't me this time, BB. I was just along for the ride. Canton deserves the praise. Him and his grandfather. Without them, we would've lost."

"See that everyone is well rested and have them study up on the Sidhe, just in case. I want them familiar with all the data up to and including the San Francisco mission. See you later, Kal."

"Bye, BB." He winked out.

There. That was done and the taste of it was rotting in my mouth. I had read Canton's debrief—no VR this time, I was getting tired of that input and the accompanying headaches—but I was able to feel his anger, his pain at the loss of Winch. I even felt his pleasure at killing the Sidhe in the tunnel, putting silver bullets into the bastard's brain. It felt *good*.

In classic literature and old movies, the hero usually chooses the side of the angels, offering mercy or compassion to his or her opponents, proving that they are worthy to be a capital H Hero. They were people of uncommon discipline and a true sense of "Justice" and they couldn't be swayed from doing what was right and proper. Big-chinned heroes who, deep down in the secret places of our hearts, we wanted to be. Those guys, man, they would never feel good about shooting a flaming scumbag in the throat. At the end of the day, there would be guilt and sorrow, and angst they would bear quietly, stoically.

They could kiss my pale Finnish ass.

If I felt bad for every evil dick I took out of this world, I'd never get out of bed in the morning, and I knew Canton felt the same way. Did this make us bad people? Were we like the monsters we hunted, too full of ourselves to feel the compassion that was so deified in literature and film?

Not in my opinion. Those heroes were ideals, archetypal humans nobody could live up to, not unless you were a cross between the real Mother Teresa, Captain Kirk, and the version of Charlemagne lionized in history. Even then it would be a stretch.

No, I'm quite comfortable with my lot in life, with my role at the Bureau. I take out the trash and I come home and sleep like a baby. Odds are that Canton does as well. And if that makes us bad guys, I can live with that. Chances are, I'm going to die with it as well.

Man, my thoughts were far too deep for a guy as bushed as I was. It was time for some ambrosia; it was time for another bowl of Lucky Charms. If they could reproduce it in liquid form, I'd be mainlining the stuff.

Everything is better with breakfast cereal.

A Sneak Peek at Kal's Next Adventure

OMAHA STAKES

T HE FAMILIAR DRONING VOICE OF Ghost came from the desk's
hidden speakers. "Kal, there's something you must see."

There ... the sinking, sick feeling I'd been dreading for the past
couple of days. "What is it, Ghost?"

A picture formed on the DRAFT, a body of a young man, throat
torn and bloody. "The police in Omaha, Nebraska, found the body of
Jacob Astorman this morning in a warehouse downtown."

I studied the boy's throat carefully. It had been savagely mauled.
"Werewolf? Vampire?"

"The manner of Mr. Astorman's death is not the relevant issue.
However, the manila envelope found on his body is." A piece of
eight-and-a-half by eleven-inch paper came into view, crammed
with writing scribbled in a tight, crabbed hand. The words seemed to
be gibberish, a language I'd never seen before.

"What is it?"

"That's the thing. It was flagged when entered into evidence, one
of my sniffer programs performing a routine search for the unusual.
This qualifies in spades."

I scratched my head, trying to make heads or tails of the note.
"Code?"

"A symmetric key algorithm."

Cryptography. Not my strongest subject. Now chemistry, there was something I could sink my teeth into. "Any clue as to who uses it? What does it say?"

A long pause. "It was used over fifteen years ago."

Uh-oh. I had a bad feeling. "One of ours?"

"No. It is an old MI-7 code and the key is one that had been used during the Lindhauer-Kowalski incident, the joint Bureau-MI-7 mission in New York. The only time a foreign Bureau operated with permission on American soil."

This was getting worse and worse. I verbally accessed the Bureau database with the DRAFT and scrolled through the relevant file while Ghost waited patiently.

"Holy crap," I muttered once I had the gist of the report, awed it what it implied. "The British Ambassador *and* the German Ambassador to the United Nations? This is friggin' unbelievable."

"Let me show you what was decoded."

"Don't suppose I can refuse to read it?"

"Not really."

Crap. It had been worth a shot. "Go ahead."

On the screen, the words faded and returned, this time forming themselves into words I could read. It turned out to be a letter. To me.

By the pricking of my thumbs ….

Kal Hakala:

I have been amusing myself in Omaha, preparing for the day when we would meet. The thought, I must confess, warms me, because I have been an admirer of yours for so long. Watching you work has been an oft-enjoyed pastime of mine.

You have been an inspiration for me. All this time I thought myself to be the perfect hunter, the ultimate predator, but we both know that is a lie, one born of arrogance. You, Kalevi Hakala, are the greatest hunter alive today, the man who can defeat any monster, the Bureau Agent all Supernaturals fear.

I cannot have that; it is intolerable to me, so we must

compete, you and I. Only the best to survive the confrontation. Nothing personal, mind you; it's simply the way things must be. There can only be one sentient Apex Predator on this planet, and I wish it to be me. Know that I hold you in the highest regard and that it will be an honor to take your life. If I should lose, it will be the highest honor to fall by your hand.

Come to Omaha within the next five days or every day thereafter I shall kill ten humans in many inventive and disturbing ways, starting a bloody spree so terrible the humans who inhabit this dungheap of a world will speak of it forever. Come soon and come alone. You may bring what weapons and magic you wish, but if I even suspect that you try to enlist assistance from the Bureau, I will commit the aforementioned killing spree. I will be watching and I will know if you disobey me. Do not force me to drastic action. Do not attempt to spoil the game.

Please do not disappoint and know that we are, at heart, kindred spirits.

No signature. Nothing.

It was creepy as hell, and, in its own way, quite terrifying. There was a mystery person or Supernatural who wanted to kill me, presumably by ripping my throat out like the man in the photo. It begged only one question: why wasn't I scared, ready to turn my shorts yellow and brown? I knew the answer straight off, without even thinking about it: I wasn't scared because I was too excited.

It was time to play.

Born in Helsinki, Finland, **Mark Everett Stone** arrived in the U.S. at a young age and promptly dove into the world of the fantastic. Starting at age seven with the *Iliad* and the *Odyssey*, he went on to consume every scrap of Norse Mythology he could get his grubby little paws on. At age thirteen he graduated to Tolkien and Heinlein, building up a book collection that soon rivaled the local public library's. In college Mark majored in Journalism and minored in English. Mark has published four other books with Camel Press: *Things to Do in Denver When You're Un-Dead*, *What Happens in Vegas Dies in Vegas*, *I Left My Haunt in San Francisco* (Books 1, 2, and 3 of the From the Files of the BSI series) as well as a standalone novel, *The Judas Line*, which was a finalist for the ForeWord Magazine Book of the Year Award in the Fantasy Category.

Mark lives in Denver with his amazingly patient wife, Brandie, and their two sons, Aeden and Gabriel. You can find Mark on the Web at www.markeverettstone.com.